14 - 6 ~ 2 same

16 - 2

AUG 0 6 2014

POWER PLAY

ALSO BY CATHERINE COULTER

POWER
PLAY

CATHERINE COULTER

G. P. PUTNAM'S SONS / NEW YORK

DOUBLEDAY LARGE PRINT HOME LIBRARY EDITION

This Large Print Edition, prepared especially for Doubleday
Large Print Home Library, contains the complete,
unabridged text of the original Publisher's Edition.

PUTNAM

G. P. PUTNAM'S SONS • Publishers since 1838
Published by the Penguin Group
Penguin Group (USA) LLC
375 Hudson Street, New York, New York 10014

USA • Canada • UK • Ireland • Australia
New Zealand • India • South Africa • China

A Penguin Random House Company

ISBN 978-1-62953-048-2

**This Large Print Book carries the
Seal of Approval of N.A.V.H.**

To my amazing husband,
who continues to pour his
heart and soul into my books.
Thank you.
—Catherine Coulter

ACKNOWLEDGEMENTS

Power Play was pure adventure to write. I would like to kiss the toes of the following people:

Kurt Crawford, Public Affairs Specialist and Media Rep for the FBI Training Division. Thank you for painting a word picture for me of Nicholas Drummond's graduation ceremony at Quantico. If I got anything wrong, I'll try to blame you, but I doubt it'll fly.

Angela Bell, Office of Public Affairs, Hoover Building, Washington, D.C. My continued thanks to you for always being available for every off-the-wall question, always enthusiastic and laughing. My only wish is to meet you face to face.

Amy Brosey, Copy Editor. My thanks to you for being as tenacious as a bulldog, never missing a thing and catching most of my brain hiccups. You are integral to making the FBI series fly high.

Karen Evans, Special Private Assistant to me. Without you I would run right off the rails; indeed, I would be in sorry shape. Bless you for always being there to fix a gnarled-up computer, deal with technology, read and edit manuscripts, give great advice, and actually, to be perfectly honest here, handle everything that comes through the door.

Perry King, Fitness and Pilates Trainer, who gave me her name. Thanks.

POWER PLAY

1

Buckner Park
Chevy Chase, Maryland
Middle of March
Saturday, late afternoon

She always ran at sunset. She rarely ran all-out, rather she maintained a smooth, steady pace because this was her thinking time. Thankfully, it wasn't freezing cold on this early evening. The two-lane trail wound in and out of oak and maple trees, the terrain not too extreme. She loved how the light played through the still-naked tree branches, and how quiet it was with so few other people out in the park this time of day. Quite different from running along the Embankment in London—a challenge, since there were always people to watch out for. Here or in London, it was still her precious thinking time. Diplomatic protocols with endless snafus, relations with Her Majesty's government, and now too often about people who wanted to blow up their neighbors, or London, still fighting out thousands of years of hatreds seemingly bred into their bones. Sometimes there were victories. Thankfully, she was good at her job, but there was always something to work through, something to make her brain ache. But not today. Today she was trying to figure out what suddenly happened in her life that had brought her here. As she ran, a constant prayer looped through her brain that she'd left the danger back in England.

Her breathing was even, her muscles warm, and she relaxed into the repetitive movement. She focused on the quiet, even heard a blue jay, the sounds of small animals moving about in the underbrush near her, the slap of her running shoes on the trail, smooth and steady.

After another quarter-mile, the trail turned back toward Nickerson Road, with its two lanes and light traffic. She ran parallel to it for a hundred yards or so.

George's face flashed in her mind. He was eating spaghetti, of all things, and smiling at something she'd said, and she felt the familiar punch of grief, raw and deep.

And that was the question she always came back to. What had she done that would make someone want her to pay with her life? With George's life? No matter how she turned it over in her mind, she simply couldn't think of anyone who possibly hated her that much.

She heard a car approaching on Nickerson Road. In that stark moment she heard the engine revving, the car accelerating toward her. She twisted to look, stumbling on a clump of rocks at the edge of the trail and falling sideways, flailing her arms to keep her balance, but still she fell hard. The car was close now, nearly on her, and it was coming fast. She didn't think, simply rolled into the bushes near several trees. She smelled the exhaust, felt the heat of that beast as it flew past her.

She heard the car brake hard, pictured the driver turning around to come after her again. She jumped to her feet and ran into the woods off the trail, the only sound in her ears the frantic beat of her heart. She plastered herself against the back of an oak tree and waited.

2

**Two Corners Mall
Washington, D.C.
Monday morning**

He turned stone-cold and his focus
narrowed laser-thin on the man who held
the woman in a choke hold. A carjacking
in the parking lot of a strip mall not a
half-mile from his town house on Euclid—
the first one he'd ever seen, and here he
was in the middle of it. He'd been walking
to his Jeep, a large Starbucks coffee in
his left hand, when he saw this man grab
the woman and jerk her out of the
driver's side of a shiny black Beemer. She
screamed once. Davis yelled at the man
to let her go and back away, but the man
dragged the woman in front of him, whirled
around to face him, and pointed a .22 at
her temple. A crap gun, but it could do
the job.

"Piss off or the bitch is dead!" the man yelled. "I don't like bitches. I don't even like my mom. I mean it, dude, walk away!"

The guy was maybe thirty, and higher than Carly from Homeland Security when she'd nabbed a terrorist in Pittsburgh. He was probably on ice, given the way he was jonesing around, his body jerking on puppet strings. Even from fifteen feet away, Davis could see his eyes were jitterbugging, the hand that held the .22 to the woman's head shaking. **Not good.**

New tactics. Davis called out, "Dude, I get it. Look, I love my Starbucks fix, too"—he waved his cup—"but you've got to let her go."

"Go away, ass-wipe, or it's brains-down-the-drain time!" Jitterbug tightened his hold around her neck, pressing the .22 hard against her cheek. The woman's hands clutched at his forearm, trying to pull it away from her neck to catch a breath. Even from this distance, it looked to Davis like she was more pissed off than afraid.

"Seriously, dude," Davis called out. "It's

really not a good idea to mess with me. I'm FBI, a walking, talking death machine. You can't hit me from fifteen feet with that popgun, but I can shoot the gold hoop out of your ear and call my mother at the same time while singing 'Happy Birthday.'" He pulled his Glock from his holster for Jitterbug to see, then held it down at his side. "You hurt this very nice lady and I'll personally stuff you in a meat grinder and make a cheap burger out of you. You got me? You need rehab, not this Beemer you'd just wreck, which really would be a shame, about the car, I mean. So put the peashooter down and let the lady go."

Jitterbug stared at him, as if trying to make sense out of his words. He was shaking his head back and forth, maybe listening to other voices, who knew? His eyes whirled, his mouth worked, his hand shook, and through all his gyrations the woman looked straight at Davis, calm as could be, and gave him a slight nod. Without a pause, she bent her head and took a deep bite out of Jitterbug's forearm, right through the tatty sweatshirt he was wearing. He yelled, loosened his grip. She pulled back inside the open car door to give herself leverage and sent her fist into his nose, then her elbow into his gut. He jerked up his .22 and fired wildly, not at the woman but at Davis, once, twice, three times. Nowhere close. Davis leaned down, carefully put his coffee cup on the ground and raised his Glock. The woman was pinned between Jitterbug and the car door, and he made another grab for her, jerking the gun up again toward her head.

"I wish you hadn't done that," Davis said, and very calmly shot the man in the shoulder. One bullet did the trick. The man lurched back and fell away from the open car door and onto his knees, howling, holding his shoulder, rocking back and forth, the gun skittering away from him. The woman shouted to Davis, "Good shot!" And she gave the guy a kick in the ribs, sending him screaming onto his side. Then she knelt down, agile as a teenager, and picked up the .22.

A good half-dozen shoppers dribbled out of the shops toward the parking lot now that it looked safe and they wouldn't get caught in anyone's crosshairs. They were brimming with excitement, chattering nervously. A woman screamed, as if for effect. Davis opened his mouth at the same moment the woman held up her hand, cleared her throat, and said in a booming voice that carried all the way to LaFleur's Dry Cleaners across the road, "Everything's okay now, people! You, sir, call nine-one-one. The rest of you, you'll want to stay and talk to the police when they get here. I mean it, this is important. I'd do it for any one of you, so do it for me, okay?" She gave them all the big stink eye, a nod, and an approving smile.

To his surprise, only two of the bystanders melted away. The others grouped together, comparing notes, still flying high on adrenaline.

Davis holstered his Glock and picked up his Starbucks coffee. He sipped it. Still hot. **Good.**

The woman started toward him. She was tall, fit, and strong, by the look of the blows she'd dealt Jitterbug. Not a coward, this woman, more a force. In that instant, he realized she reminded him of Sherlock, or Sherlock's mom, all the way to the red hair bouncing around on her head. It was kind of scary. She was smiling big, showing lovely white teeth, and her red hair seemed to turn redder as the sun suddenly broke through the clouds overhead. She handed him Jitterbug's .22, butt first, barrel to the ground, smooth and easy. She knew gun safety. Even more scary.

"A meat grinder? Really?" She quirked a dark red eyebrow at him, leaned forward, and kissed him soundly on the cheek.

She smelled like honey. "Well," he said, "the thing is, my granny always used a meat grinder when I visited her as a kid. I remember she threatened my granddad with it when he smoked his cigar in the kitchen. Why weren't you scared?"

"Believe me, I was scared to my toes, until I realized he was only a pathetic guy high on drugs," and she looked back at Jitterbug, lying there holding his shoulder, moaning.

Criminal Apprehension Unit
Hoover Building

An hour later in the CAU, Davis said to the gathered agents, "Metro showed up two minutes later, along with an ambulance that hauled Jitterbug to the hospital. Some of the cops questioned the bystanders, others questioned the woman, and another two questioned me until I wanted to hurl. I even mentioned Savich a couple of times, but all I got for dropping the Big Dog's name was one guy who rolled his eyes and one big-deal grunt. They kept asking me the same questions over and over as they usually do. The woman finally broke in and said enough was enough and we were in need of a nice strong morning shot of bourbon and I was to follow her back home in case she fainted—not likely—where we'd toast our mutual good luck and competence. She shoved her card into one of their hands and smiled at them. The two cops were so taken aback, they let us both leave, and I followed her home."

Davis grinned around the room. "So that's the story of why I'm late, and I'm sticking to it."

Savich said, "Really? Nah, that can't be true. You're actually saying one of the cops rolled his eyes and the other one only grunted when you said my name?"

"Yeah, couldn't believe it myself. You'd think maybe they'd have some respect."

Savich grinned, shook his head. "I can confirm that Jitterbug—name's Paul Jones—is in surgery at Washington Memorial to remove the bullet from his shoulder. Metro's in charge."

Special Agent Lucy Carlyle, soon to be Lucy McKnight, was shaking her head. "Davis, listen to me. You could be in the bed next to Mr. Bug at Washington Memorial instead of sitting here trying to make us laugh. I can see it all: you're moseying to your Jeep, sipping your latte, thinking about who you've got a date with tonight, when that idiot grabs the lady."

"It was not a latte."

"Yeah, yeah, macho black. One part of your brain is trying out jokes to tell your girlfriend tonight and all of a sudden, your manic brain snaps to figuring out angles and distances, the drugged psychology of Mr. Bug, and calculating probabilities for survival, right?"

Davis said, "Hey, I already know what jokes work." He paused for a moment. "And my brain isn't manic. It's a finely tuned instrument. Do you know, though, I think she'd have taken Jitterbug down herself once she got over her surprise at his popping out of the box like that. I gotta say it's possible she really didn't need me. Tough, that one. Lots of red hair, like yours, Sherlock. I bet she'd impress you.

"I did follow her home to this swank gated mansion on a huge lot in Chevy Chase, halfway down Ridgewood Road, through this big secure gate with a guardhouse, cameras, and an intercom. It's all woods out there, with very few houses. The ones that are there are big and set back and very private. The guardhouse was empty, but she didn't have to speak to anyone on the intercom. Nope, the gate opened up fast, which means there were cameras inside monitoring. I was right behind her in my plebian Jeep on her big circular driveway. Before we'd even stopped, this big guy comes running out of the house, makes a beeline right at me like he's going to rip my tonsils out. She climbs out of her BMW and calls out something like 'Hooley, it's okay.'

"Since I had to come to work and couldn't toast her with the bourbon, she patted my face and gave me another kiss. Hooley's standing only six feet away, his arms crossed over his chest, measuring me for a coffin. He was a bodyguard, I'm sure of it. I'm thinking maybe she's someone important."

"Well, what's her name?" Coop McKnight said.

"Does anyone recognize the name Natalie Black?"

Sherlock stared at him. "You've got to be kidding me."

3

**Davis's town house
Euclid Avenue, Washington, D.C.
Monday, early evening**

When Davis pulled his Jeep into his driveway, he saw a big yellow Harley idling at the curb, the rider still astride it all in punk-black, from boots to helmet to thin black leather gloves. Now, what was all this? Maybe it was Jitterbug's brother, out for revenge. He ambled over to where the Harley and its driver sat waiting. As he neared, the driver revved a loud scare-the-birds-out-of-the-trees hello. He loved the sound of the Blockhead engine.

It wasn't Jitterbug or one of Davis's informants—none of them had that kind of juice, and the Sportster 1200 Custom was a nice one, a hog right up there in the Harley food chain. Who, then? He smiled as he came to a stop a foot from that gorgeous machine with its beefy front end. "I like the hissy-fit yellow paint job. Haven't seen that color before. You like the pull-back handlebars?"

Off came the helmet and out fell a reddish-brown braid, thick and heavy past her shoulders. He'd heard one of the agents in the unit call the braid a fishtail. Okay, he could see that. She was wearing dark sunglasses. She pulled off her leather gloves and began drumming her fingers on the fuel tank. Her nails were clean and buffed, and she wore no rings. "The handlebars were a pain until I got used to them. Now they're good." She eyed him up and down. "Mom said you sort of moseyed, like you had all the time in the world. I told her you sounded like a druggie yourself. She said no, couldn't be, you were an FBI agent, plus you were too cute to be stupid. You're Special Agent Davis Sullivan?"

"Yeah, that's me. Who are you?"

She pulled off her sunglasses. Would you look at those pale green eyes. He'd never seen that color before, well, yeah, he had, that very morning. She was striking, like her mother.

"I'm her one and only kid." She leaned over and shook his hand. "Thank you for keeping my mom out of deep doodoo this morning. She seems to be getting herself into weird situations lately, and I try to be around to help her out, only I wasn't this morning, so thank you again. She couldn't believe that little twerp wanted to carjack her new Beemer, right in front of the shopping mall. All she was doing there was picking up her dry cleaning."

Even though she'd thanked him— twice—Davis could tell Biker Babe wished she could have been the one to be there to do the saving, not him. Her hair wasn't as stark red as her mom's. Her dad must have diluted the mix, but she was pale-skinned like her mom, with nary a freckle in sight. He smiled. "You're welcome. So she said I saved her?"

"Not exactly, but close enough. She said you never dropped your cup of coffee, said you calmly put it down, and when it was over you picked it up and took a sip. She admired that. She said you smelled like cordite and lime, like the aftershave my father used to use. I can still see him, patting his face with it while he hummed show tunes." She stopped, shook her head, reset. "From what she said, I think the guy's brain was on overload and he'd probably have crashed and burned without your help."

Yeah, that's what he'd thought, too, but he couldn't help himself. He said, "Nah, the guy was still in the manic stage, unpredictable, on the edge, but you're right, Ms. Black. You look like your mother."

She gave him a lazy smile. "Thank you."

"If I hadn't been there, Ms. Black, I think your mom would have cleaned Jitterbug's clock herself, made him very sorry he was in that particular shopping mall and had a hankering to joyride in a shiny black Beemer."

"Jitterbug—good name. I went by Washington Memorial to check on him, found out the moron's real name is Paul

Jones. I hope he's not a descendant of a very fine American hero John Paul Jones."

"If so, it's time the gene line closed its doors. You want to come in? Give the beast here a rest? You can pull him in behind my Jeep."

She looked at his town house, then at him, up and down, and revved the engine. "Mom said you had a real smart mouth."

"Me? Never. And my place is clean since my housekeeper was here today, so even the john sparkles. No food, though, since Monroe doesn't cook."

"Monroe?"

"He's a retired firefighter and my housekeeper, what you'd call real anal. I once saw him using an ancient tooth-brush he'd pulled off his tool belt to get after some dirty grout in the shower."

She grinned. "Don't you just hate that dirty grout?"

"Never really noticed it until Monroe pointed it out."

She studied him a moment longer, then pulled her helmet back on, fastened the strap, and pulled on her gloves. "I'd like to, but I can't. Can I have a rain check?"

"Any day but Sunday, that's my busting-around-with-family day."

She nodded. "Thanks again, Agent Sullivan, for helping my mom. I gotta go." She roared away from the curb and down Euclid Avenue like she owned it.

"Who was that hot cracker?"

Davis turned to see Mr. Mulroney standing right behind him, a bag of groceries from the Mini-Mart cradled in his bony arms, a bag of Fritos Scoops! sticking out the top. And was that a can of bean dip? His mouth watered.

"Do you know, I never found out her name."

"What's wrong with you, boy? I never thought you'd be that turtle-slow."

"I guess all that black body armor on that sweet hog sizzled my brain."

Mr. Mulroney, eighty-four and a half, said as he turned away, "At least she wears a helmet, and that's gotta mean her brain's not a bowl of cold oatmeal."

When had that saying been popular? He watched Mr. Mulroney navigate himself and his groceries safely into the town house two doors down from his, then he glanced once more down Euclid, but she was long gone. He liked her smart mouth and her sense of humor. He pulled off his leather jacket, slung it over his shoulder, and whistled as he walked into his spanking-clean entrance hall. He looked around, breathing in the scent of Pine Sol, Monroe's favorite cleaner. He walked into his shiny kitchen, pulled a bottle of water from the spotless refrigerator and drank deep. He said to the bottle, as he wiped his mouth, "Curiouser and curiouser."

4

**England
Two weeks ago**

Natalie was driving a steady fifty miles per hour in a light rain on the M2, heading south from London toward Canterbury, handling her sporty dark green Jaguar with a good deal of skill since she'd taken defensive driving lessons, thanks to Brundage's endless nagging. She loved the Jag, even driving on the wrong side of the road, and called her Nancy.

The rain picked up, nothing new in that, and the traffic remained on the heavy side, nothing new in that, either, but smooth and steady on the major thoroughfares. After living in London for more than a year, an umbrella—brolly—was as much a staple of her wardrobe as her shoes or her purse. She'd had nearly an hour and a half to think about what she was going to say to George's mother. Vivian had liked her, at least before George's death, had told her in her rasping smoker's voice that she was a modern young woman with spunk and spit. Since Vivian was older than dirt, she naturally saw even a menopausal woman as young.

Natalie turned off the M2 onto A2 before Dunkirk, then some minutes later she turned left onto the narrow two-lane country road. Another ten minutes and she'd reach the small town of Blean, not ten miles from Canterbury, and George's country home.

Her windshield wipers moved rhythmically, a steady metronome, the sound oddly comforting, and the Good Lord knew comfort was in short supply these days. There was no traffic on this pretty stretch, lots of tree-covered hills and patchwork fields and valleys, and some scary windy roads, several sharp curves above deep gullies, and few guardrails. She was only a few miles from Whitstable when she became aware of the big black sedan behind her, closing fast. Okay, so the idiot wanted to pass, on this road, in this weather, at this particular spot. It didn't make much sense to her, but she slowed and pulled over since she was near the deep curve that gave onto a thirty-foot drop. There wasn't a guardrail here, so she had to pay attention.

But the sedan didn't pull out to pass, it pulled closer until it was maybe six feet from the Jag's rear bumper. She couldn't see the driver, the windows were dark-tinted, but she knew to her gut that someone in this car wanted to hurt her, maybe even send her over the cliff edge, down, down, to the bottom of the deep gully.

The big Mercedes slammed into her and she was thrown hard against her seat belt. Her Jaguar shuddered with the force of the hit, the wheel jerking her onto the gravel on the shoulder, the wheels spinning out, so close to the edge. The air bag deployed, blinding her, but she knew exactly where she was, and saw the cliff edge looming, saw herself going over, striking the huge boulders on the way down, tumbling over and over until she hit the bottom of that rock-strewn gully. She didn't want to die, didn't want her life to end like this, at the hands of someone who hated her, someone she didn't know. She fought to straighten the wheel as the air bag collapsed and she could see again. She managed to ease the wheels off the deadly gravel and back onto the road. She saw the Mercedes coming up alongside her, waited, waited, then an instant before he struck her, she stomped hard on the accelerator. Her Jag shot forward, swerving to hug the centerline. She saw the Mercedes in her rearview mirror, accelerating to catch her. She waited, waited until he was ready to come alongside, then jerked her wheel inward, sending her vehicle straight toward the stretch of hillside. The Mercedes hit her rear bumper and went airborne, nearly flying off the cliff, but the driver somehow managed to pull the car back into the road.

He was better than she was. No choice now, she floored it. The Jaguar gave her its all, but still he came on, faster now, more determined, and she could smell the exhaust from the big engine. She saw her life, fleeting moments that held only deadening fear, and she knew she was going to die, braced herself for it, and whispered, **Perry, I'm so sorry.**

5

Davis's town house
Washington, D.C.
Tuesday morning

When Davis's cell sang out the awesome beginning of "Psycho Killer" at seven a.m., he was wet to his skivvies, sailing an America's Cup catamaran, its huge sail spearing up into the blue sky, flapping loud overhead. They were heeling so far to port he feared they were going to capsize. Odd thing was, a huge custom yellow Harley was lashed to the low side of the boat, adding five hundred and something pounds. He jerked awake, let the Talking Heads clear out his mind. When he answered, his voice rough and deep from sleep, he supposed he really wasn't surprised to hear Natalie Black's voice. "Special Agent Sullivan. I know it's Tuesday morning and your alarm will go off in precisely fifteen minutes, right?"

He stared at his cell. "No. Seven-thirty."

"A lovely morning hour. It's time to rise and shine and sally forth into this very fine day, but dress warmly or you'll chilblain your toes. I let you sleep in since you enjoyed such a lovely fun-filled Monday night with a very pretty blonde, oddly enough, of Latin origin. You might want to call your boss, tell him you'll be late again. I'll expect you at my house for breakfast in an hour." And she rang off.

He called Savich, who was eating Cheerios, and heard Sean in the background saying he wanted to play tight end for the Patriots like the Gronk, maybe in a couple years when he got big enough. Davis told him about Ms. Black's call. All Savich said was "I hope there's not another Jitterbug waiting for you, Davis."

Thirty minutes later, as Davis drove his Jeep toward Chevy Chase, he wondered if Ms. Black Leather Biker Babe would be eating grapefruit with them. And how had Mrs. Black known about Elena from Treasury?

6

Natalie Black's house
Chevy Chase, Maryland
Tuesday morning

Davis pulled his Jeep close to the discreetly inset intercom next to the huge wrought-iron gate on Ridgewood Road, saw the guardhouse was empty, and pushed the button. He looked up, smiled into the camera, and tried to look as nonthreatening as a sheepdog.

A man's deep voice came through the intercom, "Yeah, I see it's you, Mr. Hotshot. Mrs. Black told me to let you in." He finished off with a snort. Davis didn't think they were going to be best buds, sharing a beer at the Feathers.

Davis pulled in front of the beautiful old house, which had probably been built around the beginning of the twentieth century. It had a full three stories with a deep wraparound porch, at least a half-dozen chimneys, and big windows everywhere. It was painted a soft light blue with chocolate trim, though he thought it could use a bit of a touch-up. He stepped out of his Jeep to see a young guy in a green feed cap riding on a mower in clean straight lines over the large front lawn. He breathed in a hint of early spring jasmine, his mom's favorite, triggering a memory of being a teenager and wanting to go back to sleep. It wasn't breath-seeing cold, but close enough. He zipped up his leather jacket.

The front door opened and there stood the big man again, Hooley, who'd come busting out of the house yesterday morning, eager and ready to jerk out his tonsils until Natalie had called him off.

Davis eyed Hooley now, his beefy arms crossed over his beefy chest, a black turtleneck stretched around his thick neck, looking like he could punch out Muhammad Ali in his heyday, and wondered if Hooley's IQ was a match for his muscles. He walked past the bodyguard, knowing the middle of his back was being tracked. It didn't occur to him that Hooley was thinking Davis looked like a pussy with a smart mouth, and not even contemplating the size of his brain until he said, "You shouldn't be here, yahoo," and he cracked his knuckles for emphasis. "We don't need you hanging around bragging about how cool you are."

Davis turned, gave Hooley an appalled look. "What? You're saying you don't think I'm cool, Beef?"

"My name's Hooley, jerk-off. My granny looks cooler than you racing in her wheelchair."

Not bad. "You should visit the Bonhomie Club sometime, meet Fuzz and Marvin. They'll tell you what a cool guy I am." He grinned.

After a moment, Hooley grinned back. It looked painful. "I've heard about the backroom poker games there. Follow me. Mrs. Black likes to have breakfast in the sunroom."

Davis followed Hooley through a maze of hallways, all wide and high-ceilinged, with original art on the walls, ancient Persian carpets on the polished wood floors. They walked through the kitchen, a modern marvel beneath carved crown moldings from ten decades ago, into the sunroom, obviously added on, a small screened-in room with space heaters going full blast, looking out over a big backyard, beautifully kept, the big stone fence covered with ivy, thick trees behind it.

"Agent Sullivan. Welcome to my home." Natalie Black rose, shook his hand, gave him a big smile, waved around the room. "I like it out here even when it's cold outside. You can be toasty with the space heaters and you feel like you're cocooned in nature's bosom. My husband always— well, never mind that."

"I should have recognized you yesterday, Mrs. Black," he said.

"Actually, I'm glad you didn't right away, Agent Sullivan. Apparently, we both know about each other now, since I checked you out as well."

She was wearing jeans, sneakers, a

loose burgundy Redskins sweatshirt, her red hair in a ponytail. If she was wearing makeup, he couldn't see it. She did indeed look like the biker babe's mom. Because he was a cop, he saw the strain in her eyes, eyes the same light green color as her kid's.

He shook her hand, waited for her to sit, then sat down himself. He drank orange juice, then his coffee, rich and thick. He could feel it hitting his bloodstream, had to be the finest feeling there was.

"Hooley, all's good here. Go to the kitchen and have some breakfast."

He said toward Hooley's retreating back, "If Hooley's a bodyguard, then why wasn't he picking up the dry cleaning yesterday morning? Or at least with you? I mean, the shopping center is a good five miles from here. Why were you alone?"

"My Beemer's new. I wanted to drive her myself. Do you like the coffee? It's a special blend."

"Sure, I was thinking it may be even better than Starbucks." He looked at her closely for a moment. She looked tired, nearly at the end of her tether. He said, "In cosmic terms, Mrs. Black, our acquaintance is what you'd call brief, so I strongly doubt you'd invite me for breakfast to discuss the upcoming midterm elections. I know you've got big problems, so that probably means you invited the cop. What's going on that you'd need a cop in addition to a bodyguard? As to that, why do you have a bodyguard?"

She was silent for a moment, handed him a covered basket. "Have a croissant. I made them." They were big, hot and flaky, and his mouth watered, they smelled so good. "Try one with the turkey bacon," and she pointed to another covered dish.

She was dithering, which meant she wasn't sure yet about him and she wanted to feel him out. Well, okay, not a problem, since he was starving, and so he gave all his attention to making a bacon croissant sandwich and stayed silent, waiting to see where she'd head.

"I understand you met my daughter yesterday evening."

He took a big bite of his croissant and fell in love. Both with the croissant and the cook. "Yep, got home and there she was on her Harley, very nearly on my nicely kept front yard."

"Do you know who she is?"

"After I Googled her, sure. Since I've been a Redskins fan from the womb on, I realized I'd read some of her bylines and some of her blogs. Actually, I remember thinking Perry Black was a guy until they started running her photo next to her byline in the **Post**. I was amazed, I mean, a woman who's a real expert on pro football? Then yesterday, of course, I found out she's related to you.

"I thought your name sounded familiar, but I couldn't put it together until one of the agents told me yesterday when I got to the Hoover Building. And then, of course, I found out all about you and your current difficulties." She looked so normal, he thought, and nice and pleasant, and yet— "Here you are, the U.S. ambassador to the United Kingdom, one of the plummiest Foreign Service assignments in the universe, right?"

"Well, except for the Vulcan ambassadorship, I'm told, which isn't in the cards, since I can't pronounce the Vulcan capital." She grinned at him, chewed on her croissant. He saw blackberry jam ooze over her lip.

He said, "I read your family in Boston is very well connected, big politicos for decades now, with their fingers in lots of local and national elections. Did their big contributions help secure that ambassadorship for you?"

She didn't throw her fork at him. No, she laughed. "Not a bad assumption, but off the mark in my case. There's quite a bit more."

"You slept with the president."

She laughed again. "Can't say I did. Nope. He's happily married, though it took him a while to take the plunge. Imagine his daughter is only twelve years old and Perry's twenty-eight. You're forgetting who my husband was, Agent Sullivan."

A smile bloomed, Davis couldn't help it.

"Dr. Brundage Black, the longtime orthopedic surgeon for the Washington Redskins, and one of the first physicians to be directly on a pro football team's payroll. He died of a heart attack when he was only fifty. I was very sorry to hear it." He found he leaned toward her, at the loss and pain in her eyes.

After a moment, he said, "So tell me, Mrs. Black—"

"Call me Natalie, please."

He nodded. "Natalie, what did your husband have to do with your appointment as the ambassador to the United Kingdom?"

"You want to go back into the mists of time?"

"Sure. I'll eat another croissant."

She handed him the covered bread basket. "Four of us—President Gilbert; Arliss Abbott—he appointed her as his secretary of state; my husband; and I all met at Yale in our sophomore year. Thornton Gilbert—Thorn—and I were both in Berkeley College. My husband, Brundage, and Arliss Abbott in Calhoun and Branford. At any rate, the four of us were tight friends from our sophomore year on, all of us full-charge types, but we laughed about it, and somehow it worked. Brundage and I married soon after we graduated, and so did Arliss, a whirlwind romance with a mining engineer, and had her son not long after that. The president went on to law school at Harvard. He met and married his wife, Joy, some fifteen years ago. We all stayed in touch over the years, even though our paths diverged."

"So your appointment as ambassador to the United Kingdom was for auld lang syne?"

"Perhaps, in part, but I've made my career in the diplomatic corps for five years now. I had two other postings before this one."

"But you have a law degree; you had a successful practice here in Washington. Why did you decide to join the Foreign Service?"

She smiled. "Thorn, President Gilbert, told me I was the natural-born diplomat in the group, that I could talk a sheik into giving up his harem and that I was wasted hammering out endless business contracts. He said it was invaluable to him to have people around him he could trust implicitly, and he trusted me. Arliss Abbott, his newly appointed secretary of state, another one of the four of us, agreed, and so I did.

"It was Brundage who first suggested I should think about becoming a diplomat. He said to forget the harems, I could talk him out of his last bite of butter-pecan ice cream. Unfortunately, he never saw it happen. He died at the beginning of President Gilbert's first term. I remember he loved dancing at the inauguration ball. He was very pleased for Thornton and for the country."

She fell silent and Davis didn't say anything, let her gather herself. He finished off his second croissant, drank more of his coffee, sat back in his chair and crossed his arms over his chest. He said finally, "Okay, I'd like to get back to today, if you don't mind. Are you ready to tell me why you wanted to see me?"

She sipped her coffee, frowned.

"Okay, perhaps you'll let me get us started. According to what I've read, you're back in the States officially on health leave, but really because of a scandal the British press created and is hounding you with. I saw they've labeled you a black widow 'before the fact,' a clever little aside they found amusing; in short, they were making your life a misery. And now there's talk here as well, since you came home. Is that fair?"

"Yes, that's right."

"I assume you expect the press here will be going after you and that's why you have a bodyguard, to keep them away? You don't have any DSS agents with you?"

"No. The Diplomatic Security Service is not normally assigned to protect me when I'm home, and I haven't made a request for them." She said nothing more.

Davis eyed her, continued. "I read the scandal in England involved the suicide of an Englishman you were engaged to marry."

She nodded.

"The English press claimed you drove him to suicide because you broke it off with him abruptly, and that's why they came up with the black widow moniker. His family was less than supportive, and some of the public seems to think you should be exiled to the Hebrides to live in a Viking hut. Not exactly a comfortable position for an ambassador to an important ally, I gathered. Did I hit the high points, Madame Ambassador?"

She studied him silently for a moment, then said, "I don't believe George McCallum, my fiancé, did commit suicide, Agent Sullivan."

7

Now that we're officially sharing secrets, Madame Ambassador, call me Davis."

"Very well. Davis."

"Is that why you asked me over today, to tell me you don't think George McCallum's death was a suicide?"

"In part. Let me add that George was the eighth Viscount Lockenby, the head of the very large McCallum family. His family seat is near Canterbury, in Kent. Lockenby Manor." She paused for a moment, and he saw grief in her eyes. She cleared her throat. "George was the polar opposite of Brundage. He didn't know or care a thing about sports. To him, Wayne Gretzky could have been a Polish astronaut. It didn't matter, he was a wonderful man. He loved life, loved his family, loved me. He paid attention to everyone, most especially me. He had this gift, I suppose you could call it. He knew, for example, when I needed to change my back tires or where I'd dropped a missing bracelet. Someone in his family was always phoning him, even about little things like a pet that couldn't be found or a horse running in the fourth race at Doncaster. He was involved in all their lives deeply, and he took his role as head of his family seriously. He protected them."

Again she paused, then met Davis's eyes. "He did not, however, foresee his own death.

"They found him in his car at the bottom of a cliff near Dover. The car was smashed, of course, but there was no evidence the car had been tampered with, and there were no skid marks to suggest he was losing control and trying to regain it. The car went straight over the cliff.

"It's true it couldn't have been an accident, since the cliffs are a goodly distance beyond the road, thus anyone would have plenty of time to stop a car— if one wanted to. At first everyone believed he'd lost consciousness, maybe suffered a heart attack. There was an autopsy, but

I was told it was difficult to determine what had happened, since his body had been so traumatized. Still, it was ruled an accidental death.

"Then the whispers started right after the funeral, whispers and tabloid stories that it was really a suicide, that George had fallen into a profound depression because I'd broken off our engagement, that I was to blame, that I drove him to kill himself. It seems I hadn't even told him to his face, no, I'd sent him an email telling him, and it broke him."

"Had you broken it off with him?"

She shook her head. "Hardly. We'd been happy, making plans. He liked the U.S. He didn't mind living here six months out of the year; he even liked the idea of being posted elsewhere in the world.

"George was in fact under a good deal of stress in the final two weeks of his life. It had to do with his eldest son and heir, William Charles—Billy. George had told me he was a troubled child throughout his school years and that despite his complete support, Billy was asked to leave Oxford in his first year. He soon cut off most contact with the family and moved to Germany. He lived in a mostly Muslim neighborhood in Hamburg and eventually courted a Lebanese girl and ended up converting to her religion. George thought that structured life seemed to help William at first, and perhaps it did, but there was more, a lot more. I realized George didn't like to talk about Billy—it was a painful subject for him, and I didn't push it.

"Two weeks before George's death, there were huge headlines in the British tabloids, such as 'Viscount's Heir a Terrorist' and 'House of Lords Member Breeds Traitor.'" She gave him a twisted smile. "That's doubtless one of the first things you read about me, isn't it?"

Davis nodded, saying nothing.

"They published a photograph of Billy taken somewhere in Syria, bearded and in local garb, armed with a Kalashnikov. We had no idea where they'd found that picture, but it was clearly Billy, no denying it, George said.

"It was a major embarrassment, needless to say, both for George and his family and for me, the United States ambassador who was engaged to him. The story was irresistible, and we came under intense scrutiny by the press. But there was no talk between us of ending our engagement. And then George died, and that faked email surfaced in the press—again, I don't know how—and it all led to the speculation that George had killed himself, that I was responsible because I sent him that email, favoring my own career in his time of need, that sort of thing.

"As you know, Davis, the English tabloid press is probably the most virulent in the world. I remember one of the headlines— that I'd gone to Paris to get away from George and meet up with my lover. The fact is I was in Paris when George died, but I was there to meet with Jean-Marc Ayrault, the French PM.

"Of course what the tabloids wrote was far sexier. I spoke to George's family— those who would speak to me, that is— but they didn't believe me when I told them I hadn't broken it off, or they were too busy fending off the media wanting to know everything about George's son—how he became a terrorist, why he became a terrorist, and what they felt about it. You get the idea.

"The tabloids even suggested that my husband, Brundage, had killed himself as well and I'd managed to get it covered up with a heart attack story, backed by the president." He saw her hands were clenched into fists, flames nearly shooting out of her red hair. "Can you imagine? Accusing me of murdering Brundage?

"The press don't have any of the famous British sense of fair play, no brakes. In England there's simply no way to set things straight. If they decide you're guilty of something, they single you out as their latest star.

"Needless to say, the whole affair embarrassed our government, the embassy staff, and many of my British friends. I offered to resign, but the president refused to accept it, told me to soldier on, that I had done nothing wrong. As for Perry, she wants to go tear out someone's throat. Soldiering on is only part of the reason I'm sitting in my lovely house with a bodyguard to protect me—" She stopped cold.

Davis said, "What would the bodyguard protect you from? The press? No, not the press. You'd chew the press up and have Hooley toss them over the fence. All right, Natalie, why do you have a bodyguard? Why did you want to see me?"

She said, "I told you I didn't believe George McCallum's death was a suicide. Actually, my strongest reason for that is because I'm sure as I can be someone is trying to kill me."

8

Natalie told him about the attempt on her life on the narrow country road on the way to George's country home, vivid in her mind since she'd awakened early that morning sweating, her heart hammering in her chest, breathing hard and fast, nearly choking on the remembered fear.

"My Jag, Nancy, has lots of oomph, thank heaven, but I knew he could catch me; the Mercedes was more powerful and the driver was really good. Then two cars came over the hill in front of us, which meant witnesses, and the driver did a fast screeching K-turn and sped back toward the M2. I pulled over and sat there, my head against the steering wheel. It didn't occur to me then to flag down those two cars, ask them what they'd seen."

"What did you do?"

"When I got myself together, I drove to the police station in Whitstable. The constable accompanied me back to the scene. There were tire marks—both cars—but there was nothing more to show them but a dent in my back fender.

"By nightfall I saw a headline: 'Swallow This: Black Widow Blames Auto Accident on Mysterious Assassin!'"

"Did you see the driver of the black sedan?"

"No, like I said, the windows were dark-tinted and the license plate was muddied, probably on purpose."

"What happened then?"

"Arliss called me back home after consulting with the British government. From their perspective, you see, I was either unstable or, worse, the focus of a plot they could not unravel. Either way, all parties sought to avoid a major international scandal. Arliss said she and the president believed me, of course, but it obviously wasn't safe for me in England. I can't tell you how glad I was to come home. I believed I would be safe here, since all the violence had happened in England, and it seemed to be tied to George."

Davis nodded. "The son's photo, the e-mail, then his death. Okay, tell me what happened back here in the States?"

"I've been home six days, conducting business by phone, or in meetings at the State Department, meanwhile dodging the press, following the papers here and in London, waiting for Arliss and the president to decide when it will be a political necessity for me to resign." She sighed, told him about her run in Buckner Park at sunset, a beautiful time of day to run, her thinking time.

"So another attempted murder using a car as the weapon?"

"It was like England. For an instant, I thought it was all over for me, but then I managed to roll behind bushes against a tree in the nick of time. It was close. I could even smell the car exhaust."

"What did the car look like?"

"Another big black sedan, and again, I couldn't make out the license plate and the windows were tinted so I couldn't see the driver or how many people were in the car. I know it can't be the same car as in

England, but it was probably the same person behind the wheel—to try to kill me with a car twice? Why the same play?"

"You called the cops?"

She shook her head. "Believe me, I thought about calling them, but I knew I couldn't risk a police report getting into the press. I had no proof, and without that, another press leak might give the secretary of state and the president no choice. And what was there to find, anyway? Maybe evidence that a drunk might have lost control, got scared, and drove off as fast as he could?"

"So you hired Hooley."

"Yes. Hooley is ex–Special Forces, and came well recommended. He wanted me to speak to the police, to the FBI, to the State Department, but as I said, I haven't even told Arliss or Thorn—President Gilbert—no one except Hooley and Connie Mendez, a former Secret Service agent Hooley recommended. And now you."

"Do you know our FBI director?"

"Yes, I've met him, but I don't know him or his loyalties. Whereas you, Special

Agent Sullivan, I saw what you're made of, how you deal with surprise and danger. Don't you see I had to decide who to turn to. I don't know any other agents in the FBI, though I've heard of that exceptional boss of yours, Agent Savich. There's no reason for any of them to believe me, not given what's happened and what's been reported. After yesterday, I thought perhaps you would."

Davis didn't hesitate. "I do believe you. But I want to bring my boss, Dillon Savich, to see you. I want you to tell him what you've told me. Believe me, Natalie, we'll do everything to find out what's going on. And there will be no press leak. Something else—Savich has a gift, like George McCallum. He seems to know things, sense things. Sometimes you don't want to think about it because it's scary, but you're glad he's on your side."

She was quiet until she'd poured him another cup of the sinful coffee from a silver carafe. "Can you guarantee me that you'll be directly involved?"

"You know I can't, but I'll try."

"Davis, look. Your being there at that shopping mall at that particular moment—the way you dealt with Jitterbug—to me it was a sign."

Now he was a sign? He said, "You weren't at all afraid of Jitterbug, not for an instant."

"Not after I realized he wasn't one of them, that he was only a pathetic addict who needed to be punched in the head. Or elsewhere."

Them? He said nothing, only looked at her. She blinked first, nodded. "All right, I'll speak to your boss, but only if you agree to do something for me first."

Now he was negotiating with an ambassador. "You want me to dismiss my harem?"

She laughed, actually laughed. "I want you to come with me tonight to a function at the secretary of state's house. It's a show of solidarity to invite me, and a sort of testing of the waters as well. If Arliss and I hadn't been friends for more than half our lives, I think she'd have asked me to resign herself by now with outward regret and inward good riddance. But she wants to go the extra mile. I want you to come with me, as my escort and bodyguard."

Why didn't she want Hooley going with her? Well, okay, dumb question—Hooley would stick out like a shark in a fishbowl. He looked like what he was, a wrecking ball, and he'd maim anything or anyone with the poor judgment to set the **Enterprise** down within three feet of Natalie Black.

"I'm not trained as a bodyguard."

"I've seen you in action, Agent Sullivan. You don't get excited and go off the deep end, you do what you have to do, nothing more. If there was an attacker, you'd deal with him, then you'd remove him from the premises, no one the wiser."

Davis liked her, really liked her, and he didn't want her to be hurt. "Is your daughter going with you? From the looks of Ms. Biker Babe, she'd keep you safe."

"Perry is not a diplomat, so it wouldn't work. I'm afraid if someone threatened me or even made a snide remark, I might end up seeing her give me her heartbreaker smile while she stood over a bleeding body.

"She'll be there, though. Actually, she's coming with the secretary of state's son. And that's another reason Arliss doesn't want to cut me loose. Her son, Day, would blow a fit. You see, Day and Perry were practically raised together. I used to think of them as brother and sister, but now, well, maybe they'll get married, but I'm by no means sure yet, since Perry's a clam on the subject."

Davis ruminated, then gave it up. "All right, tonight I'll be your bodyguard with the understanding that first thing tomorrow, you speak to my boss, Agent Dillon Savich. Shall we shake hands?"

She gave him a patrician down-the-nose stare, but he stared back. He knew all it would take would be for her to be with Savich for two minutes to change her mind. Davis wondered if Hooley would think Savich was a pretty-boy tool. Somehow he didn't think so.

"Very well," she said, rose, and stuck out her hand.

9

<u>Washington Post</u> offices
1150 15th Street NW, Washington, D.C.
Tuesday, late afternoon

Bennett John Bennett was a ferocious linebacker at Ohio until he wrecked his knee during a snowboard competition at Squaw Valley. After a six-month funk he decided that writing about sports was the way to go, since playing pro ball wasn't in his future. Now he was the top sports editor at the **Post**, had four flat-screen TVs in his living room all set to sports channels, and was lucky enough to have a very tolerant wife. He was picked for his job because he was smart and focused and dealt with his staff like a magician with his deck of cards.

He now looked around at each of them in turn. "We've got a situation here—any of you read Walt Derwent's tweet from half an hour ago that just came up on ESPN? Yeah, of course you have, Perry. Okay, for the rest of you, here it is:

"Is Tebow returning to Patriots to become Brady's heir? Sources say yes. Sounds right to me."

"Now, all Walt has at this point— **Sources say yes**—and what does that mean?"

Alonzo Petri, aka Einstein, said, "Probably something he overheard in the ESPN men's room." Alonzo was known as Einstein for two reasons: he was always spouting esoteric trivia about baseball and his hair looked like it had been fried in an electrical socket.

Bennett said, "Could be, but I'll bet it comes from someone more reputable, otherwise old Walt wouldn't go out on a limb like that. You can bet he'll continue to milk this, now that he's whetted everyone's interest. We'll be fighting every sportswriter and announcer you can think of to get to Tebow, his agent, and the Patriots' coaching staff. This story will build and build, until someone gets an absolute denial or an absolute confirmation."

He looked at each of them again, then focused on Perry. He said, "Perry, I gotta tell you, you know the make of the towels in the Steelers' locker room, but you didn't know about this? What's going on here?"

"Sorry, boss, but nothing came my way," Perry said. "The first I heard about it was from Walt's tweet. I was on it when you called us all in."

Einstein said, "Easy enough to tweet, boss, as you know. Walt's blog is close to tanking; he needs to regain reader interest. Maybe he made it up. Perry and the rest of us can dig out the real facts, if there are any. Everyone will forget that Walt Derwent ever floated the rumor."

Lolita Barcas, aging hippie and world-wide soccer maven, said, "What are you going to do next, Einstein, ask Perry out? I say go out with him, Perry, and thank him because, fact is, you blew it. If this had anything to do with the Mexican soccer team, I would have known about it instantly and tweeted it myself."

Einstein sneered. "Yeah, Lolita, but who gives a flying hoot about the Mexican soccer team?"

Lolita tossed her long, thick gray braid. "My readers and most of the world, numb nuts. If only you'd had the brain to bet on the U.S. team when they played Mexico last year at Estadio Azteca, like I told you to, you could have taken us all out to dinner."

Einstein raised his hands, palms out. "Yeah, yeah, I should have listened, okay? How about I say you're right, Lolita, Perry blew this one."

Bennett said, "This isn't about blame, people. We don't have much time. Perry, who do you think gave Derwent this juicy morsel?"

"I'm thinking it was someone in Kary Munson's office," she said, and added for those in the room who didn't know who he was, "He's Tebow's agent. I heard a couple of months ago Kary owed Walt a favor for something, I don't know what. Still, it would take guts for Kary to risk any of his people calling Derwent to even float this rumor. Is it true? Have the Patriots decided to bring him back, coach him up, see if he can eventually take Brady's place after he retires? I don't know, but there's something that doesn't feel right. I mean, if it's true, why not an official announcement?"

Lolita said, "I can't see it being Tebow's agent. Why would he? Maybe Belichick is still thinking about bringing Tebow back, and the agent leaked it to force his hand."

"Kary Munson will deny to his dying day his office was the leak," Bennett said. "Beyond his dying day."

Perry thought she might have picked something up, that was the truth, if she'd been on her game. But she'd been worried about her mom, of course, and now about this FBI agent her mom thought was her special knight from God. A rumor about Tebow going back to the Patriots didn't even come close. But it was her job to care, her livelihood, and she was fiercely proud of it. She had to stay more turned in. It was one thing that her mom was a huge distraction, but that clean-bathroom-shower-grout FBI agent who'd saved her mom's bacon yesterday? She'd have been all over the Tebow news, antennas buzzing, if she hadn't given that moron with his come-hither saunter more than a passing thought. It was the cardinal rule in sportswriting: **the more outlandish the rumor, the more important if it's true.**

"So I guess we all need to get on this, Perry," Lolita said, giving her thick hippie braid another flip, "before this big whomping story blasts out all over ESPN and its dozens of talking heads and leaves the **Post** on the sidelines."

Bennett said, "Perry, you have twenty minutes to find out if this rumor is true and give me two hundred words. We can be online within the hour and get a longer piece going for tomorrow's paper.

"People, this is hair-on-fire time, so every one of you, go get comments, interesting takes we can use for tomorrow's story."

Perry was on her cell in under a minute. She started with assistant coaches, got the runaround, which she expected. Of course Walt Derwent had done the same thing, and four dozen other sportswriters as well.

Why not go to the Top Dog? She called Robert Kraft, owner of the Patriots, while she poured creamer into her coffee. Kraft had to know about the rumor, because no doubt every coach in the organization was talking about it and a gazillion sports people had called. But she'd bet he hadn't spoken to any of them. Maybe he'd realize the best thing to do was be up front with her, not let the media chew on it and come up with absurd conclusions.

It was a huge relief when Mr. Kraft took her call and came clean with her. From experience, he knew she'd get everything right. Of course, it didn't hurt that Kraft had known and liked her father, even remembered her as a skinny kid on the Redskins sideline.

She waited exactly six minutes before calling Belichick, time for Mr. Kraft to pave her way. He took her call, said since she'd already spoken to Kraft, what was there for him to say? And so he'd said only one word: no. No surprise, since Belichick was known for speaking only one word when fifteen would be better. He kept things close to the hoodie, his signature garb.

She was typing her story when she finally got ahold of Kary Munson, Tim Tebow's agent. "Hey, Kary, I finally realized why you had one of your people feed Walt the rumor that Tim was being called back to the Patriots."

"I don't know what you're talking about, Black. That rumor didn't come from me or my office—"

She rode right over him. "Turns out it wasn't a very smart move on your part. You've got to know Tim is going to roast you when he finds out what you did, all in hopes of raising his price tag for the CFL, specifically, for the Toronto Argonauts, by floating the rumor that he was going back to the Patriots. I know from my own sources Tim is talking to them and he isn't going to like this a bit; he might fire you for it."

And here came the music to her ears.

"No, he won't! I mean, it wasn't even my idea—" Long pause, then Munson's voice fell off the cliff. "Ah, damn, Perry. How'd you find out?"

"I spoke to Damien Cox with the **Toronto Star**. He knows everything that's going on in Canadian football, plus I figured you wouldn't shop Tim to any but the biggest team in the CFL, and that's the Toronto Argonauts. How many Grey Cup championship victories do they have now?"

"Fifteen."

"To make sure, I called one of the assistant coaches up there and he didn't deny it. Hang it up, Kary, I called to tell you I'm putting the truth on my blog in seven minutes, and there'll be a lovely headline in tomorrow's Sports section in the **Post**. Fair warning."

She grinned as she hung up.

She handed her story in to Bennett five minutes later. "Kary Munson's going to be in deep caca," she said, and she told him what she'd found out.

"So it all boiled down to Munson wanting

to soak the Toronto Argonauts for more money?"

She shrugged. "Looks like."

"Okay, then, we're good." He nodded up at the TV screen on the wall in his office. "It was reported again about two minutes ago on ESPN as a rumor that's 'flying around' the league. You know how that works, the more it's repeated and speculated on, the better the chance of it coming true. Morons." He took a minute to clean up her copy, then said, "Get this up on the Internet immediately. Get it on Twitter. Get it on Facebook. It'll go viral in three minutes."

She raced to the door of his office.

"Perry? I know this deal going on with your mother makes it tough for you to concentrate. You did a good job with this, in spite of that."

When she got home to change for the A-list party at the secretary of state's incredible antiques-filled Federal-style home on Caldicott Road, she was feeling pretty good, except for the greasy slick of fear always there deep inside, for her mother.

She wondered if Tebow and the Toronto Argonauts would close a deal. Damien Cox said Tebow was as big a deal in Canada as he was in the United States. She hoped it would work out for him. She remembered one sportswriter on the football channel say that if he was a coach he'd want Tebow to marry his daughter, not play on his team. Ah, well, fans who continued to root for Tebow would have something to follow. At least she'd set things straight.

She wondered if Tebow would ever have the chance to be the Seabiscuit of the NFL.

10

**Criminal Apprehension Unit
Hoover Building
Tuesday afternoon**

I should have told Dillon over tacos at lunch. But she hadn't. A moment of honesty. Sherlock hadn't told him because he wouldn't have let her go to the women's room without an escort, so she'd kept quiet, but only until after she took her stalwart Volvo in to get serviced. Tonight, she'd tell him after they'd gotten Sean down, when the house was settling around them, when it would be quiet and there would be time to talk. She pulled out of the Hoover Building's garage, managed with little finger waves and big pleading smiles to squeeze herself between an SUV and a tiny Fiat. It was four o'clock in the afternoon, and government employees were pouring out of buildings like a tide. Cars gridlocked the streets, people were thick on the sidewalks and at the crosswalks. The temperature had plummeted again. It was so cold she could see her breath.

Sherlock turned up the heater and drove to Georgetown, to her service station on Prospect Street. She left her baby with Honest Bob, the owner she now trusted since he knew she carried a gun. She stepped off the sidewalk to flag down a taxi even though she wasn't more than a quarter-mile from home, and she'd walked it before. She was more worried than she'd realized, more than she'd let on to herself. But there were no taxis to be had, and after five minutes, she gave up. She didn't want to walk home in the dark. She pulled her small Lady Colt from her ankle holster and slipped it inside her coat pocket. She felt stupid, particularly since her new-issue Glock was clipped to her belt. **You're still healing from that gunshot wound. It makes sense you're still paranoid, picturing a rifle sighting in on you, and blah, blah, blah.** She was being ridiculous. She was in the middle of Georgetown, the streets crowded with people huddled in their coats, heads down, all moving fast. No one was looking at her, no one was stalking her, no one was out to kill her. It was here and now, not San Francisco three weeks ago.

She crossed Wisconsin and began walking quickly down O Street NW, thinking about dinner. Dillon had made an eggplant Parmesan the night before, so all she had to do was warm it up along with a baguette, throw some tomatoes in lettuce, and not forget the croutons. Sean loved croutons and lots of ranch dressing. No problem, thirty minutes, tops.

One block away from Wisconsin Avenue, the crowds began to thin out. Sherlock walked faster. She was cold, walking into the wind, but the lovely leather gloves Sean and Dillon had gotten her for Christmas were warm enough.

She felt a single set of eyes staring at her, as she had two days ago at Chad's Market in Georgetown and again yesterday afternoon when she was out buying a baby gift for Dillon's sister Lily's new little boy, Ethan. Sherlock felt the same thing again, a sense of knowing that someone was staring at her fixedly, and only her. She whipped around, bumping into a young mother with a toddler in her arms, and apologized. She stood perfectly still and slowly looked at the circle around her. A college student from Georgetown University, a ratty backpack hooked over his shoulder, several couples laughing and talking, an older man walking a teacup poodle. No one watched her, no one stared at her, no one wanted anything. Everything was perfectly normal. **Are you on edge or what? Stop it, get yourself home where it's safe—no, don't think that, either.**

As she was crossing 33rd Street, she heard the roar of a motorcycle and whipped around to see a Kawasaki coming directly at her. The rider was all bundled up, a dark wool scarf covering his mouth, and wearing, of all things, sunglasses. He held a gun in his hand, aimed at her.

11

A woman behind her screamed. Sherlock shoved her to the ground and fell on top of her as the man fired, the bullet chipping a shard of concrete from the sidewalk. The man was only twenty feet away, but thankfully he had to handle the moving motorcycle. Sherlock pulled her Glock and fired off her magazine at him as he fired off five shots at her. A revolver, she thought, when he fired again, but nothing happened. He stuffed the gun back in his coat, swerved away from her, and accelerated. With her final shot, Sherlock got the front tire and the motorcycle weaved and lurched out of control, threading through honking horns and yelling people to the far side of the street, and hit a fire hydrant, luckily enough for an old couple standing a few feet behind it. The shooter managed to jump off before the motorcycle slammed against the hydrant and the guy jumped, fell, landing hard, then managed to get himself together and run.

The crying woman was on her feet, yelling as she grabbed Sherlock's arm, "That idiot! He was going to shoot me! You stopped him. That was a great shot. Are you a cop?"

"Yes. FBI. Stay!" Sherlock managed to break free and took off after the man. After running full-out for a half-block, she slowed and leaned down, her hands on her knees. Then she straightened and slowly looked around. No sight of him. The woman had cost her valuable seconds. He hadn't seemed very agile or fast, so she imagined he'd hidden himself behind one of the bushes that surrounded many of the houses that lined the block. He could have gone anywhere from there. She jogged back and nodded to the old couple standing by the wrecked motorcycle, called out for them to please stay. She ran back to the woman, who was hugging herself, shaking. She was on the small side, in her thirties, all bundled up and shivering, not with cold, Sherlock knew, but from fear. As for herself, after all the running, she was toasty warm, her adrenaline level now starting its way back down. She knew exhaustion would follow later.

It would be full-on dark in maybe fifteen minutes.

"You're okay," she said, and because the woman looked to be on the bitter edge, Sherlock pulled her against her, rubbed her hands down her back, smoothed out her voice. "It's all right now. He's gone."

Between bursts of sobs and moans, she said, "He was going to shoot me, kill me." She shook. "I know who it was—" Her voice firmed up, became fierce. "It was that bastard husband of mine, Lou. He told me he would kill me if I left him, but I didn't think he meant it. I mean, he hit me once and I punched him back hard in the face. Boy, did that feel good. I left him last week, and would you look, he did mean it, he tried to kill me." Her voice was rising—not good. Sherlock rubbed her arms, said over and over, "No, Lou didn't do this. Lou didn't try to kill you. The man on the motorcycle, he was shooting at me."

"If you weren't here right at this minute, right at this spot—" Her breath hitched and she grew perfectly still.

Sherlock tried again. "Listen to me now, Mrs.—"

"Glory, my name is Glory Cudlow, and that jerkface—"

"No, Glory," she repeated very slowly, spacing out her words to break through, "the bastard wasn't your ex-husband. Lou wasn't after you. Whoever it was, he was after me."

Glory looked at her, slack-jawed. Was that disappointment she saw? Surely not. Sherlock lightly touched her flushed cold face. "Believe me. Okay, tell me, Mrs. Cudlow, did you recognize that motorcycle?"

"No, I've never seen it before."

"So it doesn't belong to Lou?"

"He could have gotten a new motorcycle, to celebrate me being gone. It'd be just like him."

A half-dozen people were crowding around now, asking questions, others looking at the Kawasaki. Thank God no one had been hurt in that rain of bullets. Sherlock dialed 911 and gave the very calm female dispatcher the particulars. When she punched off her cell, she asked everyone to stick around to talk to the police. She remembered Davis telling how Natalie Black done the very same thing yesterday morning.

There was grumbling, but four people stayed, bless them. Sherlock got Mrs. Cudlow's cell number and her address. It was only two blocks away. Sherlock sent her home with an order to calm herself with a water glass full of merlot, assured her for a third time it wasn't Lou who'd shot at her.

She waved at the older couple across the street, who were still staring at the crumpled motorcycle when two Metro cop cars screeched around the corner. Two and a half minutes, good time. Sherlock showed them her creds, asked one of the officers to go over immediately to the couple before they left, since they'd seen the man closer than anyone. "Tell them to describe him as exactly as they can while he's still fresh in their minds. I'll come see them as soon as I can."

"Yeah, yeah," one young officer said. "Glad to be reminded how to do the job."

Two veteran cops arrived in a second Crown Vic. She introduced herself and showed them her creds. While Officer Newberg interviewed the witnesses, Sherlock walked to the motorcycle beside Officer Clooney. It was wrapped around the fire hydrant, a double helix of black smoke curling out of the smashed engine, and the smell of burned rubber was thick and nasty in the cold air. Thankfully, the fire hydrant hadn't burst and flooded the area with a gusher of freezing water.

"And that's the problem trying to do nasty deeds from a motorcycle," Officer Clooney said. "Not enough control, and if a tire goes, the sucker's down and out. The guy was lucky to be able to run off. Could you tell what kind of gun he was using?"

"Probably a revolver since he fired off six shots, then shoved the gun back in his coat," she said, "so no shells.

"As to the make—this is an impression, since it happened so fast, but what my brain picked up was that it wasn't new, it looked big and worn, like one of those Colt New Service revolvers, you know, the kind your great-granddaddy brought back from the Great War? Maybe a Colt M1917 you'd find mounted on the wall or a Colt official police revolver. Maybe the guy bought it at an antique-gun show." She sighed. "Or maybe I imagined the whole thing and it will turn out to be a Beretta."

Officer Clooney asked for a description and Sherlock told him the man was wearing a camel wool coat, his face covered up, and he was wearing sunglasses, adding, "I couldn't tell his age, but when the motorcycle hit the fire hydrant, he was pretty fast jumping off and getting out of there."

Officer Clooney jotted this down. "Okay,

I'll put out an APD, our people will canvass the neighborhood, but you know as well as I do it doesn't look promising.

Officer Clooney called in the motorcycle's license plate. A moment later, he said, "The Kawasaki belongs to Don E. Huzar, Farlow, Maryland, reported stolen early this morning. You have any idea why this guy would try to kill you, Agent Sherlock? Is there some gnarly case you're working on? Maybe a drug gang?"

"I honestly don't know who it was." She started to tell Officer Clooney about her feeling someone had been staring at her, then stopped at the roar of the Porsche engine taking a corner too fast onto 34th.

She smiled. "That's my husband. I guess your nine-one-one operator called him."

Officer Clooney grinned. "Agent Savich, right?"

"Right."

"You bet it was all over the air. You and your husband are always good business."

Savich pulled the Porsche with great precision close to the opposite curb, burst out and hit the pavement running. He stopped six inches from her, saw she was all right, and took several deep breaths. Slowly he reached out his hand and cupped her face, studied her.

Officer Clooney said, "She gave as good as she got, Agent Savich. Look where the bozo's ride ended up."

Savich glanced over at the wrecked motorcycle.

Sherlock said, "Turned out okay, but I was aiming at him, of course. At least I got a tire."

Savich took her arms in his hands. And felt something wet. His heart jittered. He looked to see her coat was ripped high on her arm. He said in a deep, calm voice, "He got you."

Sherlock looked down at her arm, and of all things, she felt a sudden stab of pain. "Isn't that a kick? I didn't feel anything at all until you pointed that out. Now it hurts. Well, I did it again."

Savich peeled off her coat, pulled her sweater off her shoulder, and saw it was only a graze, really, the bullet scratching through her skin. No need for stitches.

Antiseptic and a small bandage should do it. Still, his heart was galloping even with the proof in front of him that it wasn't much of anything, thank the Good Lord. It wasn't even bleeding now. He pulled her sweater and coat back into place. He stood there with her hands now in his and wondered where his brain had gone. "You're all right," he said finally. "You're all right."

She knew he was scared, knew he was remembering San Francisco, knew that if it had been him, she'd be a mess. She smiled. "Yeah, no worries, I promise. We'll take care of it at home. You made really good time, Dillon."

"The nine-one-one operator called me."

Officer Clooney smiled. "Which one, Agent Savich?"

"Jodie."

Officer Clooney nodded. "Well, Agent, we've got two women, Agent Sherlock one of them, who both claim to be the guy's intended victim."

Savich stared hard at Sherlock. Her nose was red from the cold. She was pale, not from what had happened, but from something else, something like guilt from some knowledge she hadn't shared with him? He looked away from her, over at the ruined tire, breathed in the smell of burning rubber, and said very calmly, "If Agent Sherlock says the shooter was after her, there's no question here."

The cop who'd been speaking to the older couple across the street jogged over. "Agent Sherlock, I asked that old couple to describe the man who jumped off the crashing motorcycle. They said they really didn't see him."

"But they were right there," Sherlock said. She weaved where she stood. It was humiliating.

Savich said, "Guys, we're going to leave the crime scene and the interviews to you because I'm taking my wife home to clean off the blood. We'll follow up with you tomorrow. Thanks for coming so quickly."

Clooney nodded toward the Porsche. "Nice car, Agent Savich."

"Thanks."

As he was leading Sherlock away, she called out over her shoulder, "Officer

Clooney, I'll personally call Glory Cudlow tomorrow and put her mind at rest. As for Mr. Huzar's Kawasaki, you'll notify him? Tell him it's sort of totaled?"

Clooney nodded. "We'll follow up on the ballistics, the witnesses while you get some iodine and a Band-Aid. I'll get back to you with what we learn. We'll need a full statement from you tomorrow."

Savich put her in the Porsche, fastened her seat belt himself. She said even before he turned on the sweet motor, "The old couple, their name is Thompson, and I have their address. We've got to speak to them. I don't understand why they told the officer they didn't see the man. We've got to go see them, Dillon. Now."

He eyed her, slowly nodded. "All right." Actually, Savich wanted to yell at her, wanted to hide her under his coat, but he couldn't, at least not right now. He pulled out his cell. "I'll call Gabriella, tell her we'll be a little late. She can wait awhile and then put the eggplant in the oven for us."

Eggplant. It was too much. She began to laugh.

12

Natalie's house
Chevy Chase, Maryland
Tuesday evening

Davis looked up to see Natalie Black glide down the posh wide staircase decked out in a long black gown, delicate strands of diamonds at her neck, her ears, and her wrist. Her incredible Sherlock-red hair was pulled back in a chignon, fastened with a diamond clip. She looked elegant, utterly certain of her world and her place in it. This was the woman who'd chomped down on Jitterbug's forearm and bounced her fist off his face.

His Glock, always his reliable friend, was secured comfortably on his belt, and he knew no one would realize he was wearing it. His tux was cut that well, thanks to his mom, who'd forced him with believable threats to his father's tailor. It wasn't Armani, but it was close. He'd forked out a month's salary for the privilege of looking like he belonged, no matter how high on the food chain a function was, and tonight's was pretty close to the top. Hooley was wrong. Tonight Davis was nothing but cool in a bespoke tux with a gun at his belt and an incredible woman walking toward him. He hummed "Come Out and Play" by The Offspring.

He smiled as he stepped onto the huge black-and-white marble square entrance hall. He said, "What would you like me to call you?"

"Natalie. The truth is, Davis, everyone will think you're my boy toy."

Hooley guffawed and smirked, leaving **wuss** hanging clear but unspoken in the air.

Davis said, "Shall I drape myself all over you?"

She laughed as he slipped a black wool cape over her shoulders, so beautifully made it almost put his tux to shame. "Give me the occasional smoldering eye, that'll do it."

He eyed the diamonds. "If there's trouble, all those rocks could be a casualty."

"I'm sure you wouldn't let a lady lose her sparklers, Davis." She gave Hooley a grin and walked out the front door to the waiting black bulletproof custom limousine. The driver was a young, smooth-faced Puerto Rican with ancient dark eyes and wearing no expression at all.

"Keep the lights on, Hooley," Natalie called back to her henchman. "Guard the manse."

Hooley nodded, standing in the open front door in his favorite pose, arms folded over his massive chest.

Natalie settled herself in the backseat and met the driver's eyes in the rearview mirror. "Luis, this is Special Agent Sullivan. Davis, this is Luis Alvarez. He's a body-guard and a professional driver. Luis, you know where we're going."

Luis looked street-smart and tough, probably had since he was a boy; maybe he'd been an alley rat in San Juan, or in

L.A. Davis met Luis's eyes in the mirror. He saw Luis was assessing him back. Luis nodded and pressed the button to raise the clear privacy shield.

"Hooley brought in Alvarez?"

"Yes, right after the incident in the park. You also haven't met Connie Mendez. She's with me when it's not comfortable for the guys to be, such as in my bedroom. Hooley told me she can shoot the ace of spades off a card while painting her toenails. You'll like her."

Three people guarding her, on her own dime. Good enough. He said, "So you said your daughter is coming with the secretary of state's son? You said they might be serious?"

"Well, as I told you, I'd always thought of them more as brother and sister. If Perry needs a last-minute date, he's the one she calls and vice versa. Maybe there's more now, but like I said, she won't talk to me about it. We'll see."

Davis said slowly, "She's unusual. I've never met anyone like her before. She looks like you."

She cocked her head at him. "For the most part, but in temperament, Perry was her father's daughter from the get-go. I'll never forget when she grabbed his finger when she was three months old and wouldn't let go.

"From the age of six, he took her to the home Redskins games. Later, she got to visit the sideline of every professional football stadium in the nation. She was in the locker room when he examined injured players, held their hands if they let her, which they usually welcomed, while her father worked on them. She told a receiver once he should have taken his option route outside, where the safety wasn't, but her dad would get him well anyway."

Davis checked out the cars driving near them on Cransford Avenue. "I wonder if her father would have managed to get her on the sideline in today's games?"

"Since Brundage was larger than life, a real presence in NFL lore, I imagine he could have managed it. He thought Perry's real love affair with football started when Joe Montana tossed her a ball on his way to the locker room at halftime, and smiled at her, and beckoned. She threw him back a perfect spiral, so her father told me. Joe carefully stood only six feet away. She grew up with the coaches and players, sat in on their meetings whenever she could get away from school, and no one stopped her from sneaking in the back of the room. I guess you could say football was in her blood.

"When she was a teenager, I suppose I expected to see girly concerns take over, you know, obsessions with makeup and boys, but not a bit of it changed."

Davis said, "Her future husband is going to be in football heaven with somebody like her as his wife. I'll bet she makes great guacamole, too, right?"

Natalie laughed. "Very true. Even if sportswriting weren't her job, I'd bet Perry would still try to keep in touch with the players and the coaches. She even makes a point of getting to know all the up-and-coming college players before they're drafted. Believe me, she has her own take on who should draft them. She's always discreet. She's never burned a coach or a player or a player's wife for telling her something off the record. And she's well liked, almost family."

"Tell me about the folks we're meeting tonight, and why you're suddenly being so cautious you've brought me along."

"I'm done with being vulnerable. You're with me at this shindig tonight because you're a trained objective other, a fresh eye. I want you to watch and listen, see if your gut tells you something I'm missing. And I want everyone to know I'm protected now."

"You honestly think it's possible one of the political guests at this function could be responsible for what's happened?"

She shrugged. "At this point I'd be stupid to rule out anyone but my closest friends." She touched her fingers to his sleeve. "You'll make sure no one poisons my rubber chicken or shoves a shiv in my back, won't you?"

"A little cyanide's always a nice choice, but a politician poisoning your chicken leg? At the secretary of state's house?

That would be rude."

Natalie smiled. "Let me tell you, Davis, politicians are many things, but one thing you can count on is that they're always self-serving. No matter what kind of dodgy acts they've committed, they will do anything to keep themselves in office. Show me a politician and I'll show you a Borgia-in-training." She sighed. "I think in another time politicians made good grave robbers. And now they don't even wait until the night to strip us to our skin."

Davis eyed a black truck that was coming up fast on Natalie's side. He met Luis's eyes in the mirror. Luis pulled forward and smoothly changed lanes. The truck changed lanes behind them. He met Luis's eyes again, and nodded.

Luis accelerated, changing lanes to turn off onto the less residential Moran Avenue, moving toward the warehouse district.

"What's wrong?"

The privacy screen came down. "Mrs. Black, that guy in the black truck. He's too interested in us."

Natalie braced herself while Davis twisted around in the seat, his Glock now in his hand. The black truck had speeded up, taken the exit too fast after them, scaring the crap out of the drivers behind him.

Natalie said, "Let's not try to lose him, Luis. Let's get him. Come on, Davis, with the two of you, I'm safe. Please, let's try to get him."

Davis gave her a look and nodded. "I got his license plate easily enough, so you bet the truck's stolen. Natalie, write this down," and he read out the license.

Luis said, "I'm turning right on High Leaf Street, up ahead, lots of warehouses for us to lie in wait. Let's get this moron. Mrs. Black, you stay down, okay?"

She said okay and Davis didn't believe her for a second.

Luis turned smoothly onto High Leaf and gunned the limo. Three dark buildings later, he pulled into a parking lot and around to the back of a darkened building with **acme blinds** in big aluminum letters across the front.

Natalie lowered her window. "He's got to know I'm not alone."

Whoever it was, Davis thought, really wanted Natalie Black dead. He felt no fear from her, no panic, like yesterday with Jitterbug. She was ready. What the driver was doing, chasing her down in a truck, when, like Natalie said, he had to know she wasn't alone, was foolhardy. Luis cut the lights. Both Davis and Luis lowered their windows as well. They were all quiet, waiting. Thick black clouds scuttled over the quarter-moon. Rain was on its way, probably later this evening.

"Davis," she said in an urgent whisper, "I can see you're still arguing with yourself about getting out of here to keep me safe. But no, let's get this guy. This is our chance. We've got to get him. Promise me."

He knew he shouldn't ever jeopardize a civilian, but she was right, and that's exactly what he'd been thinking. If they could catch this guy, then it would be over. He nodded. He'd keep her safe. One look at Luis and Davis knew he was as committed.

They waited, breathing in the silent air, seeing no one, all the office workers long gone. The black truck drove slowly by.

Natalie shouted, "Get him, Luis!"

The limo lights went on bright and the big Mercedes shot out from behind the Acme warehouse, blinding the driver of the black truck.

Davis leaned out the window, took careful aim, and shot out the driver's-side front tire. The truck screeched out, rubber flapping around the wheel, but the guy didn't slow.

Both Davis and Luis continued shooting, emptying their magazines, but the truck was moving too erratically for any of the shots to count. "He's heading back to Marlow," Natalie shouted.

But no, he strong-armed the truck left and accelerated into the empty parking lot behind a trio of warehouses, the truck now riding on the rim, the limo not twenty yards away.

Luis slammed on the brakes when they saw the truck with the driver's-side door open.

Silence: sudden, absolute silence.

Luis pulled up behind the truck and both men carefully made their way toward the front cab. The smell of burned rubber and scorched metal hung in the air. The truck was empty.

Natalie was right on their heels. "He's gone," she said. "We'll never find him, too dark, and too many warehouses along this route." She nodded to Luis and Davis. "Well, we tried. I'm glad Perry wasn't with me, she'd have jumped out of the limo and leapt through the cab of the truck and torn the guy apart."

13

Savich home
Georgetown
Tuesday night

Gabriella watched Sean downstairs while Savich washed Sherlock's arm, applied antiseptic cream thickly over the thin red gash, and covered it with a wide adhesive bandage. It had taken only ten minutes, but when they were back in the kitchen, ready to start dinner with Sean, he was too excited to sit because of a **big** problem at school that Gabriella couldn't help him with. This last part he told them in a whisper, believing Gabriella couldn't hear him, though of course she could. Turned out a girl had hit Sean in the shoulder because Sean had beaten her in an Inspector Milo Bork on Planet Tubor computer game. Marty from next door, whom Sean considered his future wife, had jumped on the girl's back and pulled her hair. Sean said, "Sammy didn't hit me hard. I mean, I get mad if someone beats me, too, but I suck it up like you told me to. Now Sammy and Marty are mad at each other and mad at me. It's not fair."

Ten minutes later, after Sean had called Marty and Marty had called Samantha, and all the respective parents were happy again, all was well in the kingdom.

Sherlock grabbed Sean up when he handed Dillon's cell back to him and kissed him all over his face before tossing him to his father, who squeezed him until he squeaked, laughing like a loon while Astro barked and jumped manically at Savich's legs. Her arm didn't hurt at all. Finally, the eggplant came out of the oven and they sat down for dinner.

Later that evening, once Savich had sung two country-and-western songs for Sean, three verses each, and Sean was down for the count, Sherlock took Savich's hand and led him to their bedroom.

They sat side by side on their bed, Sherlock looking straight ahead. "It started two days ago. I didn't tell you because it was so stupid, really, not much of anything, only something a little out of the ordinary."

"What, exactly, do you mean by 'not much of anything'? Apparently it wasn't that because a guy tried to kill you today." He kept his voice low and calm, hard even though hours had passed since they'd gotten home. He kept looking at her arm, remembering his gut-wrenching fear when she'd been shot in San Francisco. It brought it all back, made it seem like yesterday.

When she only stared at him, he said, "I'm not going to throw a fit like Sammy did with Sean's computer game. Sweetheart, come on, tell me what you mean."

She said, "Okay. I was in Chad's Market, for heaven's sake, two afternoons ago buying some vegetables. You know that feeling you get that someone is looking at you, checking you out? Well, that's what I felt. I was deciding between two heads of lettuce when I knew to my gut that someone was staring at me. I looked around at the dozen or so people in my immediate vicinity but didn't see anyone paying any particular attention to me. I mean, the guy behind the meat counter sometimes flirts with me, called me the hot lady with the badge once, but he wasn't even around. I forgot about it.

"Yesterday, when I was at the Olive's Baby Boutique over on M Street buying a present for Lily's baby, I felt the same thing again—eyes on me. It spooked me this time, and I turned around fast to see who it was. There were four mothers, three of them carrying babies, and one older gentleman inspecting a blue baby blanket. I didn't see anyone else. Then I looked out the big front glass window and saw a shoulder moving out of sight. I ran out of the store, but whoever the shoulder belonged to was gone. I assumed I was overreacting, Dillon. To be honest, though, I was ready to tell you I might have a budding stalker on my hands."

"And you didn't tell me about this budding stalker yesterday because?"

"Because after what happened in San

Francisco, I knew you'd lock me in a closet to keep me safe and only let me out to go to the bathroom. I needed time to weigh things out in my mind, Dillon, and decide whether it was worthwhile to worry you about it."

"It's definitely a closet for you now, and guards outside the door who'll have Uzis all around." She felt his fingers lace through hers. She looked down at their hands. "I was going to tell you over tacos at lunch, but Davis started telling about how he was going out with Natalie Black to that function this evening, and I decided not to push it, to wait until tonight. Big mistake.

"What I don't understand is why this person gave up staring at me and decided on a drive-by on a motorcycle. That doesn't sound like a stalker to me. It's too soon for that kind of escalation. I mean, two days of watching, then kill me?"

He hugged her close. "No, not a stalker, but he was casing you out for a hit, and it was a clumsy one at that, so he's not a professional. It's obvious he had to be hanging around the Hoover Building today, watching for you, following you. You never noticed anyone while you were driving?"

"No. But you know, I was thinking about Lily and Simon and how it's so great Ethan was born healthy and how over-the-moon both of them are—and how your sister deserves happiness. I wasn't concentrating on anyone possibly tailing me. I mean, why would I?"

"He was at the grocery store, then outside that baby store. We've got to figure out what changed between yesterday and today to make him go after you. And in a busy spot with lots of people around."

"Maybe he was waiting for a chance, and today was his first opportunity. He must have followed me from the service station, thought I was an easy target and thought, **Wowee, rev up the cycle, cruise right up to her, shoot her down.**"

He pressed his face against her hair, breathing in slowly, getting control of himself. He said against her ear, "So who have you pissed off lately?"

She spurted out a laugh, pulled back in his arms. "Well, there's Alex Benedict, Esquire, isn't there? That smarmy lawyer has been threatening me he'd have my job for harassing his thug client, Tommy Cohen."

"I can't see either Teflon Tommy or his lawyer calling for a hit on you. Bad for business. And they wouldn't have hired a bozo like the guy who shot at you today."

Sherlock leaned into him, resting her cheek against his shoulder. "I was sort of joking. I've given this a lot of thought and I can't come up with anyone, Dillon. If you want the truth, that's depressing. I mean, I've been a special agent for a good amount of time and yet I don't have anyone in my past who hates me so much they'd go out of their way to put me down. There's only Marlin Jones, and that was a long time ago. You'd think I could at least come up with a couple of enemies."

He laughed at her outrage.

"I really thought we'd get a good description from the Thompson couple who were right there close up when the guy jumped off that Kawasaki after I shot out his tire." She sighed again. "I was sure they'd be able to give us at least a flash of something about the man while he ran past them. How could they say they didn't see him? How's that possible?"

"They're both nearing ninety, Sherlock. One has macular degeneration and the other is swimming in cataracts. They're really a nice old couple," he added, "and they wanted to help, but the fact is I don't even think the Thompsons even realized you were shot at, from what they said."

"I wish I'd gotten a better look at him myself. I've been going over what I saw of him all evening, and there's nothing more. Like I told the officers, he was on the tall side and kind of thin. A really nice camel wool coat, khakis, and boots. I couldn't tell his age because he was wearing sunglasses and had his head all bundled up. That's all I've got." She sighed again. "Well, the forensics team might find some fingerprints on the motorcycle or DNA, if the gods are smiling on us. With any luck, he'll be in the database."

"We'll check the street cameras outside the Hoover Building, and any along Prospect Street near the service station. If you're right, and it was an old Colt M1917, but I doubt he bought the gun on the street. I wonder how he got hold of such an old weapon."

"He probably didn't know how to buy a throwaway. Maybe it belonged to his grandfather. Hey, where are you going?"

Savich turned to look down at her. He saw the slight bulge of the bandage beneath her nightgown sleeve and felt a spurt of fear. "I was going to put a brighter lightbulb in the closet so you won't strain your eyes reading when I lock you in."

14

Secretary of state's home
Caldicott Road, Washington, D.C.
Tuesday night

It appeared to Davis that Arliss Goddard Abbott's second husband was a booze hound, but then he supposed he'd have to consider that Brooxey Wallingford, of the Philadelphia mainline Wallingfords, could support one or two third-world countries. Davis thought the elder Wallingford seniors must have hated him to pin such a ridiculous name on him. He'd obviously drunk one too many shots of Glenfiddich that evening and was ogling the women, particularly Natalie, that or her diamonds, Davis wasn't sure which. He and the secretary of state, who'd kept her own name, had been married less than a year, Natalie had told him, and said only, "He was always nice and charming the half-dozen times I was with him socially. He was a prince at their wedding." She looked from Arliss to Wallingford, sighed. "I wonder if Arliss knew he was such a drinker before they got married."

Cynical to the bone, Davis said, "It may be a huge mitigating factor that he and his family are almost as rich as Bill Gates."

Natalie shook her head. "Doesn't matter, it's none of my business."

When they reached Arliss Abbott in the receiving line, she cheek-kissed Natalie and gave Davis a cool smile and a firm handshake. She was a tall, elegant woman in her long black designer gown, similar in age and as beautifully presented as Natalie. She was, Davis thought, the undisputed queen of her kingdom. It was odd though, that Natalie seemed to radiate warmth and interest, whereas Abbott gave off an "I'm in charge and don't you forget it" vibe. Maybe, he thought, she had learned to project that image on the job, but he doubted it. He rather thought she'd learned it in the cradle. He saw her give a nearly imperceptible nod to one of her aides. Davis watched the young man discreetly lead second husband Wallingford away, with some practiced excuse, no doubt. What would the aide do? Put him in his jammies and tuck him in bed?

He felt her powerful intelligence focus on him. "Natalie tells me you're a special agent with the FBI. I understand you work for Dillon Savich, and everyone is impressed with him, the president included."

Maybe Davis was impressive by extension? "Yes, ma'am," he said, and left it at that.

"However did you hook up with Natalie?"

Hook up? Well, she was sitting in a smoky bar over on K Street, drinking alone, and I—"Natalie tells it better than I do, ma'am. I guess you could say I protect her from unwanted attention."

Davis kept his eyes firmly on her face, not about to see if Mr. Brooxey Wallingford was still in sight. It was Madame Secretary of State Abbott who snuck a look toward the door her aide and her husband were currently negotiating, Brooxey swaying a bit, the aide speaking to him quietly.

Natalie said, "Arliss, I'll tell you about it later. Oh, yes, Perry told me she's coming with Day."

Arliss Abbott placed a beautifully manicured white hand on Natalie's arm and moved in close, her voice pitched low. "We need to talk. I don't think in my office, it would invite speculation. Some afternoon we can both get away?"

Natalie kept her voice steady. "Of course. We need to discuss this— situation." She drew a deep breath, her head very close to the secretary's. "I need to hear your advice about what I should do."

Arliss Abbott nodded, beamed a practiced, smooth smile at Davis, and turned to greet a plump older woman with a smoker's wrinkled face, a congresswoman from Connecticut, Natalie whispered to him.

Natalie moved gracefully from one small conversation group to another, all in all about thirty A-list men and women, as jeweled up and beautifully turned out as she was. Davis noticed when Natalie neared, conversation stopped for half a second, all eyes focused on her, until the guests remembered their manners and responded as naturally as they could to her greeting. Davis kept a bland smile planted on his face. He was sure they were burning to know what the secretary of state had said to her and what they were planning. He wondered if she would still be ambassador if the two women hadn't been best friends since college, along with the president of the United States. Davis had a feeling that despite that fact, this roomful of politicians would bet their galoshes that Natalie would end up thrown under the bus.

Davis stood a little behind her, aware of everyone who came near her. Of course, information was the currency in

Washington, and everyone wanted a big chunk, but they weren't rude enough or honest enough to ask Natalie directly. She smiled and nodded, ignored the covert stares, and her voice was cultured and beautifully pitched, but she wasn't saying what they really wanted to hear. She deflected supportive comments about the events in England with great skill and charm—**events**—as if that was the only polite word for a man's death and Natalie's attempted murder. If her laughter was a bit thin at times, no one let on that they wondered why, but of course they did. She continued from one group to another and neither her conversation nor her expression revealed that her reputation, and her life, in fact, was in the balance.

She always carefully introduced him whenever she came into a new group, referring to him only as her "friend." She'd been right about how he'd be perceived. He'd never considered what it would be like to be a boy toy. It was a novel experience, particularly since he was the youngest person at this fancy party, except for a couple twentysomething trophy wives. He was given sideways looks by some of the men, who apparently wondered what he had going for him. The women were assessing him, too, in a different way, maybe wondering if he was good in bed. But always, everyone's gaze returned to Natalie, the poor beleaguered woman they seemed to think would be cut loose long before the midterm elections.

He might have known there would be talk about football, too, an easy subject for Natalie and everyone else. From a congressman he learned Perry had rocked the football world that very day with the actual facts about the Tim Tebow rumors flying around.

And then, speak of the devil, Biker Babe waltzed in, not in a black leather jacket, black jeans, and boots, but in a long shimmery dark green gown that left her tanned shoulders bare. Where'd she get that tan? Her thick brownish-red hair was loose, pulled back with gold clips, a mess of lazy curls falling to below her shoulders. Black dangly earrings nearly touched those very nice shoulders. He realized she was as tall as her mother, those skinny-heeled stilts shooting her up to nearly six feet. Perry was on the arm of a man he assumed was Day Abbott, the secretary of state's son. He was about Davis's own age and looked quite the bruiser, like he might have played football in college. He was thick through the chest and shoulders, fit and toned, with a strong, stubborn jaw and dark eyes that never left Perry's face. His look wasn't brotherly. It was odd, but Davis knew on the spot he and Day Abbott wouldn't ever be best buds watching a hockey game, sharing a beer. He saw Perry give him a little finger wave, her eyebrow arched in question.

Evidently, her mother hadn't told her he would be her bodyguard tonight.

Natalie lightly touched his arm as an older gentleman quickly walked up to her and embraced her without much enthusiasm. "Davis, this is my half-brother, Milton Hinton Holmes." Now, that was an impressive handle. "Milton is one of the senators of the General Court—in Massachusetts the General Court is made up of the Senate and the House of Representatives."

Milt didn't shake his hand, merely gave him a patrician nod and ignored him. Davis said, all bonhomie, "General Court? I've never heard of that before."

Milt said, civil but cold, his Boston accent pronounced, "No one has. The name is a holdover from Colonial times. It's what we call our state legislature."

Milt had scarlet-red hair, threaded through with white. He was a distin-guished-looking sixtysomething gentle-man who looked reasonably fit, with no saggy jowls, probably because of some nice pull-up face work he'd had done. He spoke quietly to Natalie, giving her troubled looks. Was he concerned about the pro-priety of Natalie bringing Davis with her to-night? He thought it might be so, because Old Milt was looking at him with seamed lips and well-bred contempt. It was, he thought, the inevitable lot of the boy toy.

They were directed toward a dining room across the hall that held three large circular tables for ten guests each, set with silver and white table linens that sparkled under special lighting that made the guests' diamonds glitter as well. Davis held Natalie's chair for her and sat down in the chair to her right. A massive-bosomed matron wearing more diamonds than Natalie sat on her left. She was the wife of the big muckety Natalie had just met, no doubt a large contributor to the party coffers. The husband was fulsome, filled every small moment of silence with great enthusiasm, and spent too much time looking at Natalie. The wife was quiet, content, Davis supposed, to let the massive quantities of diamonds she wore speak for her. Perry sat across from them. To her left was a four-star from the Joint Chiefs who didn't seem all that happy to be there, and on her right sat Day Abbott. But when the four-star suddenly realized who Perry was, everything changed. He took over the conversation entirely, talking mostly about the Patriots, the general's favorite team. Day Abbott slugged down a straight whiskey and looked like he was used to this and didn't particularly like it.

When Natalie's salad was served, Davis discreetly exchanged plates. The same with her dinner plate that held a finely cut filet mignon and potatoes whipped up so high they looked sprayed in place. And there were dainty little lemon tarts that followed for dessert, only enough to tease the taste buds. If anyone noticed what he'd done with the plates, no one said anything. Davis's feeling was that no one had noticed, either because they were too self-absorbed or he was good at it. When he looked up from a bite of a lemon tart, he saw Perry's head was cocked at him. He grinned at her.

After dinner, Madame Secretary rose, tapped her goblet with her fork, and announced to the group that she had a surprise. They were going to enjoy an hour of dancing—to work off all the calories from dinner, she said, earning a few laughs and a couple of male groans. And so the group walked back into the large living room, where a small dance band had settled on a dais at the far end, all the furniture moved out of the way. A slow, easy dance song, one Davis hadn't heard before, started up, and most of the guests stepped out onto the floor. Davis danced the first number with Natalie, and spent the next few minutes watching everyone around her watching her, or them. What did they expect? Coitus in the middle of the dance floor?

When the song came to an end, the speaker of the House, Herbert McGuffen, lightly touched her arm to get her attention and asked her to dance. Tall enough to carry off his weight, and looking as arrogant as a French aristocrat, the speaker wore a very finely made rug that blended well with his own light-colored hair. Davis was sure no one had ever said a word about it. The speaker seemed to be arguing with her about something, very discreetly, of course, but Davis was paying attention. Natalie shook her head at him, and he didn't seem to like her reply. Her half-brother, Milt, was on the spot when the song finished, and she smiled at the speaker, added a light laugh, and traded partners. For a moment her eyes followed the speaker of the House, who didn't appear to be at all happy. What would her half-brother have to say? Then it was Davis's turn again.

"Trying to pump you for information?"

She laughed. "Yes, both of them are very good at it. But I'm the master. Davis, it was close tonight, but we nearly got him. He's here and he's close."

"I took a call a couple minutes ago. The black truck belongs to a Mrs. Betty Steffens, of Nantuck, Maryland, reported stolen early this morning right out of her garage. We'll go over it for fingerprints, but I doubt there'll be any. What's that song? I mean, it isn't hot and fast like the Sex Pistols."

Natalie laughed. "Nope, it's soft and flowy, from ancient times. You've never heard it?"

"No, but then again, it's easy to dance to, I don't have to concentrate and can keep my eyes on all the desperate characters around us. Why was the speaker of the House upset with you?"

"You saw that? You're good, Davis. Let's say he's not happy with a stand the president's taken on a particular trade bill that affects his district. Despite the current situation, he knows I'm close to the president and he wanted me to help him change his mind, which I refused to do." She shrugged. "He'll get over it, since he's got to know it's going to be a no-go without the president's backing. I think his biggest wish, though, is that I'll be resigning to keep the party safe."

She smiled up at him. "Any symptoms of poisoning?"

Davis grinned at her. "Not yet. Why is your kid giving me black looks? She was all smiles earlier."

Natalie looked over at her daughter, now dancing with her uncle Milt. "She heard the gossip floating around tonight, told me in the ladies' room I should have come with her and Day tonight, not drag you here to add to the gossip, what with your being so hot."

"She thinks I'm hot?"

Natalie laughed. "Guys—you never change. I think she said hot, but, hmmm, maybe it was something else. I'm getting old, my hearing's on the wane."

"Yeah, right."

"She thinks I bought your tux."

"She doesn't have a very good eye."

"Not in this case, evidently. Your tux is obviously bespoke."

"Yeah, my mom forced me to my dad's

tailor, told me if I ever gained weight, she'd shoot me."

"Somehow I don't think that's ever going to happen. You dance well, Davis."

"Thanks. I haven't heard music this old in forever. What is that song? So she thinks I'm hot? Do you know I invited her to come into my house for a cool drink?"

"The song is 'Moon River.' It's been popular for decades. Maybe she thinks you're hot because of your derring-do yesterday morning. I told her it was probably an everyday sort of deal for you, particularly the part about the Starbucks in one hand and a gun in the other. You're perfectly right, though, 'Moon River' sure isn't James Taylor." She gave him a fat grin.

"James Taylor? You mean that balding guy who played hippie ballads back in the Stone Age?"

She lightly smacked his arm. "Don't be snarky. He was my favorite back in the day—not quite the Stone Age. He still is. Hey, I like 'California über Alles' as well as the next person, but it's sometimes nice to slow-dance. You don't have to perform, and you can actually talk to your partner without shaking anything loose. Believe me, that's a concern as you get older."

Mom would really like Natalie. "What's up with Old Milt, your half-brother?"

She spurted out a laugh. "He'd have you measured for concrete boots if he heard you call him old. He looks good, actually, after he got his face perked up last year, and he's very proud of that. He said he stood ready to support me in my time of need." A small resigned sigh escaped. "He's fully capable of Victorian sentiments like that when it comes time to ask me for help to bankroll one of his campaigns. He really hates to delve into his own coffers or hoof it out on the streets for his contributions. He hates asking for money, always has. He's simply no good at it, and he knows it."

"Except you, right?"

She began tapping her fingertips on his shoulder. "He hasn't yet. I think he's trying to assess the damage my situation will have on him. Obviously, I speak to my parents quite often, and I know Milton has been pestering them for information about me. They listen and thank him for his visits and go about their business. Dad's eighty-five, my mom's nearly eighty, and both of them are still healthy and bright-eyed. Milt hates it, but they're the ones who hold the reins, since they hold most of the assets. The truth is both of them are stronger and more competent than he is."

She tap-tapped again on his shoulder. "Have you noticed anyone behaving not quite as they should? Anyone looking at me with burning rage in his eyes?"

"Not any rage I can see, more like rampant curiosity and speculation. No surprise there, since you're the latest scandal inside the Beltway."

She grinned. "I'm enjoying all the speculation about you, the looks. You'd think they'd understand why you're with me with all that's happened, despite what you look like."

Davis said, "You should meet Agent

Griffin Hammersmith, the newest agent in the CAU—that's the Criminal Apprehension Unit. Women look right past me if he's in the room. I have fielded a couple of questions about how you and I know each other. One of the ladies asked if I worked in one of the local clubs.

"Perry's been besieged about football all night, and not just by the four-star general at the dinner table. Day Abbott doesn't look very happy about that. I mean, they're talking sports here, all about quarterback stats and the latest injuries, and it's his date they're talking to. He's left out of it. I'd say his ego is hurting."

Natalie paused for a moment. "Of course Perry gets all the sports questions since Brundage was a legend, as well as her father. He should be used to it. Maybe you're right, maybe Day's tired of her claiming the spotlight. To top it off, Day himself is a sports nut; like most guys, give him a beer and some nuts and a football game and he's a happy camper. He followed his own father's footsteps and attended the West Virginia School of

Mines, which wasn't a choice his mother expected, since it isn't much of a big-time sports school."

Davis said, "Well, if the guy wants to get anywhere with your kid, he needs to get a grip, join in the conversation instead of looking pissed off, and start treating her like the expert she is," and then he dipped her.

She came up laughing. "You're not bad, Davis."

He gave her a nice twirl, slowed again. "Do you think Perry and Madame Secretary's son are headed toward an engagement?"

She was silent for a moment, again tapping her fingertips on his shoulder. "As I told you, she resists talking to me about Day. I can still remember the screaming matches between the two of them when he was fifteen or so and she was ten or eleven, exactly like a brother and sister. Ah, the song is winding down. Why not go ask her to dance before someone else snaps her up. I'll go stand over there, my back to the fireplace."

Davis asked Perry to dance, smiling at Day Abbott, who didn't look particularly happy at his showing up. Actually, he looked like he wished he had Darth Vader's lightsaber with him. Luckily, it was another slow number they could talk over without his worrying about stepping on the toes peeking out of her black stilettos. He was beginning to like the oldies, even though he didn't know any of the words and recognized the music mostly from elevators.

The first thing she said was, "I saw you changing your plates with my mom's."

"I liked the looks of her steak better than mine."

"Yeah, right. She's made you a deal, hasn't she? To keep away nosy people, right? Like the media? No, that's all right, you don't have to say anything, I'll get it out of her later. I wish she hadn't brought you. It's adding to the gossip that you're her lover."

"Yeah, so what?" So Natalie hadn't told her about the black truck after them on the way to the party. He grinned down at her, but not all that far down, maybe two inches at most. "Was your dad tall?"

She pulled back. "What? My dad? Well, about six feet, I guess. Why?"

"Without those towering stilettos, you're what, maybe five foot two?"

"You pinhead. Stop trying to distract me."

"I like your dress. You look pretty dishy. Isn't that an 1890s phrase, like this music? I hardly recognized you without the leather, the helmet, and the fishtail braid. And I'm hot, right?"

"How does an FBI agent afford a tux like that? Did you borrow it? Is it your dad's?"

Of all things, his cell belted out "I Wanna Be Sedated" by Ramones. People around them turned and stared. He immediately turned the cell to vibrate, checked the screen. Cindy from the FDA. He let it go to voice mail. Perry saw Cindy's name, looked up at him, and laughed.

"One of your girlfriends?"

"Nah, my aunt."

"Yeah, right. Why would Mom think she

needed a bodyguard here, of all places? The car that tried to run her off the road — that was four thousand miles away, in England."

Natalie hasn't told her daughter about Buckner Park, either.

"Has something happened since then?" She stopped dead in her tracks. He saw fear flash in her eyes. "All right, what hasn't she told me?"

He dipped her and pretended to nearly drop her, which made her grab on to his arms, and said, still balancing her low, "You gotta ask your mom. I'm only her boy toy."

"Pull me up."

He did, and whirled her around in a fast twirl. "Really, Perry, ask your mom."

"It isn't right. She shouldn't keep things from me. She's only known you a day and she's known me all my life."

"True, but I know how to use a gun."

"So do I, and I know where you live."

He wondered why Natalie had kept her daughter in the dark. Probably because she didn't want to scare her more than she was already. Perry wasn't a kid. She was an adult. Davis made a decision. "I'm sure your mom's told you everything that happened in England."

"Yes, yes, she told me, and the cops didn't believe her and the British press called her a liar. She wouldn't let me come over."

"Someone tried to run your mom down while she was running in Buckner Park last Saturday. It was her decision not to tell you."

"But you just did."

"I think it's important you know what's going on here. But listen, Perry, it's critical you not tell anyone else about this, though, not even Day Abbott. I'll speak to your mother and she'll explain it all to you, even about what happened on the way here tonight."

She grabbed his arm. "What happened?"

"Your mother will explain. Personally, I think the more people who know, the better. You're right, I did make a bargain with her. I would protect her tonight and she will tell everything to my boss, Special

Agent Dillon Savich. Come to her house tomorrow morning at nine o'clock. You can meet him, ask all the questions you want. If you want to tear a strip off your mom for not telling you about the latest two attempts on her life, please do it when you're alone. I don't like shouting matches. They give me indigestion."

They danced in silence, Perry stiff, her breathing choppy. Finally, the music came to a predictable end, soft and smooth, with a final trickling series of notes. She said, "I've heard of Agent Savich. Do you really think he can help?"

He squeezed her hand. "I'll bet my bespoke tux on it. Don't worry, we'll get this all figured out."

16

Natalie Black's house
Chevy Chase, Maryland
Wednesday morning

Savich and Sherlock kept a sharp eye out on their drive to Natalie Black's house. They'd seen no one suspicious following them. Savich's GPS announced they'd arrived at their destination, 2318 Ridgewood Road.

Sherlock surveyed the empty guardhouse, the high stone fence, the intercom with the camera mounted beside it aimed at the driver. "Anyone could avoid that camera, climb over the wall, no problem. There must be another camera—there, in the lower branches of that oak. Someone needs to dirty it up, it's a dead giveaway, so nice and sparkly new. Installed this week, I'll bet."

Savich pressed the button, identified

himself and Sherlock.

A man's deep voice came from the speaker. "Agent Savich, please hold your ID up toward the camera."

Savich did, and the gate swung in quickly and smoothly away from them, and the Porsche cruised through. "Lovely grounds," Sherlock said. "I can picture a tire hanging from that low oak branch over there. Sean would really like that."

"I can see him and Marty fighting over who can spin faster." There was a low branch on the maple tree in their backyard, actually. Maybe it was time to hang a tire.

He pulled up the circular driveway and stopped at the front door. "Ah, here's our questioner from the gate."

Hooley stood in the open front door, arms crossed over his massive chest, looking them over thoroughly as they walked toward him.

He said to Savich, "I know who you are, Agent Savich. Who is she?"

Sherlock gave him her sunny smile. "I'm his keeper," she said, and stuck out her hand. "You must be Mr. Hooley. I'm Agent

Sherlock. He never goes anywhere without me. It's in my employment contract."

Hooley stared at her for a long moment and shook her hand. "Your hair is an even brighter red than Mrs. Black's. Curlier, too." He said to Savich, "You've got quite a rep. Is it deserved?"

Savich said, "Rep for what, exactly?"

"Not wrestling, that's for sure," Sherlock said. "I've got that gold medal."

Hooley looked like he wanted to laugh but didn't. "A rep as a hotshot, like when you were in the papers for bringing down those bank robbers in Georgetown. Follow me. Your boy and Mrs. Black are in the sunroom." He paused for a moment. "I'm glad Mrs. Black consented to bringing you in. What's going on isn't good, and there are only three of us to watch her. Beautiful machine," he added, nodding toward the Porsche.

Savich said, "Thanks. Davis makes four professionals protecting her, but you're right, it's time to figure out how to deal with this and put a stop to it. You can thank Agent Sullivan for talking her into seeing me."

Hooley looked unconvinced. After a long trek, he showed them into the sunroom door. "Mrs. Black. There are two agents here. This one with your hair is Agent Sherlock; she says she's his keeper, contractually."

Davis laughed.

Natalie stood up, looked straight at Savich, trying to get his measure? Probably. He supposed she was very good at reading people; she'd have to be. He stuck out his hand. "Davis has told us about your situation, Mrs. Black. This is Agent Sherlock."

They shook hands. Natalie smiled at Sherlock. "Hooley's right. You do have my hair, ah, but the shine." She sighed. "That was a long time ago." Out of habit, Savich and Sherlock showed her their creds as she spoke.

Davis introduced Perry, who nodded to them, watching them closely. Natalie said, "Please sit down. Davis asked me to make croissants, and so I did. Help yourselves. I understand, Agent Savich, that you prefer tea, straight—say, Earl Grey?"

Savich nodded.

Perry said, "You're partners?"

"Partners in everything," Davis said. "They're married."

Perry examined Savich, a big man with a dark complexion who looked tough to his marrow, but with a strong, very fine face, nearly black hair and eyes. The woman was tall, dressed in black pants, a crisp white shirt, black boots on her feet. She looked like a sprite or a redheaded fairy princess with blue eyes, a lovely smile, and no hard edges to her. "Married," she repeated. "I can't imagine how that could possibly work."

Three minutes passed discussing this anomaly while Natalie passed them their croissants. Davis finally said, "Let's get to it, then. I told Savich everything you said, Natalie. I'm sure he has questions."

Savich set down his teacup and looked over at Mrs. Natalie Black, the ambassador to the United Kingdom. "First of all, I've had a full rundown on what happened last night. Whoever is behind this is getting desperate to take that kind of chance, knowing you had protection with you in the car. No fingerprints, so that also means our person is very careful.

"What I find interesting is how every-thing that happened seems perfectly coordinated, from the release of the ter-rorist son's photo followed by the infam-ous email to the whispers about your guilt over George McCallum's supposed suicide, as if someone was leaking them information in a well-planned smear campaign. After your near brush with death on the A2 to Canterbury, it's even more surprising the papers insin-uated you'd lied, that there'd been no attempt on your life, that you were simply trying to deflect attention away from your respon-sibility over George McCallum's suicide. I don't think it was piling on, I think that, too, was planted.

"Whoever this person is, Mrs. Black, they want to not only destroy you and ruin your reputation, it seems they want you dead. Do you agree?"

Natalie lightly tapped her knife on the white tablecloth. She nodded. "Cut it to the bare bones, yes, I agree. The problem is I have no idea who it could be."

Savich said, "Let's start with basics. The death of your fiancé, George McCallum."

"George knew the email was fake so there was no reason for him to commit suicide, not that he would have killed himself even if I had kissed him off. George wasn't like that. He gobbled up life, thought every moment of life precious, even if they held pain for him.

"You see, George was a colon cancer survivor, six years and counting. Even though the doctors believed he was clear, he told me his disease still hung over him like the sword of Damocles, always in the back of his mind, influencing every word he spoke, every action he took, even six years after the dreadful course of chemo. He said the experience had changed him, made him grateful for every single day. He was a thankful man, he considered himself a blessed man. And he felt close to his very large family, all except his son.

Can you imagine a man like this killing himself? No matter what happened?"

Perry said, "I didn't know about the cancer."

"It was private. Only his family knew."

Savich said, "I read the police report, Mrs. Black. The physical evidence was ambiguous. The Dover Cliffs are at least thirty feet from the road in that particular spot. The ground is flat and smooth, with plenty of time to stop if traveling within the speed limit, or to jump from the vehicle, if need be. But the tire tracks showed no evidence he'd tried to stop. The car drove straight at the cliff and went over. Now, I'm sure you discussed the possibility that he fell asleep or that he passed out from any number of medical reasons."

"I accepted that, Agent Savich, until someone tried to kill me. Then it seems to make sense that someone might have knocked George unconscious, put his Jaguar in gear, aimed it at the cliffs and let it go over. The autopsy would have been of no help because of his massive injuries. A bump on the head would have gone unnoticed."

Sherlock said, "Let me stop you for a moment, Mrs. Black. The faked email to George breaking off your engagement to him. It was sent from your personal email account. That requires a user name and a password. You didn't send that email. So who did? Who has your private information?"

"No one—at least, that's what I thought. I changed it immediately, of course."

"What exactly did the email say?" Davis asked.

"I went into my sent mail and there it was." She pulled a folded piece of paper out of her sweater pocket and read:

Dear George: You must know after all this unpleasantness you and I cannot possibly marry. Consider who I am and where my loyalties must lie. If it's any consolation, I never loved you, so perhaps it's for the best. Good-bye, Natalie.

Savich said, "I suppose this person realized George might call you immediately, but by leaking the email, he was assured the damage to your own reputation would be done. Either George's death was unexpected or this person hates you enough to have set everything in motion by killing an innocent man."

Perry, her face white, said, "All to get you blamed for it, disgraced, and try to kill you?"

"Yes, so it would seem," Natalie said, and wished she could hug her daughter, reassure her, but she couldn't even reassure herself.

"Had George been in contact with his son William?" Sherlock asked.

"As I said, George was uncomfortable talking to me about Billy, so I really don't know if there was any communication or not."

Savich said, "And the rest of George's family? Is it possible any of them could have found out your private email password? Any wild hairs in the group?"

"No, I doubt it. Wild hairs? No more than any other family. Besides, why would any of them write something so cruel, even if they could? Why would any of them want to kill him?

"The fact is I think George was sacrificed to get to me." She banged her fist on the table, making the croissant on her plate jump. Tears blurred her eyes.

Sherlock was shaking her head. "I don't think this is all about money. This is personal. Can you think of anything you've done that could lead to this elaborate revenge, with your death as the final prize? Is there anyone who hates you that much?"

17

Natalie was thoughtful for a moment. "How many of us can even conceive of a hatred that deep pointed at us? That we ourselves could have brought on? Honestly, there isn't anyone I can point to. The Foreign Service has its share of political backstabbing, jealousies and resentments over appointments, awards someone else wanted, but what field doesn't? Is someone after my job? Well, sure, hundreds of people might want to be the ambassador to the United Kingdom. But enough for"—she waved her hands—"for all this?" She looked at her daughter. "Perry, do you resent me for not joining you on the sidelines with your father at football games?"

Perry said, "The only thing I resent is you chose not to tell me about Buckner Park until I found out about it from Davis last night. And about that black truck."

Perry took her mother's hand. "Mom, I'm scared. That black truck last night? It's too much. He's here, close by, waiting. I wish you'd trusted me, told me everything. No, I know, you were trying to protect me, but no more, all right?"

Natalie slowly nodded.

Sherlock studied Natalie Black. She liked her poise, her intelligence. She was keeping herself together and focused, despite all the misery that was being visited on her. Sherlock thought she was one of the good ones. She had a strong notion if Natalie Black had been carrying a gun as Sherlock had yesterday, that black sedan would be a wreck now, like the Kawasaki. Sherlock rather hoped she could be like Natalie Black one day. Odd how they both had red hair.

Perry said, "About George's death. Maybe it was someone after him, an enemy."

Natalie said, "I can't think of anyone who would want him dead. Certainly not the McCallums. They're a large family, and their many homes and Lockenby Manor are expensive to keep up. George wasn't rich, very few of the old families are nowadays, and now there'll be George's death taxes to pay. If I had married George, some of my own money would have been available to them, and they knew that. But if George died first, they also knew the money would stay with me."

Savich said slowly, "Let's place it back at you. Tell us about your own family."

"There's only my half-brother, Milton, and his family," Natalie said. "And, of course, my parents."

Perry said, "Uncle Milt was the crown prince until Mom was born. He always resented her. He was at the party last night. He's not staying with you, is he?"

Natalie said, "No, he very much prefers The Willard. Milton showed up Monday without bothering to let me know he was coming. He claimed he wanted to share my burden, but I know him too well to confide in him. He went on about how worried he, his wife, and our parents are, patted my back and looked sorrowful, you get the picture. I didn't tell him anything he hadn't read about, not then or at the party last night.

"Perry's right, he never liked me. Actually, as far as I can tell, he's never been happy. He's always wanted more than he has, spent more than he has. He's weak, dependent on our father and his stepmother financially. I've always thought him harmless. He swims well in state political waters, but now he wants to try for Congress, and he needs money to do that. It's a level Milton couldn't manage, I'm afraid." She paused. "He doesn't have the guts for those sharks. I'd say that would pertain both to politics and to killing his half-sister."

Savich poured more tea from the Georgian silver pot. "Milt's married? Kids?"

"Yes. He went through his wife's trust fund before the end of his second campaign for state office. He's always got his hat in his hands to our parents.

"He's got a son, Allan, who's an MBA, stolid and unimaginative—like his father, really—but unlike his father, he does have a backbone. He's thirty-five, married, a couple of kids."

Davis was wiping croissant crumbs off his fingers. "Natalie, if you died, what would Milt get?"

"Nothing. Perry gets everything."

Sherlock said, "If Perry were to die, would he get something?"

That was a conversation stopper.

Perry said, "What a fun thought. I don't have a will. If I were to die tomorrow, I suppose Mom would get my money, what there is of it. If she were dead, I suppose it would go to my grandparents, who, believe me, don't need it. But if Uncle Milton was willing to kill someone for money, why wouldn't he go after my grandparents? They're swimming in it, and he'd inherit half of it if they died, wouldn't he, Mom?" She paused. "That's a gruesome thought."

Natalie cleared her throat. "My mother told me their will gives Milton a set amount, a goodly amount, don't get me wrong, but the bulk of their estate comes to me."

This was a kicker. Savich said, "Why? He's their son, the first born."

"I believe," Natalie said, "that he's disappointed them too often and they want the estate preserved for the family."

Perry said, "Mom is being too nice. My grandparents don't want their estate flushed down the political rat hole."

Savich sat back and drank his tea. When he and Sherlock left, he knew what he was going to set MAX to do.

18

<u>Washington Post</u> offices
Wednesday afternoon

Bennett John Bennett looked at Perry over the top of his glasses. "Lolita tells me you're a mess, what with all this talk surrounding your mother. Care to explain this to me?"

Note to self: punch out Lolita. She didn't want to punch Bennett out because he was sincerely unaware of the world outside of sports. What had bigmouthed Lolita told him? "I'm not a mess. I don't know where Lolita gets her information. Nothing to worry about, Boss."

"Whatever that means—all right, here's the deal: I'm only asking because I can't have you distracted by all your mother's troubles."

"You don't have to worry about anything like that. I've got two different brain compartments. The football compartment has a locked-door policy."

"Look, Perry, maybe Lolita's right. I read your blog this morning and I gotta tell you, you wrote way too many lines praising John Clayton. Three words, not three sentences. I'm hoping you did it because Clayton shot off firecrackers to you on ESPN about the Tebow scoop, your setting everything straight. A little tit for tat is always a good thing, but if you did it because you're off your game, well, I can't have you twisted up. You've got to keep on top of your story. I don't want to get beat out by those two big scoopers Shefter and Mortensen. You know they're working this around the clock, trying to find another angle on what you wrote or found something you got wrong."

Had she praised Clayton because he'd credited her? Well, yeah, probably so. He'd commented on her **acumen**. What a fine word that was. Had she really given Clayton three whole sentences? She hadn't realized—not good. "I promise, sir. No more than three glowing words about any competitors, even if they tell me I'm the greatest sportswriter born in the last century."

Bennett grunted. "I heard it really pissed Walt off when Clayton blew your horn. I thought you'd appreciate knowing that. You got anything else on the burner besides what's in your blog? Something new, another perspective? Some doomsayer predicting Toronto will lose all its upcoming games with a QB who should really be playing tight end?"

"I'm exchanging texts with an Argonaut assistant coach who tells me they're going to find the perfect coach for Tebow, train him up and watch him fly. In short, nothing but enthusiasm about him. However, as everyone knows, this is all still only talk, since they haven't signed him yet. It's all so obvious I didn't bother to mention it in my post."

"Even though you've gotten a gazillion tweets? Everyone wants more, obvious or not. Dig deeper, Perry, question everyone. And fast. You've got the markers, call 'em in.

"Oh, by the way, you're going to get an offer from ESPN, maybe a sideline job on the Sunday-night game, maybe a part-time anchor. Heard that at the sports bar from a reliable source."

Perry shook her head. "TV? You know I'm not interested, not in this lifetime. Can you imagine suffering all that crap female sports announcers have to go through to get camera-ready? And then they get to spend all their time on the sidelines no matter what kind of weather? No, thank you. I'd probably also be as wooden as a chair leg as an anchor and get booed off the set.

"Listen, sir, about my mother. Things are all tangled up, that's true, but I'll keep it away from my job."

"I know, in your other compartment." Then Bennett asked, sounding as if the words were being pulled forcibly out of his mouth, "Do you need time off to take care of this?"

"No, sir, don't worry. I'm fine."

"Stay fine or I might have Alonzo write your byline for a week or two."

Perry actually paled. "Would you put up his Einstein photo under the byline?"

Bennett laughed. "You know the score with the fans, Perry, it's always what have you done for me lately? Now get out of here and think fresh and new and exciting thoughts."

She gave him a salute, turned on her heel, and walked back toward her cubicle, considering running through her Rolodex for anyone she could bribe, threaten, or cajole.

Alonzo called out as she passed his desk, "Hey, Perry, you need to see the graffiti in the men's room. At first I thought it was a joke, from some sicko like Walt, but it's not funny. You need to see it."

Graffiti about her in the men's room? Here at the **Post**? That would be pretty outrageous, even from Walt, though he'd already threatened to steal her Harley and run off to Mexico with it. But Walt worked for ESPN, and he couldn't walk through this huge room without sirens going off, without people bringing out fire extinguishers. So, no, it couldn't be Walt. At the dead-serious look on Alonzo's face, she turned and walked straight into the men's room. Only one guy there, Potwin from the crime desk, and thank heaven he was through with his business and washing his hands. Good to see a guy washing his hands. She ignored him and looked at the block letters written in red Magic Marker above one of the urinals:

YOU'RE NEXT, PERRY. BUTT OUT.

What kind of graffiti was that? The threat was obvious, no mystery there, but back off of what, exactly? The Tebow story? That was silly, no one would get his nose out of joint that much, and besides, the feel of it wasn't like a beer tossed in her face or a threat to pull her tonsils out through her ear. No, this was scary; it made the hair stand up on the back of her neck. Was it about her **mom**? But why a freaking message left for her in the men's room about her mom?

Potwin strolled over as he wiped his hands on a paper towel. He looked at the message. "You must have written a really good story to merit this little gem. The guy's rancor made it all the way to the men's room. Good job, Black." He started to stroll out, whistling, but then he stopped, turned slowly. "It's got a strange feel to it, Perry. You want I should talk to some of my detective buddies at Metro?"

And here she'd turned him down for a dinner date three months before. "Thanks, Tommy, but I'll take care of it."

He cocked his head to one side. "I'm sorry about all the trouble your mom's been having." He gave her a small wave and left.

Alone again, she looked closely at the words and felt a punch of fear. No way was this about her Tebow story.

But she'd hardly stuck her oar in at all about her mom. She surfed a wave of cold anger and wanted to strike out, but at whom? Someone was trying to keep her out of her mom's business? Yeah, right, like this moronic message on a men's room wall would do that. Why, then?

Her cell rang, an old-fashioned ringtone

that made everyone under thirty look her way.

"Yo, Perry. My boss wants to speak to you. Only you this time, you by yourself, without your mom."

It was Davis. "Why on earth would Agent Savich want to see me again? I told him everything I knew this morning. I'm on salary here, Davis, I got things to do, a dozen calls to make, scoops to, well, scoop, a byline to write. Unlike you, I'm in a cutthroat business. Have him call me." Then she realized she really needed to see him.

"Wait, I'll be there. You're not going to believe what's happened."

She said nothing more and had the pleasure of listening to his indrawn breath and a lovely sputter. "What? Are you all right? Come on, Perry, what happened?"

"Tell you when I see you."

She'd gotten him. Even with the threat of the graffiti stuck in her throat, she smiled briefly.

"All right, get your butt to the Hoover Building now. Third floor—everyone knows where the CAU unit is." And the jerk hung up on her.

Perry shrugged into her leather jacket, slipped her cell into her pocket, and said to Leon, her assistant, and also Alonzo's assistant, "Gotta go. Back in an hour," and she was out of there.

Forty-five minutes later, she was sitting in Special Agent Dillon Savich's office in the CAU on the third floor of the Hoover Building.

"—and it was block-printed in big red Magic Marker. That's it, all that was written. Why would someone come into the men's room on my floor in the **Washington Post** building and write nonsense like that?"

Savich said, "They could be sure whatever they wrote in the men's room would get all over the workplace, and they didn't need to risk getting close to your work area to deliver the message. I assume everyone in the sports section knows all about your mother's troubles?"

"I think everyone in the known world knows about them."

"Nah," Davis said. "Everyone in the known world knows about your report on Tebow. Your mom's small potatoes in comparison." In the next moment, he was dead serious. "I don't like this. The feel of those words, it isn't good."

Perry said, "You're right about that. That message really creeps me out."

Savich said, "I'll send some agents over there to see if we can lift any fingerprints, ask the staff if they saw anything unusual."

Wonderful. Bennett's going to love this. "Let me give my boss a heads-up, okay, so he doesn't freak?"

She and Savich made their calls together. Bennett had already heard about the message above the urinal in the men's room. He didn't blow a fit when she told him the FBI were on their way to 15th Street NW to the **Post** building, he remained quiet, and that worried her maybe more.

Savich rose. "Perry, I'd wanted to ask you more follow-up questions, but that can wait. This graffiti at the **Post** is more important now. Go back to work and check in with the FBI agents there, all right?"

19

Savich, Sherlock, and Davis sat in the CAU conference room, waiting. Savich looked down at his Mickey Mouse watch. "Nicholas Drummond should be here any minute now—at least, he'd better be, since his former boss, Superintendent Hamish Penderley of Scotland Yard, is calling in about nine minutes." He added to Davis, "Drummond's an agent-in-training at Quantico. As luck would have it, his family and the McCallums go way back, according to Penderley, and that's one of the reasons he believes Nicholas could assist us."

Sherlock said, "Nicholas is very punctual, he should be here in about—"

Both Sherlock and Savich grinned when they saw a big man striding through the unit, wearing a blue shirt and khakis—the Academy uniform—a bomber jacket, and boots, his focus entirely on Savich through the glass in the conference room. Davis thought the guy looked like a pirate: cocky walk, swarthy coloring, and eyes as dark as Savich's. He knew to his gut there was a brawler lurking beneath that smooth exterior. **Hmmm.** And the man waltzed into the conference room, all smiles, handshakes, and a big hug for Sherlock. Savich said to Davis, "This is Nicholas Drummond, the first Brit in the FBI. Nicholas, this is Agent Davis Sullivan."

The two men shook hands. Davis said, "But if you're English, then how—"

Sherlock said, "His mother is American."

Savich studied him for a moment. "You're still walking so I guess they're easing off in the training."

Nicholas rubbed his back. "Well, just barely."

Savich nodded to a chair. "Sit down, Nicholas."

Nicholas sat next to Sherlock. "Do you know they're still talking at Quantico about your taking Savich down in that Hogan's Alley exercise when you were at the Academy?"

Sherlock grinned over her shoulder at Dillon. "My best memory is the rip I left in his trousers showing off his blue boxer shorts."

Savich said, "Yeah, well, I remember you ending up flat on your back in Mrs. Shaw's petunias."

"We all have our own special memories." She patted Nicholas's arm. "How's it going at Quantico?"

"No worries. Lots of good people. Mrs. Shaw tells us all she's been at Quantico since Hogan's Alley was built and everyone is inclined to believe her."

Davis said, "I know who you are—you brought back the Koh-i-Noor diamond, didn't you?"

Nicholas nodded. "Special Agent Mike Caine of the New York Field Office was front and center, as were Savich and Sherlock here. Actually, lots of folks were involved in the recovery of the diamond."

He spoke in a cool, upper-class Brit accent that never failed to charm Sherlock. She felt she could wallow in those lovely sounds and wrap herself in them, like a big warm spa robe.

Nicholas turned to Davis, a man his own age; he read the powerful intelligence in his eyes. "Are you the Agent Sullivan I have heard about?"

Davis looked wary. "No, not me. Maybe."

"They say you slipped into the martial arts instructor's bedroom and put a tranquilized rooster under his bed. And when the rooster woke up and sang out at dawn, he nearly had a heart attack— the instructor, not the rooster. You're that Sullivan, right?"

Davis said without pause, "Nah, I had nothing to do with that stunt. That was another Sullivan, some clown they sent to the Anchorage Field Office."

Savich said to Davis, "Until recently, Nicholas worked at Scotland Yard under Superintendent Penderley, whose call I am expecting"—his cell phone rang, and he put it on speaker—"and here he is.

"Superintendent Penderley, thank you for calling. Let me say again I'm pleased to be working with you. As I told you yesterday, we have very few avenues of investigation open to us here in Washington, despite the recent attack on Ambassador Black here, since the major leads in these crimes are under your jurisdiction in England. Believe me, we are grateful for your assistance. At your suggestion, I've invited Nicholas Drummond to join us. You're on speakerphone, if you don't mind."

"Certainly not, Agent Savich," said an imperious old voice Nicholas knew very well. "Nicholas, I trust you're acquitting yourself well at Quantico with the Yanks?"

Nicholas said, "Sir, every day it is my goal not to shame Her Majesty."

"Good, good. Now, Agent Savich, let me start by assuring you that Scotland Yard has been front and center in investigating the death of George McCallum, Viscount Lockenby. We do not take the unexplained death of a peer lightly, despite all the scandal mongering about him and Ambassador Black. She will tell you herself that Her Majesty's government assigned a special detail to protect her from the moment she reported the attempt on her own life, in addition to the protection provided by the Diplomatic Security Service. It would not have done to allow a United States ambassador to be murdered on British soil. Perhaps that is why whoever is behind these attacks waited until she left Britain to try again." A small pause, then, "I have reviewed both cases. First, as for the report Mrs. Black made about the car that nearly ran her over a cliff near Canterbury, naturally, it was treated seriously by the local constabulary, despite there being no actual evidence of any such attack except for the very common brand of tire tracks that could or could not be relevant. I personally sent an inspector to Canterbury to reexamine the scene. My inspector was unable to find any other evidence, and thus, there is nothing more we can do."

Savich said, "Very well. Tell us, sir, about your investigation into George McCallum's death."

"As you know, our people decided to resolve the issue with a ruling of accidental death, to spare the family a verdict of suicide. The determination was made after the autopsy. Now that you have informed us of the new attempt on Mrs. Black's life in the United States, we are revisiting the case. I've assigned two of my best people. They will conduct further interviews with his family, friends, and business associates; review his recent correspondence and emails, the scene of his death, and his autopsy results again. The usual, Agent Savich."

"And the email that supposedly led to McCallum's death?" Savich asked.

"Yes. Interesting news there. The email purportedly sent by Mrs. Black to Viscount Lockenby from her personal account was in fact sent from the Agatha Christie Cyber Café on Shaftesbury Avenue. Anyone with her password could have managed it. We are well equipped with street cameras in Central London, but thousands of people pass by there every day, and we have no clue who to look for, since we showed Mrs. Black's photo as well as all her embassy staff to all the staff at the café, and no one recognized any of

the photos. I fear that is a dead end."
Penderley paused for a moment, then
added, "However, the fact that the email
wasn't sent from Mrs. Black's own laptop
and was instead sent anonymously from
a cyber café gives more credence to her
assertion that the viscount was murdered,
that something bigger was afoot here.
That said, I will continue the McCallum
investigation.

"Now, that email was forwarded from
the same café, again anonymously, to
Frederick Stickle at **The Sun**, along with
links to articles about Mrs. Black and the
viscount's engagement, as if a newsper-
son at **The Sun** could fail to identify the
George and Natalie of the email after the
headlines they had run about him.

"The photograph of Viscount Lockenby's
son, William Charles, garbed and armed
as a purported jihadist, was sent anonymously to Charlotte Tewks at **The Mirror**
as a simple color printout from an inkjet
printer. That, too, was clever, because a
digital image might have contained tags
identifying the camera or the service and

account used to upload it. Ms. Tewks showed my inspectors the accompanying note pasted together from newsprint stating William's name, the GPS coordinates, and the date of the photo. The picture was quite clear enough to identify William Charles McCallum. Tewks said she could hardly have taken the chance of getting hauled into the Old Bailey for printing something so inflammatory if she was in doubt it was true. The viscount never denied it."

"Sir," Nicholas said, "do you know where exactly the picture was taken?"

"Northeast of Aleppo in Syria several weeks ago, in an area of rebel strength. We confirmed that William used his British passport to travel from Hamburg to Ankara, Turkey, about eight months ago. However, there has been no sign of him since, until now, with the photograph. It seems he has joined hundreds of other Europeans who have taken up the fight against the Assad regime. One hopes he has chosen to fight with the democratic coalition government and not Al-Nusra or the other radicals. But

Syria is in chaos, and we don't have the assets on the ground to find him, nor any legal reason to do so. If he is fighting, he may well be dead now. The casualties have been horrendous.

"That is all we know, Agent Savich. I will, naturally, alert you to anything new we discover, and I will rely on you to share any information you develop with us promptly."

"Yes, of course, Superintendent. You have been most helpful, sir, thank you," Savich said.

"Drummond, give your family my best."

"I will, sir, and thank you."

"Good luck with the Yanks."

Nicholas was grinning as Savich punched off his cell.

Savich said, "What I told Penderley about having little to offer him is unfortunately true. Have you had a chance to speak again with your father, Nick?"

Nicholas nodded. "And to my grandfather as well. He and Everard Stewart McCallum, the future Viscount Lockenby, attended Eton together, then Oxford back before the war. From that point on, the families became close. My father and grandfather were both well aware of the distress George, the current Viscount Lockenby, has felt concerning his son, William Charles, ever since William was forced to leave Oxford some years ago. He never spoke of his son after that, and my father said he didn't pry, he knew it was too painful.

"My family was delighted for the viscount when he announced his engagement to Mrs. Black. My father already knew her well through his contacts at the Home Office and embassy gatherings. They all quite liked her, especially my mum, who said she was exactly the firecracker the viscount needed in his life, high praise indeed.

"I was surprised to hear something from my father that Mrs. Black may not be aware of. He got a call from McCallum about a week before he died, asking his advice. You see, the viscount had received some death threats, block-printed, without postmarks. They were amateurish, complete with misspellings. Regardless, my father strongly advised him to bring in Scotland Yard, but his lordship decided against it. He didn't wish to upset Mrs. Black further, or his family, or bring on more attention from the press."

Davis sat forward. "So George McCallum ignored the threats?"

Nicholas nodded. "My grandfather believes, of course, that George McCallum's death and the attempt on the ambassador's life in England are connected. Oh, yes, he never doubted her story about the attack on the A2 for an instant, said she wasn't the sort to raise a ruckus to cover any malfeasance. He and my father both believe it's possible George McCallum's son, William Charles —Billy—is responsible for his death, which puts him in the center of a bigger storm. They cannot fathom the motive, but there is no one else they can think of if George's death was intentional."

Davis said, "To murder his own father— and if William Charles did kill his father, why would he try to shift the blame to

Mrs. Black? Don't jihadists pride themselves on taking credit? And then he attacked her as well?"

Nicholas paused for a moment, threading a pen between his fingers. "I really can't see it myself, even though the times I saw Billy when we were both teenagers—and self-absorbed as only teenagers can be—I could tell he was troubled, at odds with his family, scorned their attitudes and their opinions. He was unhappy and sullen. I do remember the viscount trying to bring him into family gatherings, but he would have none of it. But again, I didn't pay much attention, since that is normal for a teenage boy."

Sherlock said, "Did he ever show any interest in joining a terrorist group when he was young?"

"Not that I recall, but to be honest, I only saw him maybe a half-dozen times before he went to Oxford, then he was sent down, and then he was gone. I do remember he had a fine mind.

"The Billy I knew, despite his unhappiness, doesn't seem to be the type to kill his own father." Nicholas shrugged. "This is my father's and grandfather's opinion, though."

Sherlock's cell must have vibrated because she pulled it out of her pocket, checked the readout, looked confused for a moment, then got up and left the conference room. Davis saw her stop beside another agent's desk, speak to him, and then leave the unit. He saw Dillon stare after her.

What was that all about?

Savich said, "Since your dad's in the middle of things, Nicholas, keep in touch with him for us."

"Yes, certainly." Nicholas checked his watch. "I've got exactly forty-nine minutes to get back to Quantico before they lock me in Hogan's Alley's jail." He rose and shook hands with Davis, nodded toward Savich. "Call me if I can be useful. I'll keep in touch with Scotland Yard."

Savich said, "Friday night, Nicholas. Don't forget you're coming over to our place for dinner."

"I hear from Dr. Hicks that your lasagna

is about the best in Washington."

"My dog, Astro, certainly thinks so. When it comes to food, that mutt is fast. You'll have to judge for yourself."

Davis was at his desk when he saw Sherlock back in Savich's office, their heads together. There was a look on Savich's face he'd never seen before. This wasn't about Natalie Black, but what? He looked over at the newest agent in the unit, Griffin Hammersmith, a recent transfer from the San Francisco Field Office, and nodded toward Savich and Sherlock. "You know what's going on in there, Griff?"

Griffin said, "No clue, but I'm wondering what's got them so worked up."

Good, Davis thought, he wasn't the only one flapping in the wind. He said, "I gotta go. See what you can find out." Davis shrugged into his jacket and took off to see about Perry at the **Post**.

20

Blessed Backman. She didn't want to believe it. Something deep inside her wanted to deny it was possible. His name brought back too clearly the insane events of a year and a half before.

She remembered the night Joanna had shot him, trying to protect her little girl, Autumn, or thought she had. But she said the room had spun around her until she was nauseated, and she'd stumbled. The world simply stopped, she'd told them, her thoughts no longer her own, and all that was left was the sight of Blessed standing in front of her, his dark eyes reaching deep into her like fingers, wrapping around her very being. Even to protect her child, even though she hated him beyond reason, she was helpless; she couldn't move, only stare back into his eyes. Until Savich had shot him.

That was his terrifying gift, and it had

eventually destroyed him and his entire family, finally sending a raving-mad Shepherd Backman, his mother, to the State Mental Institution in Atlanta and Blessed to the same facility's medical ward, sunk in a deep coma. She'd been surprised he'd survived.

Sherlock walked to the window, stared out at the mess of government buildings wreathed in chilly sunlight. She saw the Washington Monument, the powerful spire that made her feel proud and blessed, but it had no such effect today. She realized she was hugging herself, shivering. She felt cold, from the inside out. Then Dillon's big hands were rubbing up and down her arms. It helped, but not much.

She felt his warm breath against her cheek. "Tell me how this happened."

She wasn't at all fooled by his calm voice. She turned to face him. "It's Blessed Backman."

"So he came out of the coma." Savich didn't want to say the words aloud; it made them true. He didn't want to believe it, but he had no choice. He said slowly,

"When?"

"Over a week ago! That's how long it took the hospital administrators to notify us."

"Okay, let's go over it. Tell me what happened."

"The doctor I spoke with, Dr. Nelson, told me the staff was surprised and happy when Blessed fully woke up again. Because he'd been under so long, in a vegetative state, he called it, Blessed wasn't cuffed down to the bed. The doctor said Blessed seemed bewildered, frightened, when he awoke, needed medications to control his blood pressure, which they expected. After that, he went quiet. They did cuff him to the bed at that point, as per standing orders. They didn't cover his eyes, though, even though the instruction was on his chart and in the admission note, in black capital letters and under-scored. Blessed had been helpless for so long that no one believed it was necessary. Everyone thought the cuffs would be enough to hold him."

Savich said, "We should have anticipated

that, what with Blessed's continuing coma, the passage of time, and the staff changing. Doctors, especially, find it hard to believe what Blessed is capable of. Remember Dr. Truitt had to see what Blessed could do for himself before he believed it?"

"I remember I wanted to punch him out," Sherlock said, "the idiot. It was the same with the staff in Atlanta. Dr. Nelson finally admitted both he and his staff still find it hard to take seriously that anyone, especially Blessed, has the ability to look at someone and tell them to do anything he wishes, including taking his handcuffs off, and they do it without hesitation. Even now, after Blessed escaped, the good doctor informed me hypnosis doesn't work like that. They thought the story was one of the classic urban legends, nothing more. They saw him as a toothless old hound, not a threat to anyone.

"Nelson insisted that when Blessed regained his wits, he hadn't had any kind of strange effect on anyone. I prodded the doctor and he finally admitted that

Blessed had stared at people intensely at times, even stared at him like that, but, naturally, nothing had happened. His unspoken conclusion was that Blessed may be deluded, believed some of this nonsense himself, but that was the end to it."

"Then what happened?"

"Blessed slept and ate and did nothing at all unexpected. He spoke when spoken to. They got him up walking to get his strength back, gave him physical therapy, and the doctor told me Blessed began to walk up and down the halls. When no one was available to help him, he pulled himself along the railings, at least a dozen times every couple of hours. They were impressed at how determined he was.

"Eventually, they told Blessed his mother, Shepherd, was in the institution, housed a floor down, that she was in poor health—slowly dying, in fact. The doctor said Blessed seemed shell-shocked at first, shaking his head back and forth, not wanting to accept it. The doctor believed Blessed thought she was dead. Blessed demanded to see her even though they told him she couldn't communicate with him, that they'd been injecting her with major drugs to keep her comfortable, but he insisted.

"The doctor took Blessed himself to see her. He said Blessed had tears running down his face when he saw her, buried his head against her shoulder. He said he was surprised when the old woman started stroking his hair. He hadn't believed she was awake enough, much less had the strength. He didn't hear what they said, since they spoke in whispers, although he heard Blessed sobbing out loud and saying over and over, 'I will, Mama, I will.' And then she fell unconscious. Dr. Nelson took him back to his room and cuffed him to the bed. Later that night, they told Blessed that Shepherd had died.

"Last Wednesday, two days later, an orderly let Blessed out to exercise without his handcuffs, and Blessed escaped."

"And they didn't call us until today?"

"I asked the doctor why, and he said they were sure they'd find him because he was still weak, sometimes disoriented;

he could still barely walk. He was out in the cold without any clothes other than his institutional pajamas and robe. At least they thought that until an orderly reported some of his clothes missing from his locker along with his wallet. They figure Blessed dressed in the orderly's clothes, got hold of someone's ID, and simply walked out. By the time they decided to notify us, he'd been on the loose for a week. Dr. Nelson—I'd like to clout him—still thinks he'll show up. 'Mr. Backman can't get far; he doesn't have any money,' he said. Well, almost no money. The orderly said he'd only had maybe ten dollars in cash in his wallet."

Savich stared at her, trying to control himself. He had to accept that Blessed was out there, free again. He wasn't a toothless old hound, not in this lifetime. He was as terrifying a monster as Savich had ever gone up against. Blessed was alone in the world now, and would do whatever his mother had asked of him. Of course Savich knew what Shepherd had asked him to do. Kill them. He'd come to

Washington and he'd attacked Sherlock, there was no doubt at all in Savich's mind, and he knew Blessed would stay on that single track until he was dead or they were.

He said, "He's tried once. He won't stop."

"I know," Sherlock said.

He began rubbing his hands over her arms again, for himself as much as for her. He felt the small bandage. He knew every agent in the CAU was looking at them, but it didn't matter. He pulled her close, felt the beat of her heart against his. He whispered against her hair, telling her it would be all right, but he knew the words meant nothing, not to either of them.

Sherlock said, "We were the ones who brought down the family. We arrested his mother, put her in that place, and you shot Blessed yourself. He came after me because I'm the easier target. You can resist him, and he knows that, but I can't. I don't understand, though, why he stalked me for two days, why he didn't simply walk up to me and tell me to do whatever he wanted me to do, like tell me to run until my heart burst. Why would he try something as pedestrian as shooting at me from a moving motorcycle in the middle of Georgetown?"

Savich said slowly, "I'm thinking he had to follow you, learn your habits, and come after you the old-fashioned way because his powers haven't come back. But wait, remember the two old people who saw him up close and personal but they said they hadn't seen anything? I didn't worry about it then, merely thought poor vision at the time, but now I'm thinking Blessed told them to forget him. And they did."

She nodded. "Maybe he still doesn't trust himself, doesn't think he's strong enough yet.

"Dillon, Autumn is his niece. She may be in danger, too. Could Shepherd have told Blessed to go after Autumn again? That's how all of this started, remember."

"I'll call Ethan and Joanna, tell them to take Autumn to Italy, or Siberia, or maybe consider one of those space flights they're selling, any place Blessed can't find them until we've got him in prison again.

"Which brings us to our bigger problem. Like Dr. Truitt and Dr. Nelson, no one will fully believe what he can do unless they see him in action. We still have that video we took of Blessed at Rockingham County Hospital a year and a half ago. We need to get that out to everyone, first of all, everyone in the CAU."

Dillon picked up his cell and dialed. As he listened to the phone ring, he said, "The Metro police need to know what Blessed looks like, what his clothes look like, need to read the report of his attack on you in Georgetown. They need to know he's not a poor old loon escaped from an asylum, down and out and raving mad because his mother died and he blames us.

"We need to show everyone involved that video." He heard a man's voice, and said, "Hello, Dr. Hicks? Dillon Savich here. I really need you to come to the CAU right away. We've got a situation here."

21

Forty-five minutes later, all available CAU agents were seated in the conference room, talking among themselves, wondering what was going on. Dr. Hicks arrived, nodded to them, then dimmed the lights and flipped on the digital projector. He looked at each of them in turn. They all knew he was the top expert in hypnosis in the FBI. What was going on here? He said, "You're here to watch a video that might save your life. I was there, I saw this. But first, let me give you a bit of background.

"This video was shot at Rockingham County Hospital in Titusville, Virginia, eighteen months ago. Let me emphasize that the nurse you will see is a professional. She has been told exactly what she can do and what she isn't to do—namely, she is not to remove the patient's blindfold or release the handcuffs. Now watch."

"Is anyone there? How can I know if anyone's there if I can't see?"

Dr. Hicks paused the video. "This is Blessed Backman. Helpless looking, isn't he? And with that poor, pathetic, whining little old man's voice. The reason he's in the hospital is that Savich shot him. This is his nurse bending over him."

"Yes, I'm here, Mr. Backman. I'm sorry about the blindfold. I'm your nurse, Cindy Maybeck. Do you need anything, sir?"

"I need you to take off this ridiculous blindfold."

All ears listened to his weak, querulous voice, heard the nurse say as she leaned close, "I'm sorry, sir, but I was told to leave it in place, for my own protection, not that I believe it, but I have to follow orders. Let me take your pulse, listen to your heart."

The blindfolded old man whispered, "It's that hick sheriff, he's torturing me because we had a disagreement. Here I'm old enough to be his daddy and he's afraid of me. Isn't that a kick? Listen,

how would you like to lie in darkness, Nurse, with your hands strapped down? I can't even scratch my nose. It's inhumane, don't you think?"

All of them listened to him moan and ask for morphine, and then he started crying.

"Don't cry, Mr. Backman, you're getting the blindfold wet."

He continued to sob. Then, **"Just wipe my eyes for me, Nurse. Please. What can I do? My hands are tied down. I'm helpless."**

Dr. Hicks paused the video. "You can see she's torn. We told her and all the staff that he could hypnotize them instantly, make them do anything he asked. You can see she doesn't want to believe it. She's never heard of such a thing. Who has? It all sounds ridiculous. This poor man had been shot, he was helpless. What could he do?" He started the video again.

"I swear I won't say anything, Nurse."

Everyone in the conference room was leaning forward, eyes on the screen. They watched her ease the blindfold over the top of his head. They watched her wipe away his tears. Real tears. They knew she believed this poor man couldn't do anything to anybody. Surely he couldn't. They saw Blessed Backman open his eyes and look up at her.

"You're a pretty helpful girl. Unfasten the straps on my wrists."

And he smiled up at her.

They saw she didn't hesitate for an instant. She unfastened the straps and straightened to stand next to him. She didn't move, didn't speak.

They watched him tell her to bring his clothes, watched her bring them to him—again, no hesitation.

Dr. Hicks paused the video again. "We were watching the feed in the next room. We waited to see what would happen to be sure Blessed Backman's primary physician, Dr. Truitt, would not accuse us of manufacturing a performance. So we waited. You can see he's in pain. See his pallor, the sweat on his forehead? But he's still functioning; amazing. Now she's helping him dress, and now he tells her to bring in the deputy from outside in the hall."

Savich stepped up. "That's when we had to act. We didn't want to take a chance that someone could be hurt." Hicks started the video again.

They watched Savich walk past Nurse Maybeck into the room as Blessed was reaching for his watch.

"You!"

"Yeah, it's me, your worst nightmare, Blessed. Go ahead, give me your best look, come on, give it a try. Sorry, not going to happen. Party's over. That was some performance you gave us."

Savich forced the restraints back on his wrists and blindfolded him again. And then it was over.

Dr. Hicks said, "I'll tell you, it was the most incredible psychic phenomenon I've ever seen."

Savich said, "This man was in a coma for a year and a half. This is the man who tried to kill Sherlock yesterday. He didn't try to attack her mind; perhaps he's still too weak, we're not sure, so he came after her with a gun, riding a motorcycle. Unfortunately, he escaped.

"This man is more dangerous than I can say. You've seen a little of what he can do."

Dane Carver said, "But he didn't seem to affect you, Savich. Why is that?"

Savich shrugged. "It appears some people are immune to him. There's only one other person I know who isn't affected by him, and that's his niece, Autumn, who's safe from him now, believe me."

"Why did he try to kill Sherlock?"

Sherlock said, "Because he knows I'm the easier target. He won't go after Dillon until—" Her throat went dry. She shook her head.

"He'll fail," Savich said. "And if any of you run into him, don't look him in the eye. Let me say it again: don't look him in the eye."

22

**L'Aubergine restaurant
Foggy Bottom, Washington, D.C.
Wednesday evening**

Yo, Perry. What's up? Where are you?"

"Hang on a moment." Perry smiled over at Day Abbott across the table, a bite of lobster dripping butter on the end of his fork. "Excuse me a minute, Day, it's business and I've got to take this," and she pushed back her chair before the waiter could rush to her side. She stepped into a wainscoted plush alcove of L'Aubergine.

"Where am I? Well, I'll give you a clue. I'm wearing high heels, a slinky black dress, a touch of gold at the ears and throat, and I was daintily forking down braised shrimp in some sort of coconut sauce until you interrupted me. Why are you calling?"

Davis said, "I myself am wearing a Redskins sweatshirt and jeans. My neighbor's shaggy dog, Smack, is sleeping on my feet."

"Sounds cozy. Was there anything else you would like to talk about, Davis, besides our wardrobe choices?"

"I'll bet the dress is too tight for you to run, right?"

"Like a glove."

Davis was still picturing her in the black dress and the nasty high heels. "You're on a date? Is this bozo you're having dinner with going to protect you if you get in trouble?"

"I'm with Day Abbott at a lovely continental restaurant in Foggy Bottom. You met him, remember? I believe it was only last night. We've been friends since we were children. He's filled out well, actually very good-looking, I'd say."

"It's more of a chummy dinner, then. Good. Because speaking as a special agent of the FBI, I advise you to keep it that way. Who does he lobby for?"

"The coal industry. Enough busting

around, Davis. Why'd you call?"

"To give you follow-up about your graffiti artist at the **Post**. We talked to an old doll who's a big flirt, has teased orange hair, a big cat brooch pinned on her blouse—I forget her name—"

"Her name's Angela Porthworthy, a society reporter. She's been at the **Post** so long she covered JFK's wedding back in the Camelot days. What'd Angela say?"

"She said she saw a young teenage boy she didn't know walk nonchalantly into the men's restroom. He came out a couple minutes later and headed for the stairs."

"Teenager? Could Angela describe him?"

"She said he looked Middle Eastern or Mexican. Dark skinned.

"Perry? Is something wrong?"

"Just a moment." Perry turned to smile at Day, who was looking at her, a dark eyebrow raised.

"I'm fine, Day, nothing's wrong. I'm speaking to an FBI agent about the graffiti in the men's room at the **Post**." Then she realized she hadn't told Day about the graffiti. "I'll tell you all about it. Give me another moment."

Day stared at her. "What graffiti? Is this about your mom?"

"No, well, I don't know. Please go back to our table, enjoy your lobster. I'll be back in a moment."

Day gave her a long look, then he grinned. "Is that the goofball with your mom last night at my mom's party?"

"That's him."

"I'm not a goofball," came clearly through Perry's cell.

"Okay, then, the ambassador's boy toy." Day laughed loud enough for Davis to hear him, nodded to Perry, and walked back to their table.

Perry said, "All right, Davis, that's not enough. Tell me more."

"Keep the graffiti under your hat, Black. Consider it confidential. Okay, for dinner I had myself delicious lasagna with crispy garlic toast, lots of Parmesan cheese on top, prepared for me by a neighbor, Janice. Unfortunately, she's a vegetarian, like Savich, so I had to cope with spinach."

"No, you fool, tell me more about the teenage boy."

"Angela's description wasn't much help, but she remembered he was wearing a green work shirt and khaki pants. We went over the security video in the **Post** building lobby, and there he was—she confirmed it. I invited Angela over to dinner with me for helping out, but she said her thighs were allergic to lasagna."

"Angela's on a low-carb diet, claims she's lost seven pounds in three weeks. You're driving me nuts. Come on, Davis, who is he?"

"Don't know yet. Wow, look at that. Carmelo Anthony shot a three-pointer. Swish."

He was watching a basketball game with a shaggy dog named Smack on his feet? "So why'd you call me?"

"To see if you like popcorn."

"I don't know of a single soul in the universe who doesn't like popcorn."

"Well, then. Could you pick some up on your way home?"

"I'm out with Day. Gotta go, Sullivan.

Thanks for the report." She punched off. She was still smiling when she returned to the table, the waiter standing back to hold out her chair for her. She thanked the waiter, took a sip of chardonnay, aware that Day Abbott was looking at her closely; he wasn't laughing any longer, he looked worried. She said, "You know I was speaking to Agent Sullivan. He told me to keep the graffiti quiet, and keep the details to myself. I'm sorry."

He cocked his head at her. "But how could that include me? I mean, we've known each other forever. You even trust me to drive your Harley."

"All true. However, when the FBI talks, I listen," she said, cutting up a cold shrimp and eating it. That had sounded righteous; she wondered if Day would buy it.

At least he smiled. "You told me the guy with your mom last night is an FBI agent, and he was protecting her. My mom told me his boss is Agent Dillon Savich. I've always wanted to meet him. Do you remember how he managed to capture Ted Bundy's crazy daughter? Don't you think I deserve to know about some graffiti at the **Post** a guy like Savich is involved in?"

He was right. But still, she shook her head. "I'll tell you as soon as I'm cleared to, Day." How had he known Dillon was Davis's boss? His mother had told him. Aunt Arliss knew all the players. She chewed on a green bean that was as cold as the shrimp.

"Okay, tell me this. Did the graffiti have anything to do with why you were at the Hoover Building this afternoon?"

23

However did you find out about that? I know, your mom told you. I'm convinced she knows everything about everyone in Washington. Yes, all right, it was about the graffiti."

"I'm waiting for you to break, Perry. Come on, you've never held out on me before."

She looked at the man she'd known since forever; she remembered his yelling at her when she was six years old when she forgot to wear panties on the seesaw, then saw him red-faced, yelling at her when she'd been a junior in high school and he'd caught her smoking marijuana behind her garage with some girlfriends. She realized he'd never yelled at her since.

Day speared a piece of lobster, waved it at her.

"Tell me when you can, okay? You know

I'll worry until you do. There's been so much happening, all the talk about your mom; you'd swear people had half a brain. Fact is, she's been a great ambassador, people really like and respect her, and she's done absolutely nothing wrong. People are morons.

"I had a prospective client a couple of days ago. You want to know how he tried to break the ice, joke around? About whether the president and your mother were lovers."

"What did you do?"

"I threw my napkin down on the table, told him we couldn't do business, and I was out of there. What do you think I'd do? Kiss him?"

Day had always been in her corner, and in her mom's corner as well. She reached over and took his hand. "You're a prince, Day. You know I've always thought that; it's time I said it."

He clasped her hand. "It's a nice beginning. I wouldn't mind if you keep saying it for a very long time. I only wish I could do something that really mattered to help her."

"Just being who you are and what you are, it's enough. Do you know, while you were talking I remembered when I hurled on you at that picnic when I was four years old—"

"And your mom scrubbed my shirt so hard with a wet tablecloth I was bruised for a week."

"And dad wouldn't stop laughing."

They laughed, drawing benign attention.

He gave her a twisted smile. "I remember when you were maybe five years old and you had your skinny little arms around your dad's waist, hanging on for dear life when he gunned the engine of that big Kawasaki Ninja of his and took off; your mom was standing there on the front porch, yelling at him to slow down, was he crazy? But you, Perry, you were laughing, your face pressed against your father's back."

That beautiful stark memory—she felt the joy of those moments again, the exhilaration. Tears stung her eyes. Her father had been gone five years now, and the Redskins had had two other team doctors since his death. She was still riding her motorcycle, but she was no longer clutching his back, shouting with the joy of it.

She felt the tears sounding in her voice. "Good times. I think I was six or seven."

"I remember thinking it was crazy he was taking you to the stadium to watch the Redskins practice, and on the back of his motorcycle, of all things. You were a little girl."

"Why would you say that, Day?" For a moment, there was a look of pain on his face.

"Your dad never took me with him, and I was a boy and my dad had walked out."

What was all this about? She said, her head cocked to one side, "I honestly don't think it occurred to him, Day. Why didn't you simply ask to go with us? He liked you, he would have said yes gladly."

He shook his head, as if surprised at himself, and looked down at his plate. "You're right, it's ancient history."

He looked up at her again. "Your mother

is very well liked, Perry. This will all turn out right, you'll see."

"Tell me, Day, do you think my mom was at fault for George McCallum's death?"

He drank some wine. "I don't know what happened, no one knows. But the fact is your mom's one of the most honorable people I've ever met. She wouldn't do anything purposefully to hurt someone, particularly someone she loved."

She wanted to kiss him. "I guess someone doesn't agree with you," she said.

Day shook his head. "And that must be why the FBI is all over this. To protect your mom."

"Yes," she said. Why couldn't she keep her lips zipped? But she knew. It was a matter of trust, of lifelong affection. She was twenty-eight years old. That was a whole lot of years of trust. She'd trust him with her life, her mother's life as well.

She said, "I don't want dessert. Do you think we could leave now? Believe me, it's been a very long day and I'm nearly ready to fall on my face."

"I guess that means you're not going to

give up your sources about Tebow's girlfriend tonight?" He saw her surprise and patted her hand. "Good job, Perry. You've got the universe quoting your blog. I'll bet the **Post** is selling out newspapers faster than they can print them. You need to ask for a raise."

They were still talking about her story in his new BMW on their way to her condo. She said, "What about you, Day? You told me you walked out on a prospective client a couple of days ago. Do you have any other irons in the fire?"

His eyes lit up, and he puffed up his chest a bit. He leaned toward her, Mr. Discreet in the flesh, and told her about several crucial congressmen who'd agreed to coauthor a bill that would greatly increase future profits for CONSOL coal mining, Day's biggest client. As he talked, she remembered how proud he'd been when he was accepted to West Virginia University for a degree in mining engin-eering, like his father, and not an Ivy League school. His father had remarried a sweet young thing—that was the only name Day ever used when talking about his stepmom. They were living outside of Denver, his father working on the board of a mining conglomerate. His father's name still counted, and he'd helped Day meet the right people at CONSOL. It had been the perfect springboard for him.

She listened as he laid out what the proposed bill would do for his client, tried to share in his budding excitement, but her mind kept going back to a big shaggy dog named Smack sleeping on Davis's feet.

When he pulled into the driveway of her condo on Vanderbilt Street, he turned in the seat and said, "Sit tight. I'll get the car door."

She waited for him to open her car door for her, as he always insisted on doing, and walked with him to the glowing porch light she always kept on. She yawned as she stuck her key into the front door.

"May I come in for a while?" he asked.

"Goodness, I'm sorry, Day, I'm stressed out, I guess, and—"

He took her shoulders in his hands,

turned her, leaned down and kissed her. She stilled. **Oh, no,** she thought. **Oh, no, this can't be happening. Not Day.** She'd sensed he'd been hinting at this, but she'd ignored it. She'd foolishly thought he would understand she wouldn't follow him there. He lifted his head and looked down at her as he splayed his hands on either side of her head. He rubbed his cheek against hers and clasped her shoulders.

"Day, please, no, I—"

"Why not? Perry, you know I've been patient. You know I've wanted this. I've given you plenty of time to see me as a man who loves you. We're not playmates any longer. It's time, really, it's time. I want you to marry me. Let's go inside."

She didn't know what to say. Years ago, as a teenager, she'd have thought about it, maybe, but that was a different world. She'd rather cut off her arm than hurt him, but she had to stop this. **Day, I'm sorry, but I don't feel the same way. You're my dear friend, you have been for my entire life, but I simply don't love you,**

not in that way, not the way a woman loves a man.

She couldn't get the words out, simply couldn't. Maybe what she felt for him could shift and change and evolve, maybe. But tonight, she couldn't handle it. She kept her voice calm and smooth. "Day, there's so much going on right now, I simply can't think of this, of us. We need to wait for this mess with my mom to get resolved, then maybe we can talk—"

He pulled back but kept his hands around her shoulders. "I'm surprised you didn't know, Perry. Even my mom knows how I feel about you. Do you know she tried to convince me it wouldn't work because we were raised together, like brother and sister, that all these feelings I have for you will go away when I meet the right girl? She loves you, though. You'll both change your mind, you'll see." He stepped back, sighed. "I told her I was going to ask you to marry me tonight. I have the ring in my pocket." He stopped, sighed again. "At least you're not turning me down flat." He gave her a twisted smile. "I don't suppose you'd like to see the ring? No, I guess not. We'll talk again when you're ready, Perry, when all this is cleared up, all right?"

She nodded. "I think my mom would agree with yours."

"All three of you are wrong." He kissed her lightly on the forehead, stared down at her for a long second, and turned away.

Perry watched him as he walked to his car, watched the car cruise slowly down her quiet street. She stepped inside her condo, punched in her alarm code, and took off her heels, her toes breathing a sigh of relief. She walked into the kitchen, pulled a bottle of water out of the fridge, and looked out over her darkened driveway as she slugged it down.

She froze. She couldn't believe it. Her beloved Harley was lying on its side, bashed to pieces.

24

Cranford Motel
Outside Mallardville, Virginia
Wednesday night

Blessed could walk now, his steps steady and smooth. He could even run if he had to, but not far, no, not too far yet. He was getting stronger by the day, though it was slow and hard going. But what was even harder to bear was realizing the part of him that was missing, a power that had bathed his very being with light and strength for as long as he could remember.

He was common now, only an ordinary man, no longer even young or strong. He wanted to howl with the loss, and with the fear he would remain common and powerless for the rest of his life.

It was cold. The old vagrant's coat he'd stolen after he'd stuck a knife in his heart smelled musty, with a layer of fruit and chewing tobacco, probably from the old man's crib. Blessed marveled at how easily the knife slipped between his ribs, directly into his heart. Of course, Blessed knew exactly where to slip the knife. His father had shown him and his brother Grace, pointing his old fingers with his sharp curved nails at what he called the X Spot. He remembered his father telling him and Grace, **"If you boys can't use your gift, then you will do what you have to do, but never forget, do it kindly."** He'd wondered whether how you killed someone would matter that much to that person, but he'd never asked. His father wasn't one to ever question. He felt a familiar tightening in his chest. Father was dead now, as was his precious mother. And his brother Grace. And Martin. Only Autumn, Martin's daughter, was alive, but that child of his blood would have killed him, if she could, and very nearly did.

He tasted the remembered fear, cold and acid in his mouth, and swallowed. A little girl had left him hollow, a shadow, a man of no account at all.

The old vagrant had given out only a short sigh, then slumped forward in Blessed's arms. He'd gently pulled out the knife he'd bought at a pawnshop for five dollars, most of the money the orderly had had in his wallet. He felt a leap of energy fill him when he'd walked out of that cold, bleak state hospital filled with crazy people and blank-eyed orderlies and nurses and doctors who looked through you, never at you. He'd wiped off the knife, slipped it back into its webbing at his waist, laid the man against the alley wall and took the heavy old coat.

Blessed missed his father. Had he smelled a whiff of him on the old man whose coat was now on his back? No, maybe that was how old people smelled. Blessed would have preferred sending the old man walking off an overpass on Highway 75 with a look, but he couldn't do that any longer. He wanted to curse until he remembered the old couple in Georgetown who'd seen him leap away from his down motorcycle and limp away.

He hadn't thought, hadn't considered, but he'd looked at them and said quickly, "You did not see me." And he'd seen something in their eyes, something that reminded him of his old self. He wondered what they'd told the police, what they'd told Agent Sherlock.

She'd shot the motorcycle right out from under him. She was still alive and walking around and his mama was dead, with only him left to care, to remember her and his family, and what they'd all been to one another. Now both that damned agent and her husband were looking for him, he knew it to his belly. But did they know who he was? They would soon, he would see to that.

He thought again of that old couple and felt his pulse leap. Maybe they hadn't seen him. Maybe his power was coming back. Maybe. But now that he thought about it, was it possible they hadn't seen him clearly enough because they were too old?

Blessed walked back to his end motel room, unlocked the door, and closed it quietly behind him. The room smelled like stale cigarette smoke and fried chicken. He tossed the motel room key on the bed. He didn't even have his stolen motorcycle now. Tomorrow, he'd steal a car, maybe an old Chevy Camaro. His daddy had loved the old Camaros. But it had to be close by. He rubbed his legs, raising one, then the other. They wobbled a bit. He had to work them more, but not tonight. He'd done enough for tonight.

He didn't take off the coat, simply stretched out on the stingy mattress, crossed his arms over his chest. He remembered his mama stroking his head in her last moments on earth, whispering to him that she loved him.

"Blessed, Blessed," she'd said, her voice wispy and soft, "I knew I would see you again. But I will have to leave you soon, Blessed, I don't have much time. My heart feels like it's slogging through thick mud and it's hard to breathe. Those two terrible people who put us here—you must promise me you will make them pay for what they did. You kill them for me.

You will give me revenge and peace. Will you promise me?"

He had cried, beside himself, the pain was so great. "No, Mama, don't go, don't die, you're all I have left. Martin is gone. Grace is gone, Father's gone. Don't leave me. Don't."

The wispy old voice grew softer, as if drifting away from him. "I wish I could stay with you, Blessed, but I can't. Your little niece, Autumn, is the only one who will be left of us, but I won't send you after her again. She's dangerous to you because she doesn't understand. After you've taken our revenge, you must find a woman of power, have your own children. Make us continue. They will have your gift, and you can build our family again. You can become the Father."

Blessed had whispered, "I will, Mama, I will, I promise."

Now he whispered again into the dark air of his motel room, "I will, Mama, I will."

25

Perry's condo
Vanderbilt Street, Washington, D.C.
Wednesday night

Perry was standing in the middle of her living room, barefoot, still wearing that black glove of a dress she'd worn to the restaurant. It hadn't taken him long to get there, not after she'd yelled into the phone, "My Harley! Someone trashed my Harley!"

Before he'd come into the condo, he'd gone around the side to see another officer with a Maglite standing over the remains. The beautiful machine wouldn't see life again; something like a sledge-hammer, he thought, heavy, repeated blows. Rage in those blows. He didn't like this, didn't like it one bit. This was a serious escalation from the note in the **Post**'s men's room.

He looked over at her, arms crossed

over her chest, seriously pissed, ready to rip someone's face off. He couldn't blame her. When she spotted him she was looking ready to blow. He looked at the dress, then up at her face. "I'm hoping you didn't put butter on your dinner roll. You couldn't afford one more pound on your butt in that dress."

She grinned, couldn't help it, and let her hands fall to her sides. It was her turn to look him up and down. Black Nikes on his big feet, a leather jacket pulled over his Redskins sweatshirt, his hair standing on end. She felt the rage ease off, began to feel relief that he was here, and wondered why.

Davis patted her face and turned to Detective Ben Raven, Metro PD. "Good to see you, Ben."

Ben Raven shook his pen at him. "Sullivan, Perry said she called you. You looked at the Harley?"

Davis nodded. "It's a shame. It was a fine machine."

"Looks like trespassing and felony destruction of private property. Unfortunately, she's been less than forthcoming with me about who might have done this, and why. I'm also wondering why you're here."

"Maybe she thinks of me as the real cavalry, Ben. Hey, Black, why did you bother calling him if you're not talking?"

Perry was down on her knees at that moment, black dress and all, striking a match at her fireplace. She had it going in a few seconds, rose gracefully and eyed him. "Ben's wife, Callie, is an investigative reporter at the **Post**, and a friend of mine. As I was telling Ben, I need a police report for my insurance, and trust him to try to keep this quiet."

"Yes, I understand that," Ben said, "but why keep it quiet? You know who did this, don't you, Perry?"

"Ask Agent Sullivan. I've been told not to talk, Ben, sorry."

"Well, Sullivan, are you going to talk? Or are we waiting for Savich?"

"Yeah, probably, since I called him," Davis said. He studied her face, knew she was okay now. "You're as tough as your mother, even though you're short."

Perry let out a little laugh, and the two other cops who'd come into her living room turned and looked at her. Davis imagined they were thinking, **Really, she's lost her Harley and she's laughing?**

Perry sat down in a deep wing chair near the fireplace, watching the officers speak in low voices to Ben. She was cold, and knew it was a mix of anger and fear of the monster who'd destroyed her Harley, who'd also probably left the graffiti in the men's room. **Why?**

Ben Raven said, "Davis, I know the Bureau has an interest here, because of Ambassador Black. But this is a property crime, and Perry doesn't appear to be in immediate danger. We're happy to accommodate her, gather the evidence for our report, and leave it at that. But you don't want to appear to upstage me, it isn't nice."

Perry rose. "He won't do any upstaging, Ben. Now, is anyone up for coffee?"

It was after midnight before Ben Raven left Perry's condo and Davis sat with

Savich and Perry in her kitchen, drinking his second cup of coffee. "Sorry there wasn't any tea, Savich, even in her junk drawer. You wouldn't believe what she has stashed in there, but not a single tea bag." He paused. "Raven's not happy, but he knows enough to keep out of it."

Perry said, "Callie tells me he mutters around the house sometimes, sorting through a case. He's got to know everything about everything, or he's seriously annoyed."

Savich said, "I spoke with Ben. It's true he isn't happy since he likes to dive headfirst into a case like this, but he's going to back off. His report will describe a simple property crime, nothing more."

Davis said, "This is Washington, which means he's got more than enough on his plate. He'll get over it."

Savich said, "I'll have Sherlock call Callie. She'll help talk him around."

"No, she won't," Perry said. "She's as bad as he is. She wants to know everything. She'll know this attack on me tonight ties in with my mom and she'll be on my case before breakfast."

Savich looked down at his Mickey Mouse watch. "I should be getting back. I left Sherlock muttering about wrecking some of my major body parts because she couldn't come with me, not with Sean asleep down the hall." He looked at Perry. "Did anything happen after you left the Hoover Building, something that could be connected to that threat in the men's room? Something that would lead that person to want to up the ante?"

Davis said, a bit of rancor in his voice, "She had dinner with the secretary of state's son, a lifelong friend, a coal lobbyist."

Perry frowned at Davis. "I'm thinking wrecking my bike was more about my mother than about me, since, really, I didn't do anything else today except work and talk to you. What do they want from us? That she should resign? Lie down in the middle of the road at rush hour? Call a press conference and tell everyone she's a lying, heartbreaking psychotic? What, exactly? Why would anyone care so much about an ambassador to go to all this trouble? Take all these crazy risks? Oh, goodness, guys, I don't want my mother to know about this. I don't know what she'd do, but I don't want them to win, not by threatening me."

Savich said, "Natalie doesn't need to know about this, at least not tonight. You're sure Callie won't report it out?"

"Callie thinks she's a great kickboxer and I take her down regularly. Plus, we eat tacos together. She won't report it out."

"There's a strong bond," Davis said.

"You bet. And Ben told me a property crime report rarely attracts any attention."

Savich said, "All right, then. Davis, can you stay? Make sure the perp doesn't come back? As long as these people are escalating, I want Perry safe. Maybe you can eat tacos together."

"Of course I will," Davis said, as he turned a paper plate loaded with Fig Newtons in his hand. He said easily, "Nice place you've got here, Black, except for the little spots of dust and grease here and there. You want me to ask Monroe if he could fit you in?"

She nodded, but it wasn't about the grease and dust, it was about Davis Sullivan staying here, with her, in her condo. Did Dillon really think she could be in danger? The graffiti, then her Harley—he could be right. She eyed Davis, saw he was thoughtfully chewing a Fig Newton, never taking his eyes off her. Slowly, she nodded again, and thought, **I really don't want someone to destroy me like they did my Harley.**

"Okay," she said, "okay. Davis can move in."

Savich eyed the two of them. People handled shock and fear in different ways. Perry was stand-up, thankfully, and Davis had a nice light hand. He said, "Good. I'm going home, try to talk Sherlock out of her snit, convince her she didn't miss any excitement. Sleep well, Perry. The bozo can sleep on your sofa with his size twelves hanging off the end." He grabbed a Fig Newton as he jerked his head toward Davis on his way to the front door.

Perry walked to the kitchen door so she could hear them talking. Dillon kept his beautiful speaking voice low, but she had no problem hearing him. "I don't like how this is developing, Davis. And we haven't identified that kid who left the graffiti yet."

"Show me his photo," Perry said, stepping into the entryway. Davis said to Savich, "I'm not surprised she's lurking. Eavesdropping, Black? Come and look."

Perry looked down at Davis's iPhone, at a color still from a lobby video camera at the **Post**. He was a tall, skinny, dark-skinned teenage boy. No, he wasn't a teenager; he was twenty years old. She couldn't believe it. She looked up.

"I know him."

26

**<u>Washington Post</u> offices
Thursday morning**

The column in **The Baltimore Sun** Sports section the following morning had no byline:

<u>POST</u> REPORTER'S HARLEY TRASHED

The story beneath the flamboyant headline appeared to have been written by someone who had stood in the middle of Perry's living room last night. At least there was no mention of her mother. In fact, the short article came across as a spoof, pretending to be straight news about a reporter who'd broken a big story before turning to ironic humor, speculating whether this is what a sportswriter should expect if she fell asleep on the job.

Bennett John Bennett nodded to the paper. "Who did this?"

"You mean trashed my motorcycle?"

"No, that's the police's deal. I want to know who gave the **Sun** this story."

Perry thought of the chill she'd felt when she'd seen her mangled Harley, the impotent rage. He didn't care about that? "I can only think that someone saw the property damage report and somehow it ended up with a **Baltimore Sun** Sports reporter."

"First the FBI invades our newsroom, now this? What are we here, writers or the story?" He tossed the paper in the trash basket beside his desk. It was already overflowing, and the paper bounced off onto the floor.

Lolita said from the doorway, "It was a cheap shot, Perry, even though it's true. I've got a call into my buddy at **The Baltimore Sun**. He'll tell me who wrote this and I'll go punch out some lights."

Alonzo peered in over Lolita's shoulder, looking like Einstein after an extra-heavy bolt of current from the light socket. "I guess that Tebow story got one of your readers really pissed off. I wonder why." He scratched his tangled mess of hair and wandered out, whistling the theme song from **A Beautiful Mind**. The song floated through the newsroom until he was back at his desk.

"This is freaking never-never land," Bennett said. "Who attacks a sports reporter? Go away, Perry. Think about whether you want to be here. We've got a new owner who's never been in the business, and soon they're going to move the **Post**, take this building away from us, and put us God knows where. I'd rather worry about this paper than about you."

Was she mistaken, or was there a flush of concern for her. "Why are you grinning?" he asked her.

She said, "I have something this morning you're going to like—Tebow's in love."

Bennett snapped his pencil in half, nearly rose out of his chair. "In love? Tebow? Who told you this? Did you tell your source to keep his mouth shut? What'd you do, offer him money? Sleep with him? Did he tell you who she is? Her name? Jeez, I do hope it's a girl. No, of course it's a girl. Find whatever you need to, Perry, flush it out. You be first on this and I'll murder anyone who writes graffiti about you in the men's room again. **Go!**"

She was still grinning when she sat down at her computer and logged on. She'd taken Buzz Callahan's call on the way in to the **Post**, with Davis, made him pull over next to a dumpster to make notes while Callahan filled her in. Callahan had been injured as a rookie this past season. She'd nurtured him since he was a sophomore at UCLA, rooted for him in print and on her blog, bemoaned the torn ACL and the year of rehab before he'd try again. He and Tebow were friends and, lo and behold, Buzz had sent her a photo of Tebow and a girl off his iPhone, taken in a tucked-away little restaurant off Mondaver Street in Boston. Was this Tebow's way of thanking her for setting things straight?

She typed: **Meet Tim Tebow's girl-friend, Marcie Curtis.**

She'd done initial research on Marcie

Curtis, a senior at Wellesley, majoring in international banking. She was a brainiac, and the adoring look she was giving Tim in the photo had nothing to do with his bank account.

She posted it to her blog with its photo of Marcie Curtis after she turned in her copy to Bennett. She left him chortling.

Her brain jumped back to last night. Not for a minute did she believe it had anything to do with a pissed-off fan. Most people who were passionate about sports weren't nuts—well, most of the time. No more than she was. No, it was about her mother. Who was doing this, and why? She could make no sense of it. She also knew she was going in circles.

She looked up to see a delivery boy with a bright yellow **MACDONALD'S FLORIST** logo on his jacket carrying a huge bouquet of red roses in a stylish green vase. He was making a beeline right for her.

What was this? Flowers? Had Davis sent her flowers, the idiot? She automatically pulled a five out of her wallet. "You Ms. Black?"

"That's me," she said, and she gave the boy the five and set the beautiful vase on her desk. He stuck the five in his pocket, gave her a salute, and took off.

She was opening the small card when her cell rang. "Yes?"

"The roses there yet?"

"Goodness, Day, your timing's incredible. I'm looking at a dozen gorgeous red roses as we speak."

"I wanted to thank you for last night, Perry, and to tell you I understand." His voice was muffled for a moment, then he was back. "That was my mother. She sends you her best, says she's worried about both you and your mom. And now your Harley's been trashed. We're all very worried. What's going on, Perry?"

She sighed. "I wish I knew, Day, but I don't."

"Say the word and I'll move in with you, protect you."

She had to smile at that. "No, no, I've got an FBI agent sticking to me like a second skin, so don't worry. What are you doing at your mom's house?"

"Lunch with her and Brooxey. I'm also trying to talk her out of my grandmother's engagement ring for you. I told her it was your size. It's even nicer than the one I got you. I think you'd really like it, Perry."

"Day, really, I—"

"I know, I know, lips are zipped until this mess is cleared up. You're sure you don't want me to come back, take care of you?"

"No, but thank you. Give my best to your mom and Brooxey."

Day laughed. "He wants me here to play billiards—not pool with actual pockets, mind you, too plebian. Nope, gotta be billiards." He was silent for a moment, then he said quietly, "I love you, Perry, and I'm worried sick. Please, keep safe."

"I will, Day, I promise. Thanks again for the beautiful roses," and she punched off her cell.

His grandmother's engagement ring? She felt disoriented for a moment, and sad. She loved Day. But how would she be able to tell him it could never be in that way?

She checked the roses for water, futzed

around in her desk and opened her computer. All of a sudden Special Agent Davis Sullivan appeared in her mind's eye, sprawled on her sofa on his back at 6:00 a.m., his big feet wrapped in a pale blue throw. Another throw her mother had knitted for her last year covered him to his neck, except for one bare arm that flopped over the side of the sofa, his open hand resting on the small Persian carpet her father had long ago brought her back from Istanbul. She'd said his name as she stood over him, a cup of black coffee in her hand, and watched him come instantly awake, focus his high beams on her face, and relax. He breathed in the coffee, sat up, the afghan falling to his waist, and smiled at her. "Good morning, princess. How's tricks?" And he'd scratched his bare chest.

27

Natalie Black's house
Thursday morning

Natalie Black held her favorite balancing-stick pose, one beautiful straight line from her pointed toes to her pointing fingers. Her hair was fastened with a rubber band, a red poof on the top of her head.

Perry watched her for a moment, unable not to smile. Her mom's breathing was slow and easy, her form right on—one perfectly straight leg holding her steady.

Hooley wasn't watching her. He showed Perry in, told her her mother didn't have much extra breath to speak to her since she'd been hunching and twisting and bowing and folding herself in two in those yoga positions of hers. Now he was standing by the big bay window on the south side of her workout room. The view was of the deep, beautifully landscaped backyard, elms and oaks surrounding the high stone fence. He seemed to be looking for any movement.

Connie Mendez, Natalie's young female bodyguard, was sitting on the small leather sofa, her eyes on Perry.

"Hi, Perry, I'll be done in a moment," Natalie said, not looking at her, holding her pose, her face down between her arms. In the next moment, Natalie slipped to her knees and went gracefully into the rabbit pose, all balled up, Hooley thought, glancing back at her—forehead on the floor, arms back to lie on top of her calves. Then she came to her feet, bent side to side a couple times, picked up a towel and wiped off her face.

"I thought you'd be hard at work, Perry. What's up? Nothing's wrong, is it?"

Her mom didn't know about her Harley, thank heavens. If Hooley or Connie had read about it in **The Baltimore Sun**, they hadn't said anything yet. She knew she'd have to tell her soon, since it was only a matter of time before someone dropped that bomb on her or she noticed on her own that Perry was driving a rental car. But not now; her mother didn't need any more bad stuff piling on her.

She'd start with the graffiti. "Mom, there's something I need to tell you."

Natalie paused in downing a huge glass of water. "You mean you finally want to tell me about the graffiti in the men's room at the **Post**? When Angela called, she naturally assumed I already knew. Of course, I called Davis right away, and naturally he, too, knew all about it. Evidently, everyone knew except me. So the guilt got to you? You finally realized keeping Mom in the dark wasn't going to work?"

"I'm sorry, Mom. I didn't want to burden you. The FBI has a photograph of the guy who wrote that graffiti in the men's room. It's Carlos Acosta, Mom."

Natalie stilled. "Carlos?"

"Yes. Didn't Angela describe him to you?"

Natalie splayed her hands. "From Angela's description, it could have been any young Hispanic male. I wondered if anyone recognized the man. Tell me why in heaven's name Carlos Acosta, my gardener's assistant, would be writing such awful nonsense in the men's room?"

"Ma'am," Hooley said. Natalie turned to him, a half-full glass of water in one hand, the towel in the other. "You know I asked Agent Sullivan to tell me about everyone coming and going. I wasn't told about Carlos. He should have alerted me immediately. Perry, you're certain Carlos was the one who posted that graffiti?"

"Yes."

Hooley pulled out his cell, punched in numbers. "Is this Special Agent Sullivan?"

Connie was looking at Hooley, listening to his low voice. She looked, Perry thought, alert and focused. Like Perry, she was probably wondering what Hooley was saying to Davis. Perry drew closer to her mother and lightly laid her hand on her shoulder.

Hooley punched off. "Agent Sullivan said he still can't reach Carlos. He said he also spoke again to Mr. Sallivar, who hadn't heard from Carlos, either. You know Carlos isn't one to stay out late and party, he's a responsible kid. Sullivan said neither of you is to leave the house. He'll be right over."

Perry said, "Mom, where is the key to dad's gun case?"

Hooley took a step toward her, held up his hand. "Whoa, Perry, no way. I'm here, Connie's here, and I'll get Luis up here from the guardhouse."

"Don't bother, Hooley. Mom?"

"Come with me," Natalie said, all business. "I'll get it for you."

Both women walked out of the workout room, Connie and Hooley on their heels. Perry kept her mouth shut—smart, since she didn't want to end up lying on her back on the floor with a bruised kidney. She never wanted to take on Connie.

Natalie walked into her study, once her father's study, no longer as imposing as it had been, with oversized dark leather sofas and chairs and shadowy chocolate-painted walls. Now it was a light, airy room, still filled with books, true, still stacked high and tight on deep inset shelves, but somehow they no longer overwhelmed. Natalie opened the drawer of an elegant Regency desk, pulled out a Redskins key ring weighted with a good half-dozen keys, and walked to a discreet cabinet beside a narrow closet door. She unlocked the doors, pulled out another key, and unlocked the glass doors inside.

Hooley was impressed by the collection. Lots of firepower. There were at least a dozen handguns—a couple S&W M625s, a Ruger Redhawk, even a Cimarron Thunderer and an American Lady Derringer. Were those Savage Weather Warriors? Yes, two of them, and there was a SIG Sauer 556 Classic Swat. He watched Perry lift out an automatic and hand it to her mother. "The Walther PPK still your favorite, Mom?"

"Oh, yes." Natalie took the Walther, racked the slide, checked that the chamber was empty—Hooley saw her whisper "clear," a well-learned habit. Then she took the magazine Perry held out to her, shoved it in, racked the slide once again to put a bullet in the chamber.

"Good to go. You're quite right, Perry. I should have armed myself the second I got back to the States, or at least after I was nearly run down in Buckner Park. It comes from spending so much time in England, where one doesn't do that sort of thing, especially not an ambassador." She patted the Walther's barrel. "It was Ian Fleming, though, who changed James Bond over to the Walther PPK. It suits me better than the Beretta 418." She grinned over at her daughter. "I always figured what was good enough for Bond was good enough for me."

Perry pulled out a nine-millimeter Kimber Sapphire, a striking handgun with its blue three-inch barrel, racked the slide, shoved in a magazine, racked the slide again, checked to see a bullet was chambered, and nodded. She took down a belt clip, fastened the Kimber to it, and clipped it to her jeans. She eased her leather jacket over it.

Natalie looked at her daughter's gun clip, and then down at her shirt and yoga pants. "Give me one, too, Perry. I'll go shower and change."

Hooley wanted to take on both of them, but he knew dead serious when he saw it. He had to admit both women handled the guns competently, with caution and respect. But still he couldn't help it, the words burst out of his mouth: "Wait a minute, Mrs. Black, Perry, you're civilians, protecting you is my job. You could hurt yourselves—"

Natalie held up her hand. "Don't worry, Hooley. We're both very good shots, and Brundage went to great lengths to secure us all licenses to carry in Maryland. Stop fussing."

Perry said to Hooley, "You don't have to worry about our shooting ourselves in the foot or you or Connie by accident. Now, as for Davis, I'll have to think about that. Mom and I used to shoot together every month or so. Right, Mom? Have you practiced lately?"

"It's been a while. You know as well as we do, Hooley, once you get good, your muscle habits are set. Now, I'd like to speak to Agent Sullivan myself."

Hooley said, his voice desperate, "Agent Sullivan should be here in fifteen minutes or so, ma'am. I don't think he's going to approve of you and Perry carrying weapons."

Perry shrugged, looked at her watch, then patted the Kimber snug against her waist. "Mom's boy toy should be here by now. Let's go see if he wastes time ranting or if he decides to be reasonable. Hooley, would you ask Mr. Sallivar to come to the house?"

When Davis walked into the living room, the first words Hooley had for him were "Be careful the clients don't shoot you, Sullivan."

28

Words jumped back and forth for a full two minutes before Davis realized this living room wasn't the best terrain for a battle. He'd pound on Perry later, after he'd separated her from the Kimber. As for Natalie and her Walther PPK, he simply couldn't imagine even Savich talking her out of anything she'd set her mind to. Better to retreat for the moment. He turned to Mr. Sallivar, who'd been watching with a fascinated eye the back-and-forth among Mrs. Black, her daughter, and these big men who were protecting them. Now he looked at Davis.

Davis said, "Sir, did Carlos know the FBI would be talking with him today? Is that why he failed to come to work?"

"If that's so, Agent Sullivan, I didn't know anything about it. Why? Is Carlos in trouble?"

"We need to ask him some questions.

Do you have any idea where he might be?"

"As I told Mr. Hooley, I know where he lives, but he is not at home."

Davis thought for a moment. "Did Carlos ever express any anger or resentment toward Mrs. Black or toward Perry?"

Mr. Sallivar looked horrified. "Oh, no, never. Carlos believes Mrs. Black is a great lady." He bobbed his head toward her. "I have heard Carlos bragging that he works for the ambassador to the United Kingdom."

Davis said, "Tell us about Carlos, sir?"

Mr. Sallivar said, "I am told Carlos looks like me. He is about my size, only he is about thirty years younger. My third daughter—I have seven, you know—Isabel is her name, she and Carlos like each other. Since I like Carlos, too, I have not interfered, except to tell Carlos to respect her, that if he didn't I would cut—" He glanced over at Natalie, cleared his throat.

Davis said smoothly, "Sir, did Carlos behave differently yesterday?"

"He was more quiet than usual. But he is usually quiet. His cell rang about noontime. He said it was his mother and she needed him to run an errand for her. Then, when he didn't come this morning, I called him, and his phone went to voice mail. I called Carlos's mother, and she told me she hadn't seen him since she had served his dinner last night."

Mr. Sallivar looked around, his face drawn and worried. "Please, tell me, what has happened."

Davis said, "I'm sorry, but I don't know where he is or if he's hurt."

Mr. Sallivar said slowly, "That phone call, it wasn't from his mother, was it?"

"I'll find out, sir. Could you please give us his mother's address?"

Once Mr. Sallivar had left, Davis said, "I'm off to see Mrs. Acosta. You two"— he pointed to Perry and Natalie—"stay here."

"Spoken like the emperor of the universe," Perry said. "You're not going to his house without me."

He opened his mouth, but she was faster. She raised her finger, wagged. "No barking. Heel," and she walked past him to the front door.

He followed her out, watched her open the front door of his Jeep and climb in. **Well, why not let her come along?** It would be easier to get the damned Kimber away from her and safe in his pocket.

29

**Gracias Madre Restaurant
Seven Corners, Virginia
Thursday, early afternoon**

Davis and Perry were eating tacos and shoveling in chips at Gracias Madre after they'd left Mrs. Acosta's home a few blocks away in a heavily Salvadoran neighborhood. Perry eyed the chip basket, sighed, and folded her hands over her stomach. She looked him straight in the eye. "Now that you've blasted my ears with that insane 'Time Bomb,' stuffed your face with fish tacos, and crowed about leaving me in the car at Mrs. Acosta's house, it's time to tell me what you found out. Don't deny it, I could tell from the wiped-clean expression on your face when you got back. You found out something. Spill it, Davis."

Davis picked up another chip, scooped

up some salsa, and seemed to stare at it before setting it down on his plate. "My gut says Carlos has gotten himself in big trouble."

"That wasn't hard to figure. Come on, what'd you find?"

"Nothing specific. Mrs. Acosta told me he didn't eat her **sopas**, which he loves, and that meant he was worried about something. Then he got a call and he went out and never came back.

"I know she's his mother, but she spoke of him in the same way as Mr. Sallivar. He's not the kind of kid to be involved in any of what's happened, unless he was in trouble, unless someone forced him to."

Perry said, "I told you I could hardly believe it last night."

"I thought to ask her if she'd called Carlos yesterday to run an errand for her, and, of course, she hadn't.

"There were no visitors, Mrs. Acosta said, but someone could have come in when she went out the previous day. I've put out a BOLO on Carlos Acosta along with his photograph. We'll check his cell phone records. If he has the phone with him, we might find Carlos, too."

Her cell rang. She looked down to see Day's name. She toyed with sending it to voice mail, but couldn't. "Day, hi. What's up?"

"I wanted to hear your voice, make sure you're okay."

She laughed. "We spoke not two hours ago. I'm fine. And yes, I have Special Agent Davis Sullivan with me, eating a very late lunch of tacos."

Davis watched her listen for a moment, then she said, "Yes, Day, it's the same guy who was with my mother at your mom's party Tuesday night. He's a pain in the butt, but he's trained at this, okay? I'm trying to help, too. No, don't worry, I'm always careful. Hey, did you beat Brooxey at billiards?" And she laughed again at what he said.

When she punched off, slipped her cell back into her bag, Davis said, "Your nose is going to grow with that lie, since I'm not a pain in the butt."

"Clearly a pain in the butt is in the eye of

the beholder."

"That your boyfriend? He unhappy with me being with you?"

"Nah, he's worried, that's all."

Davis chewed on a chip, handed her the basket. "Have you told your mother about the Harley yet?"

She fiddled with a chip, radiating guilt. "No, not yet. But I will when we get back. I don't want to, but I know it's got to be done."

"I'll tell you something else that's got to be done. You're going to unload that weapon, put it in a locked box, and take it home with you. If you carry it in Washington, D.C., I'll have to arrest you."

Davis stood, pulled a twenty out of his wallet, and tossed it on the table. "So are you coming? Or should I bark at you?"

30

Savich turned into the parking lot of
Metzer's Grocers on Prospect Street.
Sean was out of Cheerios, so there was
nothing else to be done. "You want me to
come in with you, Sherlock?"

She laughed. "To buy a box of Cheerios?
I think I can handle that, Dillon. Give me
ten minutes."

He looked around the parking lot before
he nodded. "Ten minutes. I'll keep watch."

Sherlock climbed out of the Porsche,
aware of everyone within a dozen feet of
her, and nodded back at Dillon as she
walked through the automatic doors.
Since she didn't know the store that well,
she stopped a clerk, then headed to aisle
nine. She bent down to pick up a box of
Cheerios when she heard a low scratchy

voice above her head. "Agent Sherlock, all that red hair, so easy to spot. I know your husband is right outside, looking like he'd tear out the throat of anyone who looks at all dangerous. I don't look dangerous.

"No, don't you move or I'll push this knife point into your scrawny neck, right above your collar. Feel that?" She felt the knife prick, the wet of her blood.

"I want you to get up, yeah, grab the Cheerios." He slipped her Glock out of her waist clip, fast and smooth. "Good, you mind your manners. You don't want to have me kill any of the nice people buying their candy and popcorn, and I will, as many as I can, before your husband comes roaring in. I'll be dead, too, but so will you and lots of others."

She stood quietly, feeling him press her own Glock against the small of her back. She felt like an idiot, a box of Cheerios in one hand, and Blessed close behind her. She said quietly, "I'm not moving, Blessed. Don't shoot anyone. How did you manage to get in here?"

"I told you I don't look dangerous. Your husband didn't pay any attention to a hunched-over little old lady, not too steady on her pins, moving slow with her cane next to her daughter and kiddos. Sweet little girl, all eager to help me, stayed real close in case I teetered. Who wouldn't help a friendly little old lady out to buy her Polident to hold her chompers in? My mama used that stuff, you know. Still clacked when she talked. Yep, this was as easy as drilling a hole in a tooth.

"No, look straight ahead. You and I are going out the back. I have a little Kia parked out there, lifted it this afternoon from a parking lot behind the bowling alley. You and I have lots to talk about, like that pretty hair of yours."

So many people, women with babies and toddlers, chatting, comparing heads of lettuce, or in a hurry, anxious to get home, none of them suspecting a thing. At least Blessed was focused on her. She had to keep it that way. She and Dillon had been right, Blessed hadn't tried to make her lose herself, to make her brain go off into the ether; he had to use a weapon to control her. It was a huge relief. He was only a middle-aged man, albeit with her gun now, pointing her gun at her and determined to shoot her, but Dillon was close. He'd said ten minutes. He'd miss her sooner than that, because it had to take less than ten minutes to buy a box of Cheerios.

"Walk, nice and easy, girl. If you try to turn on me, if you even twitch, I will kill you, then I will blast a bunch of mothers and their little kiddies."

"I'll walk." Sherlock walked slowly in front of Blessed and wondered exactly what he looked like walking behind her.

"You need to pay for that, ma'am."

A young voice brought her up short. She realized she was still carrying the box of Cheerios.

Blessed's gun pressed hard against her spine.

Sherlock gave the teenage clerk with his moon-round face and buzzed black hair a big smile. "Sorry," she said, and handed him the box of Cheerios. "I met up with my aunt here and forgot I still had it."

Blessed didn't say a word until the clerk, who, after one long, suspicious look, took himself off to aisle nine to restock the Cheerios. "See that restroom sign back there? That's where we're going. Walk."

"Why didn't you hypnotize me—stymie me, as you call it?"

The gun pressed harder against her back. "None of your business. Shut up."

"No more juice, Blessed? So now you're like everyone else, aren't you? How does it feel, Blessed, to be normal and vulnerable?"

She felt him jerk behind her. He said, low, against her hair, "It feels bad."

He sounded shaken; she supposed. In theory, she understood. His gift had been part of him all his life, and now he felt like a man with one leg. Did he even know how to operate in a world where he couldn't simply tell anyone to do what he wished and see it done? "Where are you getting your money, Blessed?"

He hissed like a snake in her ear, "Ain't none of your business," he said again. "I can see your brain squirreling around, trying to figure out how to take me, but there's nothing you can do. Don't forget, I can shoot you right here, mow down a good dozen folk. That what you want?"

"No, I don't want that. Why do you want to kill me, Blessed?"

"My ma didn't like you, said you had no respect. Now shut your trap and keep walking."

"I can't believe Shepherd said that. Why, I told her how beautiful her house was, and I meant it. So why?"

She heard his scratchy old breath, then he said, "Ma was smart. She said you had to be killed first. She said once you were gone, Savich would freak out and I'd be able to get him easier."

She thought she'd choke on her fear. Shepherd was right, Dillon would freak. But she was also wrong. Dillon would hunt Blessed down like a rabid dog. She felt him turning slightly, one way and then the other. He was looking at the people around them. He laughed, a raw, low sound that was hardly a laugh, really.

"I can't wait to kill that man of yours. Mano a mano, hand to hand, that's how it will be, but on my terms. It won't be nice and quick like that bum."

What bum?

Blessed said, "Autumn's my niece. When she gets older, I'll make her understand that."

"You remember Ethan Merriweather, the Titusville sheriff? He and Joanna married. The three of them are a family now. I believe they're expecting another child. You need to forget about Autumn, or I promise, you'll end up dead this time."

"Autumn is no concern of yours. If I ever see her again I'll make her see me, really see me, this time."

Believe me, she really saw you the last time.

"Keep going. We weave down the aisle through all those storage racks, right toward that exit sign and out the back door."

She walked through a swinging door into a huge back storeroom with the restrooms to the right and row after row of heavy metal racks filled with stock straight ahead. Blessed was so close he was nearly pressed against her back. He said, "She made me promise to find a wife for myself."

He was talking without her questioning him, but why? And then she realized he was completely alone. Blessed had no one else to talk to, no one who knew him or had any kind of tie to his life before.

Sherlock saw a lone clerk off to her left, some ten or so feet away, a clipboard in his hand, counting cans of pork and beans. He paid no attention to them.

"Look at that!"

The gun jerked.

Sherlock grabbed the corner of one of the metal storage racks and jerked it forward with all her strength.

It teetered, sending cans and boxes tumbling off, raining down on both of them, but the huge structure didn't fall.

"No more of that! Walk, you bitch," and he shoved her forward with her Glock.

"Hey! What do you think you're doing? You shouldn't be in here." The clerk with the clipboard was marching toward him, his anger giving way to fear when he saw the gun.

Sherlock grabbed a can of okra and hurled it at Blessed. It struck him hard on the forehead at the same time he fired at her. The bullet went wide, tore through a big box of oatmeal and slammed deep into a concrete wall. The sound was deafening. She slipped around the storage rack for cover, yelling at the clerk, "Get out now!" She heard him yell again as he ran toward the swinging doors. She whirled about and peeked between boxes of soap to see Blessed. What she saw was an old woman leaning back against a storage rack, holding her head. And over her tatty gray crocheted sweater covering a lacy blouse, baggy flowered skirt, and sneakers, she was wearing a camel wool coat.

An old man peered out of the unisex restroom. She yelled, "Get back inside and lock the door!" Blessed, still shaking his head, jerked toward the man, but the man moved fast, the door slamming loud as Blessed fired two bullets, one of them hitting the bathroom door dead center. She heard the old man yell, not in pain, thank heavens, heard the clerk yelling back in the store. She grabbed a can of creamed corn, hurled it at Blessed, smacking him in the middle of his back. Blessed stumbled and jerked about to face her, his old woman's seamed face tight with fury.

She was in big trouble. She grabbed another can and hurled it at him as he charged toward her and fired.

31

Sherlock dropped to her knees and rolled as he fired. He missed her. She jumped to her feet, grabbed the corner of a storage rack and pulled hard. Cans and boxes hurled outward, slowly at first, then in an avalanche, striking the bare concrete floor like claps of thunder and pelting the goods on the rack opposite. Bags of candy rained down on her. She heard yells and shouts from people outside the storeroom. She gave another final jerk to the storage rack, and the huge metal rack fell over, smacked hard against the rack next to it. She heard a low rumble, then saw the next rack topple, and the next one, a domino effect. She dropped to the floor as each of the great racks unbalanced the next, and one by one the racks went over. The noise was deafening, even louder than the bullets in the closed space. She tried to scramble away, but the floor was covered with rolling cans and she couldn't gain purchase. It hurt, slipping and sliding over the rolling cans.

She heard Dillon's voice above the din of shouts.

She'd lost sight of Blessed. But she thought she heard him now, a low, feral cry, harsh breathing, and then she saw the exit door open and close and knew he was gone. Before she could call out to Dillon, she fell on her face among the still-moving sea of canned goods, and smashed her temple against a fallen metal rack.

She shook her head to clear it. She had to get out of there or she'd be crushed. She felt hands pulling her up, felt pain from her fall, but at last she was free. Savich drew her against him and they picked their way carefully through the ruins of the storeroom and out the swinging door. A lone rolling can of pineapple struck his foot and he nearly went over, but he never let go of her. They walked right past the store manager, who stood staring helplessly through the storeroom doorway, blank-faced with shock at the devastation.

When they were back to safety, his hands were all over her, feeling and pressing every inch of her. "Are you all right? Do you hurt anywhere?"

"I'm okay. A rack got me against the temple, so I'm a bit woozy. Blessed, do you see him?"

He stared at her. "Blessed? No, of course not. He couldn't have gotten past me."

"Did you see a little old lady? Sort of bent over, walking with a cane? A camel coat? With a woman and kids?"

He cursed. She was so surprised she stepped onto a can of tomato paste and went down. Before she landed on her back, Savich lifted her under her armpits and pulled her up. People crowded in on them, everyone talking at once. Several more cans rolled out of the storeroom and down aisle five, where they were picked up by startled customers.

Savich said, "Is he in there somewhere?"

"He went out the rear exit. Said he had a stolen Kia waiting."

They ran out of the store and around to the back door, but Blessed and his stolen car were gone.

"He'll switch cars, fast," Sherlock said.

A dozen customers had called 911, and cops were soon swarming all over the store. Before they were pulled into endless interviews, Sherlock called in the Kia and Blessed's description herself.

It took time to deal with the police, the manager, the customers. Too much time. It was twenty minutes before Savich could start a grid search around Metzer's Grocers, looking for Blessed in a stolen Kia.

32

Natalie Black's house
Thursday afternoon

Carlos Acosta could be anywhere, even back in El Salvador."

Conversation died, and everyone turned to stare at Natalie. She continued. "I hope he ran because he knew you were looking for him. I hope they didn't kill him. And all for some stupid graffiti!" She looked ineffably sad, her shoulders slumped, her head down. Then anger took over, and she smashed her hand against the back of a chair. "Who are 'they'? Who could have coerced Carlos into writing that message, and probably destroying Perry's motorcycle?"

Perry said, "I can't imagine killing the delivery boy, namely Carlos, without a reason for it."

"There's always a reason," Hooley said,

"unless these people are psychopaths, then the sky's the limit."

Davis said calmly, "If he's dead, then that would mean he found out who they are. They couldn't risk his telling the police what he knew. Who knows? Maybe Carlos decided to try some blackmail."

Perry jumped to her feet and started pacing the living room. Davis watched her for a moment, then said, "I spoke to Savich. He and Sherlock are up to their eyebrows with another case. Some lunatic they arrested last year tried to kill Sherlock in a grocery store, of all places, but they're both all right. They're looking for the bozo, and will be out for a while."

He shot a look toward Hooley. "It's you and me for a while, Beef."

Hooley flexed his big hands and gave him a ferocious grin, nodded to Connie. "The three of us."

Perry dusted off her jeans. "You three and the rest of us," she said, and patted the Kimber, still on her belt. She stopped talking because Davis was no longer paying any attention to her. He was looking down at his cell. He raised dazed and disbelieving eyes to her face.

Natalie stood halfway up. "What is it? What's wrong?"

He said, his voice outraged, "Got a text from the CAU. Your daughter reported today that Tebow's got a girlfriend and she didn't tell me about it."

"You've got to be kidding me," Hooley said, blinking. "No, really, it's true? Tebow fell?"

"Tell **you**? She didn't tell her own mother," Natalie said.

Connie Mendez called out from the living room doorway. "Mrs. Black, you have a visitor. I believe it's the secretary of state."

"Oh, dear, I forgot Arliss was coming. Okay, all of you, out. No, stay here. I'd like her to meet you. Then she and I will speak in my study."

Davis turned to see Secretary of State Arliss Abbott enter the room. She was dressed in a business suit that shouted boardroom and designer, and she was eyeing all of them, an elegant eyebrow raised. "A party, Natalie? And I wasn't invited?"

"Anyone who dresses as elegantly as you is always invited," Natalie said, smiling as she walked to her. "Good afternoon, Madame Secretary."

Arliss Abbott smiled at her longtime friend, nodded, greeted Perry, Connie, Hooley, and Davis with great charm. No one mentioned Carlos Acosta or Tebow's girlfriend.

A few minutes later, the two women were alone in Natalie's study, each with a cup of Earl Grey. They made quite a pair, Natalie thought, with Arliss dressed to kill and she herself in casual slacks, a gun clipped at her waist. Arliss looked tired—wrung out, really—and Natalie felt guilty because she knew she was primarily to blame.

Arliss said, "It's been too long since we really talked, Natalie. I'm sorry for that."

Natalie said, her voice calm, steady, "You know I understand. Now, you're here to tell me Thorn has determined I'm to resign, aren't you?"

Arliss very slowly lowered her lovely Meissen cup to its saucer. "Thorn refuses to ask you to resign."

Natalie sat back. "I was certain that by now he would realize he didn't have a choice but to cut me loose. You know as well as I do that in politics and in business, personal feelings count for nothing, at least not for long. He's the president. Events are spiraling out of control, like a tidal wave gathering force and speed. Surely it would be a relief to put all this behind him—and you as well. I don't understand his thinking."

Arliss sighed. "Thorn said, and I quote, 'Natalie has never lied about anything. If she said she didn't break it off with George McCallum, then she didn't. If she said a car tried to force her off a road in England, then it did. Well, I've got to amend that. I do know of one white lie—that was to Perry when she was twelve, I think, about sex.' He grinned that famous grin of his, unrepentant, because he told me the First Lady had lied to their own daughter about the same thing, just last year."

It sounded like him. She knew their friendship was bone-deep. She felt abiding gratitude to Thornton Gilbert. But she didn't want him to suffer for this mess, her mess. "Am I hurting him, Arliss? You? The party?"

Arliss looked her straight in the eye. "Unfortunately, yes. You know how much I hate saying this. As your friend, as someone who's known you as long as Thorn has, as someone who'd like to support you to the death—" She shrugged. "I can't. I'm sure if you put aside your own wishes, it would be clear to you that Thorn is not acting in his own best interest.

"You're underestimating the situation, Natalie, you're not seeing how devastating the decisions you've made and their consequences have become. His enemies in the press use every opportunity to undermine him, and us. They're starting to bray already about his straining our strong ties with our most important ally for the sake of a personal friend. They're accusing him of carrying friendship too far, and why is that? They're still stopping short of saying you and Thorn had sex in college and maybe even now are conducting an affair, but it could come. They're hinting at a cover-up, laying out all sorts of scenarios.

"They'll be digging into your past, Natalie, all the way back to college. As I said, they would be delighted to find someone who claims you slept with him. Tell me the truth, did you ever have sex with Thorn?"

Natalie was amazed. Arliss, of all people, should have known that Brundage had been the only boy she'd ever wanted, the only man she'd ever loved. But had others wondered if she'd had sex with Thorn? She'd known, of course, that he'd cared for her back then, but he and Brundage had been best friends, and nothing was ever said about it. If it had, Brundage had never told her. Thorn and Brundage had remained friends until Brundage had died. Natalie remembered how pleased she and Brundage had been when Thornton finally married in his late thirties. He picked a lovely woman, and now First Lady, who'd proved to be a huge political asset, a nice bonus, he'd once told her and Brundage. She kept her voice calm and steady. "No, Thorn and I never had sex, nor would I have ever considered it. It was a long time ago, ancient history. I'm sure Thorn got over his feelings for me very quickly."

"Not all that quickly, given he didn't marry until his late thirties. But that would mean the feelings were all on his side, wouldn't it, and not on yours?"

Natalie nodded; her voice became brisk. "Arliss, I want the truth to come out. Really, that's all I want."

"Perhaps that would happen in a perfect world, Natalie, but Scotland Yard investigated George McCallum's death. I understand they're looking into it again at the behest of the FBI. From what I've been told, there was nothing more found to change their ruling of accidental death, if a ruling made because of his family and because he was a peer of the realm, otherwise, a probable suicide.

"They also investigated your claim that

someone tried to run you off a cliff. They couldn't find any evidence to support your claim, the first time and again when the FBI asked them to look into it again. So there's nothing new in either case."

All true, Natalie thought. Natalie didn't want to accept what she saw on her friend's face. She said slowly, as she studied Arliss, "Do you believe me, Arliss, about all of this? Because if you told me someone was trying to kill you, I would believe you, no matter what anyone said."

Arliss cocked her head to one side, sending her chic bob sliding across her cheek. "Of course I believe you, Natalie. But don't you see? What I believe simply isn't relevant; it doesn't matter. What matters is what the public believes. Since no one was there with you to verify what you said, since there was no evidence to back up your claims, you know the public leap toward the titillating, the scandalous."

Natalie saw a high, thick brick wall rising in front of Arliss's face, and knew she would never scale it. Still she couldn't help herself, she had to try. "Since you believe me, Arliss, I will tell you that someone tried to kill me again last week. They tried to run me over while I was jogging in Buckner Park."

The Meissen teacup rattled. Arliss stared at her, shaking her head. "Oh, Natalie, no, that's horrible. But you weren't hurt, were you?"

"I was lucky" was all Natalie said. She didn't want to go through it again, didn't want to feel the same fear, the same hot rage. Did Arliss believe her?

Arliss set her cup and saucer down on the beautiful Regency end table, once again poised and calm. "Thank heavens you're all right. There hasn't been anything in the press. Did you make a police report?"

"I wasn't about to do that again, not without proof. Only you and the FBI know, and my own staff, of course."

"How did you manage to get the FBI involved?"

Natalie smiled. "It was happenstance. I believe if anyone has a chance of discovering the truth, it'll be Agent Sullivan and Agent Savich."

"It's also wise that you've hired body-guards," Arliss said. She looked at the Walther. "Though you're carrying that pistol on your belt." She took Natalie's hand, squeezed it. "Natalie, what you're doing, it's smart, it's what I'd do in your place. You know I'll have to tell the president about this."

"Good. I want him to know."

Arliss leaned toward her again and lightly laid her hand on Natalie's arm. "I am so sorry this is happening to you, but you must keep in mind that Thorn has immense responsibilities, not only to you, but to a great many other people he cares for, and of course to his office. He has to make his decisions based on political realities, not on what he thought of a twenty-year-old girl at Yale.

"He is the president; it is not my role to dictate to him, but surely you see that you must take the decision out of his hands."

Arliss sat back in her chair again. She studied Natalie's face, then said, "Do not wait for Thorn to ask for your resignation.

I think you should offer me your resignation right now. It's best for Thorn, you know it is, and best for the country, and perhaps it's also the best for you."

But it's not best for me! It's not right, not fair!

"Are you saying you think the attempts on my life will stop if I resign?"

Arliss slowly rose. "I don't know, Natalie, but listen to me. We've been friends since the ark landed. I remember those years we spent together at college as the best years of my life. What I've had to say today doesn't change that. What we're facing is a political imperative, and politics, as you know, is never fair. I can see you're not ready, that you'll have to think about this. Take a couple of days, but no longer. I will expect to hear from you on Saturday, all right? My private cell is still the same."

She turned and left Natalie in her study, her heels sounding sharply on the marble tiles.

33

Georgetown
Thursday, late afternoon

Savich and Sherlock spotted the stolen Kia on a quiet residential street six blocks from Metzer's Grocers, neatly parked between two big SUVs. Savich called it in. He was certain there'd be no finger-prints. Blessed had never been stupid.

"Blessed is long gone," Sherlock said. "I'll bet when Ben Raven's people canvass the neighborhood, they'll find another car's been stolen close by. I forgot to tell you, Blessed mentioned a man he called a bum. We need to check with Ben, see if they've found a homeless person murdered very recently either here in Washington or in Atlanta." She mumbled something under her breath and looked like she wanted to holler.

"What?"

She shook her head at herself. "Blessed got my Glock. I can't tell you how angry I am about that."

"The first rule is to stay alive. I'd say what you did was brilliant. Forget the Glock."

Savich was on the phone to Ben Raven when they walked through their own front door. Gabriella and Sean were in the kitchen, Sean still flying high after a hard-fought basketball game with Marty next door, quite an accomplishment, since Marty was a killer. Sean was dirty and sweaty and kid-happy about winning, and so they let him regale them with a play-by-play until it was time for him to wash up for dinner. Then he wanted to talk about Marty's little brother, who was a real pain in the patoot.

Sean wasn't upset there would be no Cheerios in the morning, since Sherlock promised to make him his favorite pecan pancakes. Only after Sean was down and out for the night and they were alone in their bedroom, Savich unbuttoning his shirt, was there mention of the world outside. "Ben got back to me. Sure enough, there was a report of a murdered homeless man in Columbia Heights. His name was Ernest Tubbs, age sixty-six, and he was found dead from a knife wound through his heart. According to the fellow in the crib next to his, all that was missing was his only valuable possession, his coat."

"The coat, I'd wager, was a camel wool coat, good and warm. Blessed was wearing that coat today over his old-lady clothes."

He stepped into their closet, punched a combination into their safe, and brought out a Stoeger Cougar Compact, a sidepiece that had belonged to his father. "Dad never liked the company SIG. I bet he'd be pleased the Bureau's switched over to the Glock. He handed her the pistol. "Use the Stoeger until they issue you a replacement. It's got lots of mileage on it, but I've kept it in good shape. You shouldn't have any problem." He handed her a couple magazines. "Nine-millimeter, thirteen plus one rounds."

She hefted the Stoeger, got the feel of

it. "I'll bet it doesn't have much kick. I can't wait to try it out at the range. Thank you, Dillon."

He grinned at her. "I might as well give you an early birthday present." He picked another gun out of the safe and handed it to her. "It's an S-and-W 380. Feel how light it is, lighter and smaller on your ankle than the Lady Colt."

She took the pistol from him and nestled it into her hand, felt the small grip. "Oh, goodness, it's a beauty." She jumped to her feet, cupped his face between her hands. "First the loan of your dad's Stoeger and now this baby for my birthday. Thank you, Dillon. I can't wait to try both of them out on the range. Maybe if I really like the Stoeger I can talk Mr. Maitland into keeping it," and she gave him a loud smacking kiss.

"Hold that thought," he said. He took both guns from her and put them back in the safe along with his Glock, and locked it. He turned back to Sherlock, smiling. "How about a hot shower? Do you want to scrub my back?"

She looked up into the face of one of the people she'd willingly give her life for. She put her fear of Blessed away, and felt the familiar leap of her pulse as she watched him unzip his pants. "Among other things," she said. They were out of their clothes and under the shower in thirty seconds.

Outside, hunkered down in a pile of box hedges close to the house, Blessed thought he heard laughter. But how could that be? That woman almost died today. They had no right to laugh when his mama was dead, when Grace was dead, when he was all alone. His niece, Autumn, was a little kid. There was no way to make her understand, no way to make her forgive him, particularly since he knew he'd have to kill her mother and that damned sheriff. He'd do what his mother said; he'd find himself a woman, maybe have kids and become the Father. Why not? A man had to have a reason to live, a reason to make his feet move in the morning.

He was cold, despite the warm coat. He

was tired, too, and angry with himself that he'd failed again. He'd let her get the better of him with those tall storage racks. Who'd have thought she'd be strong enough to shove one over? And she'd been lucky when she'd hurled that can at him, really lucky. He touched his fingers to the knot on his forehead. That can had dazed him pretty good.

Blessed rose, all stiff and frozen, and stretched. They were in for the night, no chance to get at them now. It was stupid to try to get past the alarm system; he'd get himself shot.

He walked one block over to the stolen Toyota he'd left on the street, started it up, and turned on the heat. He drove toward Virginia and didn't stop until he reached Mama Taco, right next to the Cranford Motel, and ordered a beef burrito with extra hot sauce.

Back in his room, he turned on the local news and lay back on his bed, shoving the two skinny pillows behind his head. Whoa, what was this? He couldn't believe it. They had the story about the old varmint he'd killed for his coat, the coat now lying over the back of the only chair in his motel room. Why would that be news? It had been days ago and the old guy was homeless. Who cared? Then, to his shock, his photo appeared on the screen along with his name, asking for information about him, calling him the suspect. How did they know? There'd been no one around, he was sure of it. He felt fear swirl in his belly. No, it'd be all right. They didn't know where he was, but he knew he'd really have to watch himself now. They said the old man's name was Ernest Tubbs. Blessed said the name out loud. He saw Ernest Tubbs's seamed old face in his mind, not saying anything. Then he saw the old man's finger pointing at his heart.

34

Perry Black's condo
Thursday night

Perry and Davis sat side by side, drinking decaf and watching the small fire in the fireplace smolder and hiss, and spurt out the occasional spark.

Perry said, "I never thought Aunt Arliss would care so little about Mom. They've been friends forever. I'm afraid of what it's going to do to her."

"It's not going to do anything. Being asked to resign won't break your mother. She's pure steel."

"What? You've known her since Monday. Listen, after Aunt Arliss left, she looked ready to throw in the towel."

Davis set down his mug, stretched his arms out along the back of the sofa. "It was a tough thing to hear, but she'll deal with it. If you'd seen her handle that addict who tried to hijack her car on Monday, you wouldn't be worried. That was your mom in action. If she goes down, it'll be fighting tooth and nail, and screw Madame Secretary."

She jumped to her feet. "You're right, that's my mom. Arliss may want to throw her to the wolves to save her own hide, but Mom will do what she thinks is right. And so will I. I don't think I'm going to call her Aunt Arliss anymore. I wonder what Day will have to say about all this? And listen, you really don't have to stay here again with me tonight."

"Yeah, I do, no choice. My boss ordered me to."

She eyed him. "All right. I cleaned the bathroom."

"I appreciate it. Monroe has made me real particular about bathrooms, right down to the shower grout."

She gave him a distracted smile, then began pacing the length of her living room. She paused at the windows and peered out into the darkness, then strode back to where he sat on the sofa, watching her.

"Don't you have your blog to write?"

She stopped, rubbed her hands in front of the fire. "It seems so trivial, given what's happening with Mom. And me. I called the insurance adjuster, and the company officially ruled my beautiful Harley totaled. Isn't it sad that's what I was thinking about, how I would replace my baby? And what about poor Carlos Acosta? No one has seen him for over twenty-four hours. Do you think he's dead, Davis?"

Davis didn't have a clue, but he said without hesitation, "No, Carlos isn't dead." He paused for a moment, seeing her slumped shoulders. "I have some better news. Savich didn't want to say anything about it himself unless it panned out."

She whirled to face him, eyes a hundred watts bright. "What? Come on, Davis, tell me."

"All right, but remember, we can't take it to the bank yet. Savich spoke with Hamish Penderley again today, you know, the big muckety-muck in Scotland Yard? Penderley got word from one of the inspectors who had been checking out automobile repair shops in the region of Kent where that black sedan collided with your mother's dark green Jaguar. There was nothing all this time, but yesterday a black sedan was brought in for repair at a small shop in Ashford. The damage matches your mother's description of the collision. They're analyzing small paint chips left on the car now to see if they match your mother's car."

"We should call my mom, right now!"

"If you do, you're going to get me in trouble with Savich. Wait until tomorrow, then we'll know for sure. I only told you because you looked so pitiful. See, Black, you've got to have some faith here. So pick your optimism up off the floor."

She squared her shoulders. The fighter was back. "Yes, all right, that's better, but I'm going to tell her first thing tomorrow. This is the greatest news." She pumped her fist in the air. "Let's hear it for Scotland Yard."

"Don't you have a blog to write?"

"Yes, but—"

"No buts."

"What I was going to say was my blog's in good shape already. Well, there is one thing. I got hold of Marcie's mom. Marcie Curtis—you remember, she's Tebow's girlfriend. The mom wouldn't talk to me, even got her husband on the phone to burn my ears, but it turns out he's a huge football fan. Even better, he likes my blog, and he liked the photo of Tim and Marcie I'd posted. After that, I couldn't shut him up. He even told me his little girl met Tim at a skating rink."

"I didn't know Tebow ice-skated."

"I didn't, either, but given how athletic he is, what couldn't he do? Marcie's dad bragged to me that Tim wasn't as good as his little girl, but that'd give her something to be better at. All right, I'll go write it. Truth is, I've never had as many comments posted about any of my sports stories."

Davis reared back. "Why? I mean, she's only a girlfriend, she's got nothing to do with football. What's up with your numb-brain readers? You're not a gossip columnist, you're a sportswriter."

She laughed at him. "I guess I'm a little of both." She walked back to the sofa and plunked herself down, put her booted feet up on the coffee table next to his. A copy of **Sports Illustrated** slid onto the floor. She said, "I was wondering if I should even be going in that direction, but, Davis, I had that photo. What was I supposed to do? Ignore it? My boss would have kicked me out of his office window if I had." She leaned forward and rubbed a smudge of dirt off her boot. "Right now in the off-season, all the readers want to hear about is Tebow and his girlfriend."

"Everyone is wondering if they've had sex."

"That, too, but I won't touch that unless Bennett John shoves me to the edge of the abyss."

Davis leaned over and kissed her. She looked at him from less than an inch away, not moving, not speaking. "Well," he said, "that wasn't half bad until I saw you looking like a deer in the headlights."

She laughed, grabbed his face between her hands, and kissed him hard. She jumped to her feet. "Enough of that, even though it felt pretty good—well, close to great, maybe. No, no, don't you move, I'm going to bed."

His eyes lit up like a beacon.

"You're such a guy. I'll get your blankets."

He said from behind her, "Is it that idiot Day Abbott?"

That stopped her in her tracks. "Day is not an idiot. He's sweet, like a brother to me." He saw the lie perching on the end of her nose.

"Nah, a brother wouldn't want to put my lights out for talking with you. You went out to a fancy restaurant, you were wearing a sexy dress and stilts. You don't do that for a brother."

He had a point, but she shook her head. Would he believe it was simply a habit, since you never knew who you'd see at a fancy place like L'Aubergine, and she didn't ever want to look like a dog on Day's arm?

He was looking at her, arms crossed over his chest, waiting. "Oh, all right," and she decided to come clean. "Day asked me to marry him, if you must know, but I turned him down. It was all a major surprise to me, like who wants to marry their brother? Then I felt so guilty because I hadn't realized—no, that isn't quite true. I did know—" She stopped, started rubbing her temples, then, of all things, she grinned at him. "Geez, I get a kiss from you. I don't suppose you want to marry me, too? I'll break a record. I swear I'll post it if it happens, with full details."

He almost said she should start the blog off with him, but instead he gathered his brain and said, "I forgot to tell you. I'm invited for dinner tomorrow at Sherlock and Savich's house. Will you come with me?"

She nodded and left the living room. She soon reappeared with two blankets and a pillow in her arms. "You can have the bathroom in ten minutes, okay?"

"Yeah, sure. Hey, Perry?"

She paused in the doorway, looked back at him.

"About that kiss—"

"I know, you didn't mean it. Like I said,

you're a guy, and like every guy, when you're close to a female of the species, you lose it, then you get it back real fast."

"What's 'it'?"

"Your sense of self-preservation."

He gave her a long look, slowly nodded. "Close enough, but I was talking about Day Abbott kissing you."

"Go to sleep."

She fell asleep listening to a branch of a big oak tree outside her bedroom window bang against the side of her condo in the late night wind.

She was jerked awake by a soft sound from close by. Her eyes flew open and her heart started to pound, but she stayed still and listened. The bedroom door slowly opened, quiet as could be. She was reaching for the Kimber at her bedside when she realized from the dim outline in the doorway that it was Davis. And she realized, too, that she recognized his scent, and wasn't that odd? Sort of musky mixed with the soft fragrance of her lavender soap. She came up on her elbows, whispered, "What is it? What's wrong?"

She saw him put his finger to his lips. He whispered back, "Stay put. No matter what you hear, stay put."

He didn't close the bedroom door, but he was gone in the next instant. She grabbed her Kimber from atop the bedside table, saw it was going on midnight, held the gun under her pillow to kill any sound, and racked the slide. She slipped out of bed and eased into the hall before she stopped to listen. She heard it then— someone at the front door, trying to get in. Then she heard the door slowly open. She readied for the alarm, but there was silence. Why hadn't it blasted out loud enough to wake the neighborhood? She had the best alarm system available, that's what the security guy had told her when he'd installed it. She heard breathing. She pressed her back to the wall, taking baby steps over the cold wooden floor.

Whoever had slithered in was through the front door now, his breathing the only thing she heard. And it wasn't Davis. Odd how she even knew the sound of his breathing. Where was Davis?

35

She eased into the living room, her back still pressed flat against the wall. The quarter-moon shone in the windows, casting the room in a soft gray glow. Now she did hear Davis's low, steady breathing.

She heard Davis say, his voice low and utterly calm, "Don't move or I'll put a bullet right through your ear. It will make a huge mess, but you won't care."

A sharp cry, then Davis called out, "Perry, I know you're there. Hit the lights."

She flipped all the switches and the living room flooded with light, bright and hard. She saw Davis had his arm locked around a young man's neck, his Glock inside his ear.

She looked into the white terrified face of Carlos Acosta.

She said, "That's the best alarm available. How'd you get in?"

The Glock came out of his ear, rested

against his temple.

"Well?" Davis asked.

The young man licked his lips, darted a look from Davis to Perry. He didn't move a muscle. "I had the code. I thought you wouldn't hear me. I didn't know he was here."

Davis patted him down, perp-walked the young man to a chair, and shoved him down. "You've learned a valuable lesson: never be the amateur in a professional's game."

Carlos didn't move. He stared at Perry as she walked toward him, her Kimber at her side. She stopped right in front of him. "It didn't matter that this guy was here. I could have taken you myself, Carlos."

She leaned over him. "Listen, Carlos, we were all worried about you, especially Mr. Sallivar. And your mother and Isabel. We were afraid you were dead." She straightened. "But you're not dead, you were waiting to come after me. Why?"

His eyes flicked to the gun held loosely in her hand, then back to her face. "I was supposed to leave a message, not hurt you. I wouldn't have hurt you, Ms. Black."

Davis said, "Where is the message?"

"In my pocket."

It was Perry who pulled out a folded note from his jacket pocket. A condom fell out with it. She held up the packet, waved it in his face. "I see, the note to me, then what? Rape?"

He looked appalled, shook his head back and forth. "No, no rape, I swear it. I bought it and slipped it into my pocket. Isabel—"

Davis raised his hand. "Enough about safe sex with Isabel for the moment. Perry, read the note."

She laid the Kimber on the coffee table, slowly pulled out a sheet of folded paper, and read:

RUN AWAY, BLACK.
YOU'RE NOT SAFE.

"Isn't that lovely," Davis said. "Who gave you the note and the code to this alarm system?"

"I wrote the note. He told me to. I don't

know who. He called me on my cell, threatened us unless I did as he said. I don't know who it was, I swear."

"Not going to fly," Davis said. He grabbed Carlos's collar and pulled him straight out of the chair and shook him like a dog. "Tell me the truth or I'm going to throw your butt in the FBI dungeon. You won't get out until you're older than your mother. Do you have any idea how many felonies you've committed? You're lucky to be alive walking in here—and all to leave a message? Has it occurred to you that the someone who sent you here wanted to get you shot? Wanted to shut you up forever? And we'd be the ones to do it, not him? No matter who's threatening you, don't you think you'd be wiser to let us protect you?"

Carlos's Adam's apple bobbed.

"I don't know who he is, really," he said again, his voice a whisper.

Perry said, "You said he threatened us. Who's 'us'?"

"If I didn't put this note here, he said he'd kill Isabel."

Perry leaned in close. "You're sure it was a he?"

Carlos nodded. "Yes, it was a man, at least I think it was. Whoever it was had a deep voice, but it was sort of muffled, like he was talking through a wadded-up handkerchief, same as the first time."

"The first time? Start at the beginning," Davis said. "When did you get the first call?"

"He called me on my cell at work, the day before yesterday. That's when he told me to write that message on the men's room wall at the **Post**. I knew it was wrong, but it didn't seem too bad. He knew all about me, about my family, and I'm not a citizen."

Davis said, "Carlos, when he first called you, didn't you wonder how he got your cell number?"

Carlos paused, frowned, then shook his head. "No, but I wondered later. I scrolled through my contacts, but it couldn't have been any of them. And they wouldn't have given out my cell number to a stranger."

Davis continued. "And it was you who

came here last night, wrecked Ms. Black's motorcycle?"

"Yes. I'm sorry, but yes. He called me again that day, told me I had to do that for him, too, or he would see to it Isabel would be buried next to her grandmother in Meadowland Cemetery. He knew everything about us."

All he had to do was a thorough Web search, Davis knew. Carlos had been too scared to realize that. But the threat to the girl he loved, that was potent, enough to terrify a young man into doing anything asked to protect her.

"And yet he called you again, is that right? Sent you here tonight?"

"No, it wasn't me he called. I threw away my cell phone, so I wouldn't hear from him again. Today he called Isabel."

Perry said, "Where have you been?"

His eyes fell to his sneakers. He mumbled something.

"What did you say?"

"In Mr. Sallivar's shed, in their backyard. Isabel brought me food. Then she found out the FBI was looking for me, and I didn't know what to do. We thought about running away, and then the man called Isabel on her own cell phone today, made her bring it to me."

Carlos shook his head back and forth. "I didn't want to take her phone because I knew it was him even though the call was blocked, but I was afraid not to answer."

"Of course you had to answer. I want you to think about this, Carlos. What did he ask you to do, exactly?"

Carlos was quiet for a minute, then he said in a singsong voice, "He told me write that note, those words exactly, and put it in an envelope. He told me to come back here to Ms. Black's house at midnight and gave me the code to the alarm, 25596. He made me write it down. He told me if I was quiet she wouldn't hear me from the bedroom. He told me to leave it against her coffeepot in the kitchen, reset the alarm, and leave.

"I didn't have a choice. I decided to do this last thing, and then to run away, by myself. It wouldn't be right to take Isabel with me. Her father would never forgive me. So I thought I might be seeing her tonight for the last time. I don't mean I planned to have sex with Isabel, but—" He fell silent, and his smooth, lean cheeks stained red.

So that's why the condom. Davis wanted to laugh, but he didn't. He shoved Carlos back into the chair, patted his jacket, and straightened. He called Savich.

"Yeah?"

Davis heard a delighted laugh in the background, a female laugh, Sherlock's laugh. He'd interrupted fun time.

"I have Carlos Acosta here at Perry's," he said. "Turns out Carlos was hiding in Mr. Sallivar's shed, with Mr. Sallivar's daughter Isabel seeing to his creature comforts."

When Davis punched off his cell a minute later, he looked down at the slender young man who did look like Mr. Sallivar, only thirty years younger. He was a soft-spoken, handsome young man, and he looked scared, really scared. As he should be. Davis said, "All right, no jail time for you yet, Carlos. But you and Isabel are both going to be in protective custody for a couple of days. We'll be going over your stories very, very carefully." He hauled Carlos to his feet.

Perry held out her hand. "Give me the condom."

Carlos gave her a long look, then looked toward Davis.

She smacked his shoulder. "No, you idiot, it's not for my use, it's to keep your paws off Isabel. That is, if you have any honor left."

"I do, I swear I do. Please, we have to hurry. When he finds out I failed, he might kill Isabel."

When he finds out you didn't get yourself killed and got caught instead, that ought to give him serious pause. Davis said, "He won't get near Isabel. I'll take care of that. Come along, Carlos."

He turned at the front door. "Keep a light on for me, Black." His eyes flicked to her Kimber still on the coffee table. "Keep the gun close and reset your alarm."

36

Washington, D.C.
Early Friday morning

Blessed was nearly out of cash again. Before the accident—that was how he liked to think of it—getting cash was never a problem. He could walk into a bank— never in his hometown, Father had said that wasn't smart—fasten his eyes on the teller, and very politely tell him or her to hand over whatever amount he wanted. He was never greedy, something Father had always preached. Of course, the teller would be short that night, and what a brouhaha that would cause, but it wasn't Blessed's problem.

He wasn't like every other pathetic human being that walked the earth, the common herd who had to work or steal what they needed. He never had been like them, and he wouldn't accept it now.

He'd had to use his knife twice to get money, and already he'd hated knowing what he'd become. At least now he had Agent Sherlock's gun. He spotted a twenty-four/seven on a side street without much traffic. He waited for one customer to close the door behind him, leaving only Blessed and an older woman behind the counter. He fingered the agent's Glock in his pocket. He knew the old biddy was eyeing him suspiciously, maybe getting scared. **Do it, do it.** And so Blessed looked her right in her dark, rheumy eyes and said quietly, "Open the register and give me all your cash."

He hadn't realized he'd be afraid, afraid she might scream and pull out a gun. He wasn't afraid she would shoot him, only afraid he'd fail. He nearly puked as he waited, his heart pounding, his eyes never leaving her face. But she smiled at him and opened the old-fashioned cash register. "No o-ones or f-f-fives," he said, stuttering with relief. He watched her pull out all the tens and twenties. Then she lifted the cash drawer and pulled out a neat pile of fifties and a couple hundred-dollar bills.

"Please put all the money in a bag."

She did, handed it to him.

"Thank you," Blessed said, and turned to leave.

"What's going on here?"

It was an old man, probably the woman's husband, and he was pointing a shotgun at Blessed. "You, jerkface, put my money back on the counter! Now, or I'll blow your head off!" The old buzzard lifted the rifle, aimed it at Blessed's head.

Blessed was ten feet away from the old man. **Too far, too far.** He laid the bag of money on the counter. The old man hollered, "What's wrong with you, Meg? Woman, get yourself together and call the cops!"

But the old woman only stood there, a small smile on her mouth. "What's wrong with you?" He turned back to Blessed, stepped toward him, his gun up. "What did you do to her?"

Blessed looked into his faded old eyes and said, "Please shoot Meg. In the head,

I think."

The old man said, "What? What did you say?" Then he blinked, turned the shotgun, and shot his wife's face off.

Blessed jumped back so he wouldn't get splattered by the mess the shotgun made. Pieces of flesh and brain matter splattered against the shelf of cigarettes behind the counter, and blood fountained in all directions. He couldn't see her now, and was grateful she'd fallen, not making a sound.

He didn't want to puke now. He wanted to shout with the pleasure and relief he felt. He'd done it; with just one look, one command, he'd made the old guy shoot her—**blam!** He was back. Blessed walked to the counter, took the bag of money, careful not to look down at the woman, and added over his shoulder as he walked out toward the door, "Now shoot yourself in the chest."

Through the glass, he saw a middle-aged couple coming toward the store, arguing about something. He walked out of the store, walked right up to the couple.

Even as the shotgun blasted out again, he said calmly, "Hi. You didn't see me."

He nodded to the couple and went on his way, whistling. He never missed a step when he heard the screams, the shouts. He was half a block away when he heard the first siren.

Blessed got into his stolen Toyota and drove to Georgetown, parking two blocks away from the Savich house, to be on the safe side. He saw Savich and Sherlock climb into the hot red Porsche and pull out of the driveway. A little boy stood beside a woman in the open doorway, waving at them.

He looked at the little boy, and wondered.

37

**Criminal Apprehension Unit
Friday morning**

Sherlock was working with Dane Carver on four bizarre strangulation murders in Omaha, Nebraska, when Savich stuck his head out of the office and called to her.

She knew immediately something was very wrong. She was inside his office in a flash. "What happened?"

Savich drew in a deep breath. "It's all right. That was Gabriella. I'd showed her Blessed's photo, told her to be on the lookout. Before she took Sean to school, she checked out the front window and saw an older man slip from behind a tree and move behind another. She recognized Blessed. She locked the doors and called the cops, without Sean ever knowing anything was wrong. Then she managed to sneak in a call to me. I kept her on the line until I heard the knock on the door and knew the police had arrived. Gabriella put an Officer Blevins on the line, and I told him about Blessed. They're out looking for him right now."

He drew a deep breath. "I told Gabriella to take Sean to school with a police escort. She's going to pick him up later, after she's packed for both of them. Then she'll drive him to his grandmother's house. I'm going to call Mom, tell her Gabriella and Sean will be there this afternoon."

Sherlock was as pale as her white shirt. He pulled her against him. He said against her temple, "Sean's okay. Blessed won't get anywhere near him. Blessed has no clue where Sean's school is, and he doesn't have the skills to find out. I asked Gabriella to have the principal keep an eye on him. Everything's handled. It's all done." He held her, slowly rubbed her back.

She said against his neck, "I'm going to kill him myself, Dillon, and do a happy dance on his grave. And then I'm going to smack you. Why didn't you tell me about Gabriella's first call?"

He told her the truth. "I didn't want both of us scared at the same time." He kissed her temple. "I hope it won't come down to your murdering Blessed. Oh, yes, I got a call from Ethan. He, pregnant Joanna, and Autumn are spring skiing in Colorado. If Blessed does head to Titusville with thoughts of nabbing Autumn, he's out of luck. He's out of luck here, too, Sherlock."

She said again, "But if he gets to Sean—"

"He won't. You know he won't."

She leaned back, aware every agent in the unit was staring at them. She gave Dillon a pat on the shoulder and a smile, and stepped back. "You know what I think? We're going about this the wrong way. I think it's time we hunted him down, don't you?"

38

**Natalie Black's house
Friday morning**

Natalie said, "Never would I have imagined Carlos Acosta breaking into Perry's condo last night."

Davis said, "He was so scared I was afraid he was going to throw up on Perry's very nice Persian carpet. In any case, now he's out at the Jefferson Dormitory at Quantico. Savich wants to keep him close and safe, see if there's something his subconscious picked up about the phone calls Carlos didn't recall right away. They'll be talking with Isabel this morning, too."

"That note he was going to deliver, it scares me, Davis. Perry's a part of this, now more than ever. And I don't understand why. **Run away, Black— You're not safe**. Why are these people after Perry? Does she know anything about this she hasn't told me? Are they pressuring me to resign by threatening her?"

Davis said, "We'll find out why, Natalie. Perry's got a shadow on her, so no one's going to get close. She'll keep sharp." Even though she hadn't gotten much sleep the night before; he knew fear had a way of goosing the brain. "I called her right before I knocked on your door. She's fine, at the **Post**, and she's working. She says she has a story to write."

Natalie gave him a dutiful grin, sighed. "I feel sorry for Carlos, and for Isabel."

"He's lucky to be alive," Davis said. "Whoever put him up to this was shrewd—it was undoubtedly an untrace-able phone. We're left with very little to go on. He knew her alarm code, which means the person who gave it to him had access to it. And that makes me think this is all closer to home than it seems. Tell me, Natalie, is your half-brother, Milton, still in Washington?"

"Yes, he's still at The Willard. He claims it's the only civilized hotel in Washington."

"I think it's time to go see him."

Davis rose. "I've already spoken to Mr. Sallivar, told him they'd be picking up Isabel to question her. I had to tell him why. Mr. Sallivar is going to see to it she spends the next few days with a relative, out of town, instead of protective custody. He was grateful. Then he asked me point blank where Carlos had been hiding, and so I told him. Isabel is in for a major scolding." He added without thinking, "I didn't tell him about the condom."

"Condom? What condom?"

"Yeah, well, no worries, Perry took it."

That got him a smack on the shoulder. Davis was explaining when his cell belted out Social Distortion's "Ball and Chain."

Davis watched her pace up and down the breakfast room, her strides as long as her daughter's. He listened, asked the occasional question. And soon he was smiling. **Finally,** she thought, something good must have happened.

Davis punched off his cell.

"Well? What was that all about?" She planted herself in front of him, hands on her hips.

"Hamish Penderley called the CAU— remember, he's the head of the Operational Command Unit at Scotland Yard."

Natalie looked ready to leap at him, pull the words right out of his mouth.

"Penderley said they've matched the paint chips to your Jaguar, Natalie, so we have confirmation they've found the car that tried to run you off the road near Canterbury."

He thought she would start dancing. "That's great. Who was the driver?"

"They've got the owner in custody, a man by the name of Graham Suddsby. He's a retired chauffeur who spends most of his time in his local pub now; that's where they found him. He claims someone must have sideswiped the car when it was parked on the street, that he found it that way. A lie, of course. Now it's a matter of the Brits convincing him he's better off telling the truth."

"Now that they've got him, Mrs. Black," Hooley said from the doorway, "it won't be long before they know everything. The coppers in England, they're tough and hard, no nonsense, if they want to get something out of you."

Connie said from behind him, "How do you know that?"

"I was married to one of them a while back," Hooley said matter-of-factly, "and she damned near killed me."

Davis stared after Hooley as he walked toward the front of the house to keep watch, whistling. He looked back at Connie, realized she was smiling after him. Really, Connie and Hooley?

"Davis, since you're going to be talking with my brother, Milt, I should tell you something. He was here to see me this morning."

39

**The Willard
Washington, D.C.
Friday, noon**

Perry stepped onto the empty elevator ahead of Davis and pushed the button. "Come on, stop sulking, Davis, I know it was hard for you to call me and admit you need me for anything, but it was the smart thing to do. And you're right, Uncle Milton will be more open to talking since I'm with you. By yourself, you'd scare him to death."

"Uncle Milt scared of me? I doubt it, since he knows me. I met him at the party Tuesday night."

"Yes, he knows you as my mother's hot boy toy. It will be a shock for him to meet you as the big FBI agent here to question him."

An eyebrow went up. "I look hot?"

She rolled her eyes. "Come on, Davis, it's time to get serious." She added with a good deal of satisfaction, "Now that they've found the car that tried to run Mom off the road in England, it shouldn't be long before all the malicious rumors die down. I mean, if they find out why, I can see this making the front page."

Davis said, "So far the only thing they can prove is that someone fled the scene of an automobile accident, and that's never been disputed. I don't know the English press, but in the U.S., the wheels leading toward corrections in print turn very slowly, if they ever turn at all. No one's ever been in a hurry to dismiss a juicy scandal with something as inconvenient as the truth."

Perry hated it, but he was right. She stepped up, knocked on the suite door.

Inside, Barnaby Eagan stood by the window, rubbing his temples. He had a headache. He didn't want to answer the knock to Mr. Holmes's suite. What he wanted was quiet, a shot of single malt, and his bed for an hour, but it wasn't to be. He looked out to see a big man in a leather jacket who wasn't smiling, and, of all things, Perry Black, Mr. Holmes's niece, standing beside him. He still couldn't get over her writing about professional football, a weird thing for a woman to do, he'd always thought, but the senator's parents raved about her. As for the senator, he'd mumble under his breath, things like the damned girl was unnatural, but what did you expect, given who her father was? He opened the door. "Ms. Black? What are you doing here? And who is this?"

"Hi, Barnaby," Perry said. "We're here to see my uncle."

"Well, he's resting now, and I think it would be better if—"

Davis held up his FBI creds.

"Oh." He glanced at Perry. "Why are you here with the FBI, Perry?"

"I'm helping him." She gave him a fat smile, then introduced the two men, adding, "Barnaby's been with Uncle Milt for nearly five years now, isn't that right, Barnaby?"

"Two months short of five years," Barnaby said, "but who's counting?" Davis heard a slight lisp that sounded charming.

"Please ask him to come out, Mr. Eagan," Davis said. "I need to speak to him."

Barnaby sighed. "He's very upset, Perry."

"Well, so are we all, and that's why Agent Sullivan is here."

Barnaby opened his mouth, then closed it, and Perry realized it wasn't his sister Uncle Milt was upset about. She searched Barnaby's ascetic face for a clue, didn't see any. On the other hand, Barnaby rarely gave anything away.

"Please fetch him, Mr. Eagan," Davis said again.

Davis and Perry were left to admire the lovely Lincoln Suite living room, all blue and gold, with beautiful striped wallpaper on one wall, and blue draperies open to the courtyard below. Davis wondered how much Milton dropped per night on this awesome place to lay his head.

"Perry."

They turned to see Uncle Milton standing in the doorway, looking like a proper Boston Brahmin. His brilliant red hair with threads of white was elegantly styled. He was wearing sharp black trousers, a crisp white shirt, and black leather loafers on his long, narrow feet. He didn't look at all like he'd been having a nice lie-down. He looked, Davis thought, like he'd made up his mind about something, like a man to lead a mission. Or was this all a part of his professional politician's bag of tricks?

"Uncle Milton. This is Davis Sullivan. He's—"

Uncle Milt nodded to the man at his side. "Barnaby said he was an FBI agent, but this is the man who was hanging all over your mother at Arliss's party Tuesday night, dancing with her like they were lovers. I thought they were outrageous—"

"Actually, sir, I was protecting Ambassador Black."

That gave Milton pause, but for only a moment. He shrugged. "I see. Surprising the FBI would condone such behavior, but be that as it may—and I'm sorry to say this, Perry—it would have been more dignified of Natalie to identify him as such at the party rather than give everyone the impression he was something else entirely. But then Natalie loves to take center court."

Davis said, "So you don't believe your sister's life is in danger, Mr. Holmes?"

"I don't think she's lying precisely about what happened to her in England, no, but I think she might well be exaggerating it. She was very upset about George McCallum's suicide, of course, and she was being blamed for it. It's likely she misinterpreted the accident as an attempt on her life, don't you think? I'm not surprised the press didn't believe her. At any rate, this has all been very upsetting. To Natalie, to me, to my parents—" By the end of this extraordinary monologue, his Boston accent was flying high.

Perry interrupted him, her voice sharp, "Of course you're right, Uncle Milton, my grandparents are very upset because they're afraid for my mother. They believe her, Uncle Milton. What I don't understand is why you don't."

Milton ignored this, waved a vague hand around him. "Arliss called me this morning, asked me to convince your mother to resign her post. That is hardly a surprise. Hard as this is for all of us, I do have my own future to think of." As if realizing how self-serving that sounded, he cleared his throat, backed up, tried for a deprecating smile. "Look, I'm up for reelection, and this sort of scandal—well, it could bury me. It's best that Natalie resign, Perry, as soon as possible, best for all of us who have supported her. It will give the voters time to forget about all that happened in England before the fall elections."

Perry said, "So she should move to Florida, wear sunglasses so the tourists don't recognize her? Maybe paint caricatures on the beach, or take up windsurfing?"

There was no humor in Milton Holmes's eyes as he looked at her. Perry's sarcasm floated unappreciated and unanswered in the room. She'd brought Milton to a dead stop. So this, Davis thought, was what it was like for a politician to have his guns spiked.

He said, "Since you mentioned your future in politics, sir, you should know that Scotland Yard has identified the car used to attack Ambassador Black in England. They have the owner in custody. Your voters may soon be seeing your sister as a victim when that crime is solved. So it may be advantageous to you to make a show of acting as the loyal brother supporting his sister through all her travails, always brave and stalwart, always at her back, rather than being seen as the jealous half-brother throwing his half-sister under the bus to protect his own hide."

Milton couldn't seem to take this in. He looked over at Barnaby, who was blinking rapidly, his eyes going from Davis back to his boss. Davis saw the instant Uncle Milt was ready to put him in his place. He drew himself up, pretty impressive, really. "Who cares what the police are doing in

England? About what they're saying, about what they're now claiming? We're here, and this mess is here since Natalie brought it all back with her."

"I thought the issue was whether she was making it up," Davis said.

Barnaby cleared his throat. His head was pounding now. All he wanted was these people gone and a nice dark corner for himself, but that wasn't going to happen. His primary duty was to protect the senator, and so he did. "Agent Sullivan, Senator Holmes never said that precisely. He's upset, as we all are, and now you're telling us that what happened in England, it's all true? There's no doubt?"

Davis saw this interview shortly flying off the rails. He said quickly, "Let's sit down and talk this out, shall we, Mr. Holmes?"

"It's Senator Holmes," Barnaby said. He exchanged glances with his employer and said, "Please, come and sit here." He pointed to a blue-and-gold sofa. "Would either of you like coffee?"

Davis shook his head. Uncle Milton sat

in one of the lovely Federal-style chairs, crossed one leg over the other, and assumed the ultimate defensive position—arms crossed over his chest. He was trying to regain control, but Davis saw the wariness in him, and what was this? Perhaps fear? He hoped so. Now it was time to focus that fear. Davis said, "Concerning your reasons for being in Washington since Monday, Senator Holmes. Our office has looked into your finances, the entire family's finances, as a matter of fact, including all your expenses here in Washington." He paused to let that fact sink in. "We know you are carrying quite a bit of personal debt. I understand your campaign is in need of money as well, and that you've asked your sister for a sizable contribution to your campaign."

Davis saw the outrage on Holmes's face at having his finances laid bare. But he managed to control himself. He said, his voice credibly calm, "Politicians ask many divergent people for money, Agent Sullivan. It is a fact of our political lives." He shrugged, tried for another depreciating smile.

"Unfortunately, my sister doesn't like my politics, so I had little reason to think she would give me any money."

"Perhaps she would because you're her brother?"

"No, that has never moved her; nothing moves Natalie when she's made up her mind."

Perry sat forward. "If you're not here to beg money off Mom, Uncle Milton, then why are you here in Washington right now?"

40

Her uncle didn't meet her eyes. He studied his fine Italian loafers, frowned. Barnaby said smoothly, "The senator is in Washington because he was invited here by very powerful people who would like him to run for the United States Senate. He has appointments"—he looked at his watch in a beautifully studied motion— "very soon now, so the senator cannot give you much more of his time."

Perry, no expression on her face, said, "Would these people you're meeting with still want you to run for the U.S. Senate if you lost the race for your state senate seat in Massachusetts?"

Milton cleared his throat, said, calm as a statesman, "It would certainly be beneficial were I to run for the U.S. Senate from a position of power."

Davis had had enough of the slither and slink. It was time to confront him head-on.

He said, "Senator Holmes, don't you think we should tell Perry what we both know?"

It was as if an electrical charge passed through Milton. He snapped up straight, threw his head back. "You know nothing I care to hear, Agent Sullivan. There is nothing I have to say to Perry. I want both of you to leave now. I have people to see."

"I will show you out," Barnaby said, and started toward the door.

But Davis didn't move, and neither did Perry. He didn't look away from Milton's face. "Actually, there is a lot more to your uncle Milton being here in Washington, Perry. He hopes to promise the party power brokers he will have all the money he needs in his campaign coffers, that he won't need their financial support if they back him as a candidate in two years. You see, your uncle Milton had a plan." He waited for a moment, but Milton didn't say a word.

Davis continued, "Natalie told me he came to see her at the house. He told your mother he would continue to back her publically, give her all the support he could, if she financed his campaign or convinced your grandparents to do it. What was wrong with their helping each other, after all? Otherwise, he told her, he would be more blunt, shall we say, with the press, separate himself from her troubles, cut the parachute lines. His reasoning being that if her own family expressed doubts about her mental health, her truthfulness, where would that leave her?"

Milton's face was alarmingly red. Davis hoped he wouldn't stroke out. He said, "We talked, sir, Natalie and I."

Milton roared to his feet. "So Natalie told you! I knew I couldn't trust her word, even though she promised me she wouldn't say anything to anyone. She's always been a liar and a cheat."

Davis smiled at him and slouched against the sofa cushions, a ploy meant to enrage. "What she promised you was not to tell your parents, Senator Holmes. That would be too humiliating for all of you.

"Your mother told me, Perry, that once

he'd ended his spiel, she laughed at him, told him to do his worst. She said it was sad, really, that it would end his own career if he tried to disgrace his own sister. She wasn't sure if he believed her."

Perry stared back and forth from Davis to her uncle. She simply couldn't get her head around his betrayal. She'd always thought of Uncle Milton as pleasant, a bit ineffectual, maybe, rather pompous, and always in the shadow of his sister, and no wonder. Natalie Black's charm and intelligence shined like a beacon compared to her brother's occasional flicker. She didn't want to accept his treachery. It was almost too much to take in.

She noticed Barnaby from the corner of her eyes. He appeared nailed to the floor, his eyes on her uncle's face, and she saw the same leveling betrayal in his eyes she knew must be in her own. She said into the cold, deafening silence. "So what you said about Mom to us, you were following your script, to see how we'd react?"

Uncle Milton stayed silent.

"No, I wouldn't say anything, either,

Uncle Milton." Perry slowly rose, stared down at him. She heard Barnaby clear his throat behind her, but she didn't turn. "Don't you say anything, either, Barnaby." She said to her uncle, her voice cold, utterly damning, "You are a pathetic worm, aren't you? I disown you." She paused for a moment, then added, "Did you try to run my mother down in Buckner Park? Is it you who have been threatening me?"

His face was ashen. He stretched a shaking hand out to Perry. "What? What did you say? No, of course not. Because my campaign needs money, you suspect me of trying to kill my own sister, and of threatening you, my niece? The situation is not what you think, Perry, really, it isn't. Listen to me, you must understand. You know you can't get elected in this country without lots of money. Of course I need money to run a successful campaign, and you know your grandparents have so much money, more than they can spend. But they refused me, their only son! How many men could get themselves elected to the General Court in Massachusetts as I have? But it wasn't enough for them." He paused, panting now, red in the face.

Milton looked straight at Perry. "Your grandmother told me if I had half your mother's talent, your mother's brains, I could manage to back my own campaign, not mooch off them and their friends." He was still panting, his mouth working, and the words hurled themselves out: "Father told me he thought the whole idea of my running for the Senate was planted by my wife." He paused, tried to get control, drew in several deep breaths.

He'd memorized what his parents had said to him, Davis realized, memorized it word for word.

Amazingly, Milton's years of training kicked in and his voice sounded more reasoned. "But I would never hurt your mother, or you, Perry. I admire Natalie, always have. It's your grandparents' fault this happened."

Perry was drowning in his excuses, in his bitterness and rage at everyone she loved, in his inability to take responsibility for what he'd done. Her stomach roiled and twisted. She swallowed bile. Barnaby moved toward her, and she saw his face was leached of color, pale as death. Like hers? She asked her uncle again, "Did you try to kill my mother in Buckner Park? Run her down?"

"Of course not! Why would I? I don't even drive in this benighted city!"

Barnaby cleared his throat, but his voice shook. "He doesn't, Ms. Black, really."

She said, her eyes on her uncle again, a man whose blood she shared, "Uncle Milton, I hope Mother tells my grandparents what you did. I hope they disown you, too." And Perry marched out the door.

Davis didn't say another word, simply followed her out of the Lincoln Suite, down the long hallway to the elevator. There were two couples on the elevator, so they stayed silent. When they reached the lobby, Perry grabbed his sleeve. "You didn't tell me."

"No."

She punched his arm. "Why not? You

should have given me some warning about what he'd done so I wouldn't be blindsided—"

Davis was aware of people looking toward them, so he kept moving. She was right on his heels through the hotel doors and out into the crisp air. Davis breathed it in, smelled the faint exhaust fumes that brushed the air. "I love this city."

She grabbed his hand, shook it. "You'd better talk to me, Sullivan, give me a sink-proof explanation, or I'm going to pulverize you."

He turned to face her. A thick hank of her hair had come loose from the fishtail braid and lay against her nose. Her eyes were dark with pain. He lightly laid his hand on her shoulder. "If I'd told you, you'd have gone after him the second you saw him. Come on, you know I'm right, you'd never have held it together. And having you with Uncle Milt when I told him was the best shot we had at getting to the truth, if there was a deeper truth and your uncle is involved. But he's not. Let it go, Perry, let it go."

She stared over his shoulder. "I want to kill him," she said slowly.

"Then I'd have to arrest you."

"He's a dishonorable toad, and I should throw him into the Potomac with a cement block tied to his Italian loafers. Hey, I could write my freaking blog from jail, no problem."

"Still, he didn't try to run down your mom or threaten you, Perry. He's all about politics, and he's neither better nor worse than most of those yahoos in Congress. If you wanted to mete out punishment, you'd run out of cement blocks. All there is to do now is walk away."

He was right. She wanted to howl, to scream, but she didn't. "If you think I forgive you, I don't," she said. "I'm heading back to the **Post** by myself." She hiked up her computer bag on her shoulder and streaked across the street to the sound of honking horns and a few curses. She yelled over her shoulder, "And I'm going to buy up all the cement in the city."

Davis didn't move. He watched her until she reached the other side unscathed, got into a taxi that had pulled up, and took off. He was worried, since he didn't know her well enough to guess how she'd deal with all that rage.

He was glad he hadn't told Perry her uncle Milton's money problems included a lady he paid each month and visited whenever he was in the capital.

41

**Savich home
Friday night**

Blessed Backman wasn't cold, since he'd bought wool-lined gloves as well as a thick fisherman's sweater at Goodwill to go under the bum's coat, but he was stiff again in his crouched position, so he stood and stretched. He took several steps toward the house, hugging trees and bushes, watchful for neighbors. Last thing he needed was for the cops to show up again.

Good thing he'd noticed the Hispanic lady watching him from the house that morning and he'd gotten out of there. It was dangerous to come back, even after dark. There would be cops around; he knew they were looking for him everywhere, and with his photo on TV, he had to be careful. But he couldn't wait them out any longer. He had to act; he had to get it done so his mother would rest in peace. Was the guardian in his dreams really his mother, that disembodied voice so soft and pure, telling him he would succeed? It gladdened his heart to think so.

The two of them, Savich and Sherlock, were always together now, and he knew he'd have to take them on together, but he'd wait until they were unarmed, maybe when they were in bed, all comfortable and cozy. He'd have to shoot Savich dead right away, and then Sherlock would be easy. He could have her shoot herself in the mouth, or blow off her own head, but he'd always wanted to strangle her, to see the life fade out of her eyes just as his mother's eyes had faded to blankness the last day he'd seen her in that god-awful hospital.

He had to step back into the bushes when he saw two cars arriving, one pulling in Savich's driveway, the other against the curb. He watched as three people went inside. He had no idea who they were, not that it mattered. Whoever they were, they were messing up his plans.

After some time, he made his way to the living room window and peered in. No one was in there, but he heard faint voices and laughter coming from another room. He moved along the house until he was looking into the dining room. He saw Savich, smiling and nodding, full of himself, chatting to a woman and the two men at the table. He couldn't make out what they were saying, but he saw spaghetti, corn on the cob, garlic bread, and a big salad bowl on the table. He could swear he smelled the garlic. His stomach growled. He hadn't realized how hungry he was.

Both of the men looked young and hard, like Savich, all sharp-eyed and confident, ready to take on the world. Probably FBI agents. One of them wore a black turtleneck sweater beneath a really sharp black jacket, the other a white shirt with the sleeves rolled up to his elbows. The young woman with them seemed buff enough to be an agent, too, he couldn't tell. Weren't they all having fun?

Agent Sherlock presided at the far end of the table, her thick red hair shining at him under the chandelier. She looked pleased and relaxed, a forkful of spaghetti in her hand, nodding at something one of the men said. She looked magnificent, he thought. She would look that way until he closed his hands around her skinny little neck and squeezed the life out of her.

Blessed straightened. It looked to him like those people would be here for a long time. Should he take the risk and stay until they left, hoping no one would see him?

His stomach growled again. He had to eat, then he'd decide whether or not to come back.

42

Natalie Black's house
Friday night

Natalie usually liked it black as pitch when she went to sleep, but not tonight. She felt too antsy, too on edge. There was something she had to figure out, something unpleasant and real just beyond her reach, but for the life of her, she couldn't grasp it. Everything that had happened, both in England and here at home, was flying about in her head like scattered bits of paper in a high wind.

She had to focus. Why was the president still defending her? She grinned—Thorn, the **president**—she clearly remembered him at twenty years old, smooth and cocky even then, always ready to break a rule, but so very smart. He'd always been there, Brundage's best friend from freshman year, then hers, too, and there had been more, on his part, but it had never been spoken of until Arliss had come out and asked her about it. The four of them had mixed together so well, settled into friendships that became deep and abiding, that had lasted.

But now Brundage was dead. Thornton was the freaking president of the United States, with the ultimate authority over her future. How much longer could he resist his advisers, all the party bigwigs, all the pressure from the public who wished her gone? And then what? Disgrace, yes, but would it end with that? If someone wanted more than to disgrace her, if they wanted her dead, what could stop them? Perhaps she could stay alive for a while, but how long could she keep bodyguards around her? Forever?

Every politician, every public figure in the world, no matter how well protected, could be killed. **There is always a way. Always.** She could see herself ending up paranoid, suspicious of all her acquaintances, all her friends.

And now they'd put Perry in the mix.

Why? How did that make any sense?

She had met so many and diverse people in the foreign service, made so many important decisions that had affected her and Perry, at least before Perry had gone to college and become independent. Would one of the decisions she'd made result in her murder? And Perry, there was always Perry, and the fear for her daughter ground deep.

Had it all begun with George McCallum? In any case, that's when it had come out in the open. Dear George, a fine man, honorable, innocent of any wrongdoing. She hadn't loved him like Brundage, not to the depths of her. She was sure there would be only one such love in her lifetime. But she had cared deeply for him. He'd given her pleasure and companionship and respect, and they both knew they would rub along very nicely together. And then he'd been, what? Sacrificed? Or was he the target? But then why blame her, why all the malicious rumors? Why come after her here, at home? Bits of paper— swirling about, never coming together.

She turned onto her side, staring in the darkness toward her window. She was making herself crazy. She had to sleep, had to have a clear head, because soon now, tomorrow, she would have to make a decision that would change the course of her life.

What would you say, Brundage? Would you tell me to resign? Would that help protect Perry? Natalie felt a shift in the cool, still air in her bedroom, a puff of a fresher and colder air. From the window. She stared toward the curtained windows though it was so dark she could barely make them out. Were they moving? She started to reach for the cell phone on top of her night table. The autodial was set to ring in Connie's and Hooley's rooms, her new-age panic button. No, not yet. If she pressed the button, both of them could come running in, and if there was someone outside her window about to come in, he'd very likely escape. Besides, she was far from helpless. She picked up her pistol and waited, breathing lightly as if she were asleep.

43

**Perry Black's condo
Friday night**

It was nearly midnight. Perry sat on the sofa, leaning over her laptop on the coffee table, a bottle of water at her right elbow. Davis sat opposite her in a wing chair directly in front of the fireplace, wishing a bit of heat would come his way. He got up, added more firewood, and sat down again. He looked over at Perry, who was drumming her fingers as she read over what she'd written on her blog. Every once in a while, she looked over at him, then down again, quickly. How much longer could she pretend she wasn't finished? She couldn't ignore him for the rest of the night, could she?

Davis watched her. She'd changed into a blue Patriots sweatshirt, a dangerous move in Washington, D.C. He wondered if she ever dared wear it to FedExField on Sundays.

Her jeans were on the baggy side and looked a decade old. She was wearing only thick white socks, her boots beside her on the floor. He realized he liked watching her, liked seeing that same hank of hair fall out of the braid and onto her cheek. Energy seemed to thrum all around her, even now, near midnight, even when he knew she'd finished the blog. A live wire, his mom would call her. Come to think of it, that was what his mom called him. Her iPod was playing "Waiting Room" by Fugazi, turned way down, and that was just plain wrong. "Waiting Room" should be on full blast while, say, a guy was painting a wall, or shooting hoops, or washing his Jeep. It was versatile music, not only for messing around but also when he was working his butt off. Play it nice and loud and it always kept his brain jiggering.

Yep, he loved punk rock, appreciated women who loved it, too. He was smart enough to know the woman bending over her laptop, shoving that hank of hair behind her ear again with an unconscious hand, could become important to him, and not only because she liked his music. He found her immensely satisfying. She'd close her eyes for a moment every now and then, frown, speak to herself as if testing out a phrase, then type quickly again. Perry Black, football maven. Who'd have thought? He remembered her straddling her Harley, pulling her black visor down, roaring off as he stood in his driveway, watching her. That had been only three days ago. Amazing.

Davis sighed, sat back and closed his eyes. Good dinner at Savich's house, nothing accomplished, really, but everyone got a little well-deserved R&R, and he'd told his story about getting smacked in the head with Mrs. Shaw's spade in Hogan's Alley. He'd found out that the Brit, Nicholas Drummond, would be assigned to the New York Field Office when he graduated from the Academy. He wondered if they would ever work together. Maybe, maybe not. Davis liked the man. In fact, he had to admit he recognized bits and pieces of himself. But he also sensed a darker history beneath Drummond's very smooth surface, something complicated, unspoken, held close.

He wondered what it was, then gave it up. He was here in Perry Black's living room, watching her go over her work, ignoring him. He could outwait her, easy. He let his brain slow and mellow as he listened to "Waiting Room."

"I'll give you blankets and a pillow and you can sack out. I can finish off the blog in the bedroom."

Her voice sounded only a bit on the snarky side. He didn't open his eyes, merely said, "You've already finished. What did you write about?"

She gave him a brooding look, then shrugged. "I wrote about the quarterbacks who run whenever they see a lane or even the whisper of a lane, like RG3 and Michael Vick, and how sad it is they're always only one hit away from ending their careers. Running is part of who they are, and you can practically feel their sheer joy when they can take off, like a greyhound out of the chute. They're exciting to watch and they're immensely talented, but they're always getting pounded and smashed into the ground. Nobody can take that kind of punishment for long. Sooner or later they go down.

"Of course, every player is one hit away, but you take quarterbacks like Russell Wilson and Colin Kaepernick. They're as fast as cornerbacks, too, but since they pick their spots more carefully, slide when they can, they're likely to last longer.

"Peyton and Eli Manning and Drew Brees—they're the ultimate passing quarterbacks. They wouldn't move out of the pocket unless threatened with dynamite or three hundred and fifty pounds of mean."

"All good points. Now I'd like to talk about something else."

"No," she said, and kept her eyes glued to her computer screen. "If you want to talk about what happened today, about Uncle Milton in particular, I'm liable to belt you. Be quiet, I'm still working."

He smiled, still didn't open his eyes. "We FBI special agents know when to keep things close to the vest. Advice? I'll say it again about your uncle—get over it, Black."

"Shut up."

"At least now you know what Uncle Senator Milton is all about. I know your mom doesn't think he's behind this, and I don't, either, not really, but I'll know for sure tomorrow."

That got her attention. She looked at him. "Oh? And how may I ask will you know tomorrow? You're going to hold a séance?"

Davis pulled a recorder out of his pocket. "I'm going to play our conversation today with Uncle Milt for Carlos Acosta, see if he can identify him as the man who called him."

Something else he hadn't told her. She'd forgotten about Carlos, forgotten he might recognize the voice. Well, that's why she wrote about football and he was a cop. "Is he still at Quantico?"

"Yeah, in the Jefferson Dormitory. I'll be

visiting him tomorrow. Savich is keeping him there, along with Isabel's cell phone. If he gets another call on that cell, we may get a chance to trace it in real time. Isabel is still off visiting her aunt in Florida for a week."

Perry sighed. "I was hoping for more than that by now. This not knowing who — it's hard."

"It's only been three days since the big guns have come in on it."

She snorted and continued to type. "Big gun — is that really how you see yourself?"

He still didn't open his eyes. "I mean the Bureau. What would you call me?"

"Me? I'm still not speaking to you."

44

**Natalie Black's house
Friday night**

Natalie's heart started to pound. Would the man outside her window hear it? It didn't matter. She held the gun pointed at the window, her eyes focused on the curtains. It wasn't fear that surged through her, it was rage. **Come on in, you bastard, come to Mama.**

The alarm blasted out, piercing, sharp, the pitch of police sirens in Europe, loud enough to shake her nearest neighbors out of a dead sleep.

Natalie jumped out of bed and ran toward the window, threw back the curtains. She saw him climbing down through the branches in the huge oak tree outside her window. She yelled for him to stop and fired once, twice, three times, chipping off bark, but she didn't hit him.

Hooley and Connie burst into her room. Connie jerked her away from the window and pressed her down onto the floor, covering her. Hooley threw the curtains wide. "He's down below!" he shouted, and climbed out after him.

Natalie shoved Connie off. "Come on, Connie, we've got to help. There's no danger now, let me up!"

The two women were at the window, watching Hooley as he climbed down from branch to branch and finally hit the ground. He sprinted after a man running full-out toward the distant front of the property, straight to the high stone fence. Hooley was wearing nothing but running shoes and pajama bottoms, his gun in his hand.

"You stay right here, Natalie." Connie climbed down from branch to branch as Hooley had done, in her dainty pink pajamas with little flowers, her Beretta in her hand.

Natalie had no intention of staying put. She jerked on a pair of sneakers and was in the tree only a few seconds after Connie, carefully navigating the branches until she dropped to the ground. She saw Connie racing after Hooley.

Hooley saw the man some twenty yards ahead grab a rope that hung down over the stone fence. **No way, buddy.** He fired into the wall and yelled, "Stop right there, bozo! You're not going anywhere."

The man stopped. He stayed pressed against the stone fence, breathing hard, holding tight to the thick rope. Hooley came to a stop ten feet away from him and aimed his Beretta center mass.

"Let go of that rope and drop. Now."

The man let go of the rope and dropped. He landed soft, knees bent. He was wearing a black ski mask over his head, all of his face covered except his eyes. He was dressed in black, supple and stretchy, so he could move and climb easily.

"Now drop your weapon, slowly. Believe me, I will shoot you dead. This close, I won't miss you, even in the dark."

The man said, voice low, scratchy, "I don't have a gun."

"You're a lousy liar. Drop the gun."

Hooley heard Connie running toward them, still some distance behind. He yelled, "Connie, go around and flank him to the right. The clown is lying to me." In the same instant the man's hand whipped up and he fired, missed, and Hooley fired back. The bullet slammed into the man's side, throwing him back against the wall. In a move so fast Hooley would swear he never saw it, the man sent a stiletto blurring through the air that struck him in his chest. Hooley dropped to his knees.

The man grabbed the hanging rope and was nearly to the top of the wall when Connie emptied her magazine at him, but she wasn't close enough, and she missed as he went over the other side. She heard Natalie panting behind her, and yelled, "See to Hooley. I'm going after him!"

Connie jumped up to grab the rope, but the man was already jerking it up and over the wall. She ran to the gate, punched in the code. Finally, she was able to squeeze through the opening, her gun up and ready, but she didn't see the man, only the black ground under a black sky, and the taillights of a car speeding away. The rope with its three-pronged anchor lay in the grass beside the wall.

45

Washington Memorial Hospital

Davis and Perry ran into the emergency room together, saw her mother standing in her blood-covered pajamas with a pair of sneakers on her feet, speaking to a nurse. Perry walked up to stand beside her and put her hand on her mother's shoulder.

Natalie turned to her daughter, tried to smile and failed. "Hooley is being prepped for surgery. This is an experienced trauma center and one of their best surgeons happened to be finishing up surgery on a car accident victim. He's scrubbing in right now. It was bad, Perry, the knife was in his chest, right over his heart. I knew better than to pull it out." She swallowed, more words beyond her.

Perry held her close. "They got him here real fast, Mom. Hooley's strong, he's got a good chance, right? Come on, we'll wait together."

Davis said, "I called Savich, told him what happened. He decided there's nothing to see tonight at the house, so he and Sherlock are coming straight here. He'll go out with the FBI techs tomorrow morning, see if the guy left anything to help us." He looked over to where a nurse was writing at the admissions desk, saw her glance up at Natalie and frown.

He patted Natalie's shoulder and walked to the nurse. "What is it you're not telling Mrs. Black? Is it about Hooley?"

Nurse Chambers looked at the tall young man standing in front of her, thought about sex, wished she was ten years younger, and realized she was so tired she was going bonkers. She cleared her throat. "No, there are no secrets here. It's serious, I know, but Mr. Hooley is in Dr. Proctor's very capable hands. It will be my job to check in with the OR and give you updates whenever I can. Are you Mrs. Black's son?"

Davis pulled his creds out of his pocket. "Special Agent Sullivan. Then why were you frowning at Mrs. Black?"

"Well, I recognized her. Her photo's been in the papers—about how her fiancé killed himself in England because of her, and she was called back to the United States—"

He cut her off. "Whatever you've read, Nurse Chambers, you should put away the frown, because that's not what happened at all. She had nothing to do with her fiancé's death. It is Mrs. Black who is under threat."

Nurse Chambers blinked. "But it's all over the Internet—"

"And you believe everything you read on the Internet?"

"Well, I suppose not. You're really an FBI agent and she's really in danger?"

Davis knew he should have kept his mouth shut. It would be hard enough to keep control of the press coverage as it was. He was a regular Don Quixote sometimes, trying to right wrongs in a world that too often didn't care who was right and who was wrong. "Yes, I am, and yes, she really is. Mr. Hooley was knifed trying to protect her."

Nurse Chambers nodded briskly. "Then we should get her out of the emergency room, I think. We have a small surgical waiting room that's very private and out of the way. She'll be safe there. If you would ask the ladies to follow me, I'll alert security." Davis stared after her as she walked smartly toward the telephone on the counter.

Nurse Chambers took them to a small green room on the third floor with a half-dozen green tweed chairs and a single stingy window that overlooked the parking lot. "I'll have coffee and rolls brought up, all right? And I'll come see you when I have any news on Mr. Hooley. Mrs. Black, I'll bring you something to put over your pajamas."

Twenty minutes later, after two detectives from Metro had left for the house, Savich and Sherlock walked into the room, their eyes on Natalie, on the soaked-through dried blood on her white lab coat. "Are you all right?" Savich asked her.

"Yes, yes. Thank you both for coming." She stopped, drew a deep breath. "I already told Perry and Davis and the two detectives who were here, but I'll tell you, too. Before Hooley blacked out, he told me the man had an odd gait, like one leg was shorter than the other. That was all he could tell me before he passed out. "I-I thought he was gone, that he was dead. There was so much blood." She shuddered. "I think he wanted to tell me something else, but he couldn't." She raised her hands. "It's still right there, Hooley's blood under my fingernails. He can't die, he just can't." Her breath hitched, and she lowered her face, looking down at her sneakers. Perry squeezed her hand. "Hooley will make it, Mom. You know how tough he is. Yes, he'll make it," and Perry prayed as hard as she'd ever prayed in her life.

Connie Mendez walked in, fiddling with the buttons on the white tech coat she was wearing over her pink pajamas, pajamas like Natalie's, also covered with Hooley's blood. Natalie went to her immediately, hugged her. "How is he, Connie?"

"They let me stay near him until they

wheeled him into the OR. He was awake again, Natalie, and he smiled at me. Then they locked me out and gave me this jacket and showed me to a bathroom to clean up.

"I called Luis at the house and spoke to Detective Fisher from Metro, Agent Savich. He wants to speak to you about the crime scene tomorrow. He said he put an APB out for the wounded man, alerted the local hospitals. I don't think there's much chance he'll show up at one, though."

Savich said, "Natalie, would you please go outside for a moment, I want to have Connie tell me exactly what happened. Then I want you to tell me. That way, we should get everything."

Natalie pulled the lab coat around her. "I'll go to the nurses' station, see if they can tell me how the surgery is going." Savich waited until she was out of the room, then said to Connie, "Tell me exactly what happened, Connie."

46

Connie drew a deep breath, gathering herself. "Okay, they shot at each other at nearly the same moment, and Hooley hit him, in the side, I think. He staggered back and threw the knife, right into Hooley's chest. The bullet didn't slow the guy. He got up that rope and over the wall as I was firing at him. I was still too far away. No, that's an excuse. I missed, I got in two shots, and I missed him. Me, who used to live at the firing range."

Sherlock said matter-of-factly, "You know as well as I do what an adrenaline rush can do to your aim, and a moving target who can fire back at you. You're never close enough, especially in the dark. We've all missed, Connie." Sherlock lightly laid her hand on her arm. She felt the rippling flesh from the adrenaline rush.

Connie slowly nodded. "But still—let me get on with it. By the time the gates opened enough for me to squeeze through, all I saw were the taillights of a car as it sped away. Even wounded, even with that uneven gait Hooley said he had, he was fast. I can't tell you the make of the car, the license, anything. He was too far away and it was too dark.

"All I'm sure about is that it was a man. He was dressed all in black, even a black ski mask. The rope he used to climb over the wall was still on the ground where he left it. I was too worried about Hooley to secure it. Natalie and I waited together with him until the ambulance arrived. Both of us kept yammering at him, but he never woke up.

"Luis—Luis Alvarez—he's the other bodyguard, and Mrs. Black's driver, stayed behind with the police. I told him about the rope. Maybe we can trace—something."

Savich said, "Davis, will you get Natalie? I've got some questions for her. Connie, thank you."

When Natalie walked back into the waiting room, Savich said, "You okay, Natalie?"

She sat down and Perry moved to sit beside her. "Yes, I'm together again."

Savich said, "Tell me about the alarm system. I assume the intruder managed to turn off the alarm?"

Natalie was getting herself together. Now she was furious. Look at her, falling apart like an idiot heroine in a gothic novel. She straightened, said in a clear, strong voice, "As you know, windows on upper levels with no external access usually aren't alarmed, but Brundage was thorough. Since I like fresh air all year around, he had a different alarm installed specifically for our bedroom, set to go off only if the window was pushed up higher than twelve inches, which it never was."

Savich said, "So this guy figured once he'd turned off the house alarm, he was home free."

Natalie nodded. "He had no way of knowing about the separate window alarm. It's powered from my bedroom."

Perry said, "The question is, how did the guy disable the house alarm?"

Davis said, "Anyone with enough

experience and the general specifications could disarm the system. Just as someone gave your own alarm code to Carlos, Perry, the person behind all this could have also given the intruder the alarm code to Natalie's house alarm."

Davis sat quietly, his hands clasped between his legs, his coffee untouched at his elbow as he listened as Savich asked Natalie to run through it all again from the moment she awoke to the arrival of the ambulance.

He looked over at Natalie, who was rubbing her arms, staring down at the faded green squiggles on the carpet beneath her sneakers, splattered red and black, still unlaced. She could have tripped and fallen on her face. But she hadn't. He admired her greatly in that moment.

Everyone had done the right thing, including Natalie, waiting to trap the intruder. Hooley and Mendez had been fast, but still it hadn't been enough. He hated that the person to pay was Hooley.

Davis realized he was beat. He looked

over at Perry, who was now quietly talking to her mother, her hand on her mother's shoulder. He saw the dark shadows beneath her eyes, saw the strain.

At last Savich said, "We've got enough to go on with this guy to search through AFIS—a young man with a noticeable odd gait, in good physical shape. Best of all, Hooley shot him. Maybe we'll get lucky with one of the ERs in the area. He sounds like a killer for hire, and if he is, it's very possible he'll be in the system. I'll get this all to Ben Raven. We'll have a lot of cops looking for him."

Nurse Chambers appeared in the doorway. She looked serious, as if she was ready to give her condolences. Then she stepped aside. "This is Dr. Proctor, everyone."

An older man walked into the room. He was perfectly bald and very short, enough to make Davis wonder if he stood on a block while operating. He looked at the clock on the wall out of habit. Davis looked with him. It was exactly 3:00 a.m. He had on a fresh white coat over fresh scrubs—

no trace of Hooley's blood on him now. He said in a very deep voice for someone so short, "Mr. Hooley is in recovery and doing well, and if he knows what's good for him, he'll stay that way. He's a young man, and strong. But I have to say it was a close thing; that knife did a lot of damage. We'll try to extubate him soon, and we'll have to watch him very carefully for any signs of bleeding. Are any of you his family?"

Natalie started. His family. She had no clue about Hooley's family. They'd met so recently they'd never spoken of siblings or parents. She said, "None of us are related by blood, but I suppose you could call us his family. I will find out—"

Connie said, "He has a sister who lives in Denver with her husband and three children. I'll find her phone number and call her."

Dr. Proctor nodded. "Yes, it's best she be here. And I don't mean to alarm you, but if he is religious, I think it wise that his pastor be notified. I understand many of you are FBI?"

Savich said, "That's right. This is Mrs. Natalie Black, and Mr. Hooley is her bodyguard. How long before you're confident he'll survive?"

"I don't want to minimize the danger. The knife tip punctured his pericardium and entered his heart muscle. The wound was within a couple of millimeters of being quickly fatal. If he hadn't gotten to me so quickly he would have died from blood loss. But he did get here and he survived the surgery, and that in itself says a lot about the young man's strength of will.

"The biggest risks now are delayed bleeding and infection in his chest or his blood. I don't expect this to happen, but we'll know much more by tomorrow. I'll have you notified when he's transferred to the ICU and he's conscious. I suggest all of you go home now and try to get some sleep."

Dr. Proctor turned on his heel, paused, turned back. "I recognize you, Mrs. Black. I'm sorry for your recent loss. The nurses told me you and Ms. Mendez saved Mr. Hooley's life, stayed with him until the paramedics could take over. You both did excellently."

Connie said, "Dr. Proctor, someone tried to kill him. He needs to be guarded. Let me stay. I won't get in anyone's way. I want to protect him, make sure no one can hurt him again."

Dr. Proctor looked at her closely, saw the fear in her eyes, the blotches of blood that had bled through to the white lab coat she was wearing. "Shouldn't the police be guarding him if there's really a need?"

"I'm his partner and a professional bodyguard. It's my responsibility." Connie fell silent, simply stared at him. She had no more arguments to make to him.

Dr. Proctor sighed, looked toward Savich, who nodded. "Very well. You can stay with him, but be ready to move out of the way fast if they need you to, okay?"

He turned to Nurse Chambers. "Mr. Hooley needs protection." And, eyes twinkling, he added, "Make it so."

Half an hour later, Connie pulled up a chair next to Hooley's bed, but she didn't sit down. Not yet. She had to look at him, watch him breathe, even though it was a machine doing the breathing for him. His face was as white as the hospital sheets. With his hair flopped over his forehead, he looked very young, helpless. She lightly laid her fingers on his forearm and she prayed, something she hadn't done in a long time. Finally, she sat down, leaned her head back against the wall, and because of her training as a Marine, she fell asleep deeply, within a few seconds, knowing she would awaken instantly if someone came into the cubicle.

47

Natalie slumped against the seat back of the Beemer aware her daughter was sending her worried looks.

Finally, when Perry coasted along an empty street, she said, "Knock it off, Perry. I'm fine, it's poor Hooley—" She broke off, cleared her throat. "Drive to your condo, then I'll drive myself home."

"Nope," Perry said.

"What do you mean, 'nope'?"

"I don't want you going back home again tonight. It's a crime scene, your bedroom probably has techs crawling all over it. There might still be police activity. You don't need to go through anything else tonight." She gave her a grin. "Besides, you're my mother. I love you more than any other soul in the world, so that means you're coming home with me—no, don't argue. I'm driving, after all."

"You know by now everyone will be gone. No one else is going to come around tonight. Besides, Luis is there to protect me."

Perry came to a smooth stop at a red light, wondering why there was a red light operating at 4:00 a.m. She turned to face her mother. "Do you remember when I was a little girl and I'd have a nightmare and crawl in with you and Dad? Well, now it's you and me and you've had a whopper of a nightmare and I've got a bed big enough for the both of us. Davis will be sleeping on the sofa. We'll be safe and sound and I won't have to worry about either of us. So no more arguments, Mom."

After a moment, Natalie said, "My sneakers still aren't laced up."

"You should try Velcro."

"Nah, those are old-lady shoes." Where had that negligent bit of humor come from? She leaned her head back against the seat and closed her eyes.

They drove through the empty streets, Davis in his Jeep behind them. Natalie said suddenly, "Perry, I remember Arliss was concerned that you and Day were getting too serious about each other."

Perry arched an eyebrow at her mother. "Why our being involved would distress Aunt Arliss is beyond me. I told you Day proposed the other night, and, knowing Day, he told her about it. You'd think she'd be cheering for him. I mean, she's known me forever, which means she's got to know I'm not a crappy person. Why did you think of this at four o'clock in the morning?"

Natalie's eyes were closed again. "It popped into my head, I don't know why. I told Arliss I would tell her today what I was going to do."

Perry made a left turn onto Vanderbilt Street. It was quiet, and dark as a pit if not for the streetlights. As she turned her mom's Beemer into her driveway, she said, "I don't want you to resign, Mother. It wouldn't be right; I don't care what sort of pressure Aunt Arliss lays on your head. Please promise me you won't let her talk you into it."

"I wish it were that simple, Perry, but you know it's not. Think about Arliss and Thorn—they have an administration to run, an election to win. Maybe my resigning is for the best. I wouldn't have to live here, not really. Maybe a horse ranch in Montana. I could raise Thoroughbreds, breed and race them. Your father always loved horses. I imagine if he hadn't died, that's what we would have done when we retired. What do you think?"

Perry turned off the engine, faced her mother. "You would be out shooting snakes within a week, you'd be so bored. It's Dad who wanted to raise horses, not you."

"I could live near Big Sky. You love to ski, as do I. We could—"

Perry leaned over and pulled her mother close. "No, absolutely not. It's out of the question. Listen to me, you will not resign. You will tell Arliss to try for a little loyalty, okay? You will tell her the FBI will figure out who's behind this and put a stop to it. You will not get out of Dodge because it would make things easier for Arliss and the president. And what happened tonight, won't that change everything? No one can doubt someone's trying to kill you, not after tonight."

Natalie felt her daughter's hair soft against her cheek, smelled the light scent of lemon, felt the strength and determination in that healthy young body. It had been only the two of them for so many years now. Life was so incalculable. Like Brundage, she could be dead tomorrow, from an accident, from a disease, if the killer didn't succeed. She hugged her daughter closer. Perry was in danger along with her and she couldn't bear it. She had to bring it to a close, had to. She saw Davis's Jeep headlights swing in behind them. She said against Perry's hair, "I was wondering if I do resign if all the attempts against both of us would stop."

Perry had wondered the same thing, but only for an instant. She said now, no doubt in her voice, "You know to your gut whoever is behind this wants you destroyed, and that includes your career,

your good name, even your life, and"—
she paused for a moment—"and me. A
very thorough revenge indeed."

"Revenge—but why? I can't think of
anyone I possibly hurt so much to bring
on this sort of—madness."

Davis stood outside the Beemer as they
talked. He'd checked all around the
building, seen no one. He waited for
another moment, then opened the door.
Slowly, the women separated.

"No one's around," he said matter-of-
factly. "Come on, let's get inside."

Ten minutes later, the condo was silent.
No one had bothered with an alarm clock.

The call with news about Hooley woke
them up at ten minutes before eight in the
morning.

48

**Washington Memorial Hospital
Saturday morning**

Connie waited as long as she could manage before she called everyone with the good news. Hooley survived the night. They'd pulled his breathing tube out at the crack of dawn and he was breathing on his own. He was stable, the nurses had said. She repeated every positive word she'd heard.

She stood over him, lightly tracing her fingers over his still face. His breathing and heart rate were steady, and he seemed comfortable. There was still a clear tube coming out of his chest to draw off fluid, and that had to hurt, but he was on heavy-duty meds and only sort of awake. She really didn't want him to wake up anytime soon, because she knew he'd be in pain. And sleep healed. He was so strong, she thought, so strong. He would pull through this, he had to.

But he did wake up. When he opened his eyes, Connie saw first blankness, then confusion, and she said quietly, "Mark, it's me, Connie. You're safe, you're going to be fine. You don't have to try to talk. Go back to sleep, it's the best thing for you."

He wasn't quite sure what she'd said, but her face and the sound of her voice so close reassured him. She was smiling, and surely that was a good sign. He didn't feel much of anything, no pain, and he wasn't about to test that out by moving. His head felt like it was stuffed with cotton—heavy and thick, with strange blurred thoughts that ricocheted here and there. He blinked, trying to clear his mind; it did, a bit. His mouth was so dry, but he couldn't say her name, but he tried, a small sound, but it got her attention.

"You're thirsty. I'm sorry," Connie said, and held a straw to his mouth. "Only a little bit, okay?"

He took a few sips, managed to whisper, "Connie."

"Yes, I'm right here. No one's going to get near you, Mark. You're perfectly safe with me."

"Good," he said. "That's good. I'm really glad I'm not dead," and he drifted away, his brain closing down, and everything was fine.

When he opened his eyes again, he saw Davis Sullivan standing over him. He was saying his name over and over. Well, not his name—

"That's right, Beef, open those baby blues because you and I have got beers to drink, hoops to shoot, wrestling to do, unless you're afraid of me."

Out came a thin gruff voice. "Afraid of you, pretty boy? In your dreams. You'd last five seconds." Was that skinny little voice really his? He sounded pathetic.

He must have barely made a sound, because Davis was leaning close to him now. "Yeah, maybe. Right now, though, you can't even pee on your own, so save your strength for the pretty nurses."

Hooley started to laugh, but it hurt so bad he gasped. He felt Sullivan's hand tighten on his forearm.

"I'm okay," he whispered. "Connie says I'll be okay."

"You'd better be okay or I'll sic Savich on you. Talk about the big mean dog, he'd put you on the mat in under five seconds at the gym. You scared the crap out of us, Beef."

Hooley wanted to laugh, this time simply because he was alive, but he knew better. He did manage a small grin without the pain slamming him again. "My older brother called me Beef—short for beef on the hoof."

"I thought you only had a sister. Did Connie tell you she's on her way from Denver to coddle you?"

It wasn't pain that made Hooley want to groan. Margie was a sweetheart, but she would fuss and bother, treat him like he was eight years old again. "Aren't you a thoughtful bastard."

"I do my best. I didn't call her, Connie did, your doctor insisted. Now, what's this about a brother?"

Hooley whispered, "Kevin. He was

career Army, a major. He died, in Iraq."
His breathing hitched for a moment, then,
"I was proud of him. Is Mrs. Black okay?"

"I'm sorry about your brother. Mrs.
Black is fine. She and Perry are on their
way in. As for Savich—ah, here he is
now."

Savich looked down at the wide band-
ages wrapped around Hooley's chest,
saw the drains were clear of blood. He
looked good, considering. Hooley would
survive this. He said quietly, "I spoke to
Dr. Proctor. He said he'd kick us out in
five because he wants to check you over.
He's pleased with how you're doing, so
keep it up. I don't want to wear you out,
Hooley, but that doesn't give us a lot of
time. If it becomes too much, you close
your eyes and we'll leave you alone. Are
you up to telling us anything about last
night? Anything Natalie and Connie don't
know?"

Hooley felt a stab of pain and stayed
silent, coming to grips with it. He nodded
toward the cup, and Davis placed the
straw on his tongue. He managed to suck

a little. Davis closed his hand around the pain medicine dispenser lying at his side. "Press the button for a shot of morphine. You don't want to chase the pain, Beef, you want to stay in front of it."

Hooley pressed the button. After a few moments, the pain seemed to float away, or maybe he was the one doing the floating, he didn't know, nor did he particularly care. He saw the two men standing beside him, looking down at him, and was baffled for a moment. Then he remembered the question. "It was so bloody dark," he said. "I don't know how he saw me well enough to throw that knife in my chest. Have you found him?"

Davis said, "Not yet. He's either gone to ground, trying to deal with it himself, or he's found himself a doctor. He hasn't been to an ER."

"He wouldn't go to an ER. That would be stupid," and Hooley closed his eyes as his head fell to the side. He wouldn't be talking anymore for a while.

49

Savich's home
Saturday morning

What would you think if we moved in with Natalie?"

"What?" Sherlock whirled around to face him, scrambled eggs falling off the spatula in her hand.

Savich fiddled with a slice of wheat toast. "Well, with Hooley down, she could use the protection of our sleeping down the hall. It's been tough to concentrate on helping her with Blessed hanging over us like a black cloud of doom."

"That's true, but moving in? No, Dillon, I don't think it'll come to that. The assassination attempt on the ambassador to the United Kingdom is all over the news, on the Internet, and that means the State Department have already sent over agents to protect her. They'll wrap her in a blanket and form a circle with H-and-Ks around her.

"Do you know, this whole deal with Natalie, it feels like Blessed in a way. Like obsession, like someone has set a course and now won't, or can't, back down until it's over. Seems to me it goes real deep."

"Like a wound that never healed, that will fester until he finds a way to make her pay?"

"Yes, that's it exactly."

Savich said, "Blessed isn't going away, either, and he knows where we live. He'll try for us here sooner or later, we both know that and need to face it head-on. It might have happened last night if we hadn't had all those people over for dinner. Sean is with his grandmother for safekeeping, but what about you? About us?"

Sherlock didn't notice the scrambled eggs on the kitchen floor. "We could ask a couple of agents to hang out with us here or, better yet, they could hunker down in a warm car outside. What'd I'd really like is for Blessed to come back to the house so we can end him. Then we can fetch Sean and Astro from your mom's and get our lives back on track."

Savich realized the eggs were burning, grabbed the skillet off the stove, turned off the flame. He took the spatula from her hand, but again Sherlock didn't notice. She started pacing the kitchen. "When you left for the hospital this morning to see Hooley, I looked around the neighborhood—yes, I was very careful—to make sure Blessed wasn't lurking around. I found a candy wrapper in the bushes. I think he was hiding here last night, waiting for a chance to get to us. We need to act, Dillon. I'm thinking Blessed will come back to the house tonight."

He sat her down and kneaded her tense shoulders. "All I know for sure is that he's committed to killing us and that's not going to happen."

Sherlock leaned her head up to look at him upside down. "Let's stay up tonight and wait for him."

He leaned down, kissed her mouth. "One thing in our favor, Blessed's a lousy shot. Let's do it."

He looked down at his watch. "Now we need to head out to Quantico if we're going to meet Davis there. He's bringing his recording of Milton Holmes's voice to play for Carlos Acosta. We can say hello to Nicholas Drummond if we have the time."

Savich waved to Mr. MacPherson catty-cornered across the street as they walked out the door. He was sitting on the top step of his porch, his new puppy, Gladys, leaping around him and chasing a bright red ball.

They hit horrendous traffic on the way to Quantico, made worse by earsplitting construction and a few dead stops for huge dump trucks filled with gravel crawling across the road. Savich got a call from Natalie as they waited. Sherlock couldn't make out what it was about. When he punched off, he said matter-of-factly, even as he steered the Porsche between two big SUVs, "Natalie and I are going to see the president at two o'clock this afternoon. He was informed about the attempt on her life last night and asked to see her. She said she was looking forward to it, now that there were no more questions about her honesty. She said it would be useful if I came along, in case he had any questions for the FBI."

Sherlock punched him in the arm. "I should have guessed what it was all about, given how excited you are."

Carlos had no idea if his caller's distorted voice was Milton Holmes or not. Savich cheered him up by leaving him Isabel's new cell number.

50

**The White House
1600 Pennsylvania Avenue
Saturday afternoon**

Savich had visited the White House twice before, both times to see the president with Director Mueller to receive congratulations from the Head Dude himself on high-profile cases resolved. As always, security was tight, thorough, polite, and fully engaged. Marines posted near the lobby, both for security and for show, watched them respectfully but closely. The Secret Service agents, Savich knew, were clustered close to wherever the president happened to be—presently, around the Oval Office. There was activity everywhere, but noise levels were low.

For Natalie, of course, this was old hat. She greeted the various staffers they saw and several of the security people, all of whom, as far as Savich could tell, were happy to see her. And worried, he saw, since by now the whole world knew about the attempt on her life right in her own home. He and Natalie were met by Chief of Staff Eric Hainny. Natalie offered her hand, nodded, and said, "Good morning, Eric."

After a brief pause, Hainny shook hers. "Good morning, Mrs. Black. Everyone is pleased you survived the attack last night. Ah, Agent Savich. It is a pleasure to see you again," Hainny shook Savich's hand.

Savich saw Hainny hadn't changed since the last time he'd seen him a year before. He was still in desperate need of a gym, a merciless trainer, and fewer helpings at the dinner table. He looked rumpled and impatient, the quintessential guard dog, only Hainny was the alpha guard dog. He cleared his throat, looked at his watch. He said, his voice neutral, "The president is exceedingly busy, Mrs. Black. He made time for you he doesn't have. Come with me."

Natalie and Savich followed him past a reception room, two senior advisers' offices, the dining room, and a study. Natalie spoke quietly to a tall, thin man who joined them, obviously one of the senior advisers. He patted her shoulder, then she double-stepped to catch up with Hainny, who never slowed. She rolled her eyes at Hainny's stiff back. It was obvious, despite the attempt on her life, that Hainny still believed Natalie should resign and get out of the president's hair, preferably far enough away to be forgotten by critics and citizens alike by the time elections rolled around.

Savich raised an eyebrow. Natalie said quietly, "I'm at the center of a firestorm, and Eric is very afraid he won't be able to control the fallout. The way he sees it, I'm still a huge liability."

Natalie let him march ahead when Mrs. Janikowski, the president's secretary, stepped out to greet her. She hugged her and patted her cheek. "I'm so sorry about what's happening, Mrs. Black, and so glad you're all right. The president has expressed supreme confidence that Agent Savich and the FBI will figure all this out." And she smiled at Savich. Now, that's how you get to be the president's secretary, Savich thought. He had to admit, hearing that made him feel quite nice.

Hainny cleared his throat, again looked at his watch, and Mrs. Janikowski stepped back. Hainny led them into the Oval Office as the clock struck two.

Savich saw Natalie pull her shoulders back, coach her expression into one of serene control. Her Armani suit was stark black, conservative, so stylish it had turned heads of passersby when she'd stepped out of her limo at the northwest gate to meet him. She wore power well, like a comfortable second skin. She added a slight, subtle smile as they walked in, a smile that said she would rule over her own reactions and her own personal universe, come what may. She was, he decided, quite remarkable.

"Mr. President, Mrs. Black and Special Agent Savich are here."

Thornton Gilbert rose from behind his desk, came forward quickly to enfold Natalie in his arms. He spoke quietly to her, then stepped back and shook

Savich's hand.

"Agent Savich, it is a pleasure to see you again. Agent Sherlock is well? And your son? Sean?" Savich answered on script, assuming that Mrs. Janikowski prepared him with personal particulars on all his visitors.

The president nodded and turned serious. "Agent Savich, I will admit I was relieved to hear you were accompanying Natalie here. I'm very pleased you're involved."

Savich had always thought this president could play the role of the president of the United States in a movie if he wished. He was tall enough—that is, over six feet— he was fit without the hint of a paunch hanging over his belt, and he was blessed with a full head of dark brown hair with gray wings at the temples. He looked competent and measured, a man who would think things through before acting, a plainspoken man you could trust. Had he practiced that look, that expression?

There was no doubt in Savich's mind that the president was genuinely pleased to see Natalie, an excellent sign. He turned to Mrs. Janikowski. "Bess, could you fetch us coffee and some of those good nutty rolls from the dining room?"

Bess Janikowski nodded, smiled at Natalie, and left. As for Chief of Staff Eric Hainny, he hovered until the president said, "Eric, would you run through the remarks they've prepared for this evening with the press secretary? I won't have the time."

It was a clear dismissal. Hainny paused for only a moment, then took himself off.

The president said, "Sit down, sit down, both of you. Nat, what's been happening to you is a nightmare. I can't tell you how sorry I am and how very worried both Joy and I are for you and for Perry as well. Director Comey has briefed me about the Scotland Yard investigation and the horrendous incident at your home last night. I asked you here to assure you we're going to keep you safe, and bring whoever did this to justice."

Natalie wanted to cry, but of course she didn't. She'd hoped he would support her, but, in truth, she hadn't expected it, not with all the political realities at play, even factoring in the events of the previous night that had shut the mouths of those who said she'd made up the attack in England.

Of course she and Thorn and Brundage and Arliss had been close for more years than any of them wished to acknowledge, but he was still the president of the United States, the most powerful man in the world, and their friendship, no matter how long or how deep, couldn't matter to any decision he made about her. She cleared her throat. "I've been wondering why I am still an ambassador after all that's happened."

He laughed, a rich baritone that filled the room. He sat forward, his hands clasped between his knees. "Nat, we've known each other since we were twenty years old. It's because I know you so well, because I know who you are and what you are, that I never doubted your word, not for an instant. Now, after last night, no one else can doubt you, either. Nat, let me say, and I plan to say this only once— you would not be helping me by resigning. I have other plans for you."

51

He broke off when Bess Janikowski slipped in carrying a beautifully worked antique silver tray. She set about giving them coffee, tea for Agent Savich, and she said when he looked surprised, "Oh, I know everything about you, Agent Savich," and she smiled at him on her way out. No one took a warm nutty roll.

As Mrs. Janikowski was leaving, Arliss Goddard Abbott came into the Oval Office, Eric Hainny lumbering behind her, both looking determined. The secretary of state walked in looking like the queen of the world, exuding arrogance and competence like a potent perfume. But, Savich decided, it was the arrogant set of her head that sealed the deal, and the aura of good old pioneer grit.

The president rose. "Arliss, I'm glad you're here, but I'd expected you a bit later. I trust Brooxey is well?"

"Brooxey provides me endless entertainment," Arliss said, not a hint of sarcasm in her smooth voice.

The president nodded. "Come and join us. Eric, you and I will meet here in thirty minutes, all right?"

It was clear to Savich the president didn't want Hainny involved in speaking with Natalie because Hainny obviously wanted her out, plain to see, and the president didn't want to have to deal with him in front of them. But what about Arliss Abbott?

Arliss nodded to Natalie and frowned at Savich, who rose. She turned to the president. "I could leave if there are things you wish to discuss with Natalie before I'm to be included." To Savich's ear, she was practically screaming to stay.

"No, no," the president said easily, and added, "Do you know Agent Dillon Savich, FBI?"

"I know of him," she said, and this time, because it was expected, she shook his hand, her voice perfectly pleasant.

"Madame Secretary," Savich said, his

voice pleasant as hers. Why had she come ten minutes earlier than expected? Did she know exactly where the president stood, and would she try to change his mind?

He saw Natalie was sitting perfectly still, her back ramrod straight, her eyes on the rich dark blue draperies behind the president's desk, changed from the bright red ones of his predecessor, or perhaps she was looking at the U.S. flag on one side of the desk, to the president's flag on the other.

"Sir," Arliss said, not sitting, "I was informed of your decision and I have some ideas to share with you both. First, Natalie, all of us are concerned for your safety. Last night shouldn't have happened. I will ensure no one can get to you again. None of us want anything to happen to you."

The president said very quietly, "Of course. Let me add that I already know what your feelings are in this matter, Arliss."

"No, you don't, sir. The press is giving heavy coverage to the intruder at Natalie's home last night. It looks to become a major story that will change the dynamics for us, and for Natalie, entirely—if handled properly. I now believe Natalie should stay the course, remain the United States ambassador to the United Kingdom, and I have a plan on how we should proceed."

Natalie said slowly, "Arliss, when you visited me Thursday afternoon at my home, you wanted me to resign."

"The president had decided to keep you on and it was hurting him politically, Natalie, and I did what I thought best. Things are different now after what happened last night. A United States ambassador was attacked in her own home, her staff injured. Whatever happened in England, there is no doubt about last night. Your surviving, and persevering in your job, can be seen as a triumph. Obviously, what happened last night validates the president's trust in you, his brave and wise decision to support you, despite the seeming impropriety.

"It's clear the attempts on your life began abroad, when you were in the field representing the United States government. Natalie, the State has no choice but to wrap you in the American flag and make you a homegrown heroine."

"And there you have it, Nat," the president said, "Washington at its finest. Arliss and her staff are right about the potential politics of this, though." He paused for a moment, grinned at Natalie. "You're a perfect heroine. Now, if you're willing, we can help you prep for the press, the news networks, put you back in the spotlight on your own terms."

Natalie wondered if Arliss would have changed her mind if Hooley weren't lying in the hospital with a knife wound in his heart, if dozens of people hadn't seen her in bloody pajamas in the ER. She said, "This is a lot to process, but you know I will do my best."

"Your best will be superb, as always," the president said. "Now, Agent Savich, what can I do to help you?"

"Actually, Mr. President, after the incident last night, Madame Secretary is providing ample security. Mrs. Black's safety was always my primary concern."

Arliss said, "That's right. Our State Department agents are already at your house, Natalie, making the necessary assessments. You know, if you'd asked me, I'd have authorized the Diplomatic Security Service to protect you as soon as you arrived home."

Natalie looked at Arliss and knew very well what her answer would have been if she had indeed asked.

"That's done, then," the president said. "Arliss, why don't you show Natalie to our press office, get her started on her work with them."

Minutes later, Natalie, Savich, and Arliss walked past Hainny's office to see him tapping his pen on a beautiful mahogany desktop. Arliss said smoothly, "He'll find out soon enough. There's a private study up ahead, and I'd like a few moments alone with Natalie. Would you mind waiting for us in the hall, Agent Savich?"

When they were alone in a small staffer's office, Arliss said, "I don't think there's much reason for me to take you all the way to the press office, Natalie. I've already made plans to have you speak at the UN on Monday. Ambassador Connor was scheduled to speak on global economic policy, and has graciously given up his time to you. I will be there with you, to introduce you."

Natalie searched her friend's, and her boss's, face. "Why?"

"It's substantial enough for your position, and it will give you a reason to agree to interviews with the press. We will announce your speech at the UN today. My staff will email you a suggested text of the speech, and I'll have the press secretary send you along some talking points. You will, of course, put your own spin on things and adjust whatever you wish to your own words."

Natalie nodded. "Why did you want to speak to me privately, Arliss?"

"To tell you I'm sorry for what's happened to you and to Perry. Day said he sent her flowers, called her several times to see if she's all right. I don't think he's particularly happy she's now being guarded by that young FBI agent who was with you at my party. What was his name?"

"Special Agent Davis Sullivan. He'll be with her until this is over, hopefully very soon now. He's a fine young man, actually, smart of mouth and fast of brain. He matches up with Perry quite well." She blinked, realizing the import of what she'd said to Day's mother. She smiled. "Day and Perry have known each other forever, and there is deep caring between them."

"Day told me he's committed to marrying Perry."

"Perry told me he proposed, but there's simply so much turmoil right now, and who can make a decision about anything? Day is a fine young man. I'd welcome him as a son-in-law. Whatever they decide, of course, I'm fine with it. Aren't you?"

"What's right is right," Arliss said. "Do you remember what Brundage always used to say?"

"Yes, but he said it in German," Natalie said. "He never wanted Perry to hear him curse."

"No, not that. He always told me he believed in karma. The only thing was that karma sometimes didn't get it done, and that was when you had to give it a good shove."

Natalie honestly couldn't remember Brundage ever saying a sentence with the word **karma** in it. She could imagine the thick contempt in his voice if he had. Brundage always sat solid and pragmatic in the world and heaped scorn on those who didn't, on those who believed in some sort of cosmic balancing of the scales. He knew where he was going, what he wanted, and he managed to get it even when he was twenty years old. And he'd wanted her, he'd told her, wanted her more than anything else in his life.

She felt the bittersweet memory fill her, felt tears sting her eyes. They'd had a lot of years together, but they should have had so many more. She said easily, "Well, possibly so, but what does karma have to do with Perry and Day, Arliss?"

Arliss lightly laid her hand on Natalie's

arm. "What I mean is that what is right will overcome, that's all. Brundage believed that, too, if I remember correctly." She turned away, then paused, said over her shoulder, "Isn't it odd how life turns out?"

52

Perry Black's condo
Saturday evening

You're making too much noise out there.
I can't sleep."

Davis was lying quietly, wrapped up in
his two blankets, watching the dying
fireplace embers fade from orange to
black. He'd barely been breathing, he
thought, listening, always listening, for
any stray sound that shouldn't be there.
He smiled into the dim firelight, called out,
"I was thinking the same thing about you,
but I was too polite to troop into your
bedroom and announce it. You know, I'd
probably have had to crawl in beside you,
shake your shoulder, tell you you're
snoring and to turn on your back. I might
have even had to wake you up."

"Oh, shut up. You weren't asleep, were
you?"

"Nah, I was lying here thinking and listening, and wondering why you wrote your last blog on Russell Wilson. You know no one outside the Beltway gives a crap about anyone but the Redskins, unless they're a threat."

He watched Perry come in wearing her ancient blue robe. He saw she was barefoot, her toes painted a pretty coral color. Her hair was all over her head in wild tangles, her face clean of makeup. He had to admit he really liked looking at her.

She yawned. "Well, there's Tebow, and he'll be front and center until he's an old man with no teeth. What with my finding out about Tebow's girlfriend, Bennett is so pleased with me I can write what I want for a week. And that's why I wrote about Wilson. He really came into his own this past season, and his dad dying young, it was a real tragedy." Like her dad, she thought, and maybe that was the real reason she'd wanted to write about him.

She walked to stand over him. "So you can't sleep? Why? Hooley looked great today with Connie hovering all over him."

"Nice to see Beef has an admirer, and Connie, of all women. I think they make a great couple."

"And Mom had a great day, meeting with the president, getting his support and all the security she needs. Even Arliss came around."

"So why don't I see you sleeping, either?"

She began to pace in front of him, then turned. "I don't know. There's lots to think about."

And it's finally getting to you. He watched her meander around her living room, pause here and there to straighten a book, a picture. "Do you know when I first saw you on your hog in my driveway, when was it—five days ago—with your punk girl boots, that space-age helmet and all the black leather, I thought, **Dear Lord, what wonderful gift have you landed in my driveway?**"

"What?" She turned so fast she hit her shin against the coffee table, yelped, and bent over, rubbing furiously.

"You heard me. Those black boots with their kick-ass little chains. You nearly stopped my heart."

"You're a pitiful liar."

"Not altogether. If you'd been humming, say, 'Time Bomb' by Rancid, I would have expired right there on the concrete with my neighbor Mr. Mulroney looking on, shaking his head, wondering if you had tattoos beneath all that black leather."

"Only one tattoo."

He cocked an eyebrow at her. "Where? What?"

"None of your business. It didn't hurt very much. No worse than childbirth, I'm told."

"I hadn't heard that, though I doubt any guy would know what to make of that comparison."

"Guys don't like to admit they feel pain of any kind. Take Hooley today, lying there all stoic, trying to smile when you called him Beef and told him you were considering becoming a vegetarian."

"He couldn't wimp out in front of Connie, could he?"

Perry paused, looked at him still lying on the sofa, relaxed and calm, watching her. "Have you ever been hurt in the FBI? Not at Quantico, I mean, on the job?"

"Not recently. Well, I gotta say that a couple of weeks ago I flew the sister of a new agent in the unit back to Washington from Maestro, Virginia. She was studying at the Stanislaus School of Music, got herself into a fix. By the end of the flight she was trying to kick me out of the plane because we disagreed on the music." Davis shook his head, picked up a glass of water from the coffee table and took a drink. "Women who can't accept good music can be unforgiving."

She wanted to laugh, maybe throw something at him, or maybe drag him onto the carpet and rip his white undershirt over his head.

Whoa.

"I'm going to bed. Alone."

A dark brow went up, but unfortunately the effect was lost in the dim light. Davis said, "I don't recall inviting myself in to spoon with you. I don't snore, by the way.

Good night."

"Great to hear, Davis. Good night." She left the living room, went down the short hall, and snapped her bedroom door shut. Davis lay back down, his head cradled in his arms, and smiled at the ceiling, but for only a moment. He had a lot to think about, too.

53

Savich's house
Saturday night, near midnight

They thought they were so smart, so sneaky, kneeling behind the thick bushes at the side of their house, pressed in close. They were waiting for him to show himself, waiting to kill him. They had no idea he'd been watching them since they'd hunkered down in those bushes. Nearly two hours now.

Blessed looked through the window of their neighbor's darkened living room, sipping a cup of hot chocolate. They had to be cold and miserable out there, as he had been the night before, standing in the shadows away from the pole lights in the hospital parking lot, pacing between the cars, watching and waiting.

He'd come back last night to this house in time to see them rush out. He'd followed them to the hospital, watched them pull up under one of the lights and hurry in, Sherlock's red hair an incredible flame under that fierce beaming light. Her face was pale, pinched. He'd never seen her look so grim. Savich showed no expression, always the hard man, no give in him at all. Blessed hated himself for the fear he felt, and that made him hate Savich more.

Somebody was hurt, somebody important to them, had to be, to bring them to the hospital so late. Blessed wondered who, but he didn't really care. It was too cold to worry about it, waiting there in the parking lot all that time. All he'd seen was half a dozen people leaving the hospital for the night, looking exhausted. There was a steadier flow of people showing up to the ER, some of them limping, moaning, crying. People had no guts anymore. Pinch them on the arm and they'd go off screaming and complaining. Damn gutless worms.

As he drank his chocolate, Blessed thought of his brother Grace, as cold as the winter ground outside, dead and buried in the wilderness. Grace had always been stronger, known what to do and how to do it. But Grace was dead, gone. For a long time now. And these FBI agents were trying to kill him dead, like his mama was, and Father. Everyone he loved was dead, except Autumn, and she wanted no part of him. Even the old bum whose coat kept him warm was dead and gone.

He wondered what had become of his mama's house—no, more a shrine, really. He sometimes wondered if his mama hadn't loved that house more than him or Grace, maybe even more than Father. He shook it away; it was disloyal. No, Mama had loved them both.

He mourned them all, and wished somehow they could know he was mourning. He didn't think there would be anyone to mourn him when his own time came. Mama wanted him to find himself a wife, but he didn't think that was going to happen.

He knew his brain was looping back and forth, had been for days now, between what he'd lost and what he had to do. Couldn't be a good thing, but what else was there? This was what his life was for now, and there was no changing it. Mama asked him for revenge, and that meant the deaths of these two agents in the bushes who'd brought his family down.

He looked out again through the winter dead branches of an oak tree, and beyond to the yew bushes. That was the right spot. He could see them moving, trying to stay warm in their dark parkas and their winter gloves. They were waiting for him to come, only he wouldn't, because two hours ago, he'd knocked on Mr. MacPherson's kitchen door. When the old man had opened it the width of the chain, he'd looked into his old rheumy eyes and told him to invite him in. Like a vampire, he thought, and wasn't that a kick? It smelled like an old guy's house, like he'd been alone for some time, but still it was nice, filled with mementos of his long-dead wife and what seemed like dozens of his grandkids, photos all over the place. His mama hadn't kept a lot of photos, preferred showing off her antiques, and Grace's soul-black paintings.

He'd walked the old man to his couch in a living room that smelled like faded violets. He didn't tie him up, no need. He'd stay there until Blessed told him otherwise. He even laid a big, soft quilt over his lap, just like his mama used to do for him in the cold months. He scooped up the yapping little mutt and tossed him in the bedroom closet. He gave the old man his ancient revolver and told him to shoot anyone who came in.

He smiled now, realizing those two had to be tired, growing careless. Unlike them, he'd slept most of the day to stay out of sight of the cops. On his way here, he'd stopped for two hamburgers at a burger place over in Foggy Bottom.

It was time for him to stop sitting and waiting. It was time to get up close and personal, from behind them, close enough to put that Glock three inches from their heads, if he could, and end this. Then he could leave this cold, ugly city with its crackheads and gangs and homeless bums roaming the streets and sleeping in the alleys, and this was the nation's capital? Marble buildings and granite monuments and thousands of worker bees and the underbelly he'd stayed in that nobody gave a crap about.

He eased quickly out of the back door of the house, bent low and started working his way through the backyards, down past a couple houses, then he'd get on his hands and knees and quietly work in behind them.

54

Sherlock had a cramp in her calf. Dillon rubbed it for her, but she had to stand up, no choice. She eased up onto her knees, looked through the bushes. All was quiet, all the houses were dark, neighbors in bed. It was cold, but the night still, with little wind. She heard the sound of an engine and tensed. She smiled when she saw an old Mustang she recognized come cruising to a halt at the curb of the Morgans' house, three houses down across the street. No wonder it was coming back late—it was Saturday night and the Morgans had three very pretty teenage girls. The boy cut his engine and coasted up to the house, lights off. Was he hoping for a little necking time? An instant later, the Morgans' living room light went on, then the porch light. The front door opened and Todd Morgan came out, pulling his robe belt tight around his waist. Six foot four inches of firefighter dad stood with his arms crossed over his chest, sending the hairy eyeball toward the Mustang.

She heard a muffled yapping sound—a dog's bark?

An instant later, in the reflected light from the Morgans' front porch, Sherlock saw movement in the bushes next to Mr. MacPherson's house, low and moving away from them. She whispered, "Dillon, there's someone bent low, in Mr. MacPherson's backyard, going or coming, I can't tell. It's got to be Blessed. I hope Mr. MacPherson's all right."

He came up on his knees and looked across the street, using his night-vision goggles. He saw perfect stillness. There was another yap—a puppy's yap—and they both realized it was Gladys, Mr. MacPherson's new puppy. "If he's backing away, it's probably because of Gladys's barking."

Gladys was barking louder now, short, high, piercing yaps. Savich said, "Blessed has either made it inside the house or he's holding perfectly still. I'll bet he was about to make his move, but with Gladys yapping her head off, he doesn't know what to do. Can you run with that cramp in your leg?"

She rubbed her knotted muscle furiously and nodded.

Suddenly, Mr. Morgan shouted at the top of his lungs, "Lindy, you get in here now!" and the Mustang door opened and the interior light flashed on to spotlight Lindy looking mad and her date looking embarrassed. The car light flashed on Blessed, pressed frozen against the wall of MacPherson's house, looking wildly around him and back to where they crouched behind the bushes. He raised a gun quickly, lowered it again, and took off around the back of the house.

Savich jumped to his feet, tossed aside his night-vision goggles, and ran toward him, shouting over his shoulder, "Stay put, get that cramp out." He juked around to the back of Mr. MacPherson's house.

When he reached the backyard, he paused, crouched low, still and listening, but he didn't hear anything. He found the back door open and pushed it slowly open. The kitchen was dark. As far as he could tell, the whole house was dark. He heard Gladys, but she wasn't running at him—no, she was in another part of the house.

"Mr. MacPherson?"

There was no answer.

Gladys was growling now. Was she coming closer? Why?

Savich pressed his back against the wall and eased down the hall toward the living room, Glock raised.

He saw a man's shadow coming out of the living room, then he saw Gladys run out, leaping and barking wildly. The man's arm was shaking as he raised a gun and fired at Savich, once, twice, three times. Wild shots, nowhere near him, but he'd already dropped and rolled back into the kitchen and hugged the refrigerator.

He heard deep, steady breathing and Gladys still yipping, sounding like she was still jumping up and down, again and again.

He heard the front door open. **Sherlock.** He felt his blood freeze. He wanted to yell at her to leave, but he knew she'd heard the gunshots, knew she'd be ready. Still, he rolled up onto his knees, saw the man's shadow again. He was standing perfectly still, Gladys jumping up and down against his leg. Savich raised his Glock, shouted, "Blessed!"

The man didn't move at the sound of Savich's yell, simply stood there.

It was Sherlock who first realized what was happening. She yelled from the front hall, "Mr. MacPherson!"

A familiar old voice said softly, "Who is that?"

In the next instant, the man went down, a light switch went on, and Savich saw Sherlock fall to her knees beside Mr. MacPherson. Gladys was no longer barking, she was wildly licking Mr. MacPherson's face, whimpering. Sherlock looked up. "He'll be okay, Dillon. Blessed got to him. I knocked him out, and he won't remember anything about this. Look at this. Blessed gave him my Glock so he could shoot us. I'll see to Mr. MacPherson. Go get Blessed. He's got to be close."

Savich had almost shot the precious old man who'd lived in this house since before Savich was born. He ran out the front door, looking for Blessed.

Blessed didn't slow until he'd run the four blocks to where he'd parked the Ford he'd stolen in Alexandria that afternoon. He had a violent stitch in his side, and his lungs were aching something fierce when he finally reached it. All the houses were quiet. Hadn't anyone heard the gunshots? They'd sounded like cannon shots to him. Had the old man managed to shoot them? Even as he thought it he knew Savich wasn't lying dead; the old man was no match for him. No, Savich was after him, even now that Porsche of his was screeching out of his driveway, but it wouldn't do him any good. He had no idea which direction Blessed had run.

He got himself together enough to climb into the car, still panting. He had to go now. Savich could get lucky enough to come his way. He coasted quietly forward without turning on the lights, happy for the bit of incline. He looked into his rearview mirror and saw only streetlights. He heard the roar of the Porsche in the distance, but it was moving away. He smiled.

He heard the sirens approaching, and he smiled once more. He'd gotten away yet again. Then he saw his dying mother's face, all gray, fanatic old eyes filming over, and her face was twisted in disappointment. At him, because he'd failed yet again? Didn't Mama want him to live? He tasted something rancid and nasty in the back of his throat. He swallowed, wishing he had some water.

How had that wretched little yapper gotten out of the closet?

55

Savich gave up after fifteen minutes of cruising every street in a mile radius. When he drove into the neighborhood, he saw an ambulance and two Metro police cars in the MacPherson driveway. Neighbors had come out of their homes to see what the trouble was, and two officers were reassuring everyone. **Good.**

He found Sherlock in the MacPherson living room, standing over Mr. MacPherson, who was lying on a gurney looking dazed, a paramedic holding his veiny wrist, taking his pulse.

Sherlock said, "Did you get him?"

He shook his head. "I didn't even see his car."

He stood over Mr. MacPherson. "I'm

very sorry, sir. How are you feeling?"

The old man's eyes sharpened on his face. "I'll live, boy, I'll live. What happened? I woke up and there's all this commotion going on and my head is fixing to burst. Can you hand me Gladys? She's barking up a storm, all scared. I need to let her know I'm okay. I am okay, aren't I?" he said to the paramedic standing over him.

"You'll be just fine, sir. Ah, here's Gladys," and the paramedic pressed the puppy against Mr. MacPherson's chest. They watched Gladys licking Mr. MacPherson's face frantically. Savich didn't think she was going to calm down anytime soon. He spoke to one of the officers as Sherlock called a MacPherson daughter to come and take Gladys.

Sherlock said, "I think Blessed tossed Gladys into the closet, only he didn't shut the door well enough and she managed to poke her way out. And that's when his plans were shot." She petted the puppy's head. "You saved the day, kiddo. All four and a half fluffy pounds of you."

They were stepping into their house

when the Oak Ridge Boys belted out "Dream On."

"Yeah?" It was Dane Carver.

Dane said, "We've got a solid lead on the assassin Hooley shot in the side last night. He broke into a doctor's house in Annandale, a Dr. Marvin Kurtz, divorced and living alone. After the good doctor fixed him up, he clobbered him over the head, tied him up, and stuffed him in a closet. Here's serendipity for you—the doc had bought one of those medical alert bracelets for his mom that day, and managed to press the button. When the cops arrived, he was still tied up and shouting his head off through the duct tape. The Annandale cops called us. The doc gave a description of the guy, and I'm betting we'll find a lot of usable DNA."

Savich said, "I'll wager he didn't expect the doctor to be found anytime soon, for at least a day, enough time so he'd be out of the area."

"Yep. I've updated the BOLO out on him with the doctor's description. Dr. Kurtz said he took codeine and antibiotics with him, enough to see him through, he said, that is, if he doesn't move around too much in the next three days. Then he shrugged, said the man didn't make a sound while he closed him up, he was tough. He also said he was lucky the bullet came close but didn't hit anything vital, only muscle. The kind of wound that hurts like the devil but usually heals all right.

"Dr. Kurtz is pretty wrung out, but hyped, you know? He won't shut up, he's too buzzed on adrenaline. Do you want to see him tonight?"

Savich glanced down at his watch. It was late and the good doctor would probably crash soon now. "No, we'll drive out to Annandale tomorrow morning. Let the good doctor have a nice night's sleep."

He raised his head to look at Sherlock. She was still bundled up in her parka and gloves. He walked to her and pulled her into his arms.

"What a night," she said against his neck.

56

Annandale, Virginia
Sunday morning

Savich pulled the Porsche into the driveway of a small 1950s faded gray clapboard cottage set amid a dozen oak trees on a cul-de-sac.

Sherlock said, "Dr. Kurtz's nurse told me he's been renting this place for the past three months, since his wife caught him cheating and kicked him out.

"I wonder how our assassin found him. Was it blind luck? What really scares me is what could have happened if he'd had his family here."

"Don't make yourself crazy with what-ifs, sweetheart." He gave her a crooked smile. "I've already done it enough for both of us."

As they walked up the ancient flagstone steps with weeds sprouting up happily between them to the weathered front door, Sherlock said, "I'm very relieved the good doctor is alive, Dillon."

Savich was, too. He knocked on the once red front door. The door opened on a tall, large-bosomed woman in her mid-thirties, her long blond hair curly around her pretty face. She stared at them from behind stylish aviator glasses, her eyes suspicious. Then she smiled. "Oh, you're from the FBI, right?"

Savich smiled back at her. "Yes, we are," and he and Sherlock showed her their creds, introduced themselves.

"And I'm Linda Rafferty, Marvin's—Dr. Kurtz's—nurse. Come in, come in. Poor man, he's lying down, a concussion, clearly, but he refused to go to the hospital last night. Doctors heal themselves, right? He's a little better this morning, thank goodness. Please, follow me."

The master bedroom was painted a soft

light brown, and not much larger than
the king-size bed, with only a flat-screen
TV on the wall across from it. Dr. Marvin
Kurtz looked surprisingly well reclining on
top of the big bed, wearing a stylish
maroon bathrobe and matching slippers.
He was looking over a pair of academic-
looking glasses perched on his nose,
watching ESPN. His only concession to
his injury seemed to be the impressive
white bandage wrapped around his head.
He didn't move to greet them, but he did
smile at them, and then he smiled at his
nurse.

Aha, Sherlock thought, **so Linda is why
your wife booted you out.** She shook
Dr. Kurtz's hand. "You were very lucky,
sir. We won't stay long. I imagine you've
got a pretty bad headache."

"It's not as bad now, thanks to some
sleep and then pain meds." He shook
Savich's hand. "I'll tell you, Agents, if my
mother hadn't broken her hip I'd never
have had that emergency alert bracelet in
the house. What are the odds I'd use it
myself? I've decided I'm going to have it

bronzed. Linda, please turn off the television so we can talk."

Linda gave him another smile and turned off the TV.

They took him through every moment of the previous evening, starting with the knock on his door announcing he had a package to sign for and he saw the gun pointed at his chest by a man whose clothes were stiff with dried blood.

He said, "He knew I was a surgeon and could help him. He told me if I didn't he would kill me and treat himself if he had to. So I did the best I could with what was here. Like many surgeons I know, I keep an emergency surgical kit at home.

"He was in a lot of pain and looked quite ill, but he'd managed to stop the bleeding from his gunshot wound by applying a pressure dressing, as good a job as a medic could have done in the field. He was at the end of his rope, though, and smart enough to realize he could die if he didn't get medical help.

"I'll tell you, while I worked on him, I kept hoping he'd pass out, but as I told

Agent Carver, he looked like ex–hardline military, a Green Beret or a Ranger or something. He was fit and tough, and he dragged his left leg, probably from a war wound. Everything I did seemed quite natural to him, like he'd seen it before. Of course, he didn't want me to give him anything intravenous that could knock him out. He had me only use lidocaine, and he took a couple of Vicodin, but he could still function, still hold it together. He was lucky the bullet didn't penetrate his abdominal wall; it only tore though some muscle.

"As I was treating his wound, picking out small foreign bodies, disinfecting and closing it, I kept thinking I could let the scalpel slip, maybe even stab him in the heart before he could bring up that gun and shoot me. But I couldn't do it, couldn't take his life, even though I knew in my gut there was a chance he was going to kill me.

"But you know what it's like, you keep hoping, keep doing what you're doing, praying the guy will have a sliver of decency, show a bit of gratitude that you saved his life. I gave him the meds and antibiotics he needed, and helped him into one of my shirts.

"Then he smiled at me and I knew that was it. Decision time. You know what he did? He said thank you, and as I helped walk him to the front door, he turned and hit me on the head hard, struck me down.

"When I came around I'll tell you I was so happy to be alive I didn't care I was tied up in the living room closet. I don't think I even realized I had blood running down my face. I was that relieved. Then I thought of the medic alert bracelet in my pocket I'd bought for my mother that very day, and wanted to sing the Hallelujah Chorus." He beamed at them.

"It's all my fault," Nurse Linda Rafferty said from the doorway. "I told Marvin, I mean Dr. Kurtz, that a man called me, asked if he could come in, that he'd had an accident, and I told him that Dr. Kurtz had been called to the hospital and he was off-call after that. I know he looked up Marvin's—Dr. Kurtz's—home address and that's how he found him. I'm so sorry, if only I'd kept my mouth shut."

"Linda," Dr. Kurtz said, "it's over now, and I don't think I've had an adventure like this one in years." He paused. "Well, never, actually."

Sherlock marveled as she watched Linda Rafferty sit on the side of the bed, stroke Dr. Kurtz's hand, and fondly call him a moron. She wondered if Linda would continue on as his nurse after they were married.

By the time FBI sketch artist Jesse Griggs arrived to work with Dr. Kurtz, they'd managed to pry Linda away and sit with her in the living room. A nice spot, Savich thought, old furniture, faded rugs on the newly buffed oak floors, and chairs whose cushions sagged in the middle after cradling all comers over how many years?

Linda Rafferty kept looking toward the bedroom. Finally, she jumped up, dashed off to the kitchen to make them coffee, and offered them apples with peanut butter, since it was nearly lunchtime.

Twenty minutes later, Dr. Kurtz appeared in the doorway beside Jesse, looking like a raffish wounded RAF pilot. He said, "I can't believe I haven't mentioned it to you or Agent Carver. My head's still foggy, I guess. The man had an accent. It wasn't all that distinctive, like he'd lost most of it over the years, but I'm in London twice a year, you see, and I wondered about it. I think he's a Brit."

Jessie walked across the room and showed them the sketch. They looked at William Charles McCallum, estranged son of the late George McCallum, Viscount Lockerby.

57

Savich's house
Sunday afternoon

They took a detour for lunch with Sean and his grandmother, featuring hot dogs and chips, and a nice homemade veggie burrito for Savich. Savich needed sleep, but what he got was a basketball game with Sean at the newly installed hoop in his mother's driveway, with his mother cheering Sean on. They went through two video games and fetch with the tireless Astro before Savich and Sherlock left for the day. They arrived home to see Perry and Davis sitting in his Jeep in their driveway.

Davis started talking even before he got out of his Jeep. "What's with all the crime scene tape across the street? What happened here? You're both okay?"

Sherlock said, "Hi, Davis, Perry. Yep,

we're fine. We had a visit from Blessed last night, but, alas, he managed to get away and is still in the wind. As for Mr. MacPherson, our elderly neighbor, he had a stressful night, but he's fine now, home and resting. The crime scene tape should be coming down tomorrow. Now, what's up with you guys?"

"I didn't call because I knew you were at your mother's with Sean. Maybe Blessed won't be in the wind for much longer; we had a sighting of him this morning."

Savich said, "Come on in. I'll make some coffee and you can tell us all about it."

Once everyone had a cup of Savich's special dark roast, Davis said, "A kid in a pawn shop—Best Deal in Town in Arlington—was robbed at gunpoint. Name's Allen Purcell, age twenty-one, son of the owner. Allen described Blessed Backman, no question it was him—an old guy with gray hair who needed a shave, ill-fitting clothes that looked too big for him, and this really pretty camel wool coat. Turned out later they got Blessed on camera, too, nice sharp black-and-white. I guess Blessed didn't think about that, or didn't care.

"Allen said Blessed wanted the forty-caliber Glock he had in the display case; he told Allen he'd given his to a friend last night and wanted to replace it. When he leaned down to show the Glock, Blessed pointed a revolver at him. Allen said he thought he was going to die right there. But Blessed didn't shoot him, only waved the gun at the ammunition in the case. While Allen was reaching for the magazine for the Glock, Blessed asked him about some rifles he had displayed over the counter, really expensive and high-quality, but he said Blessed didn't take them. After Allen gave him the boxed ammo for the Glock, Blessed thanked him, locked him in the storeroom, and walked out. Of course, Allen had his cell phone in his pocket and called the cops. They were there in under four minutes, but Blessed was gone. Metro put it together that it was Blessed right away and called us.

Ollie said you and Sherlock were out in Annandale this morning with Dr. Kurtz, who fixed up the guy Hooley shot, so we handled it ourselves." He smiled at Perry, who was sipping at the wonderful coffee. "Since I wasn't letting Perry out of my sight, I schlepped her with me to speak to Allen. Our football writer asked Allen a good question."

Perry shrugged. "Well, Davis told me all about Blessed and what he can do, and so I asked Allen if the man stared at him or if anything strange happened while Blessed was there."

Davis said, "Allen thought about it, then said the old guy did stare at him, kind of gave him the creeps, but apart from being scared to death, nothing strange happened, like what was supposed to happen."

Savich said, "Looks like Blessed was tired, or maybe his ability still doesn't necessarily come when he calls. About Allen's cell, Blessed's not used to them, so I bet he didn't even think about it."

Sherlock said, "Would you guys like me

to make some sandwiches? I think Dillon could use a veggie wrap after his basketball workout with Sean."

Savich thought about that for a moment, then said, "How about grilled cheese?"

When they were seated around the kitchen table with the requested hot grilled sandwiches on their plates, Savich gave them the news about William Charles McCallum as they'd heard it from Dr. Kurtz and Nurse Linda.

As Davis lifted the top of his grilled cheese and added more mustard, he said, "Can you imagine? Natalie's almost stepson, and the heir to an English peer turned Muslim, maybe a terrorist, and she's never met him?"

Perry was shaking her head, her toasted cheese sandwich untouched on her plate. "But why? I mean, according to my mom, he'd abandoned his father, his whole family. So why in heaven's name would he try to kill the woman his father was going to marry? Why would he suddenly care about what happened to his father?"

"I put in a call to Natalie," Sherlock said.

"She'll be taking a break from her interviews to visit Hooley in about an hour. We'll head over there when you've finished your lunch. Perry, eat your grilled cheese before it hardens up on you."

58

Washington Memorial Hospital
Sunday afternoon

Hooley was awake and in pain, but so stoic Natalie wanted to smack him. She walked to the nursing station with her newly assigned Diplomatic Security agent in tow to throw her weight around. A nurse told Natalie they'd been asked to try to switch him to oral meds, and maybe it was too fast too soon. She appeared in under a minute to inject morphine into his IV.

Natalie lightly tapped his arm. "Next time, don't be a brainless macho. Pain isn't fun, even for tough guys like you. Promise me you'll ask when you need more pain meds."

"Yeah, okay, I promise," Hooley said, then added, "Hey, I'm feeling better already."

Connie was standing at the foot of his bed, her arms crossed over her chest. "I'll make sure he keeps that promise."

The FBI arrived, Perry in their wake. Savich said, "That's good, Connie, keep an eagle eye on him because you know very well Hooley would rather hang it up than complain. It's not in his genes."

Hooley smiled at that.

Davis said, "A man's brains don't always connect to his genes, right, Beef?"

"What would a pretty boy like you know about it?"

Davis grinned down at him. "Take the meds; otherwise, I'll feel guilty busting your chops."

Connie didn't say anything more about Hooley sucking in the pain. She knew pride when she saw it wearing size twelves. Instead, she said, "Since the DSS agents joined us, Mrs. Black's house is pretty much in lockdown. So I have more time to spend here with Mark. Luis is still doing the driving, though."

Savich said, "Good. Everything sounds under control. Now, if you and Hooley would excuse Natalie for a moment," and Natalie followed Savich and Sherlock out of the room.

A nurse directed them to an empty room down the hall. The DSS agent remained by the door. Savich said, "Natalie, this is about your fiancé's eldest son and heir, William Charles McCallum. You said you'd never met him, that George never said much about him?"

"No. William—Billy—wasn't in England by the time George and I met. Of course, we talked about him, after that picture of him in Syria surfaced in the press. Since I was going to be his wife, I had to understand more about what had happened."

Savich said, "Did he tell you the last time he met his son, spoke with him?"

"No, he didn't."

Sherlock said, "Did he ever mention any sort of accident Billy was in before he left for Oxford?"

"No, but I suppose if it had been a minor accident of some sort, George wouldn't have seen any reason to mention it to me." Natalie looked back and forth between them. "What's this all about?"

Savich lightly laid his hand on her arm. "We're almost certain now that the man who attacked you Friday night was William Charles McCallum, George's son. Billy."

Natalie stared at them, slowly shook her head back and forth. "But that makes no sense. I've never even met him, as I told you. George's son has turned into some kind of terrorist assassin trying to murder an ambassador?"

Sherlock said, "Since there have been no calls to kill you, Natalie, even from the most radical imam in London, we think this is personal."

"Then did he kill his father as well? Or does he think I did? Does he think I was responsible for driving George to kill himself? He wants revenge? By killing me?"

"Think back, Natalie," Davis said. "Think back to when you were talking to George about his son. Did he look devastated? Did he look like he hated his son? What?"

Natalie's world had turned upside down.

She dashed her fingers through her hair, trying to come to grips with the thought that George's son had tried to kill her. She drew in a deep breath. "All right. Not hated, no, but sure, I saw the disappointment on his face, the devastation. I mean, there had to be, hadn't there? George felt he'd failed his son, failed to realize he needed help, and then he left, became something his father couldn't begin to understand."

Savich set MAX on the table beside the hospital bed, lifted the lid, typed a few strokes. "Hamish Penderley of Scotland Yard uncovered a number of cellular communications between George McCallum and his son over the last two years." He typed a bit more. "Come look."

59

Savich said, "Calls between George McCallum and William's cell phone in Hamburg stopped only for a few months. George flew to Hamburg two years ago and William started accepting his father's calls again. They talked about once a week, for about ten minutes, on average. I imagine George tried to convince his son to return home, or at least accept his help. William had a new wife in Hamburg by then, with a family of refugees from Lebanon. I don't know why George failed to tell his family or you about William's marriage, but perhaps William insisted. I doubt his new family and community knew who he was, that is, heir to an English title. It's very probable William didn't want anyone to know.

"About eight months ago, George started making calls to a satellite phone registered to his own name, first in Turkey, and then in Syria. The dates match William's movements. Then, six weeks ago, after William's picture surfaced in the press, the calls were more frequent."

Perry walked to her mother, who looked shell-shocked as she stared down at MAX's screen at the steady flow of calls from a man she'd believed she knew to her soul. Perry pulled her mother against her. "Did George show you photos of Billy?"

Natalie pulled back, shook her head. She said, "I visited Lockenby Manor maybe two dozen times and I remember seeing some pictures of Billy as a child. Of course, I saw the picture of him the papers were showing."

Davis held up a photo. "Here he is at eighteen, Natalie, and this is the more recent photo you saw in the press. It's magnified and a bit blurry, but he looks more or less like this now. He's thirty, hardened and seasoned by eight months of combat in Syria. Why does he want to kill you? I'd say he believed the rumors that you were responsible. He isn't likely to give up, so we've got to find him before he comes back at you. They say he goes by the name Khalid now."

Natalie looked down at the photo of a handsome, fresh-faced eighteen-year-old, happy and excited, starting out a life filled with promise. Odd, he didn't look a thing like his father. Then she looked closely at the photo of the grown man. He was no longer fresh-faced; he looked gaunt, resolute, his skin etched by the sun, his eyes opaque, hardened, she thought, by the savagery and death around him. She handed the photo back to Davis.

Savich said, "He took a big risk coming into the country. His passport was flagged, both here and in England, and there's no record of him coming through customs. Homeland Security is all over that now, as you can imagine. We're scouring the area for where William—Billy—Khalid—could be holed up, probably in an out-of-the-way motel somewhere locally.

"According to the surgeon who took care of his bullet wound, he'll be down for only a couple of days, if he's lucky."

Perry still held her mother. She said, "If he took such a risk coming here, he must not have a single doubt in his mind that Mom caused his father's death."

Natalie said, "George's son believed the tabloids? Why didn't Billy simply call me, ask me what happened? He's not a boy, he's an adult. Why?"

"He's a disturbed man, Natalie," Savich said. "George knew that very well. He called his son three times the week before he died, probably trying to convince Billy to come home. Once that picture came out, it became dangerous for Billy in Syria. I'm thinking it was easier for Billy to blame you rather than himself."

Natalie said, "I wonder if he could be convinced his father was murdered rather than driven to suicide by me."

Davis said, "I wouldn't count on it."

"No, let's not," Perry said. "Mom, you and I are going to fly to Hawaii, under assumed names, or maybe Bali or Australia. What do you think?"

Incredibly, Natalie laughed. "A fine idea, but do you know what I'm doing in about three hours? More interviews with the major news networks, and then with the BBC. I have a live speech at the UN tomorrow morning, so I don't see Bali or Australia in my immediate future." She paused. "No, I'm not going to disappoint the president. I've got top-notch security, and an important job to do. William or no William, I'm going to be on my way to the United Nations tomorrow morning."

60

Marilyn's B&B
Bowie, Maryland
Sunday, early evening

He wasn't in nearly as much pain as he had been that October evening last year when a trainee, a sixteen-year-old boy from Beirut, had accidently set off a bomb too close to him and he'd been thrown a good six feet against a pile of rocks and felt like his guts had been punched in. He'd broken his leg then, and it hadn't set right.

He lifted off the bandage and lightly laid his fingertips over the neat row of stitches on his side. Only slight swelling, only a bit of heat. The small blood collection that showed purple beneath the wound was expected and would fade. But there was no sign of infection. The antibiotics were working fine. He scratched around the stitches. It felt good because it itched already, and it didn't feel particularly tender. He smeared more antibiotic ointment over the wound, then flattened down a new bandage. He took two pain pills and laid back down on his bed, closed his eyes.

The doctor had done an excellent job since he hadn't wanted to die. He'd seemed to be a good man who didn't deserve to die because he'd had the bad luck to be home and alone.

He wondered if the doctor had helped them identify him as William Charles McCallum. He knew they would, sooner or later. It made no difference. If he was digging his own grave as well as Mrs. Black's, so be it.

He shouldn't have gone out so soon, nor should he have performed the postures of the salat, the ritual prayer. It wasn't required of an injured man. He would rest now, a day more, maybe two; that was all he needed.

He heard a knock on his door, grabbed the Beretta 418 from beneath his pillow, bought off a hood in Baltimore the week before. He felt the stitches pull and moved slowly.

"Mr. Garber? It's Marilyn. Would you care for some dinner?"

He wasn't hungry, but he knew he had to eat. He tucked the gun back beneath his pillow. "Yes, thank you, Ms. Marilyn." She was a big woman, angular and nosy. He'd bet if she could, she'd sneak into his room, see what she could find. He'd left a sign on the door saying he was sleeping and wasn't to be disturbed, and hoped that would keep her outside. "Would you please put a tray right outside the door? I'd appreciate it."

He tried to speak in an American accent hinting of a childhood in the South. He thought he sounded down-home, but he couldn't be sure. Still, no reason to announce himself as British. He was glad Marilyn hadn't seemed to notice.

"Not a problem, Mr. Garber. I'll bring it right up for you. I hope you feel better. Do you have the flu? Would you like me to contact a physician for you?"

"No, thank you, Ms. Marilyn. I need rest and your delicious cooking. Thank you."

He heard her heavy footsteps retreating away from the door, past the two other bedrooms, down the single flight of stairs, and back to her kitchen.

There were two other couples staying at the B&B, both older, both out all day, sightseeing, he supposed. He'd heard one couple arguing through the walls.

His stomach rumbled. When he heard her call out again that she had his tray, he thanked her once more, asked her to leave it, and waited to hear her hulking steps back down the stairs. He swung his legs over the side of the bed and gingerly rose. He stretched carefully, only a little, not too much, and walked to the door. He listened, heard nothing. He opened the door to see the tray covered with a large sheet of aluminum foil. He smelled spaghetti and garlic bread. Good, he needed the calories.

He watched TV while he ate, scanned the news stations for any stories about Mrs. Black or her attacker. He was happy to see no leads were mentioned, that he had not been identified, at least publicly.

He saw Natalie Black being interviewed on three channels, by the usual talking heads. Not a single one of them seemed to doubt any part of the story she was telling, the credulous fools. The showed a clip of her meeting with the British prime minister, all big smiles. They didn't ask her why she was gracing them with an interview, tried instead to outdo one another with the warmth of their reception of the damsel in distress. She was good, yes, he'd give her that, very good indeed, smooth and believable.

Only he knew the whole truth, only he had heard his father's breaking voice when he told him on his sat phone that he simply didn't see how he could marry Natalie now, that he knew it would ruin her career and he simply couldn't do that to her, not after his photo had been published. He heard the pain and soul-deep anguish in his father's voice. And what could he say? That what he was doing was righteous? That he had nothing to be sorry for, that he was fighting in a just war against a tyrant and a murderer

of his own people as well as his own wife's
family, a war he'd volunteered to join
because his conscience demanded it?
He'd told his father this many times, and
then the photograph of him in the tabloid—
if he hadn't known the truth, he would
believe he was looking at a terrorist, just
as the British people now believed. What
was amazing was that his father didn't
blame him. His father wanted him home,
out of harm's way, but he didn't blame
him. And that was how they'd left it at the
end of that last call—his father trying to
come to grips with what he was going to
do and assuring his son, as he always
did, that he loved him.

Then Natalie Black's email had appeared
in the British tabloid and his father was
dead. There was no doubt in his mind
that she was responsible for his father's
killing himself, that she'd driven him to it.
His father had loved her, would have
willingly given his life for her, but she'd broken their engagement to protect herself in
an email! And then she'd leaked it to the
press. It was unconscionable. He hated

her more than the U.S. government, whose operatives he was sure had been taking photographs of him and his closest friends in Syria. Why they'd leaked his picture to the tabloids he didn't know, and he didn't really care. He didn't care about their unending petty intrigues and machinations on the sidelines of this bloody war, that they should be fighting, didn't really care his life would be in danger if he was ever able to return to Syria because his former friends knew now he was a peer of the English realm, and he was anathema to them. He barely cared that the relationship with his wife and family in Hamburg was strained to the breaking point because they had found out who he really was on the television. He cared only that his father was dead and that bitch who'd supposedly loved him had driven him to kill himself. An email! A soulless, dismissive email that bitch had sent him. He'd failed before, but he wouldn't fail again.

When Khalid Al-Jabiri—William McCallum —finished chewing on the last meatball, he knew exactly what he was going to do.

61

**Perry Black's condo
Sunday evening**

Perry was looking at photos of Colin
Kaepernick taken with fans at the game
in London with the Jaguars this past
October, and she smiled. The English
loved him—understandable, since he was
cute, well, downright sexy, and he looked
different enough to fascinate. And all
those tattoos—they fascinated the English
as well. Perry wondered what Colin would
think of his tats in twenty-five years or so,
say, when his own son graduated from
high school.

She laughed at herself. Who cared
about twenty-five years from now? He
was young and that was wonderful, even
with all its stupidities. And talk about
stupidities, look at her. She had this guy
sleeping on her sofa she hadn't known

existed a week ago and yet here he was, protecting her and giving her grief. She had to admit he appealed to her right down to her toes.

She realized she wasn't concentrating, looked at her watch, turned off her notebook, and flicked on the TV. It was time.

The man himself came out of the kitchen, wearing jeans, boots, and a white shirt rolled up to his elbows, his Glock on a clip at his waist, a cup of tea in each hand. The whole package was as potent as a guy in a sparkling white navy dress uniform. She frowned at him. "I see I'm starting to train you pretty well. Shut up, sit down, and watch with me."

He merely grinned at her, handed her a cup of tea, and slouched beside her on the sofa, his feet plopped up atop a pile of magazines on her coffee table. In another minute, Edward Rose of Fox News was welcoming her mother in the studio here in Washington. Her mom looked great, in charge as usual, Perry thought, dressed in a navy-blue suit and a white blouse with a multicolored scarf that showed off her vivid hair. Perry sipped her tea and sat forward.

Rose said, "Ambassador Black, thank you for being here tonight. And I must say we all as a nation are happy to see you are looking well. There have been news reports of an assassination attempt on you at your home as recently as this past Friday. Can you verify this and tell us what is being done to find the person or people responsible for these continuing attacks on you?"

So there would be no more questions about her lying, Natalie thought, no more hints she was making anything up. After Friday night, she would be treated as a brave victim, a heroine. She remembered Hooley's blood on her pajamas, the gut-wrenching fear and anger. She looked at Edward Rose's carefully made-up handsome face with the touch of gray at his temples, and into his sincere blue eyes. She smiled. "I'm not at liberty to discuss the details of an ongoing investigation, but I will say, though, that the president and I both have confidence the

FBI will find the person or people behind these attacks."

"Attacks, Ambassador Black. You were also attacked in England, were you not?"

"Yes, that's right. There was a hit-and-run attack on me there that Scotland Yard is investigating. I have been assured they are cooperating closely with the FBI."

"And we all hope they succeed. Ambassador Black, I understand you will be speaking tomorrow morning at the United Nations. Will you be discussing your thoughts about these events on that world stage?"

Natalie smiled. "No, that will not be part of my address. I will not be asking the UN to take up my personal troubles. Tomorrow I will be doing my job, as always. The State Department has asked me to address the General Assembly about the status of bilateral tariff reductions we've been exploring"—she spoke fluently and quickly, expecting Rose to interrupt her if she gave him the chance. It was "dead air" time for Fox, the concession to her the network had to make before Edward Rose could continue asking her questions the viewers really wanted to hear.

When she closed, he said, "I imagine many of the UN representatives will want to know about all your personal difficulties, Ambassador Black, as do many of our viewers."

She shook her head. "I tend to doubt that, Mr. Rose."

"How will you deal with those questions if asked?"

"I'll tell them what I'm telling you, that all the weight of the United States government and the FBI are behind me."

"Ambassador Black, Viscount George McCallum, your fiancé, his death marked the beginning of these attacks on you, did it not?"

She let a punch of grief pass, then answered, "George McCallum was a wonderful man. His death was a great loss to me. Scotland Yard is investigating how and why that accident occurred. There is speculation his death and the attacks on my life may be connected, but

I don't know how or why." She hadn't meant to say that; it gave away too much. To her surprise and relief, Rose let it go.

Instead, Rose brought up the press release of William's photo, identifying him as an insurgent fighting in Syria. "Two weeks before the viscount's tragic death, is that correct? And the rumors of your own culpability began?"

Natalie said, "That's correct. William Charles McCallum is now Viscount Lockenby himself after his father's death. We understand he was seen fighting in Syria against the Assad regime. That is a conflict with many factions, and, of course, a great tragedy.

"Since I have not been in touch with William—indeed, I've never met him—I have no personal information to offer as to his current whereabouts or his intentions." She looked directly into the camera. "I do know William loved his father and he grieves as deeply as I do. I hope he will contact me so that we may grieve together. I hope he stays safe."

"And you stay safe as well, Ambassador

Black."

"I'll certainly do my best. You know, Mr. Rose, some of the English people still like to refer to us as Yanks. And one of the things they know about us is that we don't run from threats."

Edward Rose wanted more, but he had run out of time. He thanked her. It was over.

Perry turned off the TV and went online to read some of the early buzz the interview had already started on YouTube and Twitter. "She's got one more interview tonight. Then it's on to New York and the UN, with Aunt Arliss paving her way."

Davis was sitting back on the sofa, his arms loose at his sides, his eyes closed, his head leaned against the cushions. He said, "I love your mother."

"I do, too," Perry said. The front window exploded inward. A bullet smashed the vase on the side table next to Davis.

62

Before they could move, bullets crashed through the front window, another hitting the coffee table, a third hitting the wall above his head. Davis jumped on Perry, knocked her to the floor, covered her.

A semiautomatic, probably a rifle, Davis thought, as more bullets hit the wall over their heads. He said against her forehead, "Don't move, you hear me?" He got to his feet, his Glock in his hand, raced crouched over across the room, and flipped off the lights. He pressed against the side of the front door, listening, and waited. Perry stayed where she was. He could hear her breathing.

He leaned over and unlocked the door, shoved it open hard and fast, and flattened his belly to the floor.

More bullets shattered a mirror on the hallway wall, blew out the lovely etched-glass panels on either side of the front door. He heard Perry move. "Perry, no, stay perfectly still. I know you're thinking about your Kimber in the bedroom, but forget it. Stay put, face against the floor."

He heard her fierce voice. "I'm calling nine-one-one. Stay put yourself, and be careful, you hear me?"

Davis didn't answer; he was looking out into the darkness. It was now dead silent. Who was out there? It was time to push. He leaned up and turned on the porch light, and fired off his entire magazine at the bushes nearby, fanning back and forth low to the ground.

He heard it—across the yard maybe, forty feet away, a muffled hiss, like a snake. Had he hit the guy?

Davis shoved a new magazine in the Glock, elbow-crawled out the front door, jumped to his feet, and ran, firing his Glock toward where he'd heard the sound. He stopped behind an oak tree and listened. The gunfire had sounded battlefield heavy, loud, sharp, and he knew a dozen neighbors had called 911. The shooter knew it, too. He couldn't stay around much longer. Davis leaned out from behind the tree, scanning for movement.

A single bullet clipped off the bark not three inches from his face. He fell belly flat to the ground, didn't move.

"Davis?"

She didn't sound scared, she sounded mad. Amazing. He called out, "Don't come out, Perry. The guy's still somewhere out here. The cops will be here in a couple of minutes."

"More like a couple of seconds, I hope. You're okay, right?"

"Yes, stay put."

They heard sirens coming.

Lights were going on all over the neighborhood, but no one appeared in their doorways or their porches just yet. They were peeking out from behind curtains, around cracked-open doors, waiting for the cops. "The shooter's got to run from those sirens, Perry. Keep down."

"That idiot destroyed my beautiful Tiffany lamp. And the etched-glass panels beside the front door? Shattered, both of them. Do you know how much I paid for those? They were a gift to me from myself when Mike Ditka called me to thank me for a story I'd done on him and the Super Bowl Bears from long ago.

"I'd like to kick his tonsils into his brain. Who was it, did you see?" **No,** she thought, it couldn't be William. He was wounded, hiding somewhere.

"I didn't see him, but I may have hit him, I don't know."

Perry came running up to him, grabbed his arm. "What did you do? How could you let this happen?"

He couldn't answer her because three cop cars screeched to a halt ten feet away, men and women were shouting as they bounded out, guns trained on him. Davis dropped his Glock and shot his hands over his head, waving his creds. He yelled, "FBI agent! Someone fired on us. FBI!"

Since the cops weren't stupid, they kept their weapons trained on him and Perry, and came steadily closer. He called out, "This is Perry Black. I'm guarding her!

The shooter's getting away. Find him!"

At a nod from the sergeant, cops fanned out into the neighborhood, shouting to neighbors to get back inside and turn the lights out. Sergeant Woollcott, carrying twenty more pounds that he should, checked Davis's creds and holstered his gun. He said in a cheery voice, "If the guy's still out there, my people will find him. Both of you are still alive, and that's got to be good, right, Agent Sullivan?"

Davis didn't have a chance to agree with him because Perry had grabbed his arm and was shaking him. "You turkey! You absolute mutton brain, really, how could you let this happen?"

He frowned down at her. "I couldn't prevent the guy from shooting at us, Perry."

"No, not that, I mean your face. You're bleeding."

"She's right, boy," Sergeant Woollcott said. "Now I've got some light, I see you're alive but you're not looking pretty. The paramedics will fix you up."

What with all the shooting, Davis knew

the paramedics, two women and a man, were expecting to see a slaughter. But all they'd get was his bloody face.

One of the paramedics ushered him inside the condo. She stepped gingerly over a crashed lamp, sat him down, positioned him under the light of the small reading lamp that had escaped destruction, and got to work. The alcohol burned, but he kept his mouth shut, aware that Perry was standing close, her arms crossed over her chest, daring him, he imagined, to make a sound. "Hmmm, it really looked impressive, but fact is, there's nothing much here. Looks like a bit of oak bark sliced you. A bit of iodine, some Steri-Strips, and you'll be good to go. We heard there was a war on out here. Lucky nobody was really hurt."

The iodine hurt, but he didn't move, didn't speak.

Perry, her sarcasm so heavy Davis was surprised it didn't flatten the paramedic, said, "Sorry we couldn't oblige you."

The woman waved her hand, impervious. "I prefer it this way, darling," she said, and continued to examine the thin slice on Davis's cheek.

"Would you like me to get you a Band-Aid?"

The paramedic grinned over at her. "Nah, we came loaded for bear, so we can handle this little cub here, no problem. Hey, Curry, want to bring over that dressing kit for our FBI agent here?"

"Look at my living room, Davis. My notebook—it's wrecked. The insurance company isn't going to be happy."

63

**Savich's house
Sunday night**

Sherlock snuggled in, pressed her cheek to his neck. Her curly hair tickled his nose, a familiar feeling, both comforting and unsettling, and he breathed in the faint rose scent that always stirred him up. He hugged her close. "We need to sleep." He kissed the top of her head.

"I know, and believe me, I'm so tired I'm ready to fall over, but I'm wired, can't seem to shut off my brain, much less slow it down. First Blessed last night, and tonight someone fires on Davis and Perry. I hate guns. Well, and motorcycles, too."

"Ben Raven has the neighborhood locked down, Sherlock. Blessed won't come back here again, not tonight. He's probably afraid of you now, after being in that grocery storage room with you and all the flying cans and shelves that weighed a ton when they toppled over."

He felt her mouth curve up. "Now, that was something. Too bad Blessed didn't get pinned under one of those shelves. I can't believe he was dolled up as a little old lady. I wonder where he got the clothes. Off a clothesline, I hope, and not off someone he killed. He's a nightmare, Dillon."

"The operative description here, sweetheart, is failed nightmare. We're still here and Blessed won't be."

"But I don't know how I'm going to get to sleep, Dillon. Too many crazy people tromping through my brain."

"What if I tell you a story about me you haven't heard yet? That's right, rest your head on my chest and close your eyes and I'll get you to sleep in no time. That includes your hand. Your hand can't be strolling downward. Really. You've got to help me out here."

"Maybe my fingers can find us a better way to relax. You think?"

He had to admit it, she had a point.

A half-hour later, Savich pulled the covers over them, kissed her forehead, squeezed her tight. "Ready to sleep now?"

She heard the lazy satisfaction in his voice, and lightly punched her fist in his belly. "Not yet. I want to hear that bedtime story you were going to tell me."

"Well, then, I'll tell you," he said, and pulled her against him. "When I was fifteen years old, my junior high school football coach, Mr. Jeffries, was in a bad car accident. A drunk driver, we heard, ran him into a bridge abutment. He went right over it, twenty feet down into the Beaver River, and you know what? He managed to get out of the car and swim to the surface. A passerby saw the whole thing and called nine-one-one. The doctors said it was a miracle he survived the fall, even more of a miracle he was able to climb out of the car with all his internal injuries and broken bones. And the biggest miracle, it looked like he might pull through. My dad went with me to visit him in the hospital. I'll tell you, to see my coach, a man about my own age now and strong as a bull, always in charge, all broken and bandaged, even his head— he looked nearly dead to me. They had sedated him and put him on a respirator. Only his eyes were open.

"His wife, Mrs. Jeffries, was standing on the opposite side of the bed when we walked up and looked down at him. I wanted to run, but I was with my dad, so I didn't. She suggested we leave, that he needed to sleep, but he saw me, recognized me. I don't know why, but I took his hand, and I waited. He looked over at his wife, then he looked at me, right into my eyes. His fingers tightened in my hand. And I knew what he was trying to communicate, as if he were speaking to me, clear as day. Of course, he wasn't speaking, wasn't even moving his mouth, since that hissing regulator in his mouth was breathing for him."

"What was he saying, I mean, what was he thinking to you?"

"That he was afraid of his wife, that she'd hired someone to run him off the bridge. He'd heard her on her cell phone when she believed he was still unconscious, talking to someone, telling him she was real mad because she'd wasted five thousand dollars.

"I remember I wasn't scared when I first heard his voice in my head. Surprised, yes, but then it felt like the most natural thing in the world. His wife was pacing. She wanted us gone. I was afraid she'd try to kill him then and there as soon as we left."

Her voice was getting low, a bit slurred. "This had never happened before?"

"No, first time. I squeezed his hand, so he'd know I'd tell my dad. On our way out, Mrs. Jeffries thanked us for coming and said she was sorry her husband hadn't been with it enough to thank us himself. But she didn't sound sorry at all.

"I knew the cops wouldn't believe me if I told them that, so I told my dad everything on the elevator back down to the hospital lobby."

He waited for her to ask what happened, but she didn't. She was down for the count. He kissed the top of her head, wishing Sean was in his bed down the hall and everything was back to normal.

"What happened then, Dillon?"

So she wasn't all the way out. "My dad never doubted me for a second. We went back up to the hospital room and he informed Mrs. Jeffries that he'd be assigning a guard to protect her husband. He held her there until he got a warrant to take her cell, one of those big suckers everyone used back in the day, and check her cell phone records, and sure enough, there was a series of calls back and forth from the man she'd hired. Later, they discovered there'd been another man in the background, a lover. My dad arrested her himself, hauled her to the New York FBI Field Office at Federal Plaza, before turning her over to the police. My coach lived, remarried two years later and has three grown kids now. He's still coaching."

He felt her mouth curve against his shoulder. She was finally asleep a couple minutes later, and soon Savich was, too. He didn't dream about the crazies who'd kept Sherlock awake, he dreamed of a long-ago evening in a man's hospital room when he'd realized what was possible.

64

Criminal Apprehension Unit
Hoover Building
Monday morning

Janice Hobbs poked her head into Savich's office. "I got blood."

"Blood from Perry's yard?" Davis said, right behind her. "I was right? I wounded the shooter last night?"

"Yep, one of the officers found a couple of bloody leaves on the ground right where you thought it would be. Had to look close, though. I had enough to type, all ready for a DNA match. We'll run it through the database, of course, but have you got a live suspect handy?"

Davis said, "Not yet, but we'll have him in twenty-four hours, okay?"

"Yeah, it'll wait, but matching DNA is like sex, you know? You get all ready, all excited, but it's no good without two people. Perry Black was there with you, right? Okay, I'll need cheek swabs from both of you to cover all the bases. I won't find my dancing partner, so you gotta make my day, Davis. Get me the bozo that'll match. Hey, I like that Band-Aid on your face. Those leopard spots look cute, like you're a little kid who got banged up on the jungle gym." Janice punched Davis's arm and took off, like she was wearing roller skates, waving to agents in the unit as she glided by. She called out as she disappeared out the door, "Hey, Davis, did you get the Sex Pistols mix I sent you?"

"Yeah, I'm already singing it in my sleep," Davis called back, but Janice was already halfway to the elevators.

Savich smiled, shook his head. "So you have someone in mind to bring in, Davis?"

Davis settled himself into a chair across from Savich. He said, "I'd bring in William Charles McCallum, if he were in reach. Has there been any word from Scotland Yard?"

"The car they tracked down appears to

be a dead end. The owner isn't talking, or doesn't know anything more. They've had no luck running down the identity William is using, and neither has Homeland Security. We can't exclude him as the attacker last night, but he's got a fresh bullet wound, and it's hard to see any strong reason for him to go after Perry like that. Sure, Natalie is well protected now and harder for him to reach, but Perry had nothing to do with what happened in England."

"I know it wasn't him. He's an experienced fighter in a bloody civil war, an expert at exploiting surprise and position. If he was the shooter and he'd wanted Perry or me or both of us dead last night, we'd be dead. Whoever that was last night squandered his chance by shooting up Perry's condo like an arcade. I suppose it could have been a hired thug who didn't know what he was doing. Or someone else entirely, with a different agenda."

Savich said, "What agenda would that be?"

"To terrify Perry? Perhaps to separate her from her mother? That's an agenda, but to what purpose?"

Savich gave him a long look. "Has it occurred to you the shooter may have been trying to separate Perry from you? Didn't you say most of the bullets hit closer to you than to Perry?"

Davis said, "All right, then. Day Abbott comes to mind. He's been calling Perry all week. She's known him since she was born, more or less, and now he's got it into his head she's going to marry him. I've been letting talking with him slide because Perry speaks very highly of him, and why would he threaten her? After last night, though, we have to interview him. There might be something there. Remember Carlos knew the alarm code to Perry's condo. It's very likely Abbott would know that code. And he knew how much she loved her Harley." He shook his head. "Was he hoping she would turn to him for help?"

Savich said, "The thought he'd be so jealous of you to put Perry at risk at the same time—it'd be insane obsession. If he's that far gone, he hides it well. Still, we should see what he has to say. Be careful, though. I get a sense you don't like him. Does he have a reason to think you're poaching on his turf?"

"I don't have any turf here. He doesn't, either, only he doesn't know it yet. Listen, Savich, sure, Perry is great, but nothing like that has happened. As for my not liking Abbott, who cares? It doesn't matter what I think of the man."

"All right, go talk to him. Take Griffin with you. Remember who the man's mother is, Davis. Tread lightly."

Davis nodded and looked down at his watch. "By this time, Natalie should be giving her speech to the General Assembly at the UN."

"An interesting venue the president picked to bring her back in the public eye. She was good with the talking heads last night. They liked her, empathized with her. So did I. I expect she'll have them all on her side in a few days." Savich typed in the URL of the direct video feed from the UN as he spoke.

They watched Secretary of State Arliss Abbott standing in front of the General Assembly, looking around at faces, acknowledging delegates she recognized before she spoke. She gave a fulsome introduction of Natalie Black, U.S. ambassador to the United Kingdom, in a strong, ringing voice. She praised her friend's courage and her outstanding service, even in the face of an assassination attempt at her home three nights before. She left little doubt they were about to hear from an American icon.

When the applause died down, Natalie thanked her and spoke for eight minutes, never mentioning the attack on her life. She spoke clearly and concisely about concrete initiatives to expand trade with emerging nations. Some of her speech was rather arcane, and none of it was entirely new, but the delegates seemed glued to her every word.

When she finished, there was more sustained applause, obviously meant to honor her. Some of the representatives from the emerging nations she'd mentioned applauded along with the rest but looked frankly bewildered at the warm response to her speech.

Davis scratched at the leopard Band-Aid from Perry's medicine cabinet she'd plastered on his face that morning. "I really do love that woman," he said.

65

Harlow, Benson, and Lerner
1980 Avenue K, Ashland Building
Washington, D.C.
Monday, noon

According to the very young, very pretty receptionist, Ms. Liu, Mr. Abbott was in his office, but he was very busy and expected in a meeting in forty-five minutes. She stammered a bit as she spoke, kept sneaking looks at Griffin. Davis was used to that. Women from fifteen to eighty seemed to fall all over Griffin at the sight of him.

"Mr. Abbott may be between clients, Agents. S-shall I see if—"

Griffin smiled at her and she simply stopped talking. "No problem, Ms. Liu. We'll announce ourselves."

Davis knew Ms. Liu was staring after Griffin all the way down the hall. He said,

"I'll bet Anna loves that." Anna was the DEA agent Griffin had met on a case not long ago in Maestro, Virginia. "Loves what?" Griffin asked, pausing for a moment to glance at one of the sepia photographs of 1850s steamships lining the walls.

Davis gave a hand wave back to the reception area. "Shall I give Ms. Liu your phone number when she asks?"

Griffin said matter-of-factly, "Anna is laid-back for a woman who carries a gun. She'll get in anyone's face if they cross her, but with me she's an angel—actually, I get my way about half the time."

A guy couldn't ask for more than that, Davis thought. Davis knocked on a door with three-inch gold letters that spelled out **dayton everard abbott**.

"Come in, Cindy."

Davis opened the door, stepped in, looked at Day Abbott across the expanse of rich pale gray carpet. He looked for some sign Abbott had been the shooter at Perry's condo last night. A bandage somewhere beneath his beautifully cut suit coat where Davis had shot him? But Day Abbott looked perfectly healthy and bewildered at seeing them. Then a look of fear leached the color out of his face. He jumped to his feet, his eyes on Davis. "It's Perry, isn't it? Did you let something happen to her?"

Davis said quickly, "No, Mr. Abbott, Perry is all right. But we were shot at last night at her condo."

"Why didn't she call me? She should have told me. Why wasn't it on the news? Who was it who shot at her? Have you caught him?"

"Let's sit down, Mr. Abbott," Griffin said. Once he and Davis were seated across from Day Abbott's beautiful antique mahogany desk, Davis said, "Perry really is all right. I'm all right as well. The shooter missed both of us."

"Did you catch the man?"

"No, not yet."

"You swear she wasn't hurt?"

"She's fine." But not the Tiffany lamp she loved, he thought, a gift she'd told him Day's own mother had given her when she graduated from college.

Day Abbott was pale, his hands fisted. "But why? It's like that bloody note—someone's trying to frighten her, trying to get to her mother through her. You know it, I know it, why can't you put a stop to this?"

"We're going to do exactly that," Davis said. "Mr. Abbott, you've known Perry for a very long time and—"

"Yes, I have. We grew up together. A nd we're going to get married and spend the rest of our lives together." He sat forward, his hands clasped in front of him. "You've been guarding Perry since last Wednesday after her Harley was trashed, right?"

Davis nodded.

"But you still haven't learned anything at all useful."

Davis ignored that. "Mr. Abbott, would you please tell us your whereabouts last night around ten o'clock?"

"Me? You're asking if I was the one who shot at Perry? That's insane. I love Perry. Why would I want to kill her?"

Griffin said, "Actually, Mr. Abbott, more of the bullets were aimed at Agent Sullivan."

Day Abbott seamed his lips in a flash of rage. "So now you have me gunning after FBI agents? I don't particularly like him, but I don't want to kill him, either."

Davis eyed this sleek young cannibal, probably a future congressman. He didn't particularly like him, either. He knew Perry hadn't told him yet she wasn't going to marry him, felt a moment of sympathy for him about it, until he saw the gleam of contempt in Day's eyes. "We don't think you're involved, Mr. Abbott. This is a necessary formality. Tell us where you were last evening."

Abbott steepled his fingertips together, tapped them to his chin. "Last night? I had planned, of course, to spend the evening with Perry, but that didn't happen." He looked at Davis for a long moment, then said, "Turns out she would have been safer with me last night than with you." He got no response, and shrugged. "I was with two friends, watching Mrs. Black's interview on Fox. I'll have Cindy give you their information."

Davis said, "You've known Perry all her life, as you have her mother. You and Perry were raised nearly as brother and sister."

Day said stiffly, "We were. That was a long time ago. Now we're adults. Now things are different. Look, Agent Sullivan, you should focus on who's trying to kill Ambassador Black, it will be the same person, then this will all be over and we can get back to our lives. Then you won't have to be near Perry anymore."

Griffin wasn't blind to Day Abbott's jealousy. He obviously wanted Davis out of her life and out of his sight. "Do you own a gun, Mr. Abbott?" he asked.

"What? A gun? Of course not. What kind of question is that?"

Griffin continued. "Again, a formality, Mr. Abbott. But your father owns a Smith and Wesson, right? Did he give it to you when he moved out and left the state, or did he forget it, leave it here?"

66

Day Abbott shrugged. "I remember my dad's gun from when I was a kid, but after he left, I never saw it again. I thought about it once or twice over the years and assumed he'd taken it with him. A lot of people own guns. How do you even know about my dad's gun?"

Davis said, "Your father registered the Smith and Wesson some thirty years ago. Do you know where it is?"

"No." Abbott gave Davis a full-bodied sneer. "The person who shot at you and Perry last night—did you get hit? Is that why you're wearing that dick Band-Aid on your face?"

Davis grinned at the man who looked about ready to burst out of his beautiful suit and leap on him. **Ready to make things personal, Day?** Davis said, "What, you don't like a jungle theme? It's from Perry's medicine cabinet, of course. She smoothed it down herself."

Griffin, his voice as smooth as the teak railing on his dad's prized sailboat, said, "The gun used last night, it was the same caliber as your father's pistol. To cut off this thread, we'd like to check it for ballistics, if you have it somewhere."

"But—"

Davis said over him, "You speak to your father often, Mr. Abbott?" Davis began writing in a black notebook, aware Abbott was watching him.

"Every week," Day said. "Thursday night, even when he's traveling or I'm traveling. My parents split up a long time ago. When he left, my dad made me promise we'd always speak once a week. We have. It's a habit. He's my dad."

Day got slowly to his feet. He was looking at them like they were a couple low-class slugs. He said, "Well, are we done here?"

Griffin said, "Perhaps you could tell us why you think all of this is happening, Mr. Abbott."

Day leaned over, splayed his palms on

the desktop. "I believe, as does my mother, that Mrs. Black unwittingly hurt someone in England and that this someone wants revenge. About the threatening notes to Perry, the shots fired at her last night, I can only think it's meant to hurt her mother." He straightened. "I really can't do your jobs for you, Agents. I know of no one who would want to hurt Perry or her mother here in the United States. Now, I have nothing more to say to either of you. I want you to leave now."

Davis said, "Mr. Abbott, what does your mother think of your marriage plans with Perry?"

Day was silent for a moment. "My mother may very nearly rule the known world, but she doesn't rule me." He caught himself. "It's obvious Perry doesn't fit the mold of the lovely young professional woman, what with her riding around on her Harley like a wannabe Hells Angel. I know my mother thinks Perry's behavior is her dad's fault. Mom said Brundage Black was selfish, that he heaped all his attention, all his pride, on the little daughter he made into his clone, and he never let her go. I don't expect you to understand any of that, Agent, since you hardly know Perry. But realize this. I do love her and she loves me. As for my mother, she'll come around."

Davis pulled a small plastic envelope from his pocket. "Would you mind giving us a cheek swab?"

Day stared at him as if he'd grown another ear.

"It won't hurt," Davis said.

Griffin saw the pulse pounding in Day Abbott's neck. His face was flushed, anger flowing hot and heavy. "You want my DNA? You've got to be joking."

"Nope, not at all."

"You like throwing around your cop's weight, Sullivan? Intimidating people? You've been trying to drive a wedge between Perry and me all along, and that's why she hasn't returned my calls. You think she'd ever have anything to do with you? Once this is over, once you're out of her life, she'll come back to me and she'll never give you another thought."

His sneer was full-blown now. "I'll bet you couldn't take her out of the States, not on your cop's salary. Tell you what, Sullivan, I'll think of you when I take Perry to Cannes, while we're wandering the beaches, while I'm making love to her. Take your stupid swab and get out of my office. You're deluded if you think I'll give you my DNA."

Davis held it together, mostly, but his voice was flippant, and he knew he was goading Day Abbott. "No, not deluded; the FBI shrinks tested me, said I was good to go," Davis said. "Whether Perry ends up with you on the beach in Cannes or with me on the Champs-Élysées in Paris, we'll get there quicker if you give us your DNA. It's a simple cheek swab. We're going to be asking everyone involved in the case, everyone with access to Perry, to give a DNA sample willingly. If you do, you'll very likely be out of the running as our shooter last night. Here."

Day Abbott never looked away from Davis. "Get out, both of you."

"You want us to think you were firing

only at me last night?"

"I didn't shoot at you!"

"You're a smart guy, Mr. Abbott. You've got to see it's the way to go. If you're cleared, you may never have to see me again."

Day Abbott said, "I am exercising my rights, nothing more. I don't know anything about my father's Smith and Wesson. You have no basis for a warrant of any kind. You have absolutely no reason to be here now. I want no more of your harassment. Leave."

Davis continued holding out the Q-tip.

Day splayed his big hands on his desktop, leaned toward them again. He said, his voice low and vicious, "You're nothing but a yahoo, Sullivan, brandishing a gun. Perry won't fall for you. You're too low-class. You're spitting in the wind. Get out of here and take pretty boy with you."

Davis said to Griffin, "Well, truth be told, I wouldn't want him for my lobbyist." He saluted Day Abbott and strolled to the door, Griffin on his heels. They heard Day Abbott's thick, fast breathing behind them. Davis opened the door, turned back. "This could be your best chance to get back with Perry quickly. Otherwise, we might have to ask you down to the Hoover Building later for more questions."

Day Abbott shook his head, gave him a disgusted look. "You know what, Sullivan? You're a liar; I'm not. Give me the swab. Believe me, you and I will never talk again without my lawyer present."

Davis handed him the swab, watched him rub it on the inside of his cheek. He carefully slid it back into the bag.

"Thank you. Won't take very long to check this out," Davis said. "Hey, it didn't hurt, did it?"

Day stood behind his desk, arms crossed tight over his chest, holding himself still. That was the last look Davis got of the man who hated him now, and who happened to be the son of the secretary of state. Savich would not be pleased. Davis closed the door behind him, with no good-byes.

Davis stood against the mirrored elevator wall, his arms crossed over his chest. "All right, Griffin, what do you think of Mr. Day Abbott?"

Griffin said slowly, "Other than he's so jealous of you he'd like to drive a stake through your heart, he's probably a decent guy.

"I think he wants this over, and that's why he gave us the cheek swab. You know as well as I do he had nothing to do with the shooting last night. You never thought he did. I'm glad it didn't get physical. Even so, it wouldn't surprise me if he tells his mama two idiot agents were all over him."

Davis said, "Unfortunately, I agree with you. Hey, Abbott nailed you, though, pretty boy. Will I see you modeling under-wear in a magazine someday?"

Griffin laughed. "Nope, I'd make a crappy model. Except maybe for Anna."

67

**Criminal Apprehension Unit
Monday afternoon**

Savich was surprised it took his boss Jimmy Maitland several hours to call him. He put the delay down to the secretary of state being in transit from New York that morning. Davis and Griffin had filled him in on their interview with Day Abbott, starting with the good news about getting a DNA sample and an alibi from him for the previous night, which they could check on. But neither of them would quite meet his eyes. The only other good news Savich heard was that Davis hadn't slugged him. Savich asked him, "So he insulted you? How?"

"Let's see, he called me a low-class slug, a liar hiding behind his shield, basically a loser, that sort of thing," Davis said.

"So you lost control of the situation. Tell me that isn't what you had in mind all along, is it, Davis?"

"No," Davis said. "Yeah, it was a mistake."

Savich sat down, waved to the chairs in front of his desk. "Tell me about it."

Maitland said now to Savich over the phone, "Director Comey relayed a call from the secretary of state. She gave him an earful about Agents Sullivan and Hammersmith doing a number on her son this morning while they were interviewing him, said they were completely inappropriate. This is, alas, the secretary of state we're talking about here, Savich, a woman with so much mojo she gets our director on the phone and reams him out. Please tell me Madame Secretary has been misinformed."

"Sir, Sullivan and Hammersmith interviewed him about the attack on Perry Black's home last night, entirely appropriate, since Day Abbott is closely involved with her. I'm told it was Abbott who started with the insults. You know Davis, though, he's not very good at lying still while getting kicked, but he didn't let things get that far out of hand. We had Griffin along as a witness."

"Whatever happened, Secretary Abbott is royally pissed. If the interview was as tame as it sounds, then why would Abbott complain to his mother about Davis?"

"The short version is that Day Abbott wants to marry Perry Black and he's very jealous of Davis, and he's not above asking his mother to hurt him."

"I don't suppose Davis—no, I'm not going there. If this guy is jealous of Davis, that kind of bad blood won't go away." Savich heard his boss curse under his breath. "You know, he couldn't have picked a better way to hurt Davis's career. If there's a formal inquiry from State alleging he behaved unprofessionally, let his personal feelings get in the way, we'll have to pull him off the case, put him through a review process that will stay on his record. I really don't want this to happen. Take care of it, Savich, get things smoothed out, all right?"

"Yes, sir. I'll deal with it. About Davis—"

"Stop. I don't want to hear anymore. The secretary of state wants to see you and Davis in her office in, ah, thirty-two minutes. You want me along to run interference?"

"No, sir, but I think I'll take Sherlock with us. She might help cool the secretary down a bit. I'll let you know what happens."

"You know what?" Maitland said. "If my mom were the secretary of state, I'd call her, too."

68

Secretary of State's office
Harry Truman Building
Washington, D.C.

Thirty-one minutes later, Savich, Sherlock, and Davis finished clearing three different security checks, all fast, efficient, but not as polite as the White House. Davis was nervous, he admitted it to himself, as they moved step by step toward the seat of power, toward the woman who could ruin his career in the FBI. Savich had told him not to worry too much, to act properly deferential, and leave most of the talking to him.

They were shown into the richly paneled office of the secretary of state. Arliss Abbott was standing behind her desk when they entered, her arms crossed over her gray Armani-suited chest. She said nothing at all until the three of them were standing directly in front of her desk, like disruptive schoolkids in front of a headmaster to be disciplined. Behind her impressive desk was a wall of solid built-in wooden bookcases filled to overflowing with books and knickknacks, probably gifts from world leaders, and a dozen shining photographic moments with various heads of state. It wasn't an overly large office, small enough to be fitting for a servant of the people, but still, it announced power, tradition, and a big fist.

An older aristocrat of a man stood at her left. He had a long face, razor-sharp cheekbones, a thin nose, and boasted a beautiful salt-and-pepper mustache above his seamed lips, perfectly matching his styled hair. He gave off the subliminal **I'm smarter than you, richer than you, more important than you.** He didn't smile at them. He did not move from where he stood, merely nodded and introduced himself as Bernard Pearson Franklyn.

A much younger man, about Davis's age, stood behind him, obviously his subordinate in billable hours, judging by where he stood. He looked dramatic, no other way to put it, with his dark, liquid eyes and glossy black hair a bit on the long side. He wore a black turtleneck beneath a black blazer. He was a sharp package, the perfect distraction, Davis thought, for a living and breathing jury. He continued to smile when he introduced himself. Sasha Powers, and what kind of name was that? Davis wondered. Like his boss, Sasha did not offer to shake hands. These two were an impressive duo.

Arliss Abbott nodded to them, only a whisper of a smile on her face and none in her voice. "You're prompt, gentlemen. And who is this?"

Sherlock pulled out her creds and handed them to her. "It is a pleasure to meet you, Madame Secretary. I'm Agent Sherlock, FBI."

Arliss Abbott looked at Davis and held out her hand even though she knew very well who he was. Savich got his creds out, but she waved his away. "I know exactly who you are, Agent Savich."

She studied them, and looked at Sherlock. "And why are you here, Agent Sherlock?"

To protect them. She said, "Agent Savich believed I could be useful."

Arliss raised a brow. "In what way, Agent Savich?"

"She's been closely involved, ma'am. Her insights are invaluable."

Whatever that meant. Sherlock returned Arliss Abbott's gaze, waiting for her to move on. She had never before been in the presence of the secretary of state, didn't know what to expect of this woman with her obvious intelligence. She was fascinated to see how she would handle this meeting—like the professional negotiator she was or like a lioness protecting her cub? She looked briefly toward the two lawyers, Franklyn leaning against the secretary's desk, the theatrical young stallion Sasha Powers with his diamond stud standing behind him at attention.

Arliss said to Davis, "Agent Sullivan, when I met you last Tuesday night with

Ambassador Black, I did not take you for a bully."

No, you took me for something else entirely.

"Indeed, after Natalie explained why you accompanied her, she assured me you have her complete confidence to keep Perry safe. I understand you saved her life last night, is that correct?"

Davis nodded. "However, the assailant escaped."

"I am grateful nonetheless," Arliss said. "Will you tell me now how those events led you to turn around and confront my son in the fashion you did?"

A smooth and flawless segue, Sherlock thought.

"After the shooting last night, ma'am, interviewing your son was standard procedure. However, he became quite upset at the nature of the questions we needed to ask him—"

She rolled right over him. "You should have notified this office as a courtesy, Agent Sullivan. You should have made an appointment to see him to give him the opportunity for legal counsel. You did neither of these things. Instead, you arrived at my son's office with no prior notification, simply barged in and accused him of trying to murder the woman he is currently viewing as his future wife. Both he and I have reason to be outraged at that behavior, Agent Sullivan."

"Madame Secretary," Savich said, "I sent Agents Sullivan and Hammersmith to interview Mr. Abbott. It is not our procedure to notify anyone of prospective interviews. Let me assure you, however, that if we need to speak to Mr. Abbott again, I will see to it we notify your office.

"As to what happened this morning, I think there are differences between what Mr. Abbott told you and what actually happened."

"Oh? My son is now a liar?"

"No, ma'am. A difference in viewpoint, I'd say."

"My viewpoint, Agent Savich, is that by not notifying my son of your planned visit, and Agent Davis's tone being what it was, the interview smacked of an attempt to intimidate, even though viewing my son as a suspect in this tragedy is ridiculous. He has loved Perry his whole life; Natalie will verify that."

Her eyes went to Davis. "My son believes you had personal motives for your questions, your tone, and your behavior, Agent Sullivan, the reason being that you have feelings for Perry Black, the woman you have been assigned by the Bureau to protect. He believes you are jealous of him, and thus your attacks and your obvious animosity. What do you have to say for yourself, Agent?"

Davis wanted to tell her that her precious son was a jackass, that he'd been the one to attack. But he knew he shouldn't have retaliated, shouldn't have provoked him. What made it worse was that Davis also knew Perry had no intention of marrying Day Abbott. Davis had been unprofessional. He'd been wrong, and it burned.

He said, "I'm sorry, ma'am. Your son is right, my behavior did border on the unseemly. There were words between us, words that shouldn't have been spoken."

He drew a deep breath. "I promise you that will never happen again."

"For the simple reason that you will never again interview my son, Agent Sullivan, unless there is a prior appointment, his lawyers are present, and you aren't. Are we clear on that, Agent?"

"Yes, ma'am."

Savich said, "The Bureau will gladly stipulate to that, ma'am. Since none of us wish either Ambassador Black or her daughter to come to any harm, we must continue in a reasonable and logical way to pursue evidence."

Arliss gave him a long look. The two lawyers took this as their cue to speak.

Mr. Bernard Franklyn said, "Since you've mentioned the matter of pursuing evidence, Agent Savich, it is our position that the DNA sample you took from our client, Mr. Dayton Abbott, was illegally obtained." He turned to the young man behind him and gave a nod.

Sasha Powers gave them a blinding white smile. "The fact is, Agent Savich, that your department had no warrant for such an invasive request, and it appears that Mr. Abbott would never have agreed to provide the sample if he had not been coerced into doing so." His dark eyes settled on Davis. "Agent Sullivan himself has agreed he behaved inappropriately while obtaining it."

Savich said, "Mr. Abbott gave Agents Sullivan and Hammersmith a sample, after, admittedly, some discussion as to the reasons for the request. The DNA is already being analyzed and matched. What is important here is that because we have Mr. Abbott's DNA, we will shortly be able to exonerate him from any suspicion. Given this positive outcome, I see no reason why there would be any legal issues in the future about how the DNA sample was obtained."

Arliss said, "This is not a game of mutual intimidation, Agent Savich. Trust me that you wouldn't fare well if it were. I understand you have a job to do, that everyone in a case such as this has to be interviewed. My son is not a boy. He is a grown man and he will deal with this.

However, you are right. The DNA my son so imprudently provided you will clear him of any involvement.

"What happened this morning is unacceptable. I believe Agent Sullivan understands that. Since I do not wish to deprive Perry of Agent Sullivan's continued protection, I am willing to let this go for now, with all the assurances you've given me. You are all excused. Thank you for coming."

On their way out, Davis saw there were coffee cups and a beautiful jug of coffee sitting on a low table. They hadn't been offered any.

Savich was bemused. The secretary of state could have lopped off their heads, but instead she'd backed off.

He wondered if Davis understood how lucky he was.

69

Natalie Black's house
Late Monday afternoon

Blessed parked his stolen Honda in the trees down the road from Ambassador Natalie Black's mansion—and that's what he'd call it, one of those huge three-storied in-your-face barns of a place they used to build a hundred years ago, with a wraparound porch and so many chimneys and big windows he'd hate to be the one to have to clean them. It was painted blue with brown trim—only two colors. His mama's big Victorian back in Bricker's Bowl was painted five different colors she'd picked out herself, and she'd had each color freshened every year. This place wasn't as nice as his mama's—how could it be, since it had only two colors and needed a paint job? It had a big, important-looking gate, though, with a call box and a guard's station, for the big yahoos who lived in this hellhole of Washington. It was easier for them than actually doing something about the criminals who littered the streets. There were cameras, too, he saw, and men in dark suits at the gate and on the grounds. They were there to protect the big-shot ambassador Black, he knew, the woman he'd seen on the TV news shows.

Well, his mama had been a big shot, too, in Bricker's Bowl, but she hadn't closed herself in with a fancy high fence and a guard gate. Nope, she'd been welcoming, especially the local folk who had touched up the paint on the house every year, planted her spring flowers, and washed her Cadillac every week, with only a little nudging reminder from Blessed. He remembered the local teenagers, probably there on a bet, to gawk at that awesome house, remembered how afraid they were that they might get caught. He'd always liked that slick of fear he saw on all those faces. He wondered what had happened to his mama's house. He wondered what Mama's house looked like now. Were there strangers living there? Or maybe it was dark and moldy now, Grace's paintings all covered with dust.

The family graveyard behind the house had to still be there. He remembered how quiet and serene it was under its canopy of trees, which always kept the gravestones cool to the touch. Grace should be buried there, comfortable in the black loamy earth with his family, but he wasn't. Mama wasn't buried there, either, and that wasn't right. He missed his family. He missed the cheesecake his mama had served him and Grace every night.

He saw a light blue Ford moving past him. It was the ambassador's daughter— Perry Black, the sportswriter, and what sort of girl did something like that? He watched her gloved hand reach out, press the intercom button, since the guardhouse was empty. The gates swung smoothly open and the car went through, the daughter giving a little wave toward the camera.

Blessed pulled a bottle of water out of the Honda and drank deep.

He was cold again, even in his beautiful camel coat, and he stuck his hands in his pockets. He wasn't here for the girl, he was here for Savich. He'd be patient and wait.

Only a few minutes later, he saw the red Porsche, Savich's red Porsche. He knew they would come. He checked his watch. He had to know how long it would take him to get to Morganville.

70

Natalie hung up her suit, placed her heels in their box in the closet, and pulled on her sweats. All the interviews here in Washington, then the trip to New York and the appearance at the General Assembly that morning, and, finally, the horrible news that someone had tried to kill Perry last night, had drained her dry. She was exhausted, her brain numb. She wanted nothing more than to crawl into bed, bury herself in a pile of blankets, and escape into blankness. That wasn't going to happen. She couldn't fall asleep if she tried. Her brain would squirrel about madly with horrible visions of Perry lying dead, with a killer standing over her she couldn't make out, only a sinister shadow. She couldn't stand it.

She'd felt only relief and hope after she'd left the podium at the UN. Her speech had gone well and Arliss had been pleased. The president had called her, congratulated her. It had felt good. It was only on her way to JFK with two DS agents escorting her that she'd had time to call Perry. Perry had kept the news from her until then.

She realized she was shaking, and drew several deep, calming breaths. Falling apart wasn't an option; it wouldn't help anything. She had to get hold of herself. Perry and Davis were both fine. Perry would be here soon and tell her all about it.

She looked toward the bedroom window, remembering the gut-churning fear when George's son William had tried to climb into her room. She wondered if he'd seen Arliss introducing her at the UN, calling her an American heroine. Had he watched any of the interviews? Did he still believe she was responsible for his father's death?

Her cell phone rang. It was Connie, at the hospital with Hooley, telling her Hooley was better today and congratulating her on her interviews. Some good news, she thought. When she punched off, she called Perry again, got voice mail.

She stood, indecisive, in the middle of her bedroom, alternately looking at the bedroom window and down at her thick white socks. She heard Luis's voice outside her bedroom door.

Perry was here. She shoved her feet into slippers and went downstairs to see Perry standing in the huge entrance hall, unwrapping the wool scarf from around her neck.

Her daughter saw her and yelled, "You were great, Mom, great!" And Perry was hugging her, kissing her, laughing, hugging her again. "You've got to be exhausted, I mean, jetting off to New York and back again. Go back on upstairs, I'll get you some tea. I'll bet you haven't eaten, either. How about some toast with peanut butter?"

Natalie stared at her, then she took Perry's beloved face between her hands and held her still. "Someone tried to kill you and Davis last night and you didn't tell me. You didn't tell me until my talk was over this morning. And you want to make me some peanut-butter toast?"

"I'm sorry, Mom, really, but the last thing you needed was to hear about the attack before you gave your speech. I talked it over with Dillon and Davis, and everyone thought it would be better to wait.

"I'm all right. Davis is all right. We spent the night here, since my condo is shot up, missing windows, and covered with crime scene tape. It's a mess." She put her hands over her mother's. "Really, Mom, I'm okay." She hugged her tightly against her. "We'll both be okay, Mom, really, you'll see."

Natalie stepped back. "I want you and Davis to remain here, with me."

"We've got to go back to my condo so I can pack some things, but yes, we'll be back here. I met your two DS agents. I'm glad Luis's still here, though. At least you're safe now. The place is a fortress."

"You'll be safe, too," Natalie said, and hugged her back.

Perry said, "I was at work this morning, but everyone stopped to watch you at the UN. You were incredible. Arliss's introduction was perfect. My mom the heroine, yes, perfect."

"What does Davis say about last night?"

Perry's face turned cold.

"What? What's wrong? Was Davis hurt?"

"No, he wasn't." She started to say something else, thought better of it, and forced a smile. Natalie merely stared at her until Perry admitted, "I need to have a discussion with him, that's all. Don't worry about it."

"What about?"

At the continued silence from her daughter, Natalie said, "Where is Davis? Is he speaking to the DS agents?"

"No. Davis had places to go, people to see this morning. I was assigned another agent."

"Where is he?"

"His name is Agent Gregory, and I, ah, left him at the **Post**."

"You ditched your guard? Why, for heaven's sake, Perry?"

Good question, Perry thought. She knew it would sound seriously lame, but still she said, "Agent Gregory is older. He meant well, I'm sure, but he wanted to play my father and give me advice on everything from crime in D.C. to my sports column. I tried to hunker down to my work, but after a while, I, well, I wanted some peace, so I left and came directly here. I called him on the way so he knows I'm okay."

"Not very adult of you, Perry."

"I know, but I was very careful, and there wasn't a problem. And now we're both surrounded by State Department agents and Luis."

Especially Luis, Natalie thought. He could probably handcuff the two DS agents together and walk away whistling. She nodded. "They've been my shadows. The woman agent even comes into public bathrooms with me. Arliss took an earlier flight, told me something had come up she had to see to. She didn't say what new world problem had jumped out from under the rug at her."

Perry knew what the problem was, but she kept still. Her mother didn't need any more to deal with at the moment. As for

Davis, the jackass, when he showed up here, and she knew he would as soon as he could, she was going to hang him out to dry. She said, "Any word on William?"

Natalie shook her head. "No one's told me."

"I'd really like to catch up with him and maybe break his legs."

Natalie cupped her daughter's face between her hands. "You sound like your father. Do you remember he used to say things like that when he was angry? As a joke, really. As for me, I want to know why he's doing this. Let's get some tea."

Luis came into the kitchen a few minutes later. "Mrs. Black, Agents Savich and Sherlock are here. They're in the living room, talking with the DS agents."

"I think hot tea is in order," Natalie said.

"Where's Davis?" she asked, the moment she stepped into the living room.

"He'll be here shortly," Savich said. He accepted a cup of the strong, rich black tea.

Sherlock said, "He's not happy, Perry. Agent Gregory called him. No, I don't want explanations; you can give them to Davis."

Savich said, "Natalie, I'm very sorry about the attack on Perry last night. Believe me, we're working hard on it."

Sherlock said, "You were magnificent, Natalie, the interviews, your speech at the UN. Please, don't worry. Perry's here now for the duration and you're both well protected."

Natalie sat forward, her own teacup on her knee. "I got the impression from Arliss—a fleeting look she gave me—that her hurrying back here might have something to do with me. Do you know anything about that?"

She was sharp, Sherlock thought, and smiled. "Davis and Agent Hammersmith interviewed Day Abbott at his office about the shooting last night. Evidently, he wasn't pleased and called his mother. That's why she came back earlier, I think, to call us into her office and introduce us to her attorneys."

Savich said, "I think Davis might be with Agent Gregory, discussing your escape."

Sherlock said, "Not very bright of you, Perry, to duck out on him."

"I texted both Agent Gregory and Davis. They know I'm fine."

Savich walked up to her, got in her face. "Listen to me, Perry, and take my words to heart. You will wear Davis like a coat. The last thing your mother needs is to have to worry more about your safety. Don't you understand she's already worried enough?"

Perry looked stricken, he saw it. **Good.** "We need to go to the office. Stay put." They nodded to Natalie and the DS agents and left.

As they heard the Porsche engine rev, Perry said to her mother, "His voice was perfectly nice, but I felt like a kid in the principal's office. I knew if I argued, I wouldn't like what happened next." She sighed. "I guess he's right. I don't want you to worry about me, Mom. Actually, I was upset at Davis—"

A metal-grinding punk-rock song blasted out of Perry's cell phone. Perry pulled it out of her leather jacket pocket and yelled into the phone, "Davis, you moron. You put 'See No Evil' on my cell? No, not important. I'm here with Mom and Luis and two DS agents. I'm fine, Mom's fine. You get your butt here, Davis. I want to talk to you."

71

Luis, open the damned gate or I'm driving my Jeep right through it!"

"Good luck with that," Luis answered through the intercom, and hit the gate button on the control pad outside the living room. Davis drove past the DS agent standing in the driveway with only a nod.

A minute later, they heard Davis say a few words to the DS agent in the foyer before he burst into the room. He looked ready to explode with righteous anger, but at the sight of Natalie and Luis together with Perry, all of them looking at him, he calmed himself. He nodded to Natalie, to Luis, walked up to Perry, looked her in the eye and said, "Agent Gregory was guarding you at the **Post** and the next thing he knows, you're gone, vanished, like some schoolkid sneaking out for a smoke.

"You planned it. You pretended you were working hard on your laptop so he would forget you for a couple of minutes. Gregory likes talking to people. You saw that, and so you waited until he got into it with a crime writer, and when he looked up, you were gone. You made him look like a fool when he had to call it in. You disrupted the CAU, forced me to come out here to find you." His voice had risen. He wanted to shake her but couldn't, not with her mother standing six feet away. "You want to tell me your problem?"

He was right, but that wasn't the point. "That's nothing compared to what you did, you jackass."

"What I did? What are you talking about?" Davis heard Natalie clear her throat and turned. "Oh, Natalie, sorry to be rude. You were great at the UN. But I gotta tell you, you should give me some help here; your rabbit-brain daughter could use a bit more discipline."

"Don't you dare bring my mother in on this!"

"All right. Tell me."

"You went to see one of my best friends for forever and you accused him of trying to murder me!"

"You mean Day Abbott? I was doing my job, and this is not the time or place to get into that." He shot a look at Natalie, who was shaking her head at him. She said, "Tell her why, Davis."

"All right. Griffin and I interviewed Day Abbott, and the interview got a bit personal, so his mama, Secretary of State Abbott, called us in on the carpet in her office. It's over and done with. I didn't accuse him of murdering anyone. Your best friend was the jackass, not me."

Davis looked at the DS agent who had followed him into the living room and at Luis, who were both trying not to be there, and said to Natalie and Perry, "The important thing is that both of you are safe. Agent Gregory's on his way over. I'm done here, and I've got stuff to do," and he turned around and walked toward the living room door.

He stopped cold when he heard the ambassador's iron voice sounding like the nuns in his Catholic grade school. "Listen to me, Davis, you walk out that door and I'll chase you down and pull out your eyebrows, one at a time."

He turned slowly to face her. "Natalie, it was your daughter who decided to play games because she's angry with me. I got the message. I don't want her killed on my watch, and that's what could have happened. She needs an agent she's willing to work with to protect her. I'm not it."

"You don't know my daughter as well as you think you do, Davis," Natalie said. "You are definitely that agent. Tell you what, I'll have Luis handcuff you to Perry and the two of you can fight it out. How does that sound? Think about this, Davis, think carefully, because I don't mean to lose this argument."

Davis couldn't help it, he smiled at her. "Would you still marry me if I didn't have any eyebrows?"

Natalie said, "Marry you, Davis? No, I wouldn't want my daughter to consider matricide."

Natalie's words bloomed tall and proud in the middle of the silent room. He heard Perry gasp and sputter behind him. Without a word, she clomped out of the living room.

72

**Perry Black's condo
Monday, late afternoon**

There was crime scene tape crisscrossed over her front door, and her shattered windows had been boarded up with plywood.

"How about we get your stuff packed up in ten minutes?" he said. "I'd like to get out of here and back to your mom's."

"I'm sure glad Dillon and Sherlock are okay." She unlocked the front door and opened it onto a disaster area. Perry felt so mad she wanted to howl with it. "Davis, look at my beautiful living room." Then she walked through the carnage, saying nothing more. She pulled a duffel bag from the hallway closet and walked into the bedroom.

Davis looked at the shattered Tiffany lamp on the living room floor. She'd really liked that lamp. He walked to the kitchen, pulled out a garbage bag, and cleaned out the refrigerator. "Eight minutes," he called out.

"Yeah, yeah, I'm hurrying."

"I'm stepping outside for a minute, but don't run out on me like you did Gregory. Remember, it's only because your mother threatened me that I'm still here guarding her pea-brained daughter." He heard her say something but didn't make out her words because he was already out her back door, dumping her kitchen garbage bag in the trash can. When he walked back into her bedroom, she was standing in the middle of the room, holding a pretty blue sweater. "I can't think what else to take," she said, and she looked miserable.

"You've got enough warm stuff?"

She nodded.

"Then come on, time's up. If you need more, we can always come back."

She grabbed her duffel bag strap and put it over her shoulder and walked past him. She said, "My Kimber's already at Mom's. I'll borrow her laptop until I can replace mine. Hey, wait up. You need another Band-Aid, the jungle leopard is peeling off." She dropped her duffel and disappeared into the bathroom. She peeled off the old one and patted down the new one. "There, you've got a monkey now. It suits you better than the leopard," and she left him to haul her duffel bag out the front door. They hadn't spoken about what Natalie had said; he knew very well it wasn't entirely a joke. They both knew it.

He saw one of her black sneakers on the floor beneath an old leather chair with a bullet hole in it that looked like a find at Goodwill from her college days—the chair, not the sneakers. He took one last look around. In her kitchen he saw the two washed cups in the drainer near the sink, one for each of them. In the bathroom he saw a black bra hanging over the shower rod along with a pair of abbreviated black panties he'd give just about anything not to have seen, and he remembered her rubbing her foot two nights ago when he'd heard a crash from the bedroom and rushed in, Glock at the ready, to see her on her back on the floor, dressed in red boxers and a red sports bra and nothing else, one leg raised and bent toward her.

He'd slipped his Glock back into the clip at his waist. "What'd you do? What's wrong?"

"I hit my foot against the dresser doing leg lifts," she said. "Nothing's broken. But, hey, you came flying in here to save me. That was fast." She sounded pleased with herself. "The fact is, I was watching TV with the sound off because it's usually annoying, and not paying attention. Entirely my fault, like everything else."

He remembered telling her he liked the boxers and bra, the red looked good against her skin, and if she was finished rubbing her foot, it was time to go to bed.

Yeah, he liked that memory.

He heard the Jeep's door slam. He followed her out, locked the door behind him, and replaced the crime scene tape.

He was at the end of the block when she said, "Day told me you'd been a horse's ass."

"Yeah, well, you can't dump that entirely on my head. What I mean is I could have been more professional, I'll admit that, but he was the one who started dishing out the insults." He sounded, even to himself, like a kid in the schoolyard.

"Insults? Don't you think you might have scared him? Two FBI agents bursting into his office with no warning? That must have been a huge shock. Listen, Day's a really nice guy, he'd never—"

"He told me I couldn't afford to take you to Cannes on a cop's salary. He said when he was making love to you in Cannes he'd think of me."

Day had said that? She didn't want to deal with that right now. She said, "Day told me you were trying to intimidate him, that you threatened to take him down to the Hoover Building."

"Day thinks I've been trying to separate the two of you all week. He's looking forward to the time when neither of you will ever have to see me again."

"Why did you go see Day in the first

place? I mean, you know as well as I do that he wouldn't have anything to do with hurting me. For heaven's sake, Davis, he thinks he's in love with me."

"Well, don't flatter yourself, he'll probably get over it." He paused for a moment. "You're not going to marry the guy, are you?"

"Do you want me to get my Kimber at Mom's and shoot off your earlobe?"

"Leave my eyebrows and earlobes out of this. Using my interview with Day Abbott as an excuse to ditch Agent Gregory doesn't fly. I'm surprised you didn't choke trying to pawn it off on me."

"How many times do I have to apologize?"

"You might consider saying it like you actually mean it and saying it to Agent Gregory. I gotta tell you, he was relieved to hand you off back to me this evening."

"He accepted my apology!"

"Not really. He's a nice guy, too." He shot her a look, sighed. "Okay, he tried to shove fatherly advice down your throat, didn't he?"

"Well, yes, and he didn't let up. This afternoon in the newsroom, it was too much. I couldn't take it anymore, that's all—and you're trying to get me on the defensive again, when you were the ass with poor Day this morning. What did Aunt Arliss do to you?"

"She started out like she was going to tear out our tonsils, but then she backed off. Why, I don't know. Maybe she saw reason."

She sighed. "I wish Day hadn't called her. He had to know it would cause trouble. And you better watch out for my mother, too." She sighed again. "I shouldn't have gotten upset with her. She doesn't need that. She's got to be on her way to see Hooley at the hospital by now. Can we stop there on the way home?"

73

Lazy Elf Motel
Morganville, Virginia
Late Monday afternoon

When the whispering call from the manager of the Lazy Elf Motel came to Savich in the CAU that Blessed Backman was there, Savich and Sherlock were in the Porsche within two minutes, siren blaring, headed for Morganville, Virginia.

They found the Lazy Elf Motel on the edge of a middle-class residential section, on the seedy side, painted a pale yellow. There were half a dozen cars parked in the parking area. The **E** in **Elf** was blinking on and off. The manager wasn't in the office. Together, they approached room 217, the end room on the second level, pressing against the dirty plaster of the outside wall. When they reached the door, Savich leaned in, listened.

He didn't hear a thing. He turned quickly and shook his head at the Morganville officer who was standing on the far side of the motel parking lot. He wasn't surprised, but he still felt a punch of disappointment. Blessed was gone. He whispered to Sherlock at his elbow, "I don't hear anyone. He's not here."

She shook her head. "You know the drill, play it safe." She nodded to the door.

Savich reared back and kicked the door in. "FBI, freeze!" The old door slammed back against the wall.

They went in high-low, fanning their Glocks, but there wasn't anyone in the tatty old room.

An ancient cathode tube TV stood drunkenly on the edge of a dresser as if someone had brushed against it and hadn't cared if it crashed to the floor. Three dresser drawers were all lopsided, shoved in carelessly. The small table beside the bed had one ashtray on it holding three butts. Sherlock scooped them into a small evidence bag. There was no sign of luggage.

As Savich went through the drawers, Sherlock checked the bathroom. Empty, two threadbare towels tossed on the floor, a squeezed tube of toothpaste on the ledge of a chipped porcelain bowl. She shook her head as she walked back into the room.

The bed was unmade; a used towel lay wrinkled on the floor. When she leaned down to pick it up, she saw something beneath the bed. She dropped to her knees and pulled out a camel wool coat. She rose, frowning. "It's Blessed's. Why would Blessed leave his coat?"

They heard a cell phone ring from the neighboring room.

Savich grabbed her around the waist and ran back through the open doorway, nearly threw her against the motel wall beside the open door, and flattened himself against her, his hands covering her head. There was an instant of silence, and then a huge blast shook the wall. A ball of orange flame exploded out the open doorway, shattered the wooden railing behind them and spurted down and out like a water hose directly onto an old Chevy in the parking lot below them. Pieces of the bed frame and the antenna from the TV flew out the door with the flames, struck what was left of the burning wooden railing and fell onto the walkway and the empty parking lot next to the burning Chevy below them. Smoke curled into the air from the doorway, black, oily, smelling like Hell itself.

They breathed in, but it was hot and the smoke burned their lungs. Savich looked down at her, made certain she was all right. He lightly touched his fingertips to her cheek, so thankful for a moment he didn't speak. His ears were ringing; he imagined hers were, too. "We're okay," he said. "Thank the Good Lord this wall is concrete block." Savich hit 911, relayed their location and reported the fire even though he knew the cops below them would already be calling for a fire truck themselves. He was on the phone when the yells and screams started and half a dozen people, some in their underwear, came bursting out of their rooms. A fire alarm went off.

Savich yelled, "FBI. The explosion is over and you're safe. But there's a fire. Leave your rooms and wait for the fire department. We'll be coming to speak to each of you as soon as we can."

As they walked down the stairs toward the still burning Chevy, they heard muttering, saw a few panicked faces and a few people shuffling back inside to get their things. Sherlock said, "I think some of them will make a run for it. This isn't what you'd call a family sort of place."

Two policemen ran up the stairs past them, broke into the room next to Blessed's when no one opened the door. Thick smoke belched out. One of them looked in, covering his face. "There's a dead man in there, looks like the manager, killed by the blast. The wall between the rooms is blown out."

Savich said, "Blessed did that. He had the manager in his control, told him to set the bomb off when he heard the phone ring. Blessed knew we were in the room. He's still got to be close by."

74

Blessed watched Savich and Sherlock burst out of the motel room and press themselves against the concrete outer wall only a second before the bomb blast. It wasn't fair. It was a fine blast, well nigh perfect, like wild orange lightning, spewing flames and black smoke. He watched it slam into the Chevy, igniting it like a torch. All it had managed to do was scare the crap out of the cheating couples with their quickies before going home to the spouse and kids. They burst out of their rooms, terrified, many in their underwear.

He cursed, then stopped. There was nothing he could do about blind luck. He realized he'd have been sorry to see them go up in the blast like that nasty-eyed manager he'd stymied into setting off the bomb when he called him. He'd hurried him along to his just reward, whatever that was. Luck wouldn't be enough for

any of them in the end. He would have to
kill them himself.

He watched the cops drive up, sirens
blaring. They scrambled out of their cars
and scattered around the motel, not
knowing what else to do until their boss,
probably the chief of police in this Podunk
town, drove up and they grouped around
him, his thick rooster tail of white hair a
kind of beacon to them. He watched
Savich and Sherlock speak to all of them,
warning them, no doubt, to be careful,
not that any of them would believe what
he could do—no one ever did until it was
too late. He smiled. He couldn't wait to
get up close and personal to some of
them. The cops fanned out, and Blessed
knew they were going to search through
the neighborhood for him. But they
wouldn't find him unless he let them, not
here, looking out at them from behind an
old lady's lace curtain, where everything
was quiet and under his own control.

He smiled. Before the sun set, some of
those cops would be shooting one
another.

He watched Savich and Sherlock walk into the motel office with the big white-haired guy. Even in the fading afternoon light, Sherlock's red hair glistened—so beautiful, her hair. When the time came, he'd make sure she didn't shoot herself in the head. He'd dreamed of the guardian again last night, whispering to him to strangle her like he'd always wanted to. He could do it, he could.

He watched a couple more cars pull into the motel parking lot and four more men pile out. No mistaking they were FBI, all formal and tough and ready to take on the world. He saw Savich come out of the motel reception area, beckon them inside. Now they had backup, but it wouldn't do them any good. Would Savich allow Sherlock to come out looking for him? He'd see soon enough. He flexed his fingers.

He saw two cops walking down the street, watched them check behind every tree, every bush. They knocked on the first door and he saw a young mother with a kid in her arms answer the door. One cop checked out the house while the other went into the garage and skirted around the yard. They were coming here next, the second house in the line of middle-class boxes, the one with the best view of the motel.

Blessed looked over at Mrs. Amity Ransom, ninety if she was a day, sitting placidly in a rocking chair, knitting needles clacking, an ancient Remington Army caplock revolver, her long dead husband's, he supposed, loaded with bullets she'd readily showed him hidden beneath some yellowed doilies in a cabinet drawer. The old dear was ready. She sneezed, once, then again.

"What's wrong?"

"It's allergies," Amity said, not looking up from her knitting, and sneezed again.

"Amity," Blessed said, bringing her face toward him, her expression as blank as her eyes. "There are two police officers at the door. I want you to invite them in to search, all right? Be nice to them. Hide the revolver under your knitting."

She did, then walked slowly and carefully to the front door, and she sneezed again.

75

Washington Memorial Hospital

Hooley's eyes were closed. He was breathing deeply and easily. Natalie was standing beside his hospital bed, thinking how much better he looked, comfortably asleep. She lightly touched her fingers to his large, strong hand, and gently stroked so as not to wake him. She looked up when Davis and Perry walked in, and smiled.

She said quietly, "Connie said he's much better, off the morphine and on oral meds now, getting down clear liquids. He nodded off just now. How did it go at the condo?"

Perry shook her head, nodded toward Davis. "We got everything I need for now, Mom," she said. "And the bozo here seems to be calming down, finally."

Davis snorted but let it go. He searched

Natalie's face, saw the strain, thought she needed some rest as much as Hooley, but knew she wouldn't want to hear that from him. He walked over to the opposite side of Hooley's bed. "Where's Connie?"

"She went to the nurse's station to ask a question. She didn't want to leave him, even with the DS agents outside, so I'd guess she'll be back in three minutes, tops. She's reading him a Dashiell Hammett mystery. Ah, he's waking up." Natalie leaned close. "I know your brain's swimming around a bit with the drugs, but don't worry about it, Mark. Can I do anything for you?"

He whispered, "I keep falling asleep. Some water would be nice, Mrs. Black."

Natalie poured him a glass and put a straw to his lips. "Slowly, that's right, and Mark, sleep is good for you."

When he finished, Hooley's brain was straight enough for him to look around and turn his eyes to Davis. "Yeah, punk, I'm surprised they let you in here."

"Gotta make sure you're behaving, Beef. It's Mrs. Black who's worried about you even though your doctor's bragging on you. I'm looking forward to your being up and ready for the gym in another week or two. Tell you what, I'll even tie my hand behind my back for you until you're a decent threat."

Hooley grinned. "You'll know I'm better when I kick your legs right out from under you, turkey brain."

"Hi, Mark," Perry said. "Trash-talking from your hospital bed? You must be feeling better."

"I'm fine. Where's Connie?"

Natalie patted his hand. "She'll be right back. You need anything else?"

"No, no, I'm fine, thank you, Mrs. Black. Any word on catching the man who's trying to kill you?"

"More to the point, the man who tried to kill you," Natalie said. "Not yet. Not since the FBI found the doctor who patched him up. You made that possible, Mark, you shot him in the side. You're the one person who's made us all safer."

"But you're not safe yet, Mrs. Black."

"I have so many guards I can't go to the

bathroom without one coming in with me and another standing outside. I'm fine, Mark, please don't worry about me."

"Connie told me they think it's George McCallum's son, William."

"It appears so," Natalie said. "They say he—William Charles—holds me responsible for his father's death. He and his father were close, but his father told me William refused to come home, that he'd made a new life for himself away from England, away from his family. The FBI thinks he's hiding somewhere nearby."

"Actually," came a sharp, clipped, upper-class British voice, "he's not hiding. He's right here."

76

Morganville, Virginia

Amity opened the door only a crack. "Officers? What's wrong?"

"Ma'am, we're looking for the man in this photo"—the cop must have held up his cell phone, Blessed thought, standing against the wall of the living room. "Have you seen him?"

Amity studied the photo carefully, shook her head. "No, young man, I haven't. What's he done?"

One officer said, "He blew up the motel. Didn't you hear the explosion, see the flames?"

"I thought I heard something, but I was watching my soap and didn't pay attention."

"Do you mind if we check your house and garage, ma'am?"

She gave them both a sweet smile and

stepped back.

Blessed waited until they were inside and close, then stepped out of the living room. "Gentlemen," he said, and looked first at one, then the other. Both stilled; both sets of eyes became blank slates. Both men belonged to him.

Blessed gave a rancid old laugh. "Well, now, here's what we're going to do. I want the two of you to go into the living room and sit down on the sofa. When the doorbell rings again, I want you both to answer the door. You will shoot whoever is standing there. Do you understand?"

Both cops nodded.

"What are your names?"

"Andrew Bibber."

"Jeff Pilson."

Boring names, Blessed thought. His mama had done better by him and Grace. Blessed watched them walk into the living room with no hesitation, sit down and look straight ahead, their faces expressionless.

"Amity, sit down and keep knitting. Keep your gun close."

She hesitated for a moment, then said in her old lady's whispery voice, "I need to use the bathroom."

"Come back soon," Blessed said, and watched her walk slowly and carefully out of the living room. He heard her soft footballs down the hallway, heard her sneeze a couple more times. He didn't have a single doubt she'd do exactly as he told her.

She was a long time coming back. **An ancient bladder,** Blessed thought, and age made her move slow; still, he was at the point of going to look for her when she appeared in the living room doorway. He said, "Sit down in your rocker and knit, Amity."

She sat, eased the old gun onto her lap, and began knitting. She rocked, back and forth. Blessed found it annoying but didn't say anything. He wondered if the old bird would survive this. He'd never before stymied anyone so old. Let her rock, settle her ancient bones. He walked into the entrance hall, looked back at the three blank-faced human beings who were his.

It wouldn't be long before someone else came. He would add them to his collection like a butterfly pinned to a board or he would let the cops with the boring names shoot them dead.

77

Washington Memorial Hospital

All of them stared at the tall, white-coated tech who stood behind Connie, the muzzle of his Beretta pointed in her ear.

Natalie said, "It's you, William? It's really you?"

"The same. And the big guy here is an FBI agent. I want you to drop your Glock on the floor and kick it over to me. Do it now or you'll see this pretty young woman's brains splatter." Khalid was annoyed it hurt him so much to talk, the pain grinding, throbbing, and it wouldn't let up. His head was starting to pound along with it. He tried not to let the FBI agent know, tried to keep upright. He had the gun, but he knew better than to take his eyes off him. He recognized what the man was capable of by looking at him, knew it from seeing other men like him, knew it to his bones. "I will not tell you again. Drop the gun now or I will put a bullet in you as well, and then into Mrs. Black."

Davis carefully pulled his Glock from his waist clip and set it on the floor. He straightened and kicked it toward McCallum, never taking his eyes off his face. It stopped six inches from his foot. McCallum looked tough as leather, not that much older than him. All that was left of the white-skinned Englishman was the flash of his blue eyes in his deeply seamed face, weathered to dark brown by the desert sun. He was a man stripped of everything he'd been, of all the comforts and baggage of being rich.

Davis saw him run his tongue over his dry lips. McCallum was in pain, no doubt about it. Davis knew he would have stopped taking his pain pills hours ago because he couldn't take the chance they would cloud his brain, slow him down. He was struggling, and that would give them a chance. He looked at Connie, knew she saw it, too. She was thinking, weighing the options just as he was.

Perry said, "William Charles, why are

you trying to murder my mother?"

"I am not William Charles any longer. I am Khalid Al-Jabiri, and that is what you will call me."

"Very well. So why are you trying to murder my mother?"

Connie tried to pull away from him and he tightened his hold around her neck until she gasped. Perry saw his gun hand shake against Connie's neck. If Connie moved again, she could die. Perry added quickly, "And why did you try to kill me?"

He cocked his head to one side, distracted. "Kill you? I don't even know you, only that you're her daughter. You're nobody to me. Whatever it is you mean, be quiet. If I wish to talk with anyone, it is with your mother, not you. It is your mother who is the murderer, who wantonly drove my father to kill himself. I am here to see she gets the justice she deserves."

Natalie said, "Billy—Khalid—your father told you we were working through the scandal together, after your photo was published in the British press."

"I am not here to debate you, Mrs. Black.

Perhaps you should listen rather than speak."

"Hooley spoke up from behind Natalie. "You're a good soldier, Khalid. You're the one who put me here."

"That I am, and you're the one who shot me. You see well in the dark. You were brave that night. What is your name?"

"Hooley. I didn't see as well as you, since I'm the one lying here. As a soldier, you've got to see you're flanked on all sides. Not only the people in this room, but you know there are the agents outside, downstairs. If you shoot anyone, you'll never make it out of here alive."

Connie tried to swing about to face him, and he dug the gun into her ear. "No, don't move! Listen, all of you. You've got to know I'm well trained, an excellent shot. I could probably kill every one of you if you came at me, even Hooley lying there staring up at me. And Mrs. Black, you will be the first to die."

He fanned his gun at them, looked back at Hooley. "I didn't come here to escape again, Hooley. I came here to end it."

78

Morganville, Virginia

Hello, Blessed."

It was her voice. He couldn't believe it. How could she be here? He whirled around, stared for all he was worth, but Sherlock was at least twelve feet away from him, and he knew she wasn't about to come any closer.

"How?" he asked. "I never saw you. How?"

Sherlock said, "We made sure all the police and agents looking for you left their radios on transmit. We heard every word you said. And Mrs. Ransom was kind enough to help me fool you, Blessed. After I hit her hard enough to bring her back, that is. Isn't that a lovely surprise?"

"No, she's in the living room, rocking and knitting! There's nothing at all on her face! Do you think I wouldn't know? She's mine as well as those two cops!" Again Blessed stared at her, stared as hard as he could, but she wasn't close enough. He felt his knife in his left jacket pocket, felt the gun in the right that would do him no good. He had to get close enough to take her over, to make her his puppet like the others. He took a step toward her. Sherlock raised her Glock, pointed it center mass. "Don't, Blessed. Step back, now. Mrs. Ransom fooled you, Blessed. She's brave and she's smart."

He was breathing hard as he stepped back, but Sherlock could see him thinking, cursing that old biddy who'd taken him in, trying to figure out what to do. Sherlock looked at him dispassionately. His teeth looked discolored. He looked, she thought, much older than his fifty-six years. His graying brown hair was thin on his head, a gray stubble dotted his sagging jowls. He looked like a harmless old dude, except for his eyes. Even from twelve feet away, she saw madness in him, bursting to get out. His eyes looked like a deep well of black, and behind those eyes crouched scary things.

It wasn't safe to try to get handcuffs on him. She could wait. Dillon had to be coming through the front door any second. He'd insisted she come through the back because he thought it would be safer. And she'd run into Mrs. Ransom coming out of the bathroom.

"You killed poor Grace and Mama!"

"What's wrong with you, Blessed? Can't you remember what really happened? I had nothing to do with either Grace's or your mother's death. It was you who killed Grace, Blessed, he was badly wounded, dying, and you used the sheriff as your weapon."

"Mama died in that miserable hospital because of you, no one else, only you and that husband of yours!"

Blessed started walking toward her, his knife clutched in his hand.

She raised the Glock. "Put down that knife, Blessed, or I'll have to shoot you."

He screamed, "Pilson, Bibber! Come here now! Get in front of me!"

She didn't have time, because the two

young men dashed out of the living room and made a wall in front of Blessed before she could react.

"Now walk toward her."

Neither man hesitated; they walked side by side directly at her. She couldn't shoot them, she couldn't.

The front door burst open and she yelled, "Dillon!"

The two men were on her, and Blessed was right in front of her, looking into her eyes. It was the last thing she remembered.

Savich saw two police officers, Blessed, and Sherlock standing like a frozen tableau. It was Blessed who said, "Bibber, Pilson, draw your weapons and aim them at that man. If he fires his gun, shoot him."

Savich looked at Sherlock, and what he saw stopped his heart. She wasn't moving, and neither was Blessed. He looked away from her and back to Blessed—he was smiling. The two cops had their Berettas aimed at his chest. Sherlock still hadn't moved, not a twitch, and she didn't speak.

Blessed said, "Well, now, Agent Savich,

looks like we've got us a situation. I say one word to either of these boys and they'll shoot you dead, or you'll shoot them, both cops, just like you. As for your wife, forget her, she's mine. Shall I have her shoot you instead?"

Sherlock stood quietly, her eyes blank, her face slack. She wasn't there. She held her Glock at her side.

Blessed looked at each of them again. He felt elated, warm to his soul. He could do anything and everything.

"Don't let him move, boys," he said, then studied Sherlock, his minion, his tool. He looked at her red hair, all the curls feathering around her face. She was so alive, so vivid, he'd always thought. It was a pity she had to pay for her sins against Grace and Mama, but Father had always taught him and Grace that the way of a just and righteous life was to make sure people took responsibility, paid for their sins. He knew then what he was going to do. It was a stroke of brilliance, really.

He moved quietly forward, stopped. He turned to look at her again. But no need, she was still gone, locked securely into him, her master in all things. It was the best feeling in the world.

"I want you to kill him," he said to Sherlock. "I want you to kill your husband. A nice clean shot through the head. Do you understand?"

"Yes," she said, "I understand."

He stroked his hand over her bright hair, then sifted the soft curls between his fingers. "Don't shoot yourself in the head. I don't want gore all over your beautiful hair. After you've killed your husband, shoot yourself in the heart."

He looked at her calm, serene face. Slowly, he leaned down and kissed her slack mouth. She made no response.

He jumped back. "Shoot him, girl, shoot him now!"

79

Washington Memorial Hospital

Connie twisted and jerked until Khalid
pulled her tight against him. He felt a
surge of crippling pain lash through him
and he stumbled back, but he managed
to grab Connie again and pull her in front
of him. She kept struggling until she felt
the cold gun press hard against her naked
neck. "Stop it, woman! You, Agent, get
back or she's dead!"

Davis was nearly on him, but that pain-
maddened voice stopped him dead in his
tracks. He felt so frustrated he wanted
to howl. He stared at William Charles—
Khalid—and saw he was not only hanging
on, he was regaining control over the pain
in his side. He could kill Connie in an
instant. Davis calmed himself, drew back.

Khalid was breathing hard through his
teeth, his voice shuddering from the pain

as he whispered against Connie's temple, "Don't do that again. My wife is a tiger like you, sharp teeth and fingernails, ready to rip out a man's throat."

Natalie's calm voice rang out: "It's me you want, Khalid, not her. Let her go."

Khalid glanced over at Natalie and felt hate roil in his belly. She was here, at last, not more than eight feet from him, and she looked as unruffled and controlled as the bloody Queen. His father had loved the faithless bitch to his very soul. It enraged him. His voice shook with pain as he screamed, "Ah, Madame Ambassador speaks! You murdered my father, you lying bitch! I watched you spin your tales to those credulous morons on the TV news stations last night, saw how they pandered to you, believed every self-serving lie that fell out of your mouth. I only wish I'd have been strong enough yesterday to kill you."

Natalie kept her voice calm. "It was you who left your father and your family, Khalid. He loved you, wanted you so badly to come home. Why didn't you?"

"Family? What a bunch of selfish little sods, with a couple of bona fide nutters thrown in. Do you think I'd join them at Ascot, or playing polo, or strut down the aisle at Saint Paul's with a whey-faced English bride on my arm? They're carrion, all of them. At least now they won't have Lockenby Hall to feast on."

"But not your father. You loved each other. Let me ask you, Khalid, why are you so certain I am responsible for his death?"

"Everyone with a brain knows it! Now you're claiming someone hacked into your email account and sent that indecent email in your name? Really? Are you ready to tell any tale that can't be disproved? And then my father was dead, dead and gone. You did that to him. Admit it!"

"You will listen to me, and this is the absolute truth. I loved your father. We would have stood together with you if you had come back to England, and we would have stood together by ourselves if you had not. Do you understand me? We loved each other. When your father died, it broke something deep inside both of us. You feel the same pain losing him as I do, I know that, but you're blaming someone else for it, and there's no one to blame, not even yourself. Your father didn't kill himself. They think now he had a problem with his heartbeat, and fell unconscious, and that's why he went over the cliffs. I know he didn't kill himself, Khalid, he cherished life. He would have never killed himself, never, even if I had broken our engagement in that ridiculous email, even if I'd announced it in Trafalgar Square. Don't you know your father well enough to realize that?"

For an instant, Khalid looked uncertain, then his eyes filled with pain again, pain for his father and the physical pain that was bowing him into himself. "So now you call it a tragic accident rather than murder? You prefer that story now? Isn't it a pity no one can prove it either way?" He had no more words. He sucked in a gasping breath, realized he was losing control of his mind and his body, and backed away from Connie. "You, get over there."

Connie moved away from him.

Davis said, "Khalid, give us a chance to prove who sent the email. Don't make another mistake before we all know the truth. Natalie was never the calculating monster you want to believe she is. Why can't you see that?"

It was hard to breathe, the pain was pulsing hard, harder still, his body struggling, fighting, but in vain. So much pain, it was going to burst out, black and hot, and he would die as his father had died, his beloved father. He couldn't stand the pain of it—he raised his gun, aimed it at Natalie. "I had to end my life because I had to avenge my father. I've lost every tie that meant anything to me, my wife, my children, my family. Killing you is all I have left."

In a smooth, precise move so fast it was a blur, Connie swung her leg out and struck him in his wounded side.

Khalid screamed and fired.

80

Morganville, Virginia

Amity Ransom shouted "No!" from the living room doorway, and fired the old revolver at Blessed. There was a clicking sound, but nothing else happened. She kept pulling the trigger as Savich dived for Blessed, grabbed him around the neck and jerked him backward against him. "All right you madman, tell the officers to drop their weapons or I'll twist your neck off."

"Shoot him!" Blessed screamed at Sherlock. Savich smashed his fist against Blessed's temple and lurched toward Sherlock. He was on top of her before she could raise her gun, but she was strong, stronger than he'd ever imagined. Slowly, inexorably, he pulled her gun arm out from beneath his chest and pinned her arm to the ground. She lay there, staring up at him with empty eyes. He slapped her hard, once, twice.

It seemed an eternity before she blinked, stared up at him. "Dillon?" Her voice was a tiny thread of a sound. "Why'd you hit me?"

"I'm sorry, I had to. You're yourself again?"

"Yes," she said, her voice filled with surprise. "Of course. I'm fine."

Bibber and Pilson stood quiescent, waiting to be told what to do. Blessed stirred and sat up. Savich walked over and pressed his Glock against his ear. "You say one word and you're a dead man."

Sherlock shook her head as she slowly got to her feet. She knew what had happened, but she had no memory of it. She didn't look at Blessed. She pulled off her jacket and ripped the sleeve off her blouse, handed it to Dillon. He wound it around Blessed's eyes, knotting it in the back. "Watch him, Sherlock." He walked to the two policemen, sent his fist into each of their jaws. They grunted in surprise, and then they were back. They straightened, looked at each other, and almost in unison said, "What happened?"

"Are you all right?" The old woman was lightly touching her fingertips to the blood on Sherlock's temple.

"Yes, ma'am, I think so."

Amity Ransom looked around her entrance hall. "Goodness, what a to-do. I think all of us need a nice cup of tea."

Blessed hurled himself up and grabbed Sherlock as he ripped the sleeve off his eyes, stared at her, and shouted, "Kill him! Kill him!"

Savich shot Blessed in the forehead as Sherlock raised her gun. Amity Ransom hit her on the temple with her heavy old revolver. Sherlock sank to the floor on her knees, holding her head and moaning. The old woman leaned down and lightly touched her shoulder. "I don't understand this, but you should be all right now. Are you back here again?"

"I think so," Sherlock said.

"I'm sorry. Your poor bruised head. Isn't that strange how this man can hypnotize you so fast? I simply looked at him and I wasn't there anymore until you hit me. Are you all right now, child?"

Sherlock's head was swimming, pain pulsing through her, she wanted to vomit, but somehow she found a smile. "Yes, ma'am, thanks to you I am. Thank you."

81

Washington Memorial Hospital

The shot hit the pitcher beside Hooley, not a foot from Natalie. Khalid wasn't screaming now, he was on his back, clutching his side, moaning, nearly un-conscious with the pain, as Davis pulled the gun from his hand. Connie was beside him, applying pressure to his bleeding side.

Davis said over his shoulder, "Perry, get a doctor in here. Connie, I think you'd make a fine FBI agent."

She never raised her hands, now red with Khalid's blood. "You think?"

Natalie walked slowly over to where William Charles lay gasping for breath on his back, his eyes glazed with pain. She saw the spreading blood through the white lab coat from his wound, saw the blood covering Connie's hand. She went down on her knees next to him, lightly touched her fingers to his face. "Billy," she said, leaning close, "I'm so sorry your father died. I'm so sorry you believed the press that I was the one who brought it about. I didn't, Billy. I loved him as much as you said." She paused for a moment, dashed the tears out of her eyes. "Medical help is on the way for you. You'll get well and I'll see what I can do for you."

Perry said, "Mom, he didn't try to kill me."

"No, he said he didn't." Natalie looked up at her daughter. "So who did?" She rose and moved back as a doctor and two orderlies pushed in to take care of his lordship, Viscount Lockenby.

82

Secretary of State's office
Tuesday noon

Theodore Reynolds, chief staffer to the secretary of state and guardian of the inner sanctum, watched the six people march up to his desk. He recognized all of them, but it was the sight of a grave-looking Eric Hainny, the president's chief of staff, that brought it all together for him. He looked over at Ambassador Black's face for confirmation, but her expression was set, giving no clue to her thoughts. Still, Theo knew this had to do with that photo of her fiancé's son, the one sent up through State from the NSA that had ended up on Mrs. Abbott's desk, and then front and center in the English papers. He knew something bad was going to happen. He tried to lick his lips, but his mouth was too dry.

Special Agent Savich stopped in front of his desk and showed him his creds. "Agent Savich, FBI."

Theo said, "Yes, sir, I know who you are." His eyes flickered to Hainny, who looked grim. Still, he had to try. He cleared his throat, hoped his voice stayed smooth. "I'm sorry, sir," he said to Hainny, "but the secretary of state is with her son at the moment. This has thrown off her schedule, and—"

Eric Hainny said, "Listen, you shite, we're here at the request of the president. Hold her calls. No, don't buzz her, I know the way in."

Theodore Reynolds shut up. He watched Hainny lead Ambassador Black; her daughter, Perry; and the three FBI agents toward his boss's office. The ambassador wore a sad expression now, and her daughter was obviously angry. Mrs. Abbott should have buried that photo, she should have alerted Mrs. Black and the president about the diplomatic problem it posed if it ever got out. He'd advised her so himself. Now the silly thing was blowing up on her. He wondered if it would mean the end of her career, and his with it. There was little he could do for her, but he had to have time to confer with Mrs. Abbott before he was questioned, evaluate their options, come up with a strategy. He pulled his recent files out of his drawers and put the contents and his laptop into his briefcase. He was waiting for an elevator to the lobby of the Truman Building, then he felt a hand on his sleeve and turned to see a serious-faced young man holding out an FBI shield. "You need to come with me to the Hoover Building, Mr. Reynolds. We have some questions for you about a criminal matter."

83

Arliss Abbott felt a surge of impatience when the door opened with no warning and without her permission. When she saw Agent Savich, her impatience morphed into rage and a dollop of fear she refused to acknowledge. She saw Eric Hainny, and stilled. He looked grimmer than he'd been when the president seemed to be losing Florida in the last election. Her heart kettle-drummed in her chest when she saw Natalie and Perry, as well as Davis Sullivan and Savich's wife, Agent Sherlock, behind them.

She quickly regained control. She was the secretary of state, she never panicked, and she wouldn't start now in front of these bureaucrats and glorified policemen. She would deal with anything this group had to say. Why was Hainny here?

She felt Day lightly lay his fingers on her arm. She saw he was staring at Perry, such hunger in his eyes it made her want to weep. Day, her son, her precious son. She took his hand, squeezed it, said low, "Listen to me, Day. This is important. Don't say anything, all right? I'll handle this."

She stepped forward, effectively blocking him. She said to Hainny, her voice brusque, "Eric, please tell me what you're doing here. What do these people want?"

Hainny said, "We're all here at the behest of the president, Mrs. Abbott. As of this moment, I am here as an observer of the FBI, to be sure you hear them out."

Day didn't understand. He stared at Perry, willing her to look at him, but she didn't. She was standing with her mother, holding her hand. She looked pale and resolute, and Mrs. Black looked immensely sad. What was this all about? He looked at Sullivan, felt a leap of anger that Sullivan knew but he didn't.

"Very well, Eric. What is it you want, then, Agent Savich?" Arliss asked him.

"Madame Secretary, we can begin with that photo of William Charles McCallum taken by a United States intelligence operative in northern Syria over a month ago. We knew it was forwarded to the NSA and it was they who identified that apparent jihadist as the son of Mrs. Black's fiancé, George McCallum. They recognized the possible repercussions of that photo to Mrs. Black and to the State Department, and so they forwarded the encrypted photo and its particulars directly to your office.

"It seemed obvious to them that you would inform Mrs. Black and the president of the photo discreetly. Instead, you arranged to leak it to the British press."

Arliss said, "Yes, of course the NSA sent me the photo. However, before I could consult with the president and Mrs. Black, it was leaked to the British press. Who was responsible for this, I don't know."

"And yet you never let Mrs. Black or the president know about the photo, even after it was released," Savich said. "You followed that with the crass email you arranged to have sent from Mrs. Black's private email account to George McCallum that made it appear she was abandoning him because of his son. You had corresponded with Natalie on that account for years, enough for you to find out her password if you didn't already know it. You forwarded that forged email to the press as well."

Arliss cocked her head to one side, then smiled at him. "Another absurd tale you're weaving without any proof? I suppose your fantasy includes some kind of motive?"

Savich said, "The motive, Mrs. Abbott, yes, the motive was the difficult part. You knew Natalie hadn't looked at another man since her husband's death until she met and fell in love with George McCallum. You knew all her hopes for the future were centered on him, as George's were centered on her. You saw that Natalie was looking forward to that future, saw that she was happy again, and how you hated that. When the photo from the NSA came to your desk, you realized William Charles McCallum's photo presented you with your chance to end it.

"The press was thrilled with the photo,

of course, with being able to label the son of a peer of the realm, the man who was slated to marry the ambassador to the United Kingdom, as a terrorist. Naturally, Natalie told you the circumstances, told you she and George were handling it. You hoped it would break them apart, hoped even more that the mounting pressure from the scandal would force her to resign her post. To make sure you upped the ante, you arranged for that email you'd forged to George McCallum to be sent anonymously to the papers.

"The point of your email wasn't to fool him. The first thing George did was call Natalie and find out it wasn't from her. The point was to leak the email to the press, to have Natalie's private life, real and imagined, dragged through the tabloids. Could she survive that?

"I imagine you were pleased with the serendipity of George McCallum's car going over a cliff near Dover, Mrs. Abbott. The autopsy was inconclusive, and his death was ruled accidental. He probably suffered some kind of cardiovascular event with all the stress he was under. Perhaps he lost consciousness. We will never know. But you didn't want the scandal to end with McCallum's death. No, you wanted it to go viral, and so you planted more rumors. Shortly after George's funeral, it didn't take the press long to happily announce that George McCallum had been driven to kill himself because Natalie had ended her engagement to him.

"You sat back and watched as the headlines made her out to be the Black Widow, a woman callous enough about her career to cause a viscount to commit suicide. She was becoming a pariah, more than you had hoped. You were thrilled the bad press embarrassed the president, embarrassed the State Department, and you tried to convince the president to call Natalie back to the U.S. and force her to resign."

Arliss said to Hainny, "Eric, you told me the president wants me to hear this man out, and I have, but he simply won't stop. Why are you a party to this . . . slander?"

"I think you will be interested to hear what he says next, Mrs. Abbott," Hainny said. "The president was."

Day stepped around his mother, his face flushed, his voice shaking with outrage. "This is crazy! Listen to me, Mr. Hainny, all of you—my mother wouldn't do anything like this. What Agent Savich is saying is insane. She doesn't hate Mrs. Black, they've been friends forever. Perry and I were practically raised together."

Savich ignored him, kept his focus on Arliss, but she said, "You will stop this now. I don't wish my son to hear any more."

"He is free to leave, Mrs. Abbott," Hainny said. "You can ask him to."

"Dammit, I'm not going anywhere!"

Arliss lightly laid her hand over his, squeezed it. Then she looked beyond Savich to Natalie. "You," she said. "You talked him into this, didn't you? I know you've hated me forever, Natalie—admit it, you've been jealous of what I've accomplished. You talked him into believing your outlandish story. I am guilty of nothing."

She turned back to Savich. "I will say, though, that I did believe it was because of Natalie that George committed suicide, and I was not alone in that opinion."

Savich nodded. "Yes, most people agreed with you, here in the U.S. as well. But the president refused to accept her resignation regardless, though you hoped he'd be forced to, sooner or later.

"That almost happened. But then, out of the blue, someone tried to kill Natalie in her car off the A2 near Canterbury. You had no idea who that was, but the press soon put it out that she was hysterical or, more likely, flat-out lying, twisting a simple accident into an alleged attempt on her life to confuse the public and gain their sympathy. Of course, you knew Natalie was too honest to make something like that up. And, naturally, since you were her friend as well as her boss, she told you all about it. What better reason for you to order her back to the United States, to keep her hidden away until you could force her to resign? Have you figured it out yet, Mrs. Abbott?

"No? George was in touch with his son, William Charles, in the last days of his life. William loved his father, knew how much his father loved Mrs. Black. He knew about the bad publicity surrounding his photo-graph, knew about the email, though evidently his father died before he could tell his son it was a hoax. So it wasn't difficult for him to believe his father had fallen apart when Natalie cut off their engagement. He believed she drove his father to kill himself. It was William who returned to England on a forged passport and tried to run her off the highway.

"It was William, too, who followed her back to the United States and tried to run her down in Buckner Park, but he failed again.

"When William Charles attacked Natalie Friday night and Hooley was shot, every-thing changed. You had to scramble then, Mrs. Abbott. It was all coming too close to home.

"All your finely executed plans, all your successes, were coming apart. Natalie was a U.S. ambassador someone had tried to assassinate—she was a heroine, and the president would back her more than ever. You decided you'd better change sides, and so you did. You joined the president and took the lead in bringing Natalie back into the public eye."

Savich waited a beat, but Arliss said nothing. She looked composed and faintly bored, her eyes flitting between him and Eric Hainny. She never once looked at Natalie. She looked down at her watch, frowned, as if she was concerned with her next appointment.

Natalie spoke for the first time. "I'm glad I was wrong that George was murdered, Arliss. I'm glad you didn't try to kill me. But we've been friends for so many years. How many years have you smiled at me, laughed with me, shared secrets and tragedies?

"Yet you hate me enough to ruin me, to destroy my reputation and my good name? When you did an about-face in Thorn's office and supported me, I was so pleased, so happy you believed in me after all. But Agent Savich is right; you had no choice but to back the president.

You were protecting yourself."

Arliss Abbott shook her head. "I don't hate you, Natalie. I could have no reason to. How could you ever come to believe that? We've been friends since we were both twenty years old, sophomores at Yale. You, Brundage, Thornton, and I, we've been close our whole lives. I do not know where this is coming from, but it is very wrong of you to be convinced by what Agent Savich is spinning."

Savich paused, studied her face. "It must have angered you beyond bearing that the president, a man you'd known since college, your most important supporter, didn't take your advice and ask for Mrs. Black's resignation as you hoped he would.

"You had to introduce her at the United Nations yourself, call her a heroine in front of the world, when she was your bitterest enemy.

"I wish ruining Natalie was the beginning and ending to it, but you know it's not. What you couldn't allow to happen was for your son to marry Perry Black."

84

Day yelled, "That is crazy! My mom's loved Perry since she was born!"

Savich waved Day to quiet. "That's why the threatening notes to Perry, the trashing of her Harley, the attack on her at her condo. Of course, you knew all about Carlos and Isabel since you and Day have been an intimate part of Natalie's life. But you wouldn't have done those things yourself, you could never manage it, anyway, with the DS agents you have guarding you all the time. So did you hire someone to terrorize Perry? Perhaps you'd gotten Natalie's half-brother, Milton Holmes, involved. Or maybe your assistant, Theodore Reynolds. But neither felt right. Who then? That was the question.

"Everything became clearer after the attack on Perry and Davis last night at her condo. Davis wounded the shooter. We managed to collect blood and get DNA.

We collected Davis and Perry's DNA, as well as yours, Mr. Abbott.

"When the DNA results came back, we knew why your mother couldn't allow you and Perry to wed. Your father, Quincy Abbott, isn't your biological father, Brundage Black is."

Perry said, "We're second-degree relatives, Day. That means you and I have to be half-brother and -sister."

Day stood there, shaking his head back and forth, so white Savich thought he might fall over. His mother turned to stone.

"Mom, tell them it's a mistake! Tell them! My dad—he's my dad! Tell them, Mom!"

"I'm very sorry, Day," Natalie said. "So very sorry. I didn't know."

Savich said, "It took me only a few minutes, Mrs. Abbott, to map your ex-husband's recent itineraries to and from Washington, D.C. We found him staying openly at the Rutherford Hotel, not doing much to hide his identity. He has a bullet wound in his upper arm, and I'm quite sure his DNA will match the blood we found at Perry's condo. We also found a Smith and Wesson we're checking for ballistics. We have him in custody, and if he's smart, he'll cooperate."

Savich hated the pain he was causing, but he had to get it done. "Day, Mr. Abbott, I am sorry, but your mother and father never wanted you to know the truth about your parentage. I doubt your father knew until recently, and he lost control. He was willing to do anything not to lose his son, or see you marry your own sister. He didn't want you to have to deal with the knowledge of any of it.

"Mrs. Black had no idea about this, either. She and Brundage had separated for a couple of months before they graduated, then made up and got married. Brundage Black never told her he'd slept with your mother."

He turned back to Arliss. "Of course, the president didn't know Brundage was Day's father, Mrs. Abbott. But he did know you loved Brundage Black back in your days at Yale. He said everyone knew it except Natalie and Brundage, because they were so involved with each other. He did remember that Brundage got drunk one night and admitted he'd slept with you during his breakup with Natalie. He didn't think Brundage ever told Natalie because he didn't want to hurt her or to hurt the friendship between the two of you. Brundage thought your time together was a mistake, and he was profoundly sorry."

Savich didn't think he'd ever seen a person stand so very silent. She'd retreated into herself, trying somehow to shield herself. He didn't want to say the rest, but he had to. "You got pregnant, Mrs. Abbott, but you couldn't tell Brundage because he and Natalie were already married. You didn't tell anyone, not even Quincy Abbott, the man you married two weeks later. You kept it from everyone for more than thirty years until you had no choice. From the moment Day told you he intended to marry Perry, and you couldn't talk him out of it, you realized you needed help, and you turned to your ex-husband, Quincy Abbott."

Day Abbott suddenly looked like a boy, afraid of what had just happened, not wanting to accept it. "Mom, tell me this isn't true. Please tell me this is all a mistake."

Arliss opened her mouth, closed it again. She reached out to her son, but he flinched away from her. He looked at Perry, whispered, "You're really my sister, Perry? I wanted to marry my sister? How can that be? No, that can't be right. My dad is the best; he's always been there for me. Even after he and mom divorced and he moved to Colorado and remarried, even after he had two kids, I was still the one closest to him. He's always helped me, even in college, he—" His voice broke off, as if he'd run out of words.

Natalie said to Arliss, "I never realized you were in love with Brundage. I suppose I should have seen it, but what Thorn said is true. Brundage and I were so involved with each other we sometimes didn't see other people clearly." She fell silent for a moment, and Perry knew she was looking into the past. "It was always like that between us until he died. Arliss, I'm very sorry we both let you down."

Arliss finally spoke again, her quiet words sounding loudly in the silent room. "Brundage did see me, Natalie, even if you didn't. After we slept together, I knew he loved me. He went back to you because he felt guilty."

Natalie said, "No, Arliss. It's what you'd like to believe, but it isn't true. We had a wonderful life together. You know his death nearly broke me, it was so sudden, and he was so very young."

"You thought you were alone? Dammit, Natalie, his dying broke me, too! I couldn't believe Brundage died, he always seemed so invincible. I hated him when he died." She looked away from all of them. "Do you know he never even thought to ask me if I'd gotten pregnant, even though he had to wonder about my sudden marriage to Quincy?"

Eric Hainny stepped forward. "Madame Secretary, I am here on the president's behalf to request your resignation, effective immediately. Your lawyers and the

White House will work out how and when your stepping down will be announced to the world." He pulled an envelope out of his pocket and handed it to her. "If you resign voluntarily, the president will see to it there is a suitable period before the Justice Department considers any criminal or civil charges."

Day Abbott said to Savich, "I want to see my father. I want to see him now." On his way out the door, he stopped beside Perry, simply looked at her. "You're my sister. I wonder if I'll ever see you as a sister," and Day Abbott walked from his mother's office.

Sherlock watched the secretary of state walk to her desk, sit down in the high-backed leather chair, take a Montblanc from her pen tray, and sign her name to the paper. She never read it.

85

**Savich's house
Wednesday evening**

Perry stood in the living room doorway for a moment, her eyes on her mother. She'd been through so much since George had died—his son William Charles, Arliss, Day, the press—but she'd kept it together, managed to protect and support Perry through all of it. And Hooley and Connie, too. Tonight, Perry thought, was for her mom.

She announced from the doorway, "I've got steaming-hot pizzas from Dizzy Dan's, veggie for Dillon and pepperoni and sausage for the rest of us, all waiting on the dining room table."

Sherlock said, "We've even got nice paper plates and a big bottle of champagne."

Pizza, Natalie thought, as she rose,

smiling, toward her daughter—when was the last time she'd bit into cheese so hot her teeth burned? She knew very well why her daughter had insisted they all come over to the Savich household tonight—to cheer her up, as well as celebrate their victory. What an odd way to think of bringing down George's son and learning her best friend had betrayed her. **Well, I'm still alive, so if that isn't a victory I don't know what is. A victory.** She'd take it. Natalie was thinking she did indeed need cheering up, maybe even a victory dance, but what she needed more was time to come to grips with all that had happened. But after the pizza and after tonight.

Once the champagne was poured, Perry raised her glass. "Mom, it's over and we're all safe, thanks to everyone here and Hooley and Connie. Let's drink up before the pizza's cold."

Halfway into her second slice of pizza, Natalie said, "Is there any more news since this morning about William?"

Savich wiped his hands on a napkin. "I

know Homeland Security spoke to him today at the federal prison infirmary at Lockport. The doctors are very encouraging about his wound. Oh, yes, and Sir Giles Lamont-Smythe, the British ambassador, visited with him and acknowledged him as Viscount Lockenby. He said the British government has no reason to bring charges against William at the moment, since they have no proof he broke any British laws. He said he'd be speaking with you, Natalie."

"Yes, Giles called me this afternoon. He's a nice man, a friend of George's for years. He was happy it's over. I'm pleased Scotland Yard has ended the investigation. If they consider any future charges that have anything to do with me, I told him I wouldn't be a party to it. I might as well tell you now—I'm going to try to get as many of the charges as I can against William dropped here at home."

"Mom, he nearly killed Hooley."

Davis said, "Natalie, are you certain about this? He's dangerous, unstable, and Perry's right, he nearly killed Hooley, not to mention a United States ambassador—namely, you."

Natalie looked at the sea of baffled faces. "I know he'll go to prison for what he did to Mark, but please try to understand. No matter what else he is, William Charles is George's son. No matter William up and left England at eighteen to search out who he was and where he belonged, George loved him dearly. And William loved him, none of you can doubt that.

"I can't, I simply can't destroy the son his father loved so very much. Yes, I know he will go to prison, but I won't contribute to throwing away the key. For George's sake, I'm going to try to help him." She smiled at all of them. "Perhaps in the process, he'll come to believe I wasn't responsible for his father's death. Perhaps soon, William and I can grieve for his father together."

She was a romantic, a complete over-the-top optimist, Savich thought. He himself couldn't begin to guess if William Charles McCallum was even capable of changing his mind, but he prayed she was right. He said, "I suppose you'll also be speaking to Director Comey?"

Natalie nodded.

Perry said, "I hope you didn't tell him to go easy on Arliss, Mom. After the lengths she went to destroy you, I hope she does go to prison. Do you think she will, Dillon?"

"Your mother can answer that better than I can, Perry."

Natalie said, "I think the president will want to remove her quietly, with the classic excuse of family obligations as the reason for her resignation, and if that's so, then the Justice Department will go along. A trial and possible jail time? I strongly doubt it."

"But still, look what she did, Mom—" Perry began.

Natalie took her hand. "She's lost everything she ever wanted, Perry, everything she had, except your father, and she never had him. Her position, her future, her reputation, and now she might lose her son. Have you spoken with Day, Perry?"

"I caught him on the phone this morning at the airport. He's in Colorado today with his dad's family, trying to explain what happened, trying to support his stepmother. He said she and his half-sisters really need him. I asked Day what his father had told him when he saw him at the Hoover Building yesterday. He told me all his father said was that he loved him, and he'd have blown up the White House to keep him from being hurt. **Hurt?** Day said he laughed when his father said that. He still doesn't understand why they didn't tell him, but his father didn't explain. I agree with him. Day's a grown man, for heaven's sake.

"As for his mother, Day thinks it had more to do with her career and her reputation than with protecting him. I know he'll always be there for his father, and I think that's very good, for both of them."

Natalie said, "I wonder how Day's life, how all of our lives, would have been different if we'd known Brundage was his father. I hope that if I'd been told, I would have come to see Day was another part of Brundage, just as you are, Perry, and I think I would have come to love him as my husband's son.

"I called Day yesterday as well. He didn't want to speak to me. It wasn't that he was mad at me, nothing like that. It was just that he sounded so very hurt, like if he didn't talk about it then it wouldn't be true. It will take him a while to come to grips with it. Day doesn't know it yet, but I'm going to call him every day."

Perry said, "Do you want to know something? I couldn't imagine finding out you're not my mother."

Natalie laughed. "Not much chance of that, sweetie." She looked over at Davis, who was smiling at her as he chewed on a slice of pepperoni. "It's been a week and a half, and our lives have changed so much. Particularly yours, Perry."

"Mom, I like the thought of having Day as my half-brother, don't ever worry about that, but I wouldn't have married him. You know that."

Natalie laughed again. "I wasn't talking

about Day, Perry. I was talking about Special Agent Davis Sullivan. It's amazing, isn't it? Neither of us would have met him if it hadn't been for that drug addict Jitterbug who wanted to steal my new Beemer." She raised her glass. "Davis, here's to your weakness for Starbucks coffee and all the good things that came out of it."

There was another round of toasts. Natalie said, "Perry, I was thinking you and Davis might enjoy visiting London together, maybe even come back with me next week. It's time I returned to the best job in the world. Ambassador to the United Kingdom. I always loved the sound of that."

Perry studied her black leather boots before she looked up and grinned at Davis. "Actually, Mr. Hot Shot, Mom and I already talked about this. So what do you say?"

"I don't know," Davis said. "I mean, I've heard all you can do is talk football, ride a Hog, wear black biker boots that send a man's heart into overdrive, make the best guacamole inside the Beltway—"

Perry burst out laughing. "I don't know about the overdrive business."

Sherlock said, "Sounds to me like she's a guy's dream come to life, Davis."

Savich said easily, "It's all right with me, Davis. You're due a week, I'd say."

Natalie said, "It's March, so of course the days will be rainy and chilly, lots of wind, but if you're lucky, there'll be a couple of days of gorgeous sunshine tossed in. There's a lot to show you, Davis, like the London Eye, and Perry would love to be your tour guide. I have lots of room, as Perry knows."

Sherlock was looking down at Astro, wagging his tail fast as a metronome set on high. She tossed him a bit of pepperoni as she heard the toilet flush upstairs. Sean was up. She knew he'd hear the conversation and creep down the stairs to see what was happening. She rose. "I'm going to get Sean, and you can tell him about this humongous Ferris wheel in London."

Savich said, "When he hears about it,

he'll want to sit on your lap on your flight back to London, Natalie."

"Why don't the three of you come to London with Perry and Davis? Maybe Hooley will be well enough in another month to come as well."

"With Connie," Perry said.

Sherlock said, "What a wonderful idea. Dillon, can you imagine Sean at the top of the Eye?"

Savich pictured it clearly in his mind. "He'll think it's better than a video game. He might even decide he wants to be English when he grows up."

Perry said, "Did you know there'll be three NFL games in London this fall? Maybe I can get the **Post** to pick up the tab and send me over. I can't wait to see in person how the Brits react to American football. Think of the interviews with the man on the street."

Sean appeared at the dining room door, holding his mother's hand. "Oh, wow, a Ferris wheel?"

Epilogue

**FBI Academy
Quantico, Virginia
Graduation Day
May**

Sherlock and Savich sat, with Sean on Savich's lap, beside the eighth Baron de Vesci, Nicholas Drummond's grandfather. Nicholas, Sherlock had told Sean, was about to become the first Brit in the FBI, since his American mother had birthed him in the United States. Nicholas's father, Harry Drummond, and his mother, Mitzie, sat beside them. Excited conversations of families and friends of new agents buzzed around them, all here to witness the new agents graduate and receive their creds and become special agents. It wasn't long before Sean was leaning toward the baron. "Papa said you were a baron. What's a baron?"

The old man with his beak nose and big ears gave Sean a startled look, then smiled and leaned close. "It means I get to eat dessert whenever I want."

Sean whispered, "Even jelly beans?"

"Even jelly beans," and the baron gave a gruff laugh. Sean thought he smelled like oatmeal and strawberries, and that was good. He leaned close again. "Let me tell you about Gargantua the octopus." Sean proceeded to explain to the baron the intricacies of his new video game starring Gargantua, Captain Nemo's pet octopus, each tentacle with a special talent. "Gargantua needs my help," Sean whispered, "or Benito the Shark sucks all the ink out of his tentacles and leaves him helpless."

The baron studied the little boy's face as he listened, surely Agent Savich's in twenty years, and remembered his own son Harry telling him stories at five years old. When Sean asked, the baron leaned close and whispered that he liked the seventh tentacle the best—who wouldn't want to be able to swim with a propeller of his own?

Sean didn't think much of that choice, but he nodded and enthusiastically embarked on Gargantua's latest adventure.

The baron's left knee hurt, but then again, every part of him hurt occasionally, only to be expected when someone approached the age of dirt. He heard Mitzie giggle at something Harry said and knew she was excited and worried and happy for her son, and what mother wouldn't be? Nicholas had become an excellent man, all Drummond he was. He'd been a fine boy; well, not to put too fine a point on it, when he'd hit his teen-age years, he'd been wild, occasionally reckless, but there was always a brain at work in there to pull him back from the biggest follies—or sometimes it was his father's brain, but Mitzie would always give Nicholas the credit.

The baron knew something had

happened to Nicholas in Afghanistan. Whatever it was, he'd left the Foreign Service and come home and signed up for Scotland Yard. Nicholas hadn't spoken of it and the baron hadn't brought it up because he knew a man had to live according to his own rules and find his own peace.

He realized Sean Savich was still telling him a story, and he patted his cheek. "I've changed my mind," he said to Sean. "I want the fourth tentacle. I want to see even in the dark."

Sean's dark eyes glistened. "Something's going to happen," Sean told the baron. Savich leaned down and whispered, "Yep, things are getting started, so listen up and watch. Don't yell at Nicholas when you see him. Wait, then wave when he looks over here."

Sherlock looked past Sean to Nigel, Nicholas's butler, his own father the Drummond family butler since the flood. Nigel had told her about the beautiful brownstone his lordship the baron had purchased for Nicholas in New York

City. He'd rubbed his hands together. "Imagine," he'd said, "I will have a floor entirely to myself." He'd smiled down at Sherlock from his great height. "The kitchen is a marvel. Ah, the meals I shall prepare for Master Nicholas."

Sherlock wondered how Nicholas would keep focused and adjust to life in New York with an English butler at home waiting to hand him tenderly into his smoking jacket. He'd been immured for four months in this vast American complex called Quantico, wearing khaki and dark blue polo shirts. She bet the thought of it made the fastidious Nigel shudder. She wondered if in the distant future, when Nicholas became the Baron de Vesci, he'd remain in the FBI. Who knew? She'd learned never to second-guess life. She looked over at Davis and Perry, who sat close by, holding hands, speaking quietly. She'd heard Davis say before they'd sat down in the auditorium, "I can't wait to see how the Brit fits in with those crazy cowboys in the New York Field Office." And he'd added to Perry, "Savich's dad had a wild rep back in the day."

Savich took Sean's hand when a hush came over the more than five hundred people in attendance, families and friends, husbands and wives and children of all the FBI graduates. The air was electric, everyone was excited, including Sean, waiting for the new agents to come down the aisle and take their seats.

When the forty-eight new agents filed in, straight-backed and serious, their eyes so bright they lit up the auditorium, families pointed and waved, children called out and applause rang out, loud and sustained.

Savich glanced at Nigel as he watched Nicholas confidently stride in with the other graduating agents, looking happy and smart in the lovely suit Nigel had prepared for him. Nicholas turned and nodded to all of them, never breaking stride. Savich squeezed Sean's hand to keep him quiet. He heard Sean whisper to his lordship, "There he is, sir, there he is. Do you think he'll be like my papa someday?" Sean shook his head. "No, that's impossible."

Savich wondered if someday Sean would be in this auditorium waiting to be named a newly minted special agent of the FBI and asking himself that same question. It was a sobering thought.

The dark blue curtains remained closed on the stage. After a short pause, the curtains opened upon a dozen people sitting on stage, among them Mr. Comey, director of the FBI; the chaplain; the class supervisor; and the special guests. One of the guests was Nicholas's uncle Bo Horsley, once the SAC of the New York Field Office. Bo looked very pleased with himself, Sherlock thought. As for the old baron, he was staring at Bo like he was the unprincipled marauder who'd seduced his grandson away from England.

The MC was the assistant director of training, McCauley Mitchell, a man Savich knew would be sharp and smooth and funny. Graduating special agents had to be one of his favorite duties, judging by how he introduced guests, counselors, then the class spokesperson. Following a brief silence, the director of the FBI walked to the lectern, tall and serious, a small smile playing on his mouth as he looked down from the stage to the new agents. He nodded. "Will the graduating class please stand, raise your right hand, and repeat after me—" He administered the oath of office and said, "Congratulations, you are now special agents of the FBI."

The applause was loud and long, and Sean tried to whistle through his teeth.

When Nicholas was presented with the top academic award, Sean's cheer was loud and clear. "Yea, Nicholas! My mama was the top shooter! She's right here!"

There were belly laughs from the stage, a few craning heads, and applause. Sherlock rolled her eyes and shook her head at her son.

When Nicholas's name was called, it was his uncle Bo Horsley who presented him with his badge and credentials from the small wooden cred holder, hugged him, gave him a big smile, and announced into the mike: "Nicholas Drummond— New York."

The FBI chaplin gave the benediction,

and the assistant director of Training announced that photos would be taken and cake and punch would be served in the Hall of Honor. "I hope it's chocolate," Sherlock heard Sean tell the baron.

Outside the main auditorium, they watched Nicholas pick up his mother, whirl her around, and give her a big kiss. He shook his father's hand, clapped Nigel on the shoulder, and turned to his grandfather. "I'm honored you came, sir. Isn't this a phenomenal place?"

The baron said grudgingly, "The oatmeal at the hotel wasn't bad," then he drew Nicholas tightly to him. "I'm proud of you," the old man said.

The two men were of a height, Savich thought, and both were impressive. One with a long, rich tapestry of a life behind him and the other, well, from what he knew about Nicholas Drummond's background in the Foreign Service, he'd already lived enough for two lives, and now he was embarking on a new one.

When Nicholas shook Savich's hand, he said, "Looks like I didn't wash out."

"I'd say you nailed the landing," Savich said. "I rather thought you would. Congratulations, Nick."

"You'll make a fine cowboy," Davis told him, and shook his hand. One of Nicholas's eyebrows shot up, and Savich laughed. "You'll soon learn what he means."

Nicholas kissed Sherlock's cheek. "Bummer, as you Yanks say, but I wasn't the top shooter, not nearly as good as you."

Sean stuck out his hand and patted Nicholas's arm. "That's all right, Nicholas, my papa says Mama can shoot out the heel of a shoe." He paused for a moment, then spit it out. "Papa said he didn't want me to yell it out so I couldn't, but he won the top smart award, too."

Nicholas smiled down at the little boy. "Would you like to win it, too, one day?"

Sean looked at his father, looked oddly adult in that moment, and announced, "I'll try."

Nicholas stilled, cocked his head to one side, and turned slowly toward Special Agent Michaela Caine, his future partner at the New York Field Office, the agent who'd been at his side for the incredible three days chasing across Europe after the Koh-i-Noor diamond. Sherlock smiled. Mike was smart, funny, and, best of all, she was a rock.

Nicholas was staring at her as if he'd never seen her before. Fact was, Sherlock thought, she looked gorgeous, her hair pulled back from her face with two gold clips, showing her fine cheekbones. She was conservatively dressed in an elegant dark blue suit, a stylish white blouse, heels on her feet that brought her nearly to Nicholas's eye level. Her eyes sparkled and she was wearing a huge smile that included everyone.

"I didn't want to miss Nicholas's ceremony, but there was work—" She threw up her hands. "Congratulations, Nicholas. Welcome to the FBI, and, better still, welcome to New York."

He walked slowly to her, studying her face. He stuck out his hand and she shook it, never looking away. "I heard you managed to snag one of the awards. What was it for? Top lamebrain stunt?"

Nicholas gave a whoop and hugged her. "Hi, partner," she said, and patted his shoulder.

Sean called out, "I don't want Nicholas to go to New York, Papa."

"Don't worry, Sean," Sherlock said, patting his hand. "You'll see Nicholas again, I promise."